PE

Siste

Praise for Elizabeth Fremantle:

'A great read. *Sisters of Treason* totally transports the reader to the Tudor court, with all its tensions and games' Katherine Webb

'An endlessly fascinating era, and Fremantle manages to combine pacey storytelling with superb background . . . it's terrifically entertaining' *The Times*

'Elizabeth Fremantle has excelled herself in this glorious second novel: the intricacies of the Tudor court were never more richly or deftly explored. Vibrant, passionate, compassionate and deeply moving, this is a fantastic read' Manda Scott

'A vivid fictional retelling of the perilous lives of Lady Jane Grey's two younger sisters' *Choice*

'A major new voice in historical fiction' *Bookseller*

By the same author

Queen's Gambit

Sisters of Treason

ELIZABETH FREMANTLE

PENGUIN BOOKS

PENGUIN BOOKS

UK | USA | Canada | Ireland | Australia
India | New Zealand | South Africa

Penguin Books is part of the Penguin Random House group of companies
whose addresses can be found at global.penguinrandomhouse.com.

Penguin
Random House
UK

First published by Michael Joseph 2014
Published in Penguin Books 2015
001

Typeset in Garamond MT Std by Palimpsest Book Production Ltd, Falkirk, Stirlingshire
Printed in Great Britain by Clays Ltd, St Ives plc

A CIP catalogue record for this book is available from the British Library

ISBN: 978-1-405-90941-9

For Raphael and Alice

Contents

THE TUDOR AND

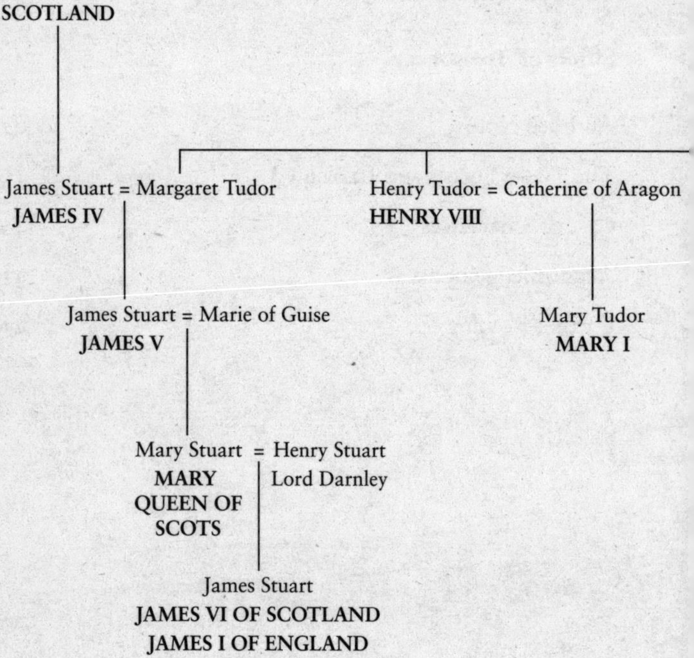

Monarchs are in bold and only marriages that produced heirs are shown

STUART SUCCESSION

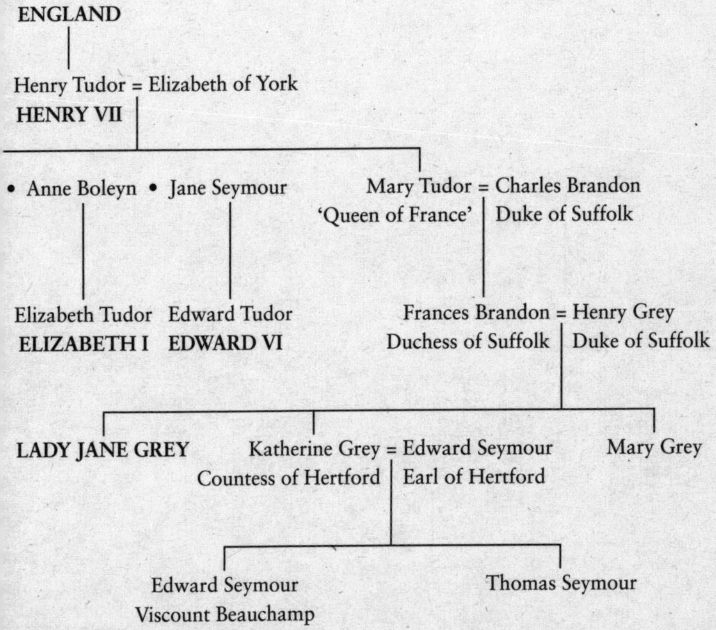

Prologue

February 1554
The Tower of London
Levina

Frances is shaking. Levina takes her arm, tucking it firmly into the crook of her elbow. A bitter wind hisses through the naked branches of the trees and smacks at the women's clothes, lifting their hoods so the ties cut into their throats. The winter sky is blotched grey, like the inside of an oyster shell, and the White Tower is a dark shape against it. A hushed collection of people shuffles about beside the scaffold, rubbing hands and stamping feet to keep warm. A couple of men trundle past pulling a cart, but Levina does not really see for she is gazing up towards a window in a building across the yard, where she thinks she can see the outline of a figure.

'Oh Lord!' murmurs Frances, slapping a hand over her mouth. 'Guildford.'

Levina looks, understanding instantly. In the cart is a bloody bundle; it is the body of Guildford Dudley. Frances's breath is shallow and fast, her face pallid, not white as one might imagine, but green. Levina takes her by her shoulders, narrow as a girl's, facing her, holding her eyes with a steady look, saying, 'Breathe deeply, Frances, breathe deeply,' doing so herself, in the hope that Frances will mimic her slow inhalations. She cannot imagine what it must be for a mother to watch her seventeen-year-old daughter die and be powerless to stop it.

'I cannot understand why Mary –' She stops to correct herself, 'why the Queen would not let us see her . . . Say goodbye.' Her eyes are bloodshot.

'Fear has made her ruthless,' Levina says. 'She must fear plots everywhere, even between a mother and her condemned daughter.' She reaches down to her greyhound, Hero, stroking the peaked landscape of his spine, feeling the reassuring press of his muzzle into her skirts.

Levina remembers painting Jane Grey in her queen's regalia, not even a year ago. She was mesmerized by the intensity of the girl's gaze, those widely set, dark eyes flecked with chestnut, her long neck and delicate hands, all somehow conspiring to give the impression of both strength and fragility. 'Painted' is perhaps not quite the word, for she had barely the chance to prick the cartoon and pounce the charcoal dust through on to the panel before Mary Tudor arrived in London with an army to pull the throne out from under her young cousin, who will meet her death today on this scaffold. It was Frances Grey who helped Levina break up that panel and throw it on the fire, along with the cartoon. The wheel of fortune turns fast in England these days

Over her shoulder Levina notices a gathering of Catholic churchmen arrive; Bonner, the Bishop of London, is amongst them, fat and smooth, like a grotesque baby. Levina knows him well enough from her own parish; he has a reputation for brutality. There is a supercilious smile pasted on his face; pleased to see a young girl lose her head – sees it as a triumph, does he? Levina would love to slap that smile away; she can imagine the ruddy mark it would leave on his cheek, the satisfying smart on her palm.

'Bonner,' she whispers to Frances. 'Don't turn. If he meets your eye he may try and greet you.'

She nods and swallows and Levina guides her away, further

from the men so she is less likely to have to confront any of them. Not many have come to see a girl that was queen for a matter of days die; not the hundreds, it is said, that came to jeer at Anne Boleyn – the one whose death started the fashion for decapitating queens. No one will heckle today, everyone is too horrified about this, except Bonner and his lot, and even they are not so crass as to overtly assert their pleasure. She thinks of the Queen at the palace, imagining how she would paint her. She must be with her closest women; they are likely at prayer. But in Levina's mind the Queen is alone in the empty expanse of her watching chamber, and has just been told that one of her favourite young cousins has been murdered at her bidding. The look on her face is not one of carefully suppressed triumph like Bonner's, nor is it one of fear, though it should be, for after all it is only days since a rebel army sought, and failed, to depose her and put her sister Elizabeth on the throne – no, her pinched face is blank as a sheet of new vellum, eyes dead, detached, suggesting that the killing has only just begun.

'This is her father's doing,' Frances mutters. 'I cannot help but blame him, Veena . . . His mindless ambition.' She spits the words out as if they taste foul. Levina glances once more towards that tower window, wondering if the figure there, watching, is Frances's husband, Jane's father, Henry Grey, who also awaits a traitor's fate. The cart has come to a halt beside a low building some distance from them. Its driver leans down to chat with a man, seeming just to pass the time of day, as if there were not a butchered boy in the back. 'It is a house of cards, Veena, a house of cards.'

'Frances, don't,' she says, putting an arm round her friend's shoulder. 'You will drive yourself mad.'

'And the Queen, where is her mercy? We are her close kin. *Elle est ma première cousine; on était presque élevée ensemble.*'

Levina grips her more tightly, without speaking. Frances often forgets that she doesn't understand much French. Levina has never asked her why, given she is English to the bone, she favours that language in spite of its being quite out of fashion at court. She assumes it has something to do with her Tudor mother, who was a French king's widow. A man approaches, his cape blowing out in the wind giving him the look of a bat. He stops before the two women with a polite bow, removing his cap, which he holds crumpled in both hands.

'My Lady,' he says, with a click of his heels. 'Sir John Brydges, Lieutenant of the Tower.' There is a sternness about him, he *is* a guardsman Levina supposes; but then his formality drops. 'My heart goes to you, My Lady. My wife and I . . .' He falters, his voice quivering slightly. 'We have become fond of your daughter these last months. She is a remarkable girl.'

Frances looks like a woman drowning and seems unable to form a response, but takes one of his hands and nods slowly.

'She is to be brought down now.' He drops his voice to little more than a whisper. 'I can give you a moment with her. She refused to see her husband before he –' He means 'before he died', but has the tact not to say it. 'She has asked for you.'

'Take me to her,' Frances manages to mumble.

'The utmost discretion is required. We do not want to attract any attention.' It is clear he refers to Bonner and the pack of Catholic hounds. 'I shall leave now. You follow me in a few moments. Take the back entrance of the building yonder.' He waves an arm towards a diminutive house tucked under the Bell Tower. 'We shall await you there.'

He turns to leave and the women follow on after a time,

giving the impression of seeking shelter from the wind. The door is low and they have to duck under the lintel, closing it behind them, finding themselves in darkness. It takes a moment for their eyes to adjust. There is a further door opposite and Levina wonders whether they should enter, feeling that she must take the initiative, as Frances seems incapable of anything. As she moves towards it, the door creaks open and Brydges peeps round. Seeing the two women, he opens it further and there is Jane, head to toe in black, holding a pair of books in her tiny white hands. She wears a smile and says, 'Maman!' as if it is any ordinary day.

'*Chérie!*' exclaims Frances, and they fall into one another's arms, Frances whispering, '*Ma petite chérie*,' over and over again. The French gives the moment a dramatic quality, as if it were a scene from a pageant. It strikes Levina, too, that Jane seems more the mother than Frances; she is so very poised, so very in control of herself.

Levina steps to one side, half turning away for decency's sake, not that they seem to even remember she is there.

'I am sorry, *chérie* . . . so, so very sorry.'

'I know, Maman.' Jane breaks away from the embrace, gathering herself, straightening her dress. '*Ne vous inquiétez pas*. God has singled me out for this. I go willingly to Him, as an envoy for the new faith.'

The girl Levina remembers drawing just a few months ago is all gone; this is a woman before them, standing straight, polished, calm. It strikes her, with a painful twist of irony, that Jane Grey would have made a far better, wiser queen than Mary Tudor will ever be. If the people had seen her as she is now, they would never have thought to raise an army to depose her and put her Catholic cousin on the throne.

'If I had but a salt-spoon's measure of your courage,' murmurs Frances.

'It is time, Maman,' Jane says, glancing towards Brydges, who nods solemnly. Then she passes one of her books to Frances, whispering the words, 'There is a letter for you within, and one for Katherine; hers is written in the book itself, for she is sure to lose it otherwise – my sister never was one for holding on to things.' She laughs, a tinkling sound that even raises something approximating a smile from Frances, and for an instant they look so like one another that Levina finds herself smiling too. But Jane's laughter drops away as quickly as it came, and she adds, 'Protect Katherine, Maman. I fear she will not stand it so well.'

Levina is struck by the horrible inevitability of Jane's younger sister becoming the new focus of reformist plots – someone will surely seek to depose Catholic Mary Tudor and put one of their own faith on the throne – like a line of dominoes, set to fall one after the other.

'And Mary? What shall I tell her from you?' Frances refers to the youngest of her three daughters.

'Mary is clever. She has no need of my advice.' Then, with a flutter of her birdlike hand, she is gone and the inner door is closed behind her. Frances, gripping the book, puts out her free hand to the wall to steady herself.

'Come,' Levina says, grasping her upper arm, leading her out, back into the wind and the waiting scaffold where a few more have gathered, though still it could not be called a crowd.

They appear then, Brydges first, ashen-faced, after him the Catholic man who was unable to convert her, both with their eyes cast down. And there she is, bold and straight, her psalter held open before her, lips moving in prayer, flanked by her two women who are barely holding back their tears. The scene engraves itself on Levina's mind: the jet black of Jane's dress against the drab stone of the Tower behind; the way the wind lifts the edges of everything, suggesting flight;

the almost weeping ladies, their gowns lurid splashes of colour; the exact pallor of Brydges's skin; the look of solemn serenity on Jane's face. She is compelled to render this in paint. A great gust of wind sends a branch of a nearby tree crashing to the ground, close enough to Bonner and his acolytes to make them jump back and scatter. She wonders how many are wishing, as she is, that it had struck a softer target.

Jane Grey mounts the few steps and stands before the onlookers to speak. She is close enough that were Levina to reach up she could touch the edge of her skirts, but the wind takes the girl's words and only snippets reach them. 'I do wash my hands thereof in innocency . . .' She makes the action, rubbing those small hands together. 'I die a true Christian woman and that I do look to be saved by no other mean, but only by the mercy of God.' She is cleaving to the new faith to the last and Levina wishes that she had a pinch of this girl's unassailable fortitude.

When Jane is done she shrugs off her gown, handing it to her women, and unties her hood. As she pulls it away from her head her hair looses itself from its ribbons and flies up, beautifully, as if it will lift her to the heavens. She turns to the headsman. Levina supposes he is begging her forgiveness; she cannot hear their exchange. But his face is utterly stricken – even the executioner is horrified by this, then. It is only Jane who seems entirely composed.

Jane then takes the blindfold from one of her ladies and, refusing help with a small shake of her head, wraps it about her eyes, then drops to her knees, pressing her hands together swiftly and mouthing out a prayer. All of a sudden, the prayer finished, her composure seems to fall away as she flounders blindly, reaching for the block, unable to find it in her sightless state. Levina is reminded of a newborn animal, eyes still welded shut, seeking, in desperation, its source of succour.

Everybody watches her but nobody moves to help. All are paralysed with horror at the sight of this young girl groping for something solid in a dark world. There is barely a sound; even the wind has dropped to a deathly hush, as if Heaven holds its breath. Still Jane seeks for the block, arms flailing now in space. Levina can bear it no longer and scrambles up on to the platform, guiding those cold little hands, a child's hands really, to the place; tears sting at her eyelids as she clambers back down to Frances, who is blanched with shock.

Then it is done, in a flash of steel and a brilliant crimson spurt. Frances collapses into Levina, who holds her upright and covers her eyes for her as the executioner holds up Jane Grey's head by the hair, to prove his job is done. Levina doesn't know why she looks up then, but what she sees when she does is not reality; it is a scene conjured in her imagination: the Queen in the place of that headsman, her fingers twisted through the bloody hair of her young cousin, her face placid, oblivious to the spill of gore over her dress. The gathering is silent, save for the desperate gusting wind, which has started up again as if in protest.

Levina steps to the side and vomits into the gutter.

I
Queen Mary

July 1554
The Bishop's Palace, Winchester
Mary

'Sit still, Mary Grey,' says Mistress Poyntz, her voice as firm as her fingers. 'You do fidget so.'

She is tugging my hair too tightly into its ribbons. I want to shout at her to stop, to not touch me.

'There,' she adds, pushing my hood over my head and tying it beneath my chin. It covers my ears. I can hear the sound of the sea, like in the big shell we used to listen to at Bradgate. I wonder what has become of that shell now Bradgate is no longer our home. 'Magdalen will help you into your gown.' She gives me a little shove towards the dark-haired girl, who offers a sideways look and a scowl.

'But I have not yet –' begins Magdalen.

'Do as I say, please,' says Mistress Poyntz, her voice firm as the brace beneath my kirtle. The girl rolls her eyes, then swaps a look with Cousin Margaret beside her.

We are surrounded by mess: trunks spill out gowns; hoods balance on sills; jewels hang carelessly from the edges of things, and the air is clogged with the reek of a dozen different perfumes. You can barely move without getting an elbow in the eye, so cramped are we, with girls clambering over each other to reach their affairs. Maman is almost as cramped as we are, sharing with five other ladies, but at least their room has a door. The maids' chamber, where fourteen of us bedded down last night, is really only a curtained-off area at the end of a corridor. All morning Mistress Poyntz has been shooing off the peeping Toms, who hope to catch a glimpse of the older girls dressing.

I hand my gown to Magdalen, who holds it up, saying with a smirk, 'How does *this* fit?' She dangles it from the tips of her fingers, away from her body.

'This part,' I explain, pointing at the high collar that has been specially tailored to fit my shape, 'goes up around here.'

'Over your hump?' Magdalen says with a snort of laughter.

I must not cry. What would my sister Jane have done, I ask myself. *Be stoic, Mouse*, she would have said. *Let no one see what you are truly feeling.*

'I don't know why the Queen would want such a creature at her wedding,' Magdalen whispers to Cousin Margaret, not so quiet that I can't hear.

I fear I will cry and make things worse, so I think up a picture of Jane. I remember her saying once: *God has chosen to make you a certain way and it cannot be without reason. In His eyes you are perfect – in mine too.* But I know I am not perfect; I am so hunched about the shoulders and crooked at the spine, I look as if I have been hung by the scruff on a hook for too long. And I am small as an infant of five, despite being almost twice that age. *Besides, it is what is in here that matters*; in my mind's eye Jane presses a fist to her heart.

'Mary Grey has more right to attend the Queen's wedding than you,' says Jane Dormer, who is the Queen's favoured maid. 'She is full of royal blood.'

Magdalen mutters, 'But what a misshapen package,' and begins lacing me into my gown with a huff.

My sister's life was the price of this wedding; it was the Queen's doing. Though it has been one hundred and sixty-four days since she was killed (I mark each day in my book of hours), the feeling of loss has not begun to wane – I think it never shall. I am like the tree struck by lightning in the park at Bradgate, its insides burned right away, black and empty.

It is a sin to hate the Queen as I do – a treasonous sin. But I cannot help the hatred welling in me. *Do not let others see what you are feeling*, Jane would have said.

'There,' says Magdalen, turning away. 'You are done.'

She has laced me in so tightly I feel like a wood pigeon stuffed and stitched for roasting.

'Will Elizabeth attend the wedding?' asks Cousin Margaret.

'Of course not,' replies Magdalen. 'She is locked up at Woodstock.'

'Poor thing,' says Jane Dormer, and a thick silence drops. Perhaps they are all thinking about my sister Jane and what can happen to girls who are too close to the throne. Elizabeth's portrait used to hang in the long gallery at Whitehall, but now there is just a dark square on the panelling where it used to be.

A thought worries at me, that my sister Katherine might now be one of those girls on the brink of the throne.

'Someone told me Elizabeth may not even walk alone in the gardens without a guard,' whispers Magdalen.

'Enough of that tittle-tattle,' says Mistress Poyntz. 'Where is your sister?'

'Katherine?' I ask, not knowing whom she addresses – the place is full of sisters.

'Do you have another sis –' she stops herself. I suppose she is remembering that my other sister is dead. She smiles at me now, with a tilted head and runs a hand over my shoulders, saying, 'This dress is well cut, Mary. It gives you a fine shape.' Her voice is sing-song, as if she is talking to an infant.

I can see the distaste behind her smile and the way she wipes the hand that has touched me over her skirts, as if to clean it. I say nothing, so she sends Jane Dormer off to seek out Katherine, who is likely up to no good.

I notice my sister Jane's Greek New Testament amongst a pile of Katherine's things and take it out to the corridor, opening it to the letter written in the inside cover, not reading, just looking at Jane's fine hand. I do not need to read it, for it is carved on my heart:

It is the book, dear sister, of the law of the Lord. It is the testament and last will, which he bequeathed unto us wretches, which shall lead you to the path of eternal joy. And if you have a good mind to read it, it shall bring you to an immortal and everlasting life. It shall teach you to live and learn you to die.

I have tried to understand why there was no letter for me. Why Jane should have written to Katherine, encouraging her to read this book, when I know for a fact that Katherine can barely read Greek at all. It is I who knows that language; it is I who used to listen to Jane read from her Greek bible each day, while Katherine chased her puppies around the gardens and made eyes at father's pages. I tell myself that Jane must have thought I had no need of guidance. But, though I know it is shameful and a sin besides, I am brimming with silent envy of Katherine, not because she is beautiful as a summer meadow and I am twisted as an espaliered fruit tree, but for being the one Jane chose to write to.

'Mary, shall we walk a little?' It is Peggy Willoughby, who takes my hand and leads me out into the cloisters that run around a garden. It has been raining heavily and everything has that fresh loamy scent of summer downpours. We perch on a stone bench under cover, taking care not to get our gowns wet, for the water would mark the silk and make trouble for us with Mistress Poyntz. We are the youngest; Peggy, who is a ward of Maman's, is just a year older than me, but is more than a head taller as I am so very small. She is fair with a snub nose and round dewy eyes, but her upper lip is divided in two and she has an odd manner of speaking.

'What do you think he will be like?' asks Peggy. She is talking of the Queen's intended, the Spanish Prince Felipe; it is all anyone has spoken of in the maids' chamber for days.

I shrug. 'You have seen the painting.'

We have all seen the painting hung at Whitehall, how the hooded eyes follow you, wherever you stand. It puts the shivers up me just thinking of it. He wears polished black armour, gilded here and there, and his stockings are whiter than swans' down. Katherine and Cousin Margaret had stood before the painting as it was being hung, nudging each other. 'Look at his fine legs, so slim,' Cousin Margaret had said. 'And the codpiece,' Katherine had added, sparking off muffled giggles.

'But what I meant,' says Peggy, 'is will he bring the *Inquisition* with him, as some say he will?' She says the word 'Inquisition' as if it is hot and must be spat out before it burns her tongue.

'Ah, that,' I say. 'Nobody knows.'

'What exactly is the *Inquisition*?'

'I do not really know, Peggy,' I say. This is a lie; I *do* know, for Maman has explained it. It is when people are hounded and burned alive for their beliefs. But I do not want to frighten Peggy, for she is already given to nightmares, and if she had an inkling of the terror that Maman says is knocking at England's door, she would never sleep a wink. 'As long as we are good Catholics, we have nothing to fear.'

Her hand moves to the rosary that hangs from her girdle. Peggy is as much a Catholic as I, which is to say not at all, but we must appear as such, for our lives depend on it. So Maman says.

'Is that why the Queen does not allow Elizabeth to court? Because she won't accept the Catholic faith?'

'How would I know?' I say, remembering my dead sister and wondering if Elizabeth will end up the same way and then Katherine too. But I swallow down that thought before it takes hold.

'You don't know anything.'

That she should think this is exactly my intention, for the truth of it is, I know far too much. This is because I listen to all the things most adults think me incapable of understanding. I know that the Spanish ambassador wants rid of Elizabeth like he wanted rid of Jane. I know too that the Queen cannot quite yet bring herself to condemn her sister. But then we had all thought that about Jane, for Jane was one of the Queen's favourite cousins. This makes me aware that though there is much I know, there is much more I don't. But another thing I do know is that England doesn't want this Spanish wedding, and fears greatly what it will bring. 'Would you help me loosen my dress?' I ask Peggy, changing the subject. 'It is intolerably tight.'

Peggy unties me a little, easing the ache in my back. I watch a blackbird pecking at something with its buttercup beak, hopping over the cobbles on legs so thin it is a marvel they can support its body. As it flits off, taking to the sky, I am reminded of Forget-me-not, the Queen's blue parakeet, a magnificent creature condemned to spend its life scratching about in a cage, mimicking words it doesn't understand.

'Do you ever imagine that animals have souls?' I ask.

'*I do not*,' she answers me. 'It is ungodly to think of such things.'

I want to ask if she ever wonders if God exists at all. She would be appalled that I ever had such a thought in me. She would surely feel compelled to tell, if only to save me from myself. I imagine Mistress Poyntz's horrified face. Who knows what might happen then. I am forming the belief that faith cannot be true until you have questioned it fully. But such ideas are heresy. That I know. I can feel Jane tapping at the edges of my mind. Did she ever question her faith? If she did she never said it. No, I think Jane believed as Katherine loves, in a way that is built on rock, like that house in the Bible.

Are you with God? I ask my dead sister silently, feeling a cool gust of air touch the skin of my face.

'Come on,' says Peggy, 'Mistress Poyntz will be asking where we have got to.'

Katherine

'Harry Herbert, Harry Herbert, Harry Herbert, Harry Herbert . . .' I whisper the name over and over again as I run around the fishpond. The ground is waterlogged and the drenched hem of my skirt slaps at my ankles.

'Lady Katherine, Katherine Grey,' Jane Dormer is calling me from the steps. I pretend not to hear.

'Harry Herbert, Harry Herbert, Harry Herbert.' I have a keepsake tucked under my stomacher next to my heart; a length of satin ribbon Harry Herbert gave me to wear for good fortune at our wedding. It was palest blue, the colour of water, but not any more, as it has sat about my person for so long now it has dirtied to a drab grey. How fitting – a grey ribbon for a Grey girl. You would never think, given the plainness of our name – grey like roof tiles, or paving slabs, or an old duchess's hair – that us Greys were such an illustrious family, that we were close cousins of the Queen. 'Harry Herbert, Harry Herbert, Harry Herbert.' I try to focus all my thoughts on him so there is no space left in me for thoughts of my sister Jane or Father, whom I miss as if there is a hole at the core of me.

I remember, with a pang of guilt, how jealous I used to feel of Jane. Your sister is a marvel, people would say, a paragon, such intelligence, such grace. It made me so jealous I felt my head would spin right off my neck. But now I miss her to the core and I cannot think of her for fear that I will drown in grief. I must keep my mind on other things. After all I am fourteen, and girls of my age are supposed to think of love, are they not? 'Harry Herbert, Harry Herbert, Harry Herbert.' And besides, everyone says that *I* am the beauty of the family and, given the fate of my poor sister, I would far rather be the beauty than the paragon.

I fling my arms out wide and spin in circles, pretending not to hear Jane Dormer, who has her skirts huffily gripped in her fists and is descending the steps towards me. I look up to the sky as I spin. The sun is a silver coin behind a down of cloud. 'Harry Herbert, Harry Herbert.' I try to picture my husband's face but it is so long since I have seen him, a full seven months, and his image has faded to little more than a vague impression. I remember his smell, though: almonds. The first time I set eyes on him was the day of our wedding. I was enraged by the whole idea, didn't want to marry at all; I was mourning a thwarted fancy for one of my cousins. I can barely remember what he looks like now, that cousin, and I once thought I would die of longing for him.

My sister Jane always told me I was too sentimental and that if I weren't careful it would be my undoing. But I cannot help it. Who can resist that feeling, the swoosh and whirl, the giddiness of love? That was what I felt when I first set eyes on Harry Herbert in his green silk doublet with green flashing eyes to match, casting themselves over me. On seeing

Harry Herbert's smile of satisfied approval, that poor cousin was cast to oblivion.

Jane Dormer looms. I stop spinning and have to hold her arm to balance myself. The for-goodness'-sake face she's wearing makes me spill out with breathless laughter. 'I don't know what you have to laugh about, Katherine.' She stops, shifting her eyes off mine, and brings a fist to her mouth as if to prevent any more words from coming out.

'I am celebrating the Queen's wedding.' I feel that even Jane would approve of this.

Jane Dormer is not so bad really, just so very unlike me.

'Mistress Poyntz asked me to fetch you, and we must hurry, for you are not even changed into your finery.' She tucks my arm under hers and leads me towards the courtyard.

'Harry Herbert will be at the wedding.'

'You're not still mooning over *him*, are you? He is not even your husband any more . . . and never was, truly.'

I can tell, from the sudden blush on her cheeks, that by this she means our marriage was unconsummated. Truth be told, I'm not sure about that. It is the official story, of course – that though I lived under his parents' roof a month or so, we were still but children and for that reason kept apart. When all the trouble started and Jane was put in the Tower, the Herberts sought to distance themselves from the Greys so I was sent back to my mother's house, a pure maid of thirteen years. But the truth of it was different, for there were occasions when we conspired to escape our chaperones and steal some moments alone. If I think of it now, his exploring hands, his tongue in my mouth, my belly slides about as if an adder is unfurling in there. I don't know exactly if that means our marriage was consummated; he certainly got his fingers to the wet part of me.

We talk a great deal about such things in the maids' chamber at night, but none of us knows for certain what happens in the marriage bed. Cousin Margaret says that the man must have his hose undone. I am fairly certain that Harry's hose stayed laced – but in the dark, when you are caught up in the heave and suck of it all, it is hard to tell. Magdalen Dacre says you can fall pregnant from a kiss, if the tongue goes in far enough, and Frances Neville says if a boy touches you down there, that will do it. We have all watched the dogs mating in the yard; but perhaps most girls cannot bear to believe that God would have us behave like beasts in order to beget children. Though I would never admit it to them, there is something oddly exciting about the idea of that.

'Oh dear, look at my slippers!' I notice the bedraggled things peeping from under my skirts as we climb the steps. They are my favourite dancing slippers. The red has seeped from the silk flowers into the pale leather and they are smeared in gritty muck. It makes me rueful that I have been so careless with something so precious.

'They are ruined,' says Jane Dormer, and I feel the sudden prick of inexplicable tears.

Two men clatter by, all togged up in the Spanish fashion. The place is seething with Spaniards. They have nut-coloured skin and dark eyes which appraise us briefly. They like what they see, if the little smile playing over the lips of the more handsome of the two is anything to go by. They bow and lift off their caps. Jane will not raise her gaze to them but I proffer a hand, which alas is snatched up by the pimply one, who gives the impression that he might swallow it whole.

Why is it with pairs of men, when one is comely he is inevitably accompanied by one who is not? The pimply one has a hungry-doggish air about him and, though I am fond of dogs (too fond, some say, for I have five altogether), I do not like this fellow, nor his greedy stare. The other one is not such a young man, about thirty-five I should say, but is quite splendid in his dress and exceedingly well built, though he only passes a cursory look over *me* and begins to goggle at Jane. Her eyes still cling modestly to the ground, while *his* are dancing over her like jumping fish.

'This is a beautiful fabric,' I say to him, running my finger lightly over his crimson sleeve in an attempt to turn his attention on to me.

'*Gracias.*' His response is perfunctory and he barely glances my way. It would seem that Jane Dormer has him firmly under her spell, for now she has allowed him a glimpse of those soft, brown eyes set into the snowy planes of her face. He cannot seem to drag himself away and I have to admit that I have lost this contest. But I concede gladly, for Jane Dormer hasn't a bad bone in her body.

'Would dew be so kindest to allow myself to intro-duct me?'

He takes an interminable time to spit this out and I struggle to keep hold of my giggles, but Jane looks up briefly, the image of self-control, and says without even the slightest hint of mirth on her face, 'It would please me greatly.'

'Gómez Suárez, Compte de Feria,' he announces with another bow, deeper this time.

Jane is quite dumbstruck so I quash my mirth and say, 'This, My Lord, is Jane Dormer and I am Lady Katherine Grey.'

'Yane Do-ma,' he says, and a further snort of laughter escapes from my nose, but he hardly seems to notice my rudeness for he is staring at Jane as if she is the Virgin herself. '*Delectata*,' he continues, in Latin.

'*Ego etiam*,' she says.

I am wishing I had paid more attention to my Latin tutor.

My nurse, when I was in frustrated tears over my studies and even my baby sister seemed cleverer than me, used to say, 'Never mind, you are pretty enough for it not to matter.'

'*Si vis, nos ignosce, serae sumus,*' Jane Dormer adds, taking me by the hand and making to leave.

'*Vos apud nuptias videbo,*' Feria says. The only word I understand is '*nuptias*', which means 'wedding'.

Once in the corridor I nudge Jane and whisper, 'Someone likes *you*.'

'You can't have them all,' she replies, with a shy smile.

'No, he is most definitely yours.'

She knows me well enough, knows that I want them all to want me. I cannot help it. It is what stops me thinking about all the things I would rather forget. I turn my mind to Harry Herbert, feeling a grip of excitement at the thought of seeing him. I know he is amongst Felipe of Spain's English entourage and I am glad I have arranged to borrow Magdalen Dacre's wooden-soled chopines, for they will make me taller. She says they are impossible to walk in sensibly, but I practised all morning, up and down the corridor until I became accustomed to the feel of them, and fancy I will manage rather well. 'Harry Herbert, Harry Herbert, Harry Herbert,' I murmur, as I rush to the maids' quarters to get changed.

By the time I get to the Queen's rooms, hurriedly tying my hood in place as I enter, everybody is almost ready to go. Susan Clarencieux is shouting out orders, telling everyone where they are supposed to be in the procession, and there are the usual disputes over precedence. Maman beckons Mary and me almost to the front where we belong, behind her and the Countess of Lennox, who is another of the Queen's cousins on the Tudor side, but Cousin Margaret starts making a fuss, as she wants to partner me. She shoulders her way in front of Mary, so, in defence of my sister, I give her a shove and a glare and, by-mistake-on-purpose, tread on her toe, which must hurt a good deal because of the chopines. But all the time I'm thinking that if my sister Jane were here *she* would be partnering me and Margaret would be with Mary. That twists me up inside, and more so when I remember that Father will not be there in the cathedral either, kitted out in his garter robes, looking magnificent, with all the others. I cannot bear to think of him. I take a deep breath to stop the tears, pinch my cheeks and bite my lips. 'Harry Herbert, Harry Herbert, Harry Herbert.'

Later, when we are all bloated with feasting, the boards are cleared and the musicians start up. The Spaniards have gathered to one side of the hall, with barely a smile between them, looking as if they'd rather be anywhere but here. The English, on the other side in a hostile cluster, eye them up. It gives more the impression of a battlefield than a wedding feast. The Queen's new husband is wearing a scowl on his Habsburg face because he was served on silver and she on gold. But scowl or not he cuts an undeniably fine figure and I wonder how the Queen, who is entirely lost in her elaborate wedding dress and weighed down by her jewels, will hold the attention of her young husband.

Harry Herbert seeks me out with his eyes for the thousandth time today. He blows me a kiss; I pretend to catch it and press it to my heart. Throughout the service, when we were supposed to be praying for the Queen to give England a string of heirs, Harry and I were exchanging looks. He was there as I arrived on the cathedral steps and it was all I could do to resist breaking rank and running to him. He flicked the dark wave of his fringe away from his eyes and threw me a smile as I passed; I thought I would faint.

The men are lining up for a pavane with the ladies opposite and I can see Harry Herbert approaching me, but his father grabs him by the wrist and pulls him over to dance with one of the Talbot girls. To make things worse, I am lined up with Feria's doggish friend who doesn't know the steps and keeps turning me the wrong way. Truth be told, I am struggling in the chopines, which have rubbed my heels raw, so I excuse myself as soon as is polite, leaving Cousin Margaret to be accosted by the pimply Spaniard, and sit to the side with Mary, who is all alone. None of the maids, save for harelipped Peggy Willoughby, who has gone to bed, would be seen dead with her. It wasn't until we came to court that I even really remarked that Mary was different – of course I could *see* she was crookbacked, but at home, no one made anything of it; she was always just Mary, our little Mouse. But here I find I have to defend her against the maids of the chamber, who are worse than a nest of snakes.

Mary leans her head against the panelling with a yawn, saying, 'I wish I could retire.' I would put my arms about her but I know she likes it not. She says she has been tugged about too much in her life, by legions of doctors and wise women. They have strapped her and stretched her and concocted foul-tasting herbs to soften her bones, all in an attempt to straighten her out. Then there have been the priests and their prayers, and even one once who performed an exorcism in the chapel at Bradgate. But Mary has remained the shape she is. I hook my little finger through hers, which is what we do in place of a hug.

I watch Harry Herbert dance with Magdalen Dacre; they are laughing at some shared joke. I cannot bear to watch, but nor can I tear my eyes away. He takes her by the hand and I am scrunched up inside.

'I have some news,' says Mary.

'About what?'

'About Maman . . .' She hesitates, which makes me think

the worst. I want to not listen, to put my fingers in my ears and hum, for I fear another piece of bad news and I might crumble altogether.

'Not something bad?'

'No, it is something good.' She looks up at me, round chestnut eyes like a just-born deer.

'What, then?' Harry Herbert is whispering something into Magdalen's ear, and I am bristling at the sight of it.

'She intends to marry.'

Now he has handed her to the doggish Spaniard and is partnering Cousin Margaret. Then it dawns on me, what Mary has just said. 'Maman, marry! No. It's just gossip, Mouse.'

'But Kitty, it came from her very lips.' How is it that Maman tells Mary everything first? Her chestnut eyes seem weaselly now and I feel a surge of the old jealousy I used to have for Jane. I try and remind myself that this is crooked little Mary and she means me no harm. 'She said to me that she has the mind to wed Mister Stokes.'

'Adrian Stokes? That can't be right. He is her *groom* . . . no more than a servant. Besides, the Queen would never allow –'

'She has permission,' cuts in Mary.

'Did she say that?' My mind is whirring and I can feel the anger bubbling up in me when I think of my magnificent father, and then of that nobody who looks after the horses. 'How could she?' The way I miss Father is like a knife to the gut. I was Father's favourite; he couldn't disguise it.

'I think,' says Mary in a small voice, 'that she has had enough. She said that married to a low-born man she could retire from court, that we could go with her, that we would be safe.'

'Safe!' I snap.

'And she loves him, Kitty.'

'That,' I reply, 'is not possible. Her mother was King Henry's sister, who was Queen Consort of France. Besides, even if it were possible, ladies such as Maman do *not* make love matches with their grooms.' But I, of all people, should know that love can alight in any surprising place, and moreover when you are in its thrall you are entirely beyond reason.

I cannot bear the thought of Maman no longer at court, living like a country housewife, Duchess of Suffolk no more, just plain Mistress Stokes – the thought of it gets under my skin like an itch. I know in my heart that I should want her happiness, but I cannot help myself. 'And will you go with her from court?'

'I don't know, Kitty. Perhaps the Queen will not allow it; after all, I am her pet monkey.' This is said with uncharacteristic bitterness.

'Mouse.' I feel now a surge of love for my little sister. The resentment for her affinity with Maman drops away when I remember the reality of Mary's existence. 'Come, I shall sneak you out of here and to bed. No one will know.'

'Look,' she says, lifting the bottom of my skirts. 'Your foot is bleeding. I blame those shoes. I will bind it for you.'

I am full of good intentions, but as we stand he is there, Harry Herbert, warm, smelling of almonds, slipping his hand about my waist, whispering in my ear, 'Come with me, outside. No one is watching.'

I know I should refuse, tell him that I must see my sister to bed, that we have important things to talk about; but I am sucked into his world, I cannot help myself.

'I will be just a moment,' I say to Mary, and I allow myself to be led away, my bloodied foot forgotten – everything forgotten.

Outside it is warm and there is a fat moon casting slivers of silver light over the courtyard.

'Here,' Harry says, passing me a flask. I put it to my lips and gulp back the liquid it contains. It burns my throat and makes me cough. I laugh then and so does he.

'Harry Herbert,' I say. 'Harry Herbert; is it really you?'

'It is really me, my pretty Kitty Grey.'

I pull his cap from his head and run my fingers through his hair.

We find ourselves in a little walled garden off the court, with yew hedges and a carpet of grass. We collapse on to it and he is at my laces with his fingers. I taste the flesh of his neck, salty. His hand is inside my shift.

'We are husband and wife still,' he says.

'So this is not a sin,' I laugh. 'What a shame.'

'Naughty Kitty. My father would whip me, were he to find us.'

I shrug off my over-gown and pull my hood away, letting my hair splay out on the damp grass, spreading my arms out wide. He is over me, smiling, silver with moonlight.

'I have wanted you, Kitty, so badly,' he murmurs, his hot breath caressing my skin, bringing his lips on to mine. I am alive at last.

Mary

I have waited an age for Katherine. I suppose she is not coming back. A worry niggles at the back of my mind, that this Harry Herbert will visit trouble on her. I watch his father, Pembroke, searching for him amongst the dancers. I think I see Katherine's pale gold hair in a crowd near the door but I am mistaken, for when the girl appears fully she doesn't have my sister's bright eyes nor her bud lips; it is just some girl who looks a little like her. I am conspicuous sitting all alone and can sense curious eyes flitting over me. I feel scrutinized for my ugliness as my sister must feel gazed upon for her beauty. My dress pinches at me and my back aches in its brace; I think about slipping away to the maids' quarters alone, but I will never reach the laces at the back of my gown without help, and Peggy is bound to be fast asleep by now. Maman is busy waiting on the Queen. I even consider seeking out Mistress Poyntz but am daunted at the idea of her sharpness.

I decide to wait a bit longer and watch the Queen gazing at her new husband. She has opened like a flower, but he cannot hide his disappointment and I wonder what he had expected of her. Had he been sent a portrait that flattered a little too much, like the one of me that Maman keeps, which makes me appear perfectly formed? The more I watch the new couple, the more I can feel my hatred for them both take hold. His dissatisfaction makes a mockery of the price that was paid for this wedding – my sister's life.

I shall never forget when I discovered the truth behind this Spanish union. It was last winter, in the aftermath of a failed reformist rebellion to snatch the throne. The court's ladies, and I with them, had sat up all night, crammed into the women's chambers at St James's, petrified, awaiting the rebel army. Father was out there somewhere with them, though I did not know it then. I overheard Maman whispering to Levina that it would be a 'bloodbath' if the insurgents made it to the palace. It was quite beyond my comprehension then, but I have learned something of the world these last months. Maman said too that we must all secretly pray that the uprising succeed, for if the Queen were ousted Jane would be released from the Tower, but that we must not whisper a word of it to anyone, save God. There is so much of all this I still do not fully understand, and try as I might I cannot put the pieces of it together. People do not tell me things; they suppose me too young. But I know more than they think.

It was in the aftermath of that night that I came upon a terrible truth. The Queen was resting in her closet; I was on her lap, as she likes it, kneading at her birdy arm. She is constantly beset with all manner of aches and pains.

'Harder, Mary.'

'Harder, Mary,' rasped Forget-me-not, strumming the bars of his cage with his beak.

I feared to snap the Queen's wrist beneath my fingers; there is no flesh on her. She hummed a fragment of tune under her breath, repeating it over and over again, while she fingered a miniature of her husband-to-be. She gazed at it, making a sigh, as if she was either very happy or very sad. That is love, I suppose. I know, from watching Katherine, that love lacks logic.

'Now like a feather, Mary,' she said. I began to stroke her lightly with the very tips of my fingers, barely touching the dark growth of hair that runs up to her elbow. She is quite hairy, the Queen; her legs are covered in a thick dark tangle. When I asked Katherine about it, she said that no, it was not normal, revealing her own fine-shaped lower leg that is smooth as butter. 'It is because she is half Spanish and the Spaniards are known to all be hairy as bears.'

I heard something then; not more than a tiny tap of sound, like the creak of a beam. The Queen stopped her humming, pricking her ears, and there it was again. Tap, a pebble against glass.

'Tie our sleeve, Mary,' the Queen said, holding her arm out for me.

Forget-me-not rapped at his bars. 'Tie our sleeve, Mary.'

I fumbled with the tapes, feeling the impatience bubbling

in her, making my fingers all thumbs. She shoved me off her lap. 'Hood! Gown!' I fetched them and helped her into them, thankful that the gown, a stiff thing made of gold cloth, covered my untidy bows. She grabbed a candle and moved to the window, stopping there a brief moment before arranging herself back in her chair. Then she asked for her bible and rosary and indicated that I sit on a cushion at her feet. She sat straight with her chin up, as if she were playing a queen in a masque and I were a favourite pet on the floor beside her.

I heard a scuffling coming from the far wall, and a figure wrapped in a cloak appeared through the panelling like a spectre. I must have been gawping, for the Queen cuffed me on the shoulder with, 'Catching flies, Mary.'

The figure strode to the centre of the chamber and bowed, throwing off his hood and flinging his cloak to the corner of the room. I recognized Renard, the imperial ambassador, standing before us. I felt the Queen come to life, like a spark in tinder. I had seen him often about the palace with his entourage, watched how refined his manners were, how perfectly turned out he always was, everything in its place, which makes you wonder what he is hiding.

'Have you something for us from our betrothed?' The Queen's voice was breathless, as if she had been running.

'I do.' He pulled a pouch from beneath his doublet.

The age dropped from the Queen's face and suddenly she was a child tempted by a sweetmeat. She took it a little more eagerly than is quite correct, pulling its neck open and tipping a ring out into her palm with a delighted sigh, then holding it up to the candle.

'An emerald, our favourite of all the stones,' she said, sliding it on, holding her hand up to admire it. 'I feel he knows me already.'

It was enormous, far too big for her tiny finger.

I remember feeling sure I had seen this ring before, on the smallest finger of Renard himself. I have always been one to notice things that others don't.

The Queen was blushing and cooing like a bride. 'Look how it catches the light,' she said. 'Is it Felipe's own, has his finger sat here where ours is? What is this engraved here? SR. What is that, Renard, is it some secret message of love?'

'*Semper regalis*.' The words spilled out of his mouth, too fast.

'Ever regal,' she echoed.

'*Semper regalis*!' cried Forget-me-not, making Renard titter politely and offer some flattery about how only *she* could have a bird that learned Latin so quickly.

I was wondering how it was possible that the woman who faced down a rebel army only the night before, a woman so greatly educated as Mary, Queen of England, had not suspected that SR might also stand for Simon Renard. I am only nine – though it is true I am not typical for my age – and it seemed clear as day to me. This was not a love token from her husband to be, but something Renard had hastily conjured up, knowing she would expect a gift from the Spanish prince.

The ring was a deceit, like when people say to me, 'You are not *so* small, Mary, and your back is only a little crooked; it will straighten out as you grow.' It is said to make me feel better about my deformities, but I would rather the truth. The Queen, though, seemed happy with Renard's lie. I have noticed people will believe what they want to believe.

'The Emperor has asked that I congratulate you on your fortitude in quelling the heretic rebels. "A finer match for his son", he said, "could not be found upon this earth. A formidable queen."'

'Indeed.' She looked like a finch fluffing its feathers.

'And, "pious".' The Queen slowly closed and then re-opened her eyes, as a small smile flickered about her mouth. 'But,' continued Renard, clearing his throat with a little cough.

'But?'

'But the girl . . . She cannot be allowed to live.'

The Queen then expelled a small groan. 'She is our family.'

'The Emperor is adamant on this point. With so much unrest, so much dissidence about – reformists, heresy.' He paused. 'She is simply too great a risk to your crown.'

I supposed they were talking of the Queen's sister, Elizabeth. The rebels would have put *her* on the throne with their uprising.

'She is so very young.' All the joy seemed to drain from the Queen then, and she began wringing her hands, rubbing and rubbing, as if washing ink from them. 'She spent many happy days with us at Beaulieu.'

I remember thinking, *I* know Beaulieu well; we used to go there often to visit Mary before she was queen. I remember her greeting us always as 'My most favourite cousins.' I remember Jane refusing to curtsy before the sacrament in the chapel there. 'She will grow out of it,' they said.

We all must take the greatest care to appear as Catholics, now Mary is queen, so Maman says all the time.

'Renard.' The Queen's voice was twisted out of its normal shape. 'We cannot.' She stood then, her bible and rosary slipping to the floor with a clatter. 'You do not understand. We love the girl. We cannot see her executed.'

The Queen dithered back and forth, turning one way and another, while Renard followed her with his eyes. They seemed to forget I was there. 'The husband's execution we can stomach. Those Dudleys are traitors to the core. But *she* . . . She is our cousin, our *child* cousin.'

It was only then that understanding came to me, like a shadow in the side of my eye. It wasn't Elizabeth they were talking of; it was my sister Jane and her husband, Guildford Dudley. A gasp escaped my mouth. The Queen and Renard turned to me together; her face was smudged with despair, Renard's with . . . What was it; was it shame? I hope it was shame.

'*Her* sister,' hissed the Queen, pointing towards me. '*Her* sister.' She crumpled into her chair, dropping her face into her hands. 'We cannot.'

'*Her* sister,' repeated Forget-me-not.

Renard was kneeling at her feet then. 'The Emperor . . .' he began. 'The Emperor would see it as a sign of commitment to his son.'

'What are you saying?' Her eyes flashed angrily. 'That it is a condition . . .' She paused, taking a deep wavering breath. 'Prince Felipe or Jane Grey?'

I wanted to shout at them, remind them I was there. But I found myself struck dumb.

'There are no conditions, as such.' Renard's voice was smooth as silk velvet. 'The Emperor – *also* Your Highness's own cousin – wishes nothing more than the security of your realm. You are a "formidable queen", as he says.'

'But . . .' she began. Then said nothing.

'The Prince Felipe, pardon my turn of phrase, madam, he itches for this wedding. He thinks of the match, of *you*, my dearest Queen, as' – he seemed to search for the word – 'peerless.'

She twisted the emerald on her finger. It seemed to me a grotesque thing. I was hollowed out by the thought of it; I still am – my kind sister, who never hurt a soul.

The Queen leant forward and grasped my under-arms, pulling me up on to her lap again, clasping me tightly to her, so tight I struggled to find my breath. She hummed a low note close to my ear, a kind of sob or moan; I could smell the sharp neroli oil she likes to dab on her breast; her stiff golden gown scratched at the skin of my face. I wanted, desperately, in that moment to feel the arms of my own Maman about me. It is only Maman's touch I can bear.

'You may leave, Renard,' the Queen said.

Only when he was gone did she release me from her grip. 'Oh, little Mary, the Lord asks much of us.' Without looking at me she took up her rosary, flicking the beads through her fingers, murmuring a prayer. I wanted to jump from her lap, run from the room, from the palace, away from her.

'May I be excused?' I whispered, in a break in her prayers.

'Of course, Mary dear, run along,' is all she said. There was no mention of my sister who was about to be executed, not a word. As I reached up to the door handle, she said, 'Mary!' and I thought, now she will say something.

I turned to look at her.

'Send in Susan Clarencieux and Jane Dormer.'

I was utterly deflated. It was almost too much for me to put one foot before the other and leave the room.

I feel a squeeze on my shoulder. 'Let me take you to your bed, *ma petite chérie*.' It is Maman. My neck is severely cricked and I realize I must have dropped off, though how, with the racket of the musicians and the stomping of the dancers, I do not know.

She scoops me up in her arms and carries me from the great hall, taking me, not to the maids' quarters, but to her own, gently depositing me on the big tester bed and beginning to undo my clothes.

'But Maman, what of your bedfellows?' I ask sleepily, remembering how many ladies are sharing this room.

'Fret not, Mouse,' she says. 'I shall see to it.' She unpeels my clothes, layer by layer, until I am just in my shift and sinking into feathers as if on a cloud. 'Better?' she asks.

'Better,' I reply. We sit in silence for a while, she stroking my hair, but I cannot stop thinking about Jane; much as I have tried to make sense of it all, I cannot fill the spaces in the story. 'Maman,' I ask. 'Why was it that Jane was made Queen?' My mind is a thicket of tangled questions.

'Oh, Mouse, I don't think –'

'Do not say I am too young. Tell me, Maman. I am old enough to know the truth.'

I have seen our great family tree, a long roll of parchment painted with meandering gilded branches, and curlicues of vegetation, with birds and small creatures scattered here and there, and what appear to be fruits hanging in clusters but are in fact tiny portraits. Father had unrolled it once for my sisters and me, on the floor of the great hall at Bradgate, and pointed out exactly how we come to have our royal blood. He showed us the first Tudor king, the seventh Henry, our great-grandfather, and then with his finger followed the meandering gilded lines, finding all our cousins so we could see how we are connected.

'Young King Edward – *pauvre petit* – he named her his heir. There were simply no boys to be had.'

'But Mary and Elizabeth?'

'His sisters? There were problems of legitimacy and *your* sister, Jane, she was perfect – of the new faith, pious, learned and of an age to birth boys: an ideal choice.' She pauses and swallows, as if to stop her feelings from spilling out.

'But why were *you* not named before Jane, Maman?'

'Oh, *chérie*,' she says, drooping visibly at the shoulders. 'I set aside my claim in favour of her.'

I am trying to tug this fact out from the tangle in my head, to get a proper look at it. 'So it was you?' I stop myself from saying it was her fault, but I am thinking it. Her eyes are glossy with tears, so I offer my handkerchief, which she takes without looking at me.

'I must live with the shame of it,' she says. '*J'ai honte, jusque au coeur.*'

'Ashamed to the heart,' I repeat. 'But why did you do it?'

She sighs again, as if the air in her is poisoned and she must get it out of her. 'Your father, Mouse, he was in the thrall of the Lord Protector, Northumberland, at the time. He was caught in Northumberland's web. I tell myself I had no choice. Whether that is the truth or not . . .' She stops. 'We all deceive ourselves sometimes, Mouse. You will learn that with age.' The candle gutters and spits, its flame diminishing. 'And when Northumberland knew the young King Edward was dying, he conspired, with your father, to wed his son, Guildford Dudley, to Jane.' There is a flash of anger in her eyes. 'I never sanctioned *that*. But my word held no weight against theirs.'

At last the knot in my head begins to untangle. 'Northumberland wanted to see *his son* as king, then?'

'Father was a fool in the face of Northumberland, became infected with his ambition. That path always leads to the block.'

Maman cradles her chin in her hands, looking at me. I notice the way the dim light enlivens her chestnut hair and sculpts the angles of her face; she is pale and finely wrought, like Jane, and I can see for an instant the way we are all undeniably tied together, seeing the golden branches of that family tree, veins of Tudor blood, joining us inextricably. The inevitable question emerges from amongst my newly ordered thoughts. 'And Kitty!' I say. 'There are so many who do not want a Catholic on the throne, will someone not try to put the crown on Kitty since she is next, after Jane?'

She looks away from me, down towards the floor, with the words, 'I hope to God not.' Then repeats more quietly, '*Dieu nous garde*.' It feels as if a great dark blanket has lowered itself over us, and she murmurs, 'Let us pray that this Spanish marriage produces an heir.'

'When you are wed,' I say, to change the subject, 'is it sure I will live with you away from court? Will the Queen not want me?'

'The Queen has her husband now, and if God is on our side will soon have an infant.'

I know she means that I will not be required to play the Queen's poppet when she has a real baby.

'It is all I want, Maman, to stay close to you.'

'And so you shall.' She unclasps the pomander from her girdle, placing it on the pillow. The scent of lavender reaches me. 'It will help you sleep, little one.'

'Sometimes I wonder though, Maman, what will become of me, for no man will want me for a wife, despite all the royal blood I contain.' Unless, I think bitterly, there is some noble boy out there with only one leg or two heads who would accept me.

'You must not vex yourself with such thoughts, Mouse. *Ne t'inquiètes pas*.'

But what I cannot say is that, having lost my father and my sister so brutally, my world seems barely strong enough to hold the remnants of our family and I wonder what will become of Katherine, who seems now teetering on the brink of safety. What if I should lose Maman too, and spend my days a ward of the crown, traipsing from palace to palace for ever? I know it is sinful to think only of myself, but the fear has got inside me like a fever, so I close my eyes firmly and force myself to think of another kind of future: a simple life, a quiet place, where girls are not used as pieces in this game of crowns.

July 1554
Ludgate
Levina

Levina watches the sleeping form of her son, Marcus, back from his studies. He is sprawled across a bench in the Ludgate yard, with Hero stretched out beside him in a pool of sun. It seems hard to believe that sixteen years ago she was cradling him, a tiny swaddled bundle, in her arms; now he is becoming a man and she has begun the process that every mother must, of letting him go. The thought squeezes her heart tightly. He was born so early no one thought he could survive. A few whispered that was what happened when a woman sought to do a man's work. Spending too much time amongst painters' materials had poisoned her womb, they said; and women like her could not birth healthy infants. But Marcus survived, and more than that he thrived; that silenced the goodwives of Bruges. Levina sometimes wonders what they would all say if they knew she had been barren since; they would have liked that – the satisfaction of being right. But London had beckoned and Bruges is nothing but a memory now. The women of Ludgate offer begrudged respect, due, she can only assume, to her success at court, but she is aware that they think her occupation displeases God. Everyone has an opinion on what God might or might not think, whether in Bruges or London, but for Levina God is a private matter – more so now, with a Catholic queen on the throne.

She unfurls a sheet of paper on to the table and begins to sketch out a rough outline of her boy and Hero, who has shifted to rest his chin on Marcus's thigh. She can hear the street sounds beyond the wall, hawkers calling their wares and a man who has been shouting his protest against the royal wedding all morning in a loud voice. Levina passed him on her way back from market and she can still hear him, though he has become quite hoarse now. There is nothing his protest can achieve – the wedding is done; England has a Spanish king whether she likes it or not. The edges of her paper refuse to stay flat, so she weighs down the corners with four large pebbles kept for that purpose. They came from her father's studio. Her husband had been puzzled at her desire to bring ordinary stones on their journey to England when they were already so laden with baggage. But, perhaps more than any other objects she has kept from the past, they serve as mementoes.

Levina doesn't miss Bruges but she misses her father. She was his special child and understood the disappointment he felt that none of his five daughters was a boy. Levina was the one he took to his workshop where, as a very small child, she would marvel at the sheets of vellum exquisitely illuminated by his hand, books of hours with intricate images and delicately etched text, the colours leaping out, vibrant, the gilding polished like solid gold. That place is etched into her memory. She used to gaze for hours at her father's work, the curlicues of vegetation branching out and around the margins of the page, with the occasional bird or creature breaking up the regular pattern. He could put a fly in the margin, so realistic that, even though she knew it was painted, she couldn't quite believe it didn't fly away when she swiped her hand over it. She was captivated by the illusion.

She hears the door bang. Hero lifts his head, alert but

unperturbed. Her husband must be home. A small niggle of irritation insinuates itself into her mind. She had been enjoying this peaceful moment and her drawing is on the brink of taking shape; an interruption now might cause it to be lost. She looks at Marcus again. The sun has moved, so shadows fall in grey lines over his skin where the light bleeds through the railings. Levina notices the new lean musculature of her son's arms where they used to be soft and pudgy as the putti in a Florentine chapel. She looks back at her drawing and sees it is wrong; there is nothing of Marcus there. She takes the paper, screws it up and tosses it to the floor. Hero, thinking it a ball, makes a sudden lunge for it and the scene is broken. Marcus twitches, half waking, then settles once more. She can hear George in the hall, talking to the servant. Taking up a new sheet of paper, she starts again, scrutinizing Marcus's striped face, feeling a warm flood of recognition, seeing the parts of him that are hers, the softly rounded cheeks, the wide-set eyes which come from her father, the generous mouth. His ears are George's though, exact facsimiles, as are his large hands, his dark hair too, for Levina's is pale and colourless as whey.

Sometimes she thinks about how she has ended up in this small family of men when she was raised in a house full to the rafters with women, but she has found women enough at court to replace her sisters. The Greys have become as close to her as family – she counts Frances very dear and witnessing with her Jane's death has knotted the bonds of their friendship even more tightly. They had first become close when comforting each other following the death of Levina's first patron, Katherine Parr. It strikes her that this unlikely friendship has been deepened more by shared grief than any other common territory. She and Frances could not be further apart in upbringing, she a common painter from

Bruges and Frances the granddaughter of a king. But sometimes friendship between women cannot be explained in the normal scheme of things.

Levina fears deeply for Frances and her girls at court, where they are forced to dance around her daughter's usurper. The memory of Jane sits in her gut like a grocer's weight. Frances is criticized, Levina has heard the whispers, for remaining at court whilst her daughter and husband went to their deaths. They call her heartless. They do not see the truth of it, that she stayed, stays, close to the Queen because the Queen demands it, but also to try and draw some mercy out of her cousin and keep the remnants of her family from the same fate – after all, Katherine Grey now has as much of a claim on the throne as poor, dead Jane had.

George has come in now and stands silently behind his wife, watching her draw. She doesn't acknowledge him. She is grateful of his respect for her work, that he never seeks to interrupt her, and she is tweaked by guilt for the annoyance she felt before. A strand of hair has fallen forward over her face, which she blows away with an upward exhalation. She can hear George's breath. Now the charcoal seems to magically obey her wishes, the image appearing on the paper as if it were there already and it is some kind of mysterious alchemy that has made it visible. She stops and turns to George with a smile.

'You have captured him, Veena,' he says, lightly placing his hand on her shoulder. It is an unfamiliar touch for her; he has been on guard duty at court, they have been apart for several weeks and will have to find one another again amongst the detritus of their separate experience.

'How are you, George? You look tired,' she says.

'Don't stop your drawing. I like to watch you draw.'

'Sit, then, and I shall draw you. Over there.' She indicates a stool in the sun by the window.

Sometimes, when she looks at her husband's face, she feels she hardly knows him, for she cannot see any more the young man who presented himself nervously to her father all those years ago in an ill-fitting but expensive doublet and with a fringe of hair severely cut across his forehead that gave him the look of a monk. Levina remembers fearing there might be a tonsure beneath his cap, which made her want to laugh. He was the nephew of her mother's friend and thought he might find a wife amongst the Bening family's abundance of daughters.

Strictly speaking they were not quite well-born enough for him, but George Teerlinc was something of an oddity, with the cowed look of a beaten dog and a stutter that made it seem impossible for him to get from one end of a word to the other. His first greeting left an excruciating hiatus in the room while they waited for him to stammer out the usual niceties. Levina's sisters, Gerte in particular, looked on anxiously, each of them silently willing him to pick one of the others. Levina felt desperately sorry for him and her sympathy must have shown on her face, for she was the one he chose.

Her father was sanguine on the outside at least – he knew he would lose her to marriage one day, though if he'd had his way he would have kept her always. But Levina was seventeen then, and it was seventeen years ago now; how time has surprised her in its passing. It was her mother who drove the deal and George Teerlinc took her without a dowry, which was unusual.

'Why so miserable?' Levina remembers her mother asking her father. 'You have four girls left still.' He turned from her and left the room without a word.

Levina followed him, catching up with him in the garden, where the leaves were falling. 'It will not be so bad, Father.'

'But Veena, you are my special one,' he replied.

'Shhh,' she remembers saying. 'The others might hear.'

'Do you think they don't know it already, Veena?' He opened his arms out to his favourite daughter then, wrapping her with them, and she was glad not to have to look at his buckled face.

'Are you not suspicious,' Gerte had said that night, 'that Teerlinc takes you without a portion? Even with that awful speech impediment – he comes from a much better family than us. Perhaps he is incapable of it.'

It was something the sisters talked of often. Levina was glad to get away from Gerte, even if it meant marrying the peculiar George Teerlinc. Gerte was wed soon after, to a cloth merchant who was wealthy enough, even for her, but she died in her first childbed. And Levina came to the English court, invited by Queen Katherine Parr, who had heard of her work, and with her came odd George Teerlinc, who was offered a position in the royal guard. She grew to love him, in the main because he tolerated her painting, as most men would not have done. George's stutter has diminished over time but occasionally reappears unexpectedly, usually in a moment of heightened emotion, great joy or great fear. He never mentions it, but Levina suspects it has made things hard amongst the ranks of guardsmen – for men together can be every bit as cruel as women. But by and large it is a good occupation for him, as it requires patience and silence, two of George's greatest talents.

'There,' she says, laying down her nub of charcoal and handing the sketch to her husband. 'What do you think?'

'I look old,' he replies. 'Do I truly look this old?'

'Since when were you so vain, George?' She laughs, and he puts his arms about her, folding her into an embrace. 'L-Levina,' he breathes, and she remembers how much she has loved him, the tenderness seeping out of her, blurring the boundaries between them. He pulls her towards the other room. She glances back at Marcus but he sleeps on, oblivious, with Hero, beside him again, now lolling on his back. The door swings shut and they fumble at each other's laces, breath shallow and urgent, pulling the clothes from each other. As her kirtle falls to the floor she feels her bulk, suddenly self-conscious, afraid perhaps that he will not like the weight that has crept on to her recently. But he seems not to notice, burying his face in her belly, inhaling deeply, as if to catch her very essence.

After they have supped and Marcus has retired, George picks up a sheaf of Levina's sketches, looking through them.

'Whose hands are these?' he asks.

Levina crosses the room to look over his shoulder where he has leaned towards the candlelight to better see. He is holding a drawing she has made of Jane Grey's hands blindly feeling for the block.

'Nobody's, they are from my imagination.' She doesn't want to explain how it was; doesn't want to remember the horror of it, nor how she cannot bring herself to recreate the whole scene.

'This is Lady Mary Grey, is it not?' He has put that sketch to the bottom of the pile and looks at another now.

'It is.' Levina has drawn her from behind, seated at a three-quarter angle. She has made sketches of Mary, dozens of them, trying to imagine her little body beneath her clothes, the spine twisted and reptilian. She remembers her father taking her to a mortuary once and there seeing the corpse of a dwarf. He had her sketch the body over and over again. It was a lesson in anatomy. 'You cannot assume the human body takes a single form,' he had said. 'Look at each line separately and how it relates to the rest.' She was young enough then to be shocked at the strangeness of the little man's proportions, the short legs, the long body, the square head. Mary Grey is different. Her proportions are perfect but miniaturized, like a marionette; her face is dominated by a pair of round liquid eyes and a mouth that sits in a smile whether she means it or not. But she is crooked, quite inhumanly so, and that is the thing that fascinates Levina, the juxtaposition of perfection and imperfection.

'I can't imagine what it must be like for her,' murmurs George. Levina wonders if he is referring to the girl's deformities or her situation.

'She is stronger than she looks,' Levina says. 'It is the other sister I worry for most.'

'Lady Katherine?'

She nods. 'Look.' Taking the sheaf of drawings from him, she shuffles through them until she finds one of Katherine.

'You have caught her fragility,' he says. 'And her beauty.' He scrutinizes the drawing, holding it closer to the light. 'I had never noticed before how she favours her father in her looks.'

'She has his charisma,' Levina says. And it is true; Henry Grey turned heads in his time.

'In the guards' room I have heard some talk of *her* rather than Elizabeth as the heir.'

'God help her.' She tries to imagine capricious Katherine Grey as Queen of England. It seems impossible but it is not, for she doesn't have the blot of illegitimacy on her as Elizabeth does, and it is she, with her abundance of Tudor blood, who comes next in the late King's Device for the Succession. 'But the Queen hopes to produce a boy to put things straight.' George throws his wife a look, rolling his eyes up.

He continues to look quietly through her drawings,

alighting on one of Frances, an image she made from memory. She is smiling. Levina hasn't seen her smile for some time now. 'Why so many drawings of the Greys?' he asks.

'Frances is making a gallery at Beaumanor. She wants me to paint portraits of them all to hang there.' The Grey estates should have been lost to the crown when the duke was executed, but the Queen reinstated most of them almost immediately, though not Frances's beloved Bradgate. Frances's relief had been palpable, it meant far more than the lands and the houses; it meant she had regained a little of the Queen's favour, but even so she still teeters on a knife-edge with her two girls. Their pretence at Catholicism is scrutinized; Frances has told Levina that she feels Susan Clarencieux's eyes on her constantly and that every last thing is reported back to the Queen – what they eat, with whom they correspond, how often they pray. It is no wonder she wants to shore herself up with images of her fragmented family.

'More portraits!' George's voice betrays his resentment. Perhaps he would like a wife at home birthing infants, one a year.

'Not this,' she says.

'What do you mean?'

'I mean that you do not have the right to complain about my painting. We live in the main from the proceeds.' She spreads her arms out to indicate that almost all they have – the silver plate stacked in the sideboard, the glass in the front windows – came largely from her labours, aware that she is being unkind in reminding him of his shortcomings. She knows most husbands would have whipped her into submission years ago.

'Is it true Frances Grey means to wed her groom?'

'Do you have nothing better to do than gossip in the

guards' room?' Her annoyance sits on the surface of her voice. She knows well enough that George is jealous of her friendship with Frances and he will know it irks her to think that they are all prattling about her friend's choice of husband. 'Stokes is a good man, a kind one, and that marriage will mean a life away from court for her and the girls.' She is almost shouting now. 'Nobody else sees it like that, though. It is as if the world will turn on its head if a duchess marries a commoner.'

'I didn't mean . . .' George begins.

'I'm sorry,' she says. 'I know.' She *is* sorry. She can't bear to argue when they are together alone so rarely.

'I worry, though . . .' He pauses, bringing a hand up to his brow. 'I fear that your connections to that family might visit trouble on us.'

'I am not a fair-weather friend, George. I would not abandon Frances. She has been good to me.' She is thinking of how little men seem to understand female friendship. 'Besides, the Queen favours her.' She is aware of being disingenuous but can't help it. She has caught herself up in this dispute and can't seem to get out of it.

'The Queen was fond of Lady Jane, you said it yourself, but it didn't stop –'

'Enough!' she says, lifting her palm as if conjuring an invisible wall between them, feeling her anger brimming again, but he is right.

'I fear the c-c-c . . .' It seems an interminable time before he can spit out the rest of the word. It no longer frustrates Levina, who has lived with her husband's stammer for so long now she barely notices, but her anger with him continues to brew for what he implies. 'The c-c-consequences of this new union, Veena.' He is talking of the Queen and her Spanish Prince Felipe. He is not the only one who fears the Catholics; many of those who cleave to the reformed faith have fled abroad, where they can practise it safely.

'If you are afraid, if you are not man enough, then go back to Bruges.' She instantly claps a hand over her mouth, admonishing herself for being sharp-tongued again. 'I didn't mean . . . That was not fair.'

She moves behind him to massage his shoulders. He is stiff and unyielding and they are silent for some time until he says, 'We have a good marriage, do we not, V-V-V –'

'We do, George,' she murmurs.

'Are you cold?' he asks. She nods. The evening has brought a chill with it.

'The Queen will be married by now,' he says, as he gathers things together to light the fire. 'God alone knows what changes will occur. I fear there will be burnings. There was a fight in Smithfield earlier today. Worse than usual.' He is hunched over the hearth with the tinderbox.

'Catholics and reformers?' Levina asks, though she does not need to, for it seems increasingly the case. There is one kind of scuffle or other between opposing religious groups most days.

'Bonner thrashed a man for not raising his eyes to the host at Mass. That started the trouble.'

'Bishop Bonner.' She has an image of him in her mind, his rotund shape and boyish expression belying a cruel streak of monstrous proportions. 'Now there is a man who will be first in line to Hell.' It all seems so distant, the time under young King Edward, when they could practise their faith openly; England is still reeling from the abrupt shift to Catholicism with the new Queen.

'Veena, do we have anything here in our house that might condemn us?'

'A few pamphlets. A bible.' George has never engaged

much in religious matters but Levina has found the reformed faith fixed into her indelibly, as egg renders paint immutable. She knows that a bible written in English is a dangerous thing to own. 'As long as we are seen to attend Mass.'

'And raise our eyes to the host.' She looks through a pile of things for a pamphlet she was handed in the market place the other day. 'Here.' She gives it to him.

'It seems fairly innocuous,' he says, scanning it then throwing it on to the fire nevertheless, 'but you never know.' She adds another to it, which she had been using to mark a page in one of her books of anatomical drawings. They have seen too many changes in the last years and caution hovers over them constantly.

'They wouldn't see harm in these, would they?' She opens a book to a drawing of a dissected corpse. 'Are they ungodly, perhaps?'

'The day those become heresy, Veena, is the day we return to Bruges.' He gives her an affectionate squeeze. 'And your bible?'

'George, you can't mean to burn that?'

'Rather *that* burn than you.'

'No!' She can't quite believe he has suggested it. 'It is God's word.'

'Yes,' he says. 'And surely God would forgive that. The reason is good enough.'

'You go too far, George.'

'Then give it me and I shall hide it somewhere outside the house. Bury it safely.'

'Has it truly come to this?' she asks.

'Not yet, but it will.'

She takes her bible from the wooden chest, kissing it before handing it to him, surprised to feel lighter for it. She is protected by her husband's cautiousness, understanding how George, Marcus and she are stronger together than the parts of them. She thinks of Frances on her own, trapped in the dissembling world of the court, trying to keep her girls out of harm's way. It is no surprise she seeks to wed her groom.

'I am so very fond of you, George,' she says.

'I know,' he replies.

November 1554
Whitehall
Mary

The Queen's hand is a claw. It clasps at my shoulder and it is all I can do to stop myself from shrugging it off. Her other hand is cradling her belly, stroking it in a circular motion, lest anyone forget that she is with child. She is radiant with it, blissful, gazing goggle-eyed at her husband.

My loathing for her is a demon squatting behind my smile. I am still her pet monkey, at her beck and call, to rub her aching arms, to read to her, to fetch and carry. It seems as if she has forgotten she murdered my sister. I wonder about her conscience; how she can live with what she has done. She thinks she has pleased God. I will not believe in her God who is pleased with such things. But I click my rosary between my fingers when we are at prayer – Mary Grey, good as gold.

Her Spaniard is beside her, stiff and awkward, leaning away, as people do when they are seated next to *me* – I of all people know what distaste looks like. She touches his sleeve and he flinches. I can see how she disappoints him, and how little she is aware of it. Felipe wears the look Katherine has when she is offered a gift that doesn't please her, but she must pretend. People seem content enough with the Spaniard now he is here all splendid and haughty; he has the look of a king. People are greatly swayed by appearance; I should know that.

We are in the stand at the Whitehall tiltyard, all here to watch the visitors show us some kind of Spanish fighting game. I have watched the English these last months, doing their very best not to be impressed by anything about the Spaniards, and today is no different. A few of the minor foreign nobles are skipping about on the field enacting a mock battle, waving their rapiers about, but no one is taking much notice. The sky is heavy with cloud and the air is cold and damp with a mizzle that threatens to turn into rain. We are wrapped in furs and under the canopy, protected from the weather, but the men on the field droop miserably and must be wishing themselves back home in the sun.

They do not like England, and complain constantly about the weather and the food and the maids. They say we are strangely dressed, too vivacious, and plain. That doesn't stop them leering like hungry dogs at my sister and Jane Dormer. Feria, who is closest to the King and the most gentle-mannered of them, seems to have taken a shine to Jane Dormer. Katherine says she would make a good wife for a man like him because she is so good and meek and kind. I know it is obedience that makes a good wife, or so Mistress Poyntz is always saying, though not to me, for everyone knows I will never be a wife. I must strive to be docile anyway, to make up for my shortcomings. But I wonder what that means for Katherine, who hasn't an obedient bone in her body.

Felipe whispers something to the Queen, so close that even I, though I am still seated upon her lap, cannot hear. As he speaks his eyes drift towards me and I can see clearly the disgust in the set of his mouth.

'Mary, dear, our knee is aching. Would you get down and sit beside us.' There is an apology in the Queen's voice. She cannot be aware of how little I enjoy all the lap-sitting, nor how much I detest her. She asks Jane Dormer to shuffle down and make space for me at her side, but her husband intervenes with another whisper. Jane Dormer is moved back beside the Queen, and I am shunted down to sit on Jane's other side, next to Magdalen Dacre – where the Spaniard can pretend I don't exist. Magdalen makes a face and, turning a shoulder to me, slides herself away as far as she can, muttering something to Cousin Margaret, who makes a snort of laughter. I pretend I do not care. I am used to it, but I do care; I just cannot let myself think of it.

I look across the stand to where my sister should be, but she has slipped away. I scan the field and spy her scarlet gown peeping out from behind the big yew hedge of the physic garden. She is likely canoodling with the Herbert boy. Half a dozen mounted Spaniards, Feria amongst them, thunder on to the field to a great cheer from the waiting crowd. The King stands, clapping his hands together above his head. The rest of us follow suit but the applause is hollow. The riders are dressed as if for battle in breastplates and boots, with odd-shaped plumed caps and voluminous black capes. Each of them makes a great deal of flicking the ends of his cape over his opposite shoulder. Instead of lances they carry long canes. Someone shouts, 'That's not much of a weapon!' which gets the crowd laughing, though I am not entirely sure what is so funny. Their weapons may be lacking but their horses are beautifully turned out, shining like polished wood, their necks curved, nostrils flared, skirts swaying, bridles and bits as complicated as the Queen's jewels.

The horses trot in formation, weaving in and out, lifting their forelegs high and flicking their tails, while their riders toss their canes one to the other, catching them deftly in mid-air.

'Is that the best you can do?' comes a cry from the crowd.

'I'm not familiar with this dance,' comes another, his voice pitched to a squeak in imitation of a woman, raising a laugh.

Felipe's jaw tightens. He is tapping the arm of his seat with the nail of his first finger. We are all silent. There are a few more jeers and heckles. Tap, tap, tap. The Queen takes her husband's hand. He snatches it back. She mumbles something about it being a spectacular display. He snorts in response, turning away from her. The Queen's closest ladies, Susan Clarencieux and Frideswide Sturley, behind us, have begun to clap in pretend eagerness. The King turns and throws them a look that stills their hands. The Queen rubs her belly. One of the horses, a bay gelding, bucks, almost unseating his rider, whose cap flies off.

Even the King laughs at this, until someone calls out, 'Has the lady lost her hat?' causing his jaw to clench once more and his eyes to simmer in anger.

But I have stopped watching whatever it is the Spaniards are doing on the field. My eyes are on a scene in the distance, over by the physic garden, involving my sister. Harry Herbert's father, who is Earl of Pembroke, has his son by the scruff of the neck. Katherine is beside them; she looks so very small next to Pembroke, like a doll, and I can see by the tilt of her head that she is pleading with him. I am silently willing her to hold her tongue, because I know only too well that Katherine is someone who speaks first and thinks after, but she seems unable to stop herself.

Pembroke then, still gripping his son's collar, takes a stride towards her and slaps her smartly across the face with his free hand. She collapses to the grass, her scarlet skirts spreading out around her. I can barely believe what I have seen, that giant of a man, who is now marching his son away, striking my sister like that. He will say she asked for it, but there is no excuse for such a thing.

What would Jane have done, I ask myself, knowing the answer before the question is out. I beg the Queen to excuse me, and clamber down from the stand without alerting Maman, for to draw attention to the incident might make the whole thing worse. My sister's reputation teeters on the brink as it is.

The mizzle has turned to a steady rain and my gown is damp and heavy by the time I reach her. She is still seated on the grass, the red of her dress is dark where it is soaked through, and she is shivering and sobbing uncontrollably.

'Come, Kitty,' I say, trying to sound older than I feel, trying to imagine what Jane would say to her. 'Let us get you inside and out of those wet clothes, before you catch your death.' Her hood has tipped back and some loose strands of yellow hair have plastered themselves to her face. There is a red mark on her cheek in the shape of that man's hand. She still sobs, her shoulders heaving, and only now do I notice that her lacings are undone, and that she is having to hold her gown in place to keep it from falling to the ground.

She allows me to fasten her up and then lead her in silence towards Maman's chambers, which are quite a distance from the tiltyard. My clothes are so heavy with wet it is hard to walk and by the time we get there we are completely bedraggled. Two of Katherine's dogs greet us in a frenzy; she crouches down cooing at them, for a moment seeming to have forgotten her grief.

'Stan, Stim, where are the others?'

'Maman left them with one of the grooms. The puppies were chewing the hangings.'

'And Hercules too?'

'Yes, your monkey too,' I nod. My sister's pets bring out an abundant tenderness in her. Sometimes I think she is so overflowing with love that she doesn't know what to do with it all, and the animals lap it up for her. I wonder what it might be like to spill over with feeling. I clutch on to my emotions so tightly. It is not to say I do not feel things, though.

I call one of the scullions, who arrives with a bucket of hot coals to get the fire going. Soon we have peeled off our wet layers and are sitting by the hearth, Katherine wearing Maman's best silk nightgown and her fine shawl while I am folded in a woollen blanket. We share a hot toddy, passing it between us, taking tiny sips for fear of burning our mouths.

'You must leave him be,' I say.

'But he is my husband,' she sniffs.

'He is *not*, Kitty. You will never win.' I know that Katherine's marriage was part of Northumberland's scheming, for Jane was wed to Guildford Dudley on the same day.

'But we are in love.'

'That doesn't make any difference,' I say. Her face is scrunched with tears.

'Pembroke said I am tainted by the treason of my father and sister, and he will not have his son sullied by it.'

I don't know how to respond but another part of my family's story is coming clear. Pembroke must have changed sides to save his skin when the Queen ousted Jane and that is why he wants no ties to the Greys – we are proof of his own disloyalty.

'At least Father had the courage to die for his beliefs,' she adds, wiping a string of mucus from her nose with her sleeve.

I am not so sure that our father was the man Katherine thinks him. He joined the rebels against the crown and was caught running away, that is what Maman has said. But I will not prick my sister's bubble by repeating it, for Katherine idolized Father. I remember something else Maman said, something about the taint of treason being the one thing that might prevent Katherine from finding herself pushed on to the throne.

'The Queen's position is fragile, *chérie*,' she said. 'And there are many reformers who would see her brought down.'

But Katherine is not thinking about the throne, nor the danger that presses silently around us. She is filled to the brim with the idea of being in love and there is no space in her for anything else. I suppose we all have our own way of forgetting, of not looking truth in the eye.

Maman seeks a way out with her marriage. 'It will put us out of harm's way,' she tells us. But there will be no marriage just yet, for it is too soon, and besides, the Queen barely lets us out of her sight. She has hidden Elizabeth away at Woodstock, in the hope that everyone will forget her. But Elizabeth is unforgettable, everyone whispers about her, and that is a good thing for us, because as long as the reformers are busy not forgetting Elizabeth, us Greys can merge into the background, or so Maman says.

'Come, Kitty, we must dress, for they will all be back soon.' I am trying to take her mind off things. 'What will you wear? Your blue dress? It is so very becoming.'

We help each other into our clean linens and kirtles, lacing one another up, tying on our sleeves, plaiting our hair and tucking it up into our coifs. I like it when Katherine helps me into my clothes, for she is accustomed to my odd shape and touches me as little as possible. Even sweet Peggy Willoughby, when she helps me dress, cannot hide her curiosity, and I can sense the effort she makes not to stare at my strange shape.

'*And* Cousin Margaret is to marry,' Katherine announces, as if she is thinking out loud. I had heard of Margaret Clifford's betrothal, but hadn't wanted to say anything for fear of upsetting my sister. 'Henry Stanley, Lord Strange – a strange match indeed,' she huffs. 'That boy can't keep his hands to himself. She's welcome to him.'

I say nothing; there is nothing to say when Katherine has a bee in her bonnet.

'*And Maman?*' She bangs a fist to her knee, and the remains of the toddy tip on to the floor so that Stan and Stim clamour to get their tongues to it. 'What could she *possibly* see in Stokes? Who *is* he, anyway?'

'He is a kind man,' I say, regretting it instantly for it pricks her further.

'*Kind*,' she says, as if the word tastes bitter. 'He is not even . . .' She doesn't bother to finish.

'I wish you could accept it, Kitty, for it will happen whether you rail against it or not. And besides, Maman seems happier these days, do you not think?'

'Pah!' she exclaims, pulling Stan up on to her lap, holding his face to hers, saying in a baby voice, 'You don't like it either, do you, Stannie?'

I stand and go to the window. 'The rain has stopped.' I make a squiggle with my finger on the misted glass.

'*And*,' Katherine continues her griping, 'that Feria, you've seen him, Mouse, the Spaniard . . . the comely one . . . He has his eye on Jane Dormer. Not that *she'd* notice . . . They *all* want to wed Jane Dormer. Thomas Howard moons at her constantly.' She shrugs off her gown, letting it fall to the floor, and chooses another, slipping it on, smoothing it down. Then she picks up one of Maman's necklaces, clipping it at her throat, taking the glass and inspecting herself in it, turning her head this way and that and pursing her lips, then says with a sigh, 'All the Queen's maids will be wed and I shall be left alone on the shelf.'

'You are only just fifteen. Hardly an old maid yet.

Besides, *I* will be on the shelf with you, so you will not be alone.'

'I am sorry, Mouse,' she says, pushing Stan to the floor and rushing to the casement, where she sits on the window seat so we are the same height and holds out her little finger for me to take. 'I wasn't thinking; it was unkind of me to be so concerned with my own woes when . . .' She doesn't say it but what she means is, when *I* am too deformed to be of interest to anyone at all, ever.

She slides her wedding ring off, saying, 'Here.' Then she lifts my hand very gently, and slips it on to my middle finger. 'You have pretty hands and a pretty face, and you may be small of stature but you have great intelligence; and you may be crooked but you are good and kind.' She pauses, and I can see that there are tears welling again in the corners of her eyes. '*I* am not good and kind. You are worth a dozen of me.'

As she is saying this I have a teary feeling in the back of my throat. I am not one for crying much but my sister's tenderness is making me go soft inside.

'*And*,' she adds, 'there is Claude, who was Queen of France once. Have you not heard of her? She was crookbacked like you and she was married to King François . . . and she was boss-eyed to boot.'

I nod, taking a breath to quell my feelings. I am not sure that I want to know about Queen Claude of France, for knowledge of a crookbacked queen makes me feel less safe in my skewed body.

'What happened to her?' I ask.

'I don't know,' she says. 'But she was mother to the next King of France and in France they named the greengage after her.'

'The greengage,' I repeat, thinking how ordinary a fruit it is. 'And what fruit will be named for me? A gooseberry? I am as sour and as prickly.'

'Mouse! This is not like you.'

But I am thinking that it *is* like me.

'Your eyes are perfect. You see, all is not lost and you are of the blood, as Queen Claude was, so . . .' She leaves her words hanging and spreads out her arms as if to show me that the whole world is mine for the taking.

'Yes, Kitty,' I say, just to please her, my resentment hiding itself once more. 'Of the blood, both of us.' This makes her smile, and when she smiles it is as if the sun is out. We can hear the clatter of people in Base Court returning from the tiltyard. 'They will be going to sup. We had better go too before we are missed.'

We walk, little fingers clasped, to the hall where the boards are laid out and people are arriving. I watch my sister crane her neck, seeking out Harry Herbert. His father is here but he is not, and I can sense Katherine's upset in her stiffness. Maman is over by the dais, beckoning us up to where the King and Queen are receiving. I take a breath and Katherine helps me up, for the steps are too high for me. We curtsy before Their Majesties and a fuss is made of the fact that we have changed, when everyone else has come straight from the jousting. Felipe moves away to where his men are gathered and the Queen pats her lap – my cue to sit myself upon it – and I am back to playing her pet monkey again.

February 1555
Smithfield/Whitehall
Levina

Levina's horse picks his way through the crowds. She is glad her groom is just up ahead for there is violence in the air. They are moving in the opposite direction to the river of people headed for Smithfield, where she has just been collecting new pigments from her supplier whose shop lies tucked in behind St Bartholomew's. She is due at Whitehall; the Cardinal is to sit for her. She fears being late for him and disgracing herself, but the crowds are thickening and increasingly frenzied. She had passed through the market square itself earlier and seen the stake at its centre waiting for the prisoner to arrive and be strapped to the post for burning. It is the prebendary of St Paul's awaiting such a fate – he refused to revoke his beliefs. Levina has seen him about the city on occasion; he always seemed a reasonable man; his manner was gentle. She tries not to think of it, but wonders if it is coincidence that the burnings have begun so soon after the return of the Cardinal from his long exile in Rome, and the reinstatement of the old heresy laws.

A great roar goes up and her horse takes fright, rearing, its flailing hooves almost striking a man's head.

'Get that blasted beast under control!' he shouts, waving his fist and baring his teeth like a cur.

Levina struggles with her nervous mount, made all the more agitated by the shouting, and is thankful when her groom grabs her bridle, coming in close, whispering in the animal's ear and soothing him.

Another roar goes up in the square. 'Oh God!' she cries, the words escaping her mouth involuntarily. The prisoner must have arrived. She had hoped to avoid this, but they are stuck and the crowds are pushing to see the spectacle before it is too late. She prays it will be over quickly, thankful for the strong breeze as the fire will burn well, and hopes that someone has thought to send the poor man a pouch of saltpetre to send him off quicker still. She feels a weight in her gut – that mild man, meeting such an end. She has never witnessed a burning and doesn't want to.

She looks behind to check that Hero has kept up with them; his ears are back and she can see the whites of his eyes; even he has a sense that something bad is afoot, more than the usual rowdy mob. He can sense the bloodlust. She hears a tortured screech and sees a coil of smoke rising, wishing she hadn't turned. It is blowing their way, catching their nostrils, woodsmoke and still that terrible screaming, striking to the heart of her. Then sickeningly there is a whiff of roast pork, which sets Levina's mouth watering involuntarily. Disgusted with her body's response, her eyes prickle and she wraps a kerchief tightly around her face to shut out the stench. Thankfully now the mob has thinned and they can pick up the pace.

Cardinal Pole sits before Levina, his hands folded in his lap. He has not spoken a single word; it is as if she doesn't exist. Perhaps he doesn't like being painted by a woman. But it is the Queen's commission so he has no choice in the matter. He avoids meeting her gaze. His hooded brown eyes give the appearance of kindness but Levina is sure they are deceiving. She cannot get that terrible stench out of her mind, it clings to her clothes; she fears it will never wash out of her and that she will be cursed with the sound of that anguished howl reverberating about her head for ever.

There are five more imprisoned awaiting the same fate next week, and that is just the beginning. Archbishop Cranmer has been taken. They will want to make an exhibition of *him* – the one who annulled the marriage of the eighth Henry and the Queen's mother, rendering Mary Tudor a bastard. The Queen will have her revenge now. Levina asks herself how much of it is driven by the man sitting before her, how much the King, how much the Queen. She has taken to attending Mass daily, even at home away from court, for you never can tell who might be watching and Bishop Bonner has eyes everywhere. George had been right to get rid of her English bible.

She puts down her brush to look at her sitter more carefully, watching the light play on the jewel in his ring, stretching her hand down absently to stroke Hero's ear. Pole has an abundance of beard, which obscures his features, making him hard to read. She tries to tease the man out from those eyes that will not look at her. But she struggles to depict him, so focuses on rendering the red of his robes, mixing a vermilion pigment paste, looking carefully at how the scarlet satin is touched with a bright sheen, almost white, where the light kisses it and how it darkens in the folds, to the colour of blood.

She cracks an egg, allowing the white to slip through her fingers into a bowl and rolling the tender glob of yolk around in her palm to dry it a little, so it takes on a thicker texture. She takes up her knife and slices through the yolk's membrane, dripping it into the pigment, stirring fast until it reaches the perfect consistency, looking again at the Cardinal's robes, adding a few grains of cadmium. She rarely uses egg tempera these days but this picture, with its crimson expanses, calls for it. She hears her father's voice: 'It will still be bright a thousand years hence.' He said it more than once of tempera.

She begins to apply the colour in tiny cross-hatched strokes. The Cardinal heaves out a deep breath, shifting in his seat. His robes settle differently, which irritates her, for she felt she was on the brink of something with her red pigments. There was a dead cat hung from a gibbet. She saw it the other day on her way to the vellum merchant at Cheapside. Someone had dressed the creature in a cardinal's habit. After six firm years of reform under the boy King Edward they do not suppose it will be such a smooth transition to return the English to the Catholic faith, do they? People are not so malleable, and Levina is beginning to believe that those who feared the Inquisition finding its way to these shores with the Spaniard might have been right. There is a palpable sense of fear hanging over the city and she is wondering too if the people have come to regret favouring Mary Tudor when there was a choice to be made; if they might not be rueing the day they rejected Jane Grey.

The English are looking for alternatives; they fear becoming an annexe of Catholic Spain. Elizabeth's name is whispered about, as is Katherine Grey's. There are many who would have either one of those girls on the throne tomorrow. It is no wonder Frances is sick with worry, and Levina wishes there were something tangible she could do to help. The King wants Elizabeth married off to the Duke of Savoy, a cousin of his, and safely packed off to the Continent. But the girl resists, and her will seems greater than the whole of the Privy Council put together, so she festers at Woodstock out of harm's way and under watchful eyes. As long as Elizabeth remains unwed and on these shores, the danger to Katherine is lessened. But the Catholic heir that the Queen has in her belly may save the Greys yet, particularly if it is a boy. She counts in her head: six full months since the wedding – that baby must be half cooked by now. She sets down the crimson paint, wiping her brush on a rag.

The Cardinal's hands are slightly clenched and his knuckles are yellow like shelled nuts. Levina looks again at the shiftiness in his eyes, the way they refuse to meet hers. What is buried beneath that beard, beyond a slash of pink mouth? She takes her fine brush to render the coarse chestnut hair, woven through with steely threads. It is an attempt to find truth in the detail. She imagines a looser style, creating more the idea of a scene or a person, rather than attempting such verisimilitude. It is something she had discussed much with her father. The way in which, however akin to life, there is something, an essence, a movement, that resists capture. Levina feels, when she is attempting a likeness, that she must render not only what can be seen but also what is hidden. The light drops quite suddenly and she looks to the window, where sodden sludge-coloured clouds are billowing, flattening the hues of the Cardinal, rendering his skin an unappealing shade of grey. She finds herself thinking it is fortunate that the rain held off this morning for that poor man's death would have taken longer still with the wood damp, then is suddenly aware of the irony of her thoughts – nothing is fortunate about it, only marginally better.

'I fear the light has gone, Your Grace,' she says. 'May I beg an hour more of your time tomorrow?'

He looks at her at last, with the words, 'Show me,' prodding a hand towards the painting.

Levina does not usually allow her sitters to see themselves unfinished, unless she knows them well, but the Cardinal's manner makes her feel unable to refuse, so she takes down the portrait, which is not large, not even a foot across. Holding it carefully by the edges, so as not to smudge the wet paint, she holds it up for him. He cranes his neck forward.

'Closer.' He speaks to her as if commanding a dog to perform a trick. She moves towards him; as she nears she can smell the incense that clings to his robes and can see more clearly the gauntness that hangs about his face. He looks in silence for some time, seeming satisfied, which is a relief to her for she has not tried to flatter him as she does with some. Then he reaches out a finger towards the close work of his beard. 'The detail,' he says, seemingly to himself. But as he speaks he over-reaches, touching the paint, smearing all the fine hairs Levina has spent the better part of the last hour rendering and leaving a russet mark on his finger. 'Oh . . . I . . . I didn't . . .' He appears unable to spit out an apology, though he is clearly embarrassed by his own clumsiness. For a fragment of time he seems just like an awkward aging man and she thinks it *may* be kindness, or something like it, she sees in those eyes after all.

'It can easily be redone, Your Grace,' she says, handing him a rag to wipe his hand. At least he can't refuse her another sitting now. She begins to clean her brushes, rubbing the excess paint off them with a rag, popping the cork out of the jar of spirit. It makes her eyes smart and the sour smell seeps out into the room. She watches from the side of her vision as the Cardinal clicks his fingers sharply to beckon his page. She wants to catch him when he thinks he is not observed, trying to discover a little more of the man through the occasional fissure in his careful veneer. As the boy helps him out of his seat, he seems to creak like an old door on the hinges of his gouty knees. The two of them cross the room, the Cardinal leaning heavily on the boy. Levina drops into a deep curtsy when they near and he surprises her by stopping and saying with a vague smile, 'You are blessed with a gift, Mistress Teerlinc. It is a sign God favours you.'

'I am most grateful for your kind words, Your Grace.' She sees that he notices, with an almost indiscernible nod, the rosary hanging from her girdle. It is an old one, a relic from her grandmother, and the wooden beads are worn down with use. She imagines he must think their erosion a sign of her faith – everyone is dissimulating in this place, one way or another.

'The Queen might find you a position as a lady-in-waiting,' he says.

'I would not assume such an honour, Your Grace, I am not so gently born.'

'Gently born,' he echoes. 'There are many well-bred ladies who are not as finely mannered.' He pauses, casting his eyes over her, then adding, 'She needs more like you about her.' With this he bends to briefly pat Hero on the head, which warms him to her minutely, then turns and exits, still leaning on the page, leaving Levina wondering if he will continue to think her such a boon when he discovers her close connection with the Greys. But perhaps now that the Greys have been almost entirely decimated and Frances and the girls are giving a convincing impression of having returned to the fold, that connection may not be the disadvantage it once might have been.

When he is gone Katherine Grey enters, sidling round the door. She looks puffy about the eyes and has a handkerchief bunched in her fist; Levina has noticed the girl weeping over Pembroke's boy a good deal of late. She tries to remember what it was like to cry over a lost love but it is hard to garner the feeling – she never was much given to grand passions. But this girl is buffeted by it.

'Can I do something for you, Katherine?' she asks.

'The Cardinal,' Katherine says, looking at the portrait. 'He looks very glum.'

'Do you not find him a rather glum kind of person?'

'I do, I suppose. Must be all that praying.' She takes a jar of pigment from the box, uncorking it and holding it to the light. 'What is this one called?'

'Lead-tin yellow,' Levina says.

'It is the colour of lemons. That is a happy colour.' As she says it her face looks fit to crumble.

'Come here, Katherine.' Levina holds out her arms and Katherine allows herself to be wrapped into them. 'There will be others,' she murmurs, stroking the girl's hair.

'But I am so very broken-hearted. I am like those maidens in the poems, rent in two.'

Levina wants to tell her it will pass, to tell her that she will look back on this one day and it will be a nothing, but she knows she won't be believed, for the girl's feelings are stubbornly fixed, so she just holds her quietly for a while until Katherine says, 'Maman was asking for you.'

Frances is in her rooms with a seamstress, poring over several bolts of fabric that are leaning up in a row against the wall.

'Veena, *ma chère*,' she says with a warm smile, 'how glad I am to see you. No one is better with colour. Mary needs a new gown for Cousin Margaret's wedding.'

Levina notices Katherine's face tighten at the mention of the marriage – it is not surprising, given the manner in which she was wrenched from her own young husband. Frances holds out a swatch of deep pink damask together with a square of buff silk. 'What is your opinion of these together?'

'I think they are too much of one tone, I would rather see the buff with this.' Levina picks up a roll of dark blue velvet. 'It will suit her colouring better.'

'You are right, always right.' Frances turns to the seamstress, instructing her to make a forepart in the silk and a high-necked gown in the velvet, explaining exactly how to best disguise Mary's crookedness, by running the back seams at an angle and making the collar stiff at the nape, with a small starched half-ruff to cover the hunch of her shoulders. 'You should measure her really, but she is with the Queen and I don't know when there will be time. Use this.' Frances hands her an old dress of Mary's.

'Upon my word, it is no bigger than a doll's gown,' the woman exclaims, provoking a sharp look from Frances. 'Begging your pardon, My Lady, I was just –'

'Yes,' interrupts Frances brusquely, turning pointedly away from the woman and to her daughter. 'Now, Katherine, should you not be in the Queen's rooms, *avec ta soeur*?' To Levina she says, 'Let us take a walk while Mistress Partridge gathers all her bits and pieces. There are things to discuss.'

Poor Mistress Partridge, scurrying about, is quite cowed in the face of Frances's firmness and efficiency. Frances can be intimidating to those who don't know her well; people are daunted by her status alone, but it is true that she has a stoniness to her demeanour that hides the depth of kindness and loyalty she harbours, and Levina is one of the few to have seen beneath the surface.

Frances throws her a squirrel wrap. 'It is cold out but the gallery is too full of prying ears. Do you mind, Veena?'

'I could do with some air,' Levina replies, as they both fold themselves into their furs.

'*Je peux imaginer* . . . you have been painting that man. I'm sure he sucks the air out of the room.'

'True,' says Levina. 'But I believe there might be more to him than meets the eye.'

'I doubt it,' Frances says with a sneer. 'The fanaticism for their faith runs through those Poles like wood-grain.' She pauses. 'The Queen seems fond of him, but then I suppose she would be; he has brought England back to the Pope.'

She leads the way out by the back, down the narrow winding steps that run from her chambers to the east entrance. In the yard a messenger has recently arrived entirely spattered with mud, vaulting from his horse and throwing the reins to one of the grooms before scaling the steps three at a time. Levina wonders what news he is bringing; something to do with the Emperor's war with the French, she supposes. The King is itching to get his sword bloody, but the word is that he will stay until his infant is born.

The trees in the orchard are dark against a February sky that is thick like soup. Moles have ruined half the grass, leaving great earthy mounds that the two women have to pick their way around, and Levina can feel the damp seep through her shoes. They arrive eventually at a pavilion. It is open on one side, affording a view of the palace, and has a dovecote at its top, a place where people meet for assignations in better weather, with the scent of the wild flowers and the coo-curoo of the doves to serenade them. Today it smells dank and vaguely of urine, though not enough for them to bother seeking out a better place. They settle on to the cold bench. There is an ominous scattering of white feathers on the floor – a fox must have got at one of the doves.

'I shall be glad to get away from this place,' says Frances. 'I sometimes feel the walls are closing in on me.' Levina looks at her friend. She is thin and pale and her eyes have circles, dark as bruises.

'When will you wed?'

'The spring, I suppose. It is a year since the duke . . .'

Levina nods, understanding that she means she has left a respectable time since the execution of her husband before marrying another.

'It will be a quiet affair.'

'And you will be Mistress Stokes.' She laughs at this, they both do, for they know that, though she will lose her position at court, all will still think of her as the Duchess of Suffolk and first cousin of the Queen, even when she is married to a commoner.

'They think him after my estates but, as far as I'm concerned, he can have them all, what's left of them – it is a small price to pay to get myself away from this *folie*.' She smiles and Levina sees the fleeting ghost of Jane in her face.

'The girls will go with you?'

'That is what I wanted to talk to you about, Veena,' she replies. 'The Queen has said she wants them, well certainly Katherine, at court.'

'She fears another uprising,' Levina says, thinking out loud. 'That a reform faction will champion Katherine for the throne.' She thinks, as she often has, about Katherine as queen and it seems quite ridiculous, but then royal blood and a functioning womb is all most care about in a princess.

'The Queen feels secure with that infant in her belly, though yes . . . I suppose so.' Frances is clenching and unclenching her hands in her lap. 'She has not said as much but that must surely be the reason.'

'People do believe Katherine turned back to Catholicism, don't they?'

'They do, *grâce à Dieu*; they think all us Greys good papists these days. But you know how it is.' Levina does indeed know how it is. 'I persuaded her to let me have Mary,' she continues. 'No one thinks Mary a threat, so she will come with me to Beaumanor and will only be required occasionally. Katherine is to be given rooms of her own.'

'So she won't be in the maids' rooms under Mistress Poyntz's sharp eye.' Levina is wondering if it is a good idea for the girl to be given so much freedom.

'I know. It is an honour.'

'More a curse than a blessing, I'd say.'

Frances nods. 'Will you keep an eye on her, Veena? I worry so that without me she may find herself caught up in God only knows what kind of trouble. She is so very impulsive.'

'Of course I will. You know your girls are like family to me. I shall treat Katherine as if she were one of my own.'

'All this business with the Herbert boy has been such a worry. Pembroke had words with me.'

'Oh dear,' Levina says. No one would welcome 'words' from Pembroke.

'He has sent the boy away. He will go to fight the French soon enough, I suppose. That will get him out of Katherine's orbit. I must put my mind to another match for her, though it might be hard to find anyone prepared to tie themselves to the Greys at the moment.'

Levina thinks of Harry Herbert; he can only be Marcus's age, still so far from manhood really. She can't help but think, too, of all those English boys, courtiers' sons, being readied to fight the Emperor's war. She sees them in the tiltyard sometimes, scrapping like puppies, laughing, their fresh faces still smooth, their slender limbs still carrying the gawkiness of youth, trying on their swagger for size like new outfits. She can't bear the thought of it, the things they will see, how they will suffer. 'I shall make sure your Katherine stays away from trouble, Frances. That is a promise.' She meets the other woman's eye to enforce her words.

'There is another thing,' Frances says, lowering her voice, though there is no one within earshot. She pulls a fold of paper from her sleeve, handing it to Levina. 'Read it.'

'What is it?' she asks, opening it up, seeing a page of carefully written text, casting her eye over it. *I have sent you, good sister Katherine, a book, which although it be not outwardly trimmed with gold, yet inwardly it is more worthy than precious stones* . . . 'It is Jane's letter.' *It shall teach you to live and learn you to die.* The memory returns to Levina unbidden, of that moment: Jane blindly floundering for the block, the crimson spurt. 'Oh Frances,' she says, her voice cracking.

'I copied it from Jane's Greek New Testament.' She pauses. 'I will ask something of you, Veena, but you must know that you are free to refuse. I will not judge you on it. Your friendship is dear to me.'

'Ask,' she says. 'Ask me.'

'Can you get this out to Bruges somehow? Perhaps it could go hidden amongst a package to your family. I can have it collected there and taken on to Geneva. There is a man in that place, Foxe, who will see it is put into print.'

Levina finds herself overwhelmed with emotion and unable to reply with more than a nod.

'Veena, *merci*. From the bottom of my heart, thank you.' She pulls the other woman into an embrace. 'I will *not* have her forgotten. She will shine as a beacon for the new faith. As the Catholics have their Virgin, the reformed Church shall have its martyred Jane Grey. *I* cannot speak out, but *Jane's* voice will sing from beyond the grave.'

Levina folds the paper carefully and tucks it away beneath her gown. However much of a risk it may be to involve herself in this, she is compelled to fulfil Frances's wish – she too needs some kind of sense to be made out of that poor child's death.

April 1555
Hampton Court
Katherine

'Harry Herbert, Harry Herbert, Harry Herbert.' I rub the piece of grey ribbon between my fingers; it is frayed almost to nothing now and I haven't seen Harry Herbert for months, nor even had a letter. I tuck the ribbon away and staunch my thoughts. If I let myself think about him for too long it will set off all that crying again, and I have only lately managed to put the parts of me back together.

Elizabeth is here, and thank God, for we are all going out of our minds with boredom waiting for the Queen's baby, which seems not to want to be born. There is no dancing, nor music; the Queen lolls on her bed and we are all to sit in silence about her for most of the day. Even when the weather without is fine and we could be riding or walking in the gardens, we must stay in that gloomy bedchamber straining our eyes in the candlelight, embroidering a cloth of state that will hang over the infant's cradle, or if not stitching, then praying for the prince's safe delivery.

But Elizabeth's presence gives us all something to talk about: how it was the King himself who insisted she come to court; how she travelled from Woodstock in a high wind and had to shelter behind a hedge to adjust her hood which had quite blown off; how she was swollen with the dropsy and could barely manage half a dozen miles a day in her litter; how when she arrived in the outskirts of the city, all in white with two hundred riders, a great crowd came out to cheer her. When the Queen heard of it, she had us dress her in her finest loose gown and stood in profile at the balcony window so the crowds below could see her great belly.

It has been like a game of trumps: Elizabeth put down her best card and the Queen had a better one, for what is better than a royal infant? It seems now though that the Queen is refusing to play; she will not give her sister an audience. Elizabeth is confined to her rooms; they are better rooms than mine, though mine are quite good, it is true, with a view of the water gardens. No one is supposed to see Elizabeth without permission, but Cousin Margaret seems quite desperate to set her eyes on our captive cousin. I pretend I do not care one way or another but truth be told I am easily as keen as Cousin Margaret to get a look at Elizabeth, for I have only ever seen her at a distance.

'I see no reason why we should not simply pay her a visit,' I say to Cousin Margaret.

'No reason?' she replies, horrified. 'The Queen has forbidden it, Katherine.'

'Are you scared?' I say, in full knowledge that Margaret cannot bear to be thought lacking in mettle.

'Of course not,' she replies with a toss of her head.

'So then you will accompany me.'

Margaret dithers a little; clearly she is having second thoughts, but she is pushed into a corner and cannot get out of it. 'Certainly,' she says with a look on her that is not at all certain.

So I take her hand and lead her to the western corridor, where Elizabeth's chambers are. There are a couple of guards at the door and happily one I know a little, as he was a page to my father at Bradgate for a while.

'Humphrey?' I say, offering him my best smile.

'My Lady,' he replies, with a flush rising through his cheeks, like wine soaking into linen, indicating that my smile has had the desired effect. I momentarily place my hand on his sleeve. His blush deepens. His companion seems even more embarrassed than he; these men are used to being invisible to girls such as we, and Cousin Margaret, acting on my instructions, has had her eyes on him for longer than is correct.

'Can you keep a secret, Humphrey?' I ask.

'If it is your secret, My Lady, then it is safe with me.'

'Good,' I say. 'Then you will admit us to see Lady Elizabeth and you will say nothing of it.'

'But, My Lady . . .' he begins.

'Humphrey,' I say in mock admonition, with a little flicker of my lashes. 'I hope you are not going to disappoint me.'

'I would rather die than disappoint you, My Lady.' I have

the feeling that there might be a grain of truth in what he says. 'But,' he continues, 'Lady Elizabeth has visitors.'

As the words leave his mouth there is a hard rap at the door. Cousin Margaret and I skitter off to an embrasure. I, suppressing my giggles, throw open the window and look out, as if quite absorbed in the view of the home paddock where the pregnant mares are grazing on the spring grass.

The door swings open and from the side of my eye I watch Bishop Gardiner and my uncle Arundel stride out with a couple of others, whom I have seen but whose names I can't remember. They are all members of the council, that much I do know.

'. . . impossible creature,' I hear Uncle Arundel saying. I suppose he is talking of Elizabeth. They approach, so we pull ourselves back in from the window and drop into polite curtsies.

'Ah, a brace of nieces,' says Arundel, turning to one of the men, whom I think I recognize, now he is in the light, as Shrewsbury. 'What would you say the collective term for female relatives was?'

'If it were wives, I'd say a yoke,' he quips. 'But since these two are so pretty then they are probably a duet.' They both laugh at this. Gardiner and the other fellow are fidgeting impatiently as if they have better things to do than pass the time of day with a couple of girls.

'And what are you doing in this part of the palace, ladies?' asks Arundel.

I fear Margaret will give us away with the guilty look she has on her, so I quickly say, 'We are looking at the Queen's palfrey that has just foaled. This is the only window in the palace with a good view on the paddock.'

The two men lean out and I point to where there is indeed a mare, that could as well as any of them be the

Queen's, with a very young foal wobbling about beside her on stick legs.

'Charming,' says Shrewsbury.

'Indeed,' says Arundel. 'Let us hope Her Majesty will foal before long.'

We are all hoping that will happen, for the baby is so very late and the Queen's temper quite foul over the discomfort and the waiting. The midwives say the dates are wrong – who knows; I don't know anything at all about birthing, though I do know a little now about how to get yourself with child, or rather how not to, for the older maids whisper about such things at night.

Gardiner clears his throat impatiently and they take their leave. I pull Cousin Margaret by the sleeve back to the door where the pliant Humphrey awaits. All that is needed is another smile and the door is opened just enough for us to slide in.

We enter so very quietly that none of the group of women across the room notices we are there. I do not recognize any of them except for Elizabeth herself. Her dress is black and quite plain, such a contrast to the Queen's overdone outfits. Two of her ladies are untying her sleeves and slipping them down her wrists, another unlaces her gown, pulling it away from her shoulders, leaving her in just her scarlet kirtle, which sets off the luminous white of her skin. Like that, with her dark eyes flashing, her hood still on and a haughty tilt to her chin, she has the look of a helmeted Athena from the myths. Her ladies, even the beauties, are all diminished beside her.

'. . . they think me foolish enough to confess to a part in Wyatt's rebellion,' she is saying. 'It is they who are the fools if they think me so stupid. I will not go the way of my cousin Jane Grey.'

I gasp to hear my sister's name on her lips, and the whole gaggle turns to face us. I swallow, for even I am intimidated in the face of such a company; they are all older by a decade, and looking at us with such a threatening aspect I am tempted to turn tail. Cousin Margaret is clasping my hand so tight I fear she will stop the blood-flow. But I find my courage and drop to my knee, glad of the fact that I have my newest gown on and Maman's pearls.

Elizabeth doesn't seem to recognize me, so I say, 'My Lady, we are your cousins. I am Katherine Grey and this is Margaret Clifford, lately become Lady Strange. We are come to welcome you to Hampton Court.'

My smile seems to have no effect whatsoever on any of them and least of all on Elizabeth, who bluntly asks, 'Did my sister send you?'

'We are come of our own accord, My Lady.' We are still on our knees and she makes no indication for us to stand.

'I don't know why you think I would have any interest in seeing you,' she says, sitting down and picking up a book.

I rack my brains to think of a reply, but truth be told I am quite out of my depth with this cousin of mine. She has started to thrum at the book with impatient fingernails and her women are still staring at us like gorgons.

'You come from a family of traitors, Katherine Grey.' Thrum, thrum, thrum. 'Your father and sister were lately executed for treason. Why do you think I would seek to consort with you?'

'He who has a glass head should beware of stones.' It slips from my mouth like a fat, ugly toad plopping on to the oak boards before me; I try to stop it, but it is too late.

'Get out!' This is not said by Elizabeth, but by one of her gorgons who marches towards us, pulling us both to our feet and giving us an unceremonious shove towards the door.

Elizabeth has turned back to her book as if nothing at all has occurred.

As we skulk out I hear her say, 'Those Greys think they will have the throne one day. They will not, I shall see to that.' Which is nonsense really, for it is the half-Spanish infant the Queen is cooking who will have the throne. Besides, I do not want the throne. But then nor did Jane.

It shames me to say, I am thoroughly intimidated by Elizabeth. But I cannot help admiring her spirit and there is a part of me that wants to rise to the challenge of winning her over, though I know in my heart it would be an impossibility, for she is more formidable by far even than the Queen. But my heart sinks when I realize that in truth I have managed to make an enemy of her before we are even acquainted. I am hoping she will be sent away again, back to Woodstock, and not be brought into the Queen's fold, or better still that she will be sent off far away to marry the Duke of Savoy.

'She's right, you know,' says Cousin Margaret, as we get to the long gallery. I am only half listening, for most of what Cousin Margaret says is nonsense. 'Your family have forfeited their right to the succession.'

I feel the anger gather in me, thinking of my murdered father and my poor sister Jane, her life cut short. It is forming a great clog in my throat so I cannot say what it is I want to say, which is to put stupid Cousin Margaret down and defend my family.

'Due to that, it is *I* who comes after Elizabeth in line,' she continues talking, will not stop, and I can't help myself as I grab her arm with my left hand and with my right I strike her across the cheek.

She squeals like a stuck pig, which is overdoing it because for a start she is a great lump of a girl and I am barely half her size. The damage one of my tiny hands could do to her ham of a cheek is negligible. There isn't even the slightest mark upon her face, but as usual I have gone and put myself on the side of wrong, for when the story gets out, I shall be the one who seems the monster. Cousin Margaret, who is fleeing down the gallery, still squealing as if pursued by a bear, will be fussed and cooed over and I shall be blamed.

God knows what will happen to me; I have managed to make adversaries of both Elizabeth and Cousin Margaret in the space of a single hour and I wish, more than anything, that Maman and Mary had not left for Beaumanor, for I do get myself into a muddle when I am left alone in this place. Such a thing would never have happened to Jane and I wish for once that I was more like her: inclined to think more of God and less of myself.

July 1555
Beaumanor
Mary

I have one end of a daisy chain in my hand; Peggy Willoughby has the other, and we are sitting on the grassy bank beside the lake. There is a swan we have named Aphrodite, who has laid claim to this stretch of the water. She has half a dozen late-hatched cygnets, and Peggy and I have taken to coming out daily after our lessons to assure ourselves that none of them has been taken by a fox overnight.

Today is the first dry day in weeks. The weather has been so bad the farmers fear the harvest will be destroyed and the villagers are worried that come winter they will not be able to feed their families. Many blame the Queen for dragging us back to the old faith – they say God is angry. Each week we hear of new arrests. The servants talk about it all the time. It will not stop at the clergy, Maman says. They will soon find a reason to start taking laymen too. Even here at Beaumanor, in the middle of nowhere, surrounded only by friends, we must mind to hear our prayers in Latin and raise our eyes to the host.

'There she is,' cries Peggy, pointing towards Aphrodite as she glides into sight. She carries three of her little ones on her back, grey fluffy heads just visible above her wing, with two more in the water behind her tail. 'One is missing,' says Peggy, reflecting my thoughts, but as the words leave her mouth the straggler comes into view beyond the reeds. We get up and walk along beside them, with Aphrodite pivoting her head to observe us from the side of her eye, assessing whether we might be a threat. Further along, where the weeping willow tumbles down to the water and the reeds are thicker, she clambers up out of the lake, all her elegance lost as she makes her ungainly waddle over to her nesting place, chicks trotting in her wake.

We lie down under the tree, gazing up at the leafy dome arching over us like a cathedral. The light filters through the leaves, falling in silvery dapples on the damp loam, and casting a greenish glow over Peggy's face. She starts singing the song we have been learning all morning with the music master.

Alas! What shall I do for love?
For love, alas! What shall I do?

I find myself plucking out the notes with my fingers on an imaginary lute, all the time thinking how content I am to be here at Beaumanor and not at court waiting for the Queen's baby to come. An announcement was made a few days ago, that a boy had been born; the church bells were rung for a four-hour stretch, but whoever proclaimed it was mistaken. The bells stopped ringing and the waiting continued.

Sith now so kin,
I do you find,
To keep you me unto. Alas!

'Why do you think it is when the poets talk of love,' Peggy muses, 'they always seem so miserable?'

'Perhaps it is the artistic temperament,' I reply. 'Maman is clearly in love with Stokes and the pair of them are not miserable.' This is true; Stokes dotes on her in a way I never saw with Father. I do not think I have ever seen Maman so content, though the other day I caught her gazing upon me with a smudgy look about the eyes and when I asked what ailed her she said, 'From certain angles you have the look of your sister Jane about you.'

'I am glad to be here with you, Mary, away from court.' Peggy rolls over on to her front to look at me with her bright eyes and cloven smile.

'And I too,' I say.

We are two days' hard riding from Hampton Court, but Maman has two brace of messengers riding back and forth so we are party to all the news. Though we are a sizeable household here at Beaumanor, it is nothing like the hurly-burly of palace life and for that I am very glad. 'I should like to always live this quiet kind of life.'

'Hmm,' she replies, lost in her own thoughts.

I imagine Katherine at Hampton Court. She has rooms of her own now. I can picture them, a chaos of discarded clothes, her pets creating havoc, the poor servants rushing about after them and Katherine there playing hostess to a gaggle of girls, all in her thrall. It is quite an honour to be assigned her own quarters and not be with Mistress Poyntz and the other maids of the chamber. She will be pleased about that.

Were it me, I would be asking myself why I deserved such an honour, what it would cost me. But Katherine is not suspicious, as I am. She sends letters, carelessly scrawled, full of gossip. She tells of how the King has an eye for the ladies, that he got Magdalen Dacre in a corner and Magdalen was all in a knot about it. (I secretly like the thought of Magdalen in a bother.) She also said she managed to catch a glimpse of Harry Herbert the other day riding in the tiltyard. But mostly Katherine talks of the Queen, how after ten and a half months even Frideswide Sturley, who is one of her closest ladies, believes she is mistaken and is not with child at all. Katherine says the Queen sits curled, her knees tucked up to her chin, rocking back and forth miserably for most of the day in a darkened room. Everyone has remarked that a woman in her condition wouldn't be able to sit in that way, and those who are not joking of it don't know what to think. I remember how desperately the Queen wanted that infant, the way she would talk of it to me.

'Mary,' she said, the day before I left, caressing her belly with the flat of her hand. 'God is showing me His gratitude for my faith, for restoring the true religion to England. Knowing that a little God-given prince germinates in me brings me more joy than I can describe.'

I cannot muster any sympathy for her; my sympathy was used up on the day Jane met her death.

Maman prays for that baby though, Spanish or not, for it will take us a step away from the throne, she says. But surely the Queen is mistaken, as no baby takes so very long to come – even I know that. Maman worries for Katherine at court, as do I, for there are signs in her letters that things are not without trouble. She has argued with Cousin Margaret, but there is nothing new in that. Worse is implied by a line in her most recent letter: *The King has taken a shine to Elizabeth, which puts the Queen in a most uneven temper. She barely acknowledges her sister. And as for Elizabeth, I do not find her one little bit friendly, given we are cousins.* She did not say more than that, but it was enough to prick Maman's concern.

'I have known Elizabeth since she was an infant, and she is not one to get on the wrong side of,' Maman had said to me. 'I hope Katherine has not spoken out of turn, for she will not gain anything from a quarrel with that girl.'

I have the impression that Maman is not at all fond of Elizabeth, but she does not speak more of it.

The pitter of rain starts up in the leaves above; a single drop lands on my throat, but our green dome protects us from the worst of the downpour. I think of the poor farmers worrying about the harvest, how glad they must have been to have a clear day at last, only to be rained upon again. People will be starving this winter, though nothing will stop the banqueting at court, the roasted fowl, dozens to a dish, the endless loaves of fine manchet bread, the marchpane fancies, the fountains of wine.

'I wonder at a world that is so unfair,' I say.

'What do you mean?' asks Peggy.

'I was thinking of the harvest, with all this rain.'

'The poor are closer to Heaven, are they not?' says Peggy, twiddling a dry leaf in her fingers.

'I'm not sure the Queen would think so,' I say, thinking of the Bible – the rich man and the eye of the needle. 'Most tailor their beliefs to fit their lives.' Maman has said this many times.

'But it is different for the Queen.' Peggy lifts herself up on to her elbows. 'We all have to accept God's will. God made us this way and He placed us in this world for His own reason. It is not to question.'

'Why, then, do you think God gave you a cloven mouth?' I ask.

'*God* did not do that,' she exclaims, quite aghast that I should not know such a thing. 'It is the mark of the Devil's claw, where He tried to take me from the womb.'

'Did your mother tell you that?'

'She did not need to, it is well known what this means.' She touches the tip of her finger to her upper lip. 'It means I was marked out as the Devil's thing and it was God that saved me.'

'I suppose the Devil tried to hook me out by my shoulders, then,' I say.

'Of course,' she replies. I envy Peggy for the straightforwardness of her world, when my own thoughts and doubts tangle themselves up in one another.

'Does that mean deep down we are both evil like the third Richard?' I have been reading Sir Thomas More's history of that wicked king, who was crookbacked like me.

'Oh no,' she exclaims, quite loudly. 'We are all the more good, for God took the trouble to save us.'

'That is certainly reassuring, Peggy,' I say. 'Does it say so in the Bible?' I do not say that I can think only of Leviticus, who says that none who are blemished may approach the altar, for I fear it would spoil her perfect version of things.

'It is a well-known thing,' is all she says. Somehow I love her the more for it, for not being beset by doubt, as I am. It is not God I doubt, but man's idea of Him. How could I explain that to Peggy, or anyone? It is only Jane whom I might have been able to talk of these things with.

'The rain has stopped,' Peggy says, looking up. My eyes follow, to see blinking shafts of golden light shining through the leaves, and I wonder if Peggy sees it as a sign that God is blessing us. She gets to her feet and helps me up, leading me by the hand to where Aphrodite is nesting with her chicks. We peep over the rushes. The great swan turns to us with a furious look, then opens her puce beak and hisses sharply, sending us skittering away, through the wet grass back to the house in giggles.

'A swan has the strength to break a man's arm, if her chicks are threatened,' gasps Peggy.

'A mother will –' I stop myself, remembering Peggy has no mother to protect her, changing the subject. 'Do you think the Queen will have this baby?'

'One thing is certain, if she does not she will want *you* back at court.'

September 1555
Greenwich
Mary

'Cardinal Pole,' says the Queen, summoning him over to where we sit, I on her knee in the place of the infant that never appeared. Peggy was right in thinking I would be called back to court. The Cardinal approaches slowly, his red robes swinging with his limp. 'Sit, sit.' She pats the empty seat beside her. It is the King's seat and the Cardinal hesitates. 'We are alone,' she adds with an encouraging nod. Her eyes are bloodshot and her skin blotched – she has been crying for days now, since the King left for the Low Countries and his war. She can be heard sobbing and moaning in her chamber at night and everyone hovers cautiously in her presence, fearing an outburst.

The Cardinal says nothing, but casts his eyes about the

chamber, where there are at least half a dozen ladies busy with one thing or another, but none looks over this way. 'Besides, our husband has abandoned us for his foreign campaign.' As she says this she brings her fist down to the arm of her chair with a great puff of breath, like a bull. 'Sit!'

The Cardinal, slightly cowed, finally places his large behind on to the seat beside us. The Queen is rubbing and patting at my back as if she were a wet nurse winding a baby, and I am racking my brains to think of any excuse I can possibly find to get myself away from her prodding hands, and out of the orbit of her rage.

I have been back at court for a week now. There never was a royal infant. The whole thing is shrouded in mystery and it is not to be mentioned, or certainly not within earshot of the Queen.

'So that was that,' Katherine had said of it. 'All that hushed waiting around in her darkened chamber for nothing.'

Whispers have been flying about: that the Queen had been bewitched, or that it was wind; most think she miscarried and said nothing. I am not supposed to know about these things, I am supposed to be too young, but I do know. Whatever it was or wasn't, the Queen is quite addled with grief. This means that I am to play the poppet again. Maman has requested I stay no more than a month but for the meantime the Queen caresses and pokes and hugs and holds me as if I were the disappeared infant itself, and with each prod my loathing grows.

Of course now there is no heir of the Queen's body there has been a great shifting at court and endless whispered discussions about the succession. Many look to Elizabeth and there is talk of a marriage between her and Edward Courtenay, some Plantagenet boy who has disappeared abroad. Cousin Margaret is convinced *she* will be named in line, though she is the only one who thinks this. Some look to Katherine. All I can think of is Jane and what became of *her*. Maman has instructed Katherine to be discreet, to not draw attention to herself; I wonder if that is possible.

'How can I be of service, Your Majesty?' The Cardinal is hovering with his hands before him, fingers steepled.

'For goodness' sake, if we can't dispense with the formalities when we are alone with you, then who? Use "madam", if you must insist on anything other than my given name.'

I want to shout, *You are not alone, I, Mary Grey, am here*, but I do not, of course.

'Madam,' he says with a fawning little dip of the head.

She grabs his hand and drops her voice to a whisper. 'God is displeased with us.'

'Madam, it cannot be so, with your devotion . . .'

She doesn't let him finish. 'No! He has taken back our infant, His gift to us. He finds us lacking.' Her whisper is like Aphrodite's angry hiss. 'We need to show our faith more profoundly. We need your help.'

'A pilgrimage, perhaps?' suggests the Cardinal.

'No, not that.' Her whispered response is firm and I can feel the heat of her breath on the back of my neck. 'A pilgrimage is to give thanks. We believe God is asking us to show our faith, like Abraham.'

I wonder which story of Abraham she means. There is only one I remember well – Abraham and Isaac. There is a tapestry at Hampton Court where the boy Isaac, open-mouthed in terror, looks up at his father, who wields a knife.

'When the monasteries are reinstated –' starts the Cardinal.

'Yes, that,' she interrupts. 'But what we must first do is hound every heretic from our kingdom. Then God will be pleased with us and send us an heir.'

The Cardinal says nothing, but in his face lies the question, 'How?'

'We want everyone held,' she continues, speaking with such force that a shower of spit lands on my cheek. 'Everyone who shows even the slightest sign of heresy. And if they will not recant they shall be burned – all of them.' The Queen's grip on his hand is so tight now that her knuckles are a row of white stones.

The Cardinal seems horrified. 'God would be pleased, madam, to see you show clemency.'

'Clemency!' There is Aphrodite's hiss again. 'Now is not the time for clemency. We want Cranmer and Latimer and Ridley to burn first and that will serve as a warning. Then we will be rid of the rest.'

'If it is Your Majesty's wish . . .'

'It is more than our wish. We command it. We will have you speak to Bishop Gardiner . . . and Bonner. Now there is a man who understands our cause.'

'He is one of the faithful, madam.'

There has been much talk of Archbishop Cranmer of late, people wondering what the Queen plans to do with him. I know these names. Latimer was my step-grandmother's chaplain; I remember him from infanthood, and Ridley too was often a visitor at Bradgate. These men are close to my own family. I touch my finger to my forehead and down to my heart, then one shoulder, then the other.

'Ah, little Mary,' says the Queen. 'You are one of the faithful too, now that traitor father of yours has been dispensed with, and . . .' She doesn't finish but I suppose she means to add Jane to the list of people the world is better off without. She looks at me with a grimace of a smile and I daren't speak for fear I will spit out the truth – that her faith is corrupt and cruel and I would have none of it. But I manage to return her smile and bow my head in what I hope appears to be acquiescence. 'You *are* one of the faithful?'

I can feel her eyes on me, as if she can see right through to my reformed soul. I daren't speak for fear of a wobble in my voice giving me away, so I nod, clutching my rosary.

'There are many about us, Cardinal, who seem as one thing but are another. Do you think Mary here is one of those?' She pokes my shoulder hard. I flinch. '*She* and her family of traitors. Look how scared she is. What do you think she is afraid of?'

I struggle to breathe and my heart is beating so hard she can surely hear it. I am thinking what Jane would have done – she would have told the truth and died for it.

'Shall we have Bonner question her, Cardinal? Bonner could tease a confession from a stone.'

'Madam,' says the Cardinal, placing a hand on her sleeve. She looks at it, and then at his face, and the hand again. 'With all respect, she is but a child. What age are you, Mary?'

'Ten.' I am barely able to squeeze out the single syllable.

'Old enough,' murmurs the Queen.

The bell in the palace chapel rings. Blood rushes in my ears. The Cardinal shuffles in his seat and the Queen pokes me, saying, 'Run along now, Mary. We want the Cardinal to hear our confession before Mass.'

I clamber off her lap and make for the door.

'And Mary?'

I turn to her, my heart stuck in my throat, clasping my hands tightly together so she cannot see how they tremble. Her gaze is hard and blank as a pane of glass.

'I have my eye on you.'

I curtsy, thinking that it is only a matter of moments before I will be out of the room. Clinging to that thought.

'Perhaps the Cardinal should hear your confession. You

have a way of sorting the wheat from the chaff, don't you, Cardinal?'

The idea of confessing to this man, who will surely see what heresies I harbour in my soul, makes my skin prick with fear. I hold an image of Jane firmly in my mind and think of what she would advise – *Be stoic, Mouse* – and somehow I find the courage to speak.

'That is an honour I do not merit, Your Majesty.'

'Why so?'

'The Cardinal's great wisdom would be wasted on such as me.'

'Pah!' She waves her hand at me as if brushing away a fly. It is my sign to leave them.

Has she changed her mind? I know not.

I rush to Katherine's rooms as fast as I can, my head spinning with thoughts of being tied to a pyre and burned alive, trying to remember the way through the labyrinthine corridors of Greenwich Palace. I arrive to find one of the pages making an attempt to gather Katherine's over-excited pack of dogs together for their evening walk. When he is gone I wriggle out of my over-gown and lie in silence, trying to steady my breath, watching the flickering pattern of light that falls through the branches of a tree beyond the window, keeping my mind on that so as not to think about what has just happened.

There is something hard beneath the pillow and, slipping my hand under it, I find a book. It is Jane's Greek New Testament. I clutch it to my heart, thinking of my dead sister's words. But it strikes me suddenly that this book might be used against us, for what Jane speaks of is heresy if you are Catholic. My head begins to spin again as I wonder how many more things we have here that might condemn us – innocent-seeming things. I open the big chest and slip the book to its very bottom beneath the clothes and blankets, resolving to take it with me to Beaumanor when I leave, which will be before too long, I hope.

Katherine arrives and on seeing me says, 'What is wrong, Mouse? You look white as a ghost. Are you ailing?'

I try to explain what happened, the words spilling out of me in a muddle. She hooks her littlest finger into mine, soothing, 'Never mind, never mind, little one,' as if I am a baby.

'But this is important, Kitty,' I say, pulling my hand away. 'We are in danger. They are burning men close to our family.'

'Vex not,' she replies, suppressing a yawn. 'Those men will burn as martyrs for their faith. They will not convert. They have chosen it, Mary.'

'As Jane did?' I snap, and watch the look of pain cross Katherine's face. 'They would not have to look so hard at us to see we are pretending in matters of faith. You know, as well as I, of the things people will do to make you tell the truth.'

'Oh Mouse.' She gives her head a little toss as if to shake my words out of it. 'Just as long as we go to Mass, and all of that. But take Jane's book to Beaumanor, if you want. If it makes you feel better.' A splinter of satisfaction finds its way to me in the idea that Jane's precious book will be in my hands now, as if it is mine. But that thought is engulfed by the feeling that my head is in a tightening vice.

'Have you anything else amongst your things that might incriminate us?' I ask.

'I don't know. I shouldn't think so.'

'But –' I stop, there is no point trying to describe the look I saw in the Queen's eyes, nor the force of her words. I am angry at Katherine's carelessness; I don't want her to 'think so' I want her to *know* so. I want her to say she will help me look through every last possession we have, just to be sure. But I don't say anything more, for there is no changing my sister.

One of my earliest memories of Katherine, and I have the image clearly in my mind, is of her with her fingers in her ears, eyes tight shut, spilling tears, humming loudly, while the head groom at Bradgate, red-eyed himself, tells her of the death of her favourite pony.

'It is best not to think about it,' she says.

II
Forget-Me-Not

January 1558
Ludgate
Levina

'V-V-Veena.' George's eyes droop like a bloodhound's. 'See reason!' This is more a plea than the order Levina supposes her husband means it to be.

She screws up a fold of paper in both hands, compressing it into a tight ball. It is a pamphlet warning of one of Bishop Bonner's book scourges. When it is not books being burned it is people – the number is near on two and a half hundred souls gone up in flames these last couple of years, since England was returned to Rome. The whole country is choked with the stench of roast pork. It started with the clerics; she remembers when she first heard that Latimer and Ridley were to go to the stake. When she thinks of it her throat feels clogged with grief, even after so much time.

She had known Latimer when she first went to Bradgate to paint the Greys. It must have been five years ago; time has slipped by without warning. She had been quite seduced by the subtlety of his mind and he had a tenderness of spirit that she found entirely disarming. They had talked much of Calvin – that was in the reign of the young King Edward, when Calvin and Luther, Zwingli even, were openly discussed, and thought of as visionaries rather than heretics. How different it is now. She can feel still the tingle of excitement such ideas had generated in her: justification by faith alone, the symbolic nature of the sacraments, a sense of personal spiritual discovery as if she were Christopher Columbus discovering the New World.

She had experienced her encounter with Latimer as one might an unexpected attraction, the feelings it conjured up, a true fascination with the man and his ideas. When she thinks about Latimer, even now, she feels something physical, a frisson of sorts, though the episode had been entirely chaste. She flings the ball of paper on to the fire, watching it, imagining what it must be like to burn alive. It is impossible to conjure up the feeling. She has the urge to press her finger against one of the bright embers and hold it there, to experience in a small way the exact nature of the sensation.

'V-V-Veena, say something.' George touches her arm; she looks at the delta of thick blue veins running towards his fingers, a liver spot that she has not noticed before. Her husband will be an old man in a few years. She is struck by the hard fact that Hugh Latimer's dotage, a time of quiet and contemplation, was so brutally brought to a close and it makes her eyes smart with sadness.

'Marcus could go to your parents in Bruges,' she says, but she is still thinking of Hugh Latimer, remembering the words he is said to have spoken as the faggots were lit: *We shall this day light such a candle as I trust will never be put out.* Such faith, such courage – the man was a true believer. She wishes her own faith were half as strong but she is filled with doubt and a desire for self-preservation. Though she *has* done her bit to keep that candle bright, has sent documents to Geneva, witness accounts, to be published for all to see what monstrous acts are rife in the reign of Catholic Mary Tudor. She has made ink drawings to go with them, one in particular of the Manx woman who birthed a child on the stake. Levina has never been to the Isle of Manx, had never even heard of it before, but she has seen burnings enough lately to imagine up the scene: the crowd encircling the fire, the flames licking at the poor woman's legs, her mouth set in a howl; it horrifies her to think of it, and the church official throwing the baby back on to the pyre to burn with its mother. The ink ran with her tears and she had to start her drawing again, more than once.

'Where *is* Marcus?' asks George in a matter-of-fact way, as if he has forgotten that they are in the middle of a dispute. But then they always seem to be in a dispute of one kind or other these days.

'He went to court the Carruth girl. Took her flowers.' A tender spot opens up in her at the thought of Marcus courting. She still finds it hard to believe her son is a man now, of nineteen years – old enough for most things, old enough to be drafted to fight in the King's war against the French. She has an image of a battlefield scattered with bodies twitching and writhing, faces riven in agony; it is like a scene from Bosch. Yes, she thinks, Marcus will be better off in Bruges, out of the way. She wonders though if even Bruges is safe. After all, it is under imperial rule. But no place could be as bad as this one.

'He could do worse than Alice Carruth,' George replies and then, as if he suddenly remembers what it is they are really discussing, adds, 'And us, Veena? We could go with him to my parents.' It is a conversation they have had over and over again.

'No,' is all she says. She cannot shake the monstrous scenes from her head. But it is not only on the battlefield that the innocent fall. Nowhere is safe. Things have never been so bad in England. Even in the last years of the eighth Henry's reign when the court tiptoed about in fear, when no one knew what they were supposed to believe, it was not as it is now. Even the slightest breath of suspicion is enough to get you burned these days. Even dear friends cannot be trusted. And God forbid you should have an altercation with a neighbour, for all they need do is make a suggestion that you are not attending Mass or that you read the Bible in English. Petty disputes, trifles, end on the stake these days, for all know, if there is a finger pointed, where it will lead. More than two years of horror. George is right, they *would* be better off away from this place.

'I am your husband,' he says. 'You are bound to do my bidding.' But his tone betrays his diffidence.

'I made a promise.'

'Yes, yes, I know about your promise. B-b-but think about it, Veena. The mother lives. Cannot she take care of her own?' He talks of Frances and her girls, her vow to keep them out of harm's way.

Levina shakes her head silently, unable to explain how attached she has become to the Greys, how fond of those girls and their mother, or the way Jane's execution – the fact she was there – has created an unassailable bond between them. She cannot leave them; she has the sense that she is holding them back from the brink, particularly Katherine. Dear, wild, Katherine, who is eighteen now, and ripe for picking; she counts back in her head, realizing that Mary must be thirteen. It is some time since she has had the chance to visit Beaumanor and see Mary and Frances.

Levina had witnessed the Queen questioning Katherine the other day, over a miniature of Jane. Sly Susan Clarencieux had discovered it amongst Katherine's things – poking her nose where it wasn't wanted.

'But it is nothing more than a memento of my sister,' Katherine had pleaded, while Levina stood on, willing the girl to hold her tongue.

'Your sister was a traitor,' snapped Susan Clarencieux.

'We will *not* be reminded of that,' said the Queen loudly. 'Burn it, Susan.'

Thank the Lord Katherine had the wherewithal to remain silent then, to keep her eyes to the floor when her sister's portrait was thrown into the flames. It was a likeness Levina herself had made. On that occasion the Queen's suspicion waned once the flames had done their work, but the Queen is becoming increasingly unpredictable and there is no way of knowing, with Katherine, if she will blurt the wrong thing out of turn.

'Are you listening, Veena?' She is jolted out of her thoughts by her husband's question. 'Frances Grey or Stokes, whatever it is she calls herself these days . . .' He is unable to hide the petulant edge in his voice. 'She has the Queen's favour. She is the Queen's cousin.'

'That never saved anyone,' Levina says harshly. 'If you'd been there to see that girl on the scaffold as I was . . . If you could see the knife-edge her sister walks on at court.'

He looks chastened.

'Anyway,' she adds, 'I am one of the Queen's ladies-in-waiting now and am not at liberty –'

'Poisoned chalice,' mutters George, but a sharp knock at the door startles them both into silence; Hero, by the hearth, lifts his head, alert. George moves to open the door, sliding out into the courtyard, pushing it ajar so all she can see is the shadow of a man and a pair of gesticulating hands, recognizing suddenly, with a lurch of her gut, the ornate garnet ring that belongs to the sacristan from St Martin's – Bonner's man.

One of her preliminary tear-blotched sketches of the Manx burning lies on the big table at the centre of the hall and she curses herself inwardly for being so remiss as to leave it on display like that. Reaching for it, she prays that George has the wherewithal to keep Bonner's man on the other side of the door for as long as possible. They are talking, but Levina can make out only the odd word above the rushing of blood in her ears. She slips the paper into the hearth, watching it blaze and curl, reminding her of that portrait of Jane that had gone the same way. Finally, there is nothing left of it but flakes floating prettily up the chimney, like black butterflies.

The door swings fully open and Bonner's man stands in the entrance, his features obscured by the light behind him. Hero raises his hackles.

She makes her greeting, 'Such a pleasure,' her voice more loud than is normal, as if she is performing in a masque, but she cannot remember his name and fears insulting him by not using it. He takes her outstretched hand, gripping it tightly, too tightly, in both of his and then raises it to his lips, planting a wet kiss on her knuckles. His eyes meet hers and he gives her a disarming smile that reveals a row of small, even teeth. She has seen him often in church. With his black robes and slender hands, he reminds her of a jackdaw, but she has never seen that smile before. George hovers. She sees beyond the door that the sacristan has not come alone and feels her throat restricting, imagining herself taken, bundled into a cart and then on to the Fleet Prison. If they search the house they will find a roll of papers hidden behind the hangings in the bedchamber, written accounts of the atrocities to be sent to Geneva with her drawings. That would see them all burn. Her breath is shallow and she is afraid that she wears her fear in the heave of her chest and in the beads of sweat she can feel accumulating on her brow.

'Byrne has come to talk to us, Levina dearest,' says George.

She is impressed at his calmness and thankful he has remembered the man's name. Byrne, how could she have forgotten? There is not even the vaguest residue of George's stutter and she feels reassured, remembers, as if a fist is squeezing her heart, that she loves him and why. 'Get the boy to bring some chilled ale, would you?'

In the passage she leans against the cold wall for a second to take a breath, thankful for this moment to collect her poise. She tucks the stray wisps of hair into her coif before calling the serving lad and returning to the hall, where George and Byrne are seated on the chairs either side of the hearth. Hero watches like a hawk with its eye on a hare. Byrne's man, whom he has not bothered to introduce and who, by the look of his clothes, is a henchman or servant of some kind, loiters in the gloom, rocking from one foot to the other. Levina sits on the low stool next to her husband, busying herself, smoothing her skirts, adjusting her sleeves, anything to avoid meeting Byrne's gaze.

'I trust your loved ones have not been touched by the influenza,' she says, by way of making polite conversation. It is what everyone talks of these days, the influenza that is wending its way through the country, taking souls in droves.

'God's revenge for heresy,' Byrne states. 'Thank you, yes, my family have been spared.'

'God has spared us too,' says George, making the sign of the cross.

Byrne watches sly-eyed. 'I believe you are familiar with the Carruth family,' he says, his voice smooth and reasonable, as if merely passing the time of day, chatting about friends in common. But there is something beneath it, a threat or an accusation.

'Our neighbours,' says George. 'We know them a little. Have they been afflicted?'

The serving lad passes Byrne a cup of ale, which he sniffs at before taking a gulp and slapping his lips. 'Good stuff, this, Teerlinc. You brew it here or buy it in?'

'I get it from –'

But Byrne interrupts before George has a chance to answer: 'Neighbours, you say?'

'That is right,' Levina says, trying to sound as if this is an ordinary conversation, trying to not look at Byrne's small, perfectly aligned teeth, to not think – suddenly, inappropriately – of them biting her. 'Our boy has taken a shine to one of their daughters.' Her mind is working, like the wheels of a mill, thinking that if the Carruths have been afflicted then Marcus is at risk. A grain of dread drops in amongst her thoughts.

But Byrne doesn't seem to be talking of the influenza any more. 'Yes,' he says. 'The Bishop is aware of that liaison.'

'It could hardly be called a liaison,' Levina says, trying to keep her voice level and not show the anxiety she feels at the turn the conversation has taken. 'We have not encouraged it.' She exchanges a glance with George, who nods minutely.

'It *should* be encouraged,' announces Byrne. They wait for him to explain himself. 'You see, the Bishop wants the Carruths watched. They seem to be . . .' He stops and twists his ring round his finger. 'How can I put it? The Carruths seem to be behaving in a manner that has aroused the Bishop's suspicion.' He lengthens the last word, stretching it out. 'If your boy is courting one of the daughters that would give a perfect vantage point from which to observe the family.'

'Unfortunately,' says George, 'Marcus is to leave for Bruges imminently. His grandfather, my father, is ailing.' He genuflects again and places his hands one on top of the other in his lap. Levina fiddles with the rosary at her waist. 'It is likely we will all be travelling there.'

'Bruges,' says Byrne slowly as if trying to place Bruges on the map, eventually giving a slight nod of approval, and Levina is thankful that Bruges is under Catholic rule. 'I am sorry to hear of your father's ill health,' he adds, without sincerity, 'but I am sure you shall find a means to keep the Bishop *au courant*.' And there is that smile again, sickeningly beguiling. He drains his cup of ale and stands in a swish of robes. 'I doubt Bishop Bonner would be happy to lose you from his parish. The truly faithful are so few and far between.'

Levina is certain she can detect a layer of sarcasm beneath his lilting words and wonders whether Bonner is testing *their* faith as much as the Carruths'. The threat of the influenza seems nothing now and is replaced with something far more sinister. She knows the Carruths to be reformers; perhaps Byrne has also paid a similar visit to them – it is certainly possible. The man makes for the door and with a bark of 'Look sharp!' to his servant is gone.

She turns to George, who is watching her as if waiting for a pronouncement, but she avoids meeting his eye and begins to collect together the ale cups.

George grabs her wrist. 'Leave that to the servant boy. It is why we pay him.'

Why *I* pay him, she wants to say, but doesn't.

'Are you still so eager to stay?' he adds. There is nothing tender in his tone.

'We *cannot* leave now. It would arouse suspicion.'

'If you hadn't –' He stops and drops his face into his hands. It is a gesture of despair that tugs horribly at her heart. 'If you hadn't insisted on sending all those papers, those drawings, to Geneva,' he mumbles, 'we wouldn't find ourselves under suspicion.'

She wants to shout at him, remind him of his own love of the new faith, call him disingenuous, but she holds her tongue. There is no point in railing at George, who loves her. He is frightened. She remarks the irony: that her guardsman husband is more afeared than she. 'I love you, George,' she whispers. He doesn't respond and for the first time she asks herself if his love for her has waned, feeling a chasm open up at the heart of her.

'And what about Marcus?'

'I don't know, George.'

'For the moment he must continue courting the girl, I suppose.'

'We can report to Byrne. Just innocuous things for the meantime and then perhaps find . . .' She can't think of a way to make her son safe.

The door swings open and Marcus appears as if on cue. His jaw is clenched, suggesting he is holding something in check, anger or upset, and he pushes past his parents with a muttered greeting, heading for the stairs, but his father puts out an arm to stop him.

'What is it, Marcus?'

He simply shakes his head in response and Levina can see that he's afraid to speak in case his emotions overwhelm him; he is a dam on the brink of bursting. She knows every little crevice of her boy's character, remembers him as a six-year-old coming a cropper to the bumps and scrapes of infancy, the way he would bite down on his trembling lower lip, his little body rigid with the effort of holding tears at bay. She knows not to try and comfort him, to allow him some distance. But George has him by the shoulders now. 'What is wrong?'

'If you must know,' Marcus spits, 'she has left.'

'The girl?' says George.

'No, not "the girl" . . . Alice, Father; her name is Alice, and they have left – all the Carruths – for God alone knows where. She did not tell me.' He is shouting now; the tears have got the better of him and are trailing down his cheeks.

George looks at Levina as if to ask, what now? But Marcus wrenches himself from his father's grip and storms up the stairs, throwing a screw of paper to the floor. Levina picks it up, unfolding it, moving closer to the window for the light. It is a letter from Alice Carruth telling little more than Marcus has said: that her family have gone. She feels, by proxy, the painful twinge of her son's first heartbreak.

'So?' says George.

'We are reprieved,' she replies, offering the paper to him. 'You can take it to Byrne later. But wait until they have had a chance to get far enough away before Bonner sends out the hounds.' George nods, then lifts his eyes up to the rafters as if to acknowledge God's hand in this. 'That way,' Levina continues, 'the Carruths will be safe and the Teerlincs will be seen to be doing as they have been asked.' George seems satisfied but she knows it is only a matter of time before he begins to plead for their own departure once more.

There is a frenzy of shouting in the street outside and from the window she can see a crowd gathering on the corner. 'Oh Good Lord, not another burning!' she says.

'I passed through the market earlier,' says George, joining her at the window. 'There was no stake built. I have heard nothing.' He has his arm round her and she tucks her head into the hollow of his shoulder, closing her eyes for a moment, trying to shut out the world. 'I had better find out what's going on.' He doesn't move, though, and they stand there still, taking comfort from the proximity of each other.

'I shall come with you,' she says.

'Marcus?'

'Leave him be. Let him cry it out in private.'

They make for the door. She offers her hand but he doesn't take it as they step into the January chill. The street is like a Breughel, teeming with people, all rushing towards Smithfield to find out what it is that's created such a commotion. A cart has been abandoned to one side, meaning the stream of humanity is forced into a bottleneck. Panic begins to spread in the crush, with men lifting children on to their shoulders for safety and lads climbing out of the way on to nearby window sills, scaling the tops of walls and over low roofs like cats. Levina can feel Hero close at heel as they are taken with the flow and eventually spat out into the market square, where there is a man on a crate shouting out to the crowd.

'What says he?' she asks a goodwife beside her.

'Calais is lost!'

Levina claps her hand to her mouth. 'No!'

Word of the loss filters through the throng and Levina's head is full of images of all those young men, boys still really, that she used to watch play-fighting in the tiltyard; she sees their smooth faces distorted with pain, their bodies twitching and mangled. She thinks of their mothers, cannot imagine the grief of losing a son in someone else's fruitless war. It is Felipe's war and Calais, England's last corner of hard-won ground on the Continent, is gone to the French. The crowd simmers. Someone presses a pamphlet into Levina's hand. On it is an image of the Queen, wizened and ugly, and beneath it are the words . . . *an utter destroyer of her own subjects, a lover of strangers, and an unusual stepdame both to these and to thy mother England.*

There is a crash; a gang of youths has toppled a goods cart. A roar goes up. Someone has clambered on to the upturned wagon and is shouting angrily, punching a fist into the air. People begin to jostle and shove and Levina feels her husband's hand firmly clasped to her shoulder.

'Come,' he says. 'Let's get away from here.'

March 1558
Whitehall
Katherine

Forget-me-not is scratching about at the bottom of his cage making little tutting noises. My hands are blue with cold; I clasp them together into a single fist and hold them to my mouth, huffing warm air into them. The weather is uncommonly bitter for March and the horizon beyond the window is thick and white and empty. Even the birds don't dare venture out for fear of freezing and dropping from the sky. That is what Juno says. Lady Jane Seymour (or Juno as everyone calls her, for court is filled to the rafters with Janes) arrived amongst us a year ago; and thank Heaven for her, as Cousin Margaret is poison these days and Jane Dormer can barely be prised away from the Queen. Besides, the latter shall be wed to Feria soon and will leave the country eventually to be a Spanish countess. It is a perfect match, given she is one of the true Catholics amongst us. Not like me or Juno; we truly couldn't give a fig if there is or isn't a purgatory, or if the host does or doesn't transform into flesh at Mass, and we try not to think too much about what happens when we die; there is plenty of time for that when we are old, and so much else to think of in the meantime.

Juno and I are often mistaken one for the other. Anyone who took the time to look closely at us, though, would see that we are only superficially alike, in our colouring and size.

Where my eyes are pale blue, hers are darker, my face is heart-shaped but hers is oval, and her mouth takes the form of a bow, whereas mine is more bud-like. But during the last year we have been so much together as to have picked up each other's little quirks and tics of speech and deportment. This gives us all the advantages of being twins – the fascination of men, the appearance of being in two places at once, the ability to cause confusion – and none of the adversities, like not being unique and having to share everything.

The Queen, whose eyesight is fading, cannot tell us apart and sometimes we swap dresses, which creates havoc and gets po-faced Susan Clarencieux's hackles up, causing us great amusement. Juno is my only ray of sunshine in this dismal place, where everyone wheels carefully around the Queen, whispering about who will succeed her. But no one dares mention it out loud for fear of upsetting her, when she is already as upset as a person can be. Besides, she believes herself to be with child again, though *she* is the only one to think so.

Some would have me as her successor, though more think it will be Elizabeth. I do imagine it sometimes, being Queen and all that goes with it – the jewels; the dresses; the splendid chambers; the men fawning, but even *I* am not silly enough to suppose it to be entirely pleasurable; I have watched the present Queen crushed by it until she is barely herself any more. The idea of it is too big to fit comfortably with all the other thoughts in my head: thoughts of my sister Jane. So I try not to think about it. Besides, the Queen suspects my faith. I know this because I feel her eyes on me when we are at Mass, as if her own prayers are less important than ensuring there is not a heretic amongst her ladies. If she were witness to my thoughts, I would burn for it. Anyway, I have concluded that Elizabeth is better suited for the role of Queen. She is returning to court soon and Maman has counselled me to repair my friendship with her – not such an easy task, I fear.

Jane Dormer is singing quietly. Juno and I are sewing small discs of gilt on to a pair of sleeves; it is dull work indeed. The Queen is slumped to one side in her chair, asleep. No one truly believes her to be with child, but it is Frideswide Sturley alone who voices her doubts. By all accounts the Queen has known Frideswide since they were girls, and she is the only one with the courage to say what she thinks. The rest of us, even Susan Clarencieux, humour her. But the Queen *is* ailing with something, for her gut is as swollen as a carnival bladder and painful too, judging by the fuss she makes when we dress her. We have all heard her retching in the morning and had to deal with the bright puddles of bile she brings up. As Jane Dormer's song comes to an end the Queen shifts and snorts, waking herself with a shudder. Juno nudges me, smirking, and I hold my breath, pressing my lips together to suppress the giggles. Levina, who sits slightly apart from us with her greyhound at her feet, is sketching the scene. She looks towards us, raising an eyebrow. In the absence of Maman Levina has been a reassuring presence indeed, always there to gather up the pieces.

'Goodness!' cries the Queen with a smile, not fully awake, as if she is still dreaming. 'The sound of angels.' Perhaps she imagines herself dead and before her maker. Then the smile drops away and she looks suddenly ancient, as if the woes of the world are on her. 'Calais,' she says, bringing the back of her hand up to her forehead. 'When I am dead and opened, you shall find Felipe and Calais lying in my heart.' I notice Frideswide Sturley, who is sewing on the other side of the hearth, exchange a look with Susan Clarencieux next to her. They barely conceal their concern. It is true, the Queen talks too much of death lately.

'Calais, Calais, Calais,' squawks Forget-me-not, swinging on his perch.

Jane Dormer offers the Queen a posset, murmuring reassurances: 'Fret not, Your Majesty, your husband will be back beside you before you know it. Your baby will be a cure . . .' The Queen's hand goes to her belly, and a flicker of a smile plays on her mouth. It is her sole joy, the idea of her imaginary infant. She takes a few sips from the cup and whispers something to Jane Dormer, who begins to sing again. The Queen falls back to sleep almost as suddenly as she woke.

It has been a miserable place indeed, the court, these recent months. Since the King returned last year the Queen has sunk into the depths of despair. He was accompanied by the Duchess of Lorraine, his mistress – though nobody actually called her such but it was plain as day, the way he looked at her as a dog drools over a bone. It has not been helped by the fact of the Duchess being such a splendid creature. If you saw the two women side by side, anyone who did not know them would think the Duchess the Queen, with her fine jewels and regal bearing, and the Queen herself, with her long face and small, cowed shape, just a sad lady-in-waiting or some such.

Anyway, the Duchess left months ago when the King departed to fight his war, taking every single young man in the land, or so it seemed. He left only ancient doddering fellows like the Cardinal hobbling about the place, and no one to dance with, not that there have been any entertainments lately. Though since Calais fell the men have returned in droves, save for those who lost their lives, of course. My mind turns often to the boys I used to dance with, who are no more. For a full month last year, after the battle of St Quentin, we were beset with wave after wave of terrible news: this person is wounded and will likely never walk again, that person is taken by the French, so-and-so is not accounted for.

I cannot forget how I felt when Cousin Margaret came running up to me in the knot garden, back then, crying out: 'Harry is killed!'

It was as if someone had taken hold of my heart and carved it up like a joint of meat. An animal moan came out of me, a sound I have never heard before, and I had to lean on Margaret for fear of collapsing to the ground.

'I don't know why you feel the need to make such a fuss,' she said. 'You hardly knew him. He was *my* friend.'

'But my husband!' I moaned, unable to contain myself, feeling uprooted, the world spinning away from me.

'Not Harry *Herbert*, you ninny. Harry Dudley,' she said.

'*Not* Harry Herbert?' Only then did the world begin to settle back into something recognizable.

'That is what I said, Cousin.' Her face was set in a kind of triumphant moue, which made me realize she had deliberately set out to confuse me.

'I knew him not,' I said, composing myself. 'Though his brother Guildford was married to my sister Jane.'

In my head I was making the calculation that Harry Dudley was just a year older than me. It pierced me right through with sadness, thinking of myself, barely out of girlhood, and he cold and beneath the ground, like my sister Jane, who was only seventeen when she died.

'Less said about those traitors the better,' muttered Margaret. 'Besides, Harry Herbert is not your husband.' As she said this she twirled her own wedding ring about her finger, smug as a pig in its own filth. 'Harry Dudley spent a summer with us at Skipton once,' she added, pulling a handkerchief from her sleeve and dabbing at her eyes. I didn't say it, but I knew the Cliffords hadn't been to Skipton since Margaret was an infant.

Jane Dormer's voice is pure as a clear pool of water. Time ekes by and it seems as if we will never finish stitching these gilt decorations – there seem to be acres of sleeve still uncovered, so when no one is watching I tip the remains of the discs into my purse. Jane nudges me with a little smirk as I tuck it under my gown, where I can feel the stiff crunch of paper. It is a letter from Harry Herbert that arrived in the bag from the Low Countries this morning.

My own dearest Kitty

I leave these blasted shores for England in a month and shall return to court where I will at last be able to rest my eyes upon my own sweet love. I have seen much here on the field of battle; base horrors that make me fear more than anything (more than my father's wrath, more than God's wrath even) wasting a single moment of precious life away from my beloved Kitty. I am determined that on my return we shall live as man and wife once more. In my mind's eye, Kitty, we are as two cherries and meant to hang together from the bough of life. Please write me a note, my sweet, that I may keep it close to my heart until we are once more united . . .

When I read it first, I felt that I might spill over with longing but I found I could not make a picture of Harry Herbert in my mind – his image had become blurred and merged with others, the mouth of Thomas Howard, the hands of Robert Dudley, the eyes . . . The eyes were always Harry's, jade green, feline, smiling, but the voice was not his; the voice had the Leicestershire burr of a page I once liked. An unsettling thought has crept over me these last hours, while sitting beside the Queen with little to do but think and sew. It would seem, despite the fact I still carry that grey fragment of ribbon buried in my undergarments, and I still read his letters over and over again, my fondness for Harry Herbert is no longer the burning passion it once was. When I think of him I am no longer stirred to the core. There is affection, certainly, but perhaps it is more the habit of love than love itself. After all, I have barely laid eyes upon his person for a full three years, unless you count the glimpse I had of him in the tiltyard last summer, in the final days before he left to fight.

Frideswide Sturley looks over at me, her brow raised, and mouths, 'Not sewing?'

I pick up the carton and tip it upside down to show that we have run out of discs. She shrugs; then the Queen, all of a sudden, sits upright as if she has woken from a nightmare.

'Get rid of it!' she shouts, seeming to stare directly at me. My stomach drops as I wonder what it is I have done. I rack my brains to think if I have said anything incriminating, remembering a joke I told recently about the Pope, which even had Frideswide Sturley reaching for kerchief to dab her eyes. Perhaps someone has told the Queen of it.

'I cannot bear to have him staring down at me,' the Queen continues, pointing to the large picture of her husband in full battle armour that hangs on the wall at my back.

I exhale, letting my shoulders drop.

'Get rid of it,' mimics the parakeet.

'Your Highness,' says Frideswide quietly. 'Do not vex yourself.'

I turn to look at the painted King; he is watching me. And before I have time to realize what is happening, the Queen has jumped from her chair, snatched up my embroidery scissors and is stabbing at the painting until great pieces of it are gouged right away. We all watch aghast except Frideswide, who grabs her wrist and prises the scissors from her fingers, handing them to me. The Queen sinks into her arms, weeping and wheezing and spluttering, while Susan Clarencieux and Jane Dormer fuss about. Levina has the wherewithal to tell one of the pages to make arrangements for the picture's removal. As the Queen is led out towards her bedchamber, I glance over at Juno; she is pale as bone and leaning against the wall.

'Juno,' I say. 'What is it?' Her eyes are glazed and there is a damp sheen over her skin. I touch her forehead. She is burning.

'I have to lie down,' she murmurs.

I loosen her gown and pull her arm over my shoulders, taking her weight, so as to manoeuvre her to the window seat. Levina places a pillow beneath her head and calls an usher, instructing him to get word to Jane's mother at Hanworth. My eyes fall on Levina's discarded drawing. It is not of the Queen as I had thought; it is of Juno and me. She has caught us in a moment of suppressed laughter, heads together, carefree, brimming with possibility. But when I look closer there is a brightness in Juno's eyes that hints at fever, and though my right hand is soft and fluttering aloft, my left, half hidden in the folds of my skirts, is fisted tight as a new bud that would break apart were you to prise it open. I don't know why but the sight of that makes my heart feel like a dead weight.

March 1558
Hanworth Manor
Katherine

'Influenza,' announces the physician. 'Without a doubt.'

He barely looked at Juno before he made his diagnosis. He didn't need to, for we knew it already. He may as well have stayed at home for all the good he can do, though he is mixing a tincture and giving instructions for its administration.

I can hardly make sense of what he is saying, so distressed am I at the thought of losing my ray of sunshine. If Juno goes it will be as if I have lost a part of myself. Sometimes I feel I love her more than I have ever loved any lad. We have slept wound together at night, so tightly I have lost sight of where I begin and she ends. I have felt her breath on my cheek and the heat of her body against mine, touching the core of me with an inexplicable desire. But there will be no intertwined nights now, for Juno lies there fighting for her life.

I nod and the physician seems satisfied with that, as he hands me a vial of green liquid. Above a thousand souls have been struck down with the influenza lately; some are saying it is a worse killer even than the sweating sickness and that there is no remedy against it. Juno's skin is a dull shade of grey and her eyes are hollow, as if she is dead already. I would cry but I notice Juno's mother, the Duchess, is stock-still and speechless, with her hands clamped over her mouth and a terrified look in her eye. One of us must hold things together, and though I am usually the one to fall apart, the Duchess appears to have given me little choice.

The doctor leaves us with the whispered words, 'She has reached the crisis. If she survives thc night all will be well.'

I try not to think too much on it and busy myself straightening the bedcovers. I ask the maid to stoke the fire, strew fresh herbs and call for a broth from the kitchens. Juno has fallen into an uneasy sleep; her breath is a shallow wheeze. I wipe a cool cloth over her brow; I must make myself busy to keep the thoughts at bay.

Turning to the Duchess, who has barely moved, I say, bossy as a nursery maid, 'You need sleep, My Lady. I shall stay up with Juno tonight.'

She is amenable as a lamb when her maidservant leads her out by the arm – which is surprising, given she has a reputation for being quite the harridan. I suppose it must be grief that has reduced her to this.

As she leaves she turns to me, face aghast, and asks, 'Why is it bad things happen to good people?'

I shrug, without a word. I do not know what to say. My sister Jane would have said something like: *We cannot know the Lord's plan for us; think of Job*, and my sister Mary might have answered: *Good and bad things happen to all, it does not bear scrutiny*. But what do I think? I know not why bad things happen to good people. I have never thought about it.

I turn back to Juno and find her deathly pallid and shivering. She must be dreaming, for she murmurs unintelligibly and there is a smile that moves briefly over her lips, which makes me think that perhaps, at least, they are happy dreams. I wonder if I am in them. I touch her forehead; her skin is damp and cold and I cannot help but think that this is how a corpse must feel. I shake that thought away and pull the plummet up and around her. She looks so fragile lying there, like a fallen leaf. I am twisted up inside with the dread that I may never see Juno awake again, and filled with a longing that is more deep and more sad and more lacking in hope than seems possible. I search the remote pockets of myself for my usual optimism, but it is nowhere to be found.

I lie on the bed, careful not to wake her, and listen to her breathing, making my breath take on the same rhythm to feel closer to her, and find I am accosted with memories. The day Juno arrived at court and Susan Clarencieux, who is as myopic as the Queen, mistook her for me, berating her for one of my misdemeanours: I watched from afar as Susan wagged her finger, barking, 'Katherine Grey, one of your dogs has done its business in the Queen's privy chamber. I shall have those infernal creatures banished if you can't keep control of them.'

Juno, rather than pointing out Susan's mistake, apologized profusely, promising it would never happen again, that the dogs would be kept strictly away from the Queen's rooms, until Susan seemed satisfied. Juno then sought me out.

'You are Lady Katherine Grey are you not?' she said, meeting my eye in a disarmingly bold fashion.

'I am. And you?' I replied, expecting trouble.

'I am Lady Jane Seymour and *you* are indebted to me.' She said this with a wide grin, continuing, 'I feel there is potential for friendship between us, Katherine Grey. We have much in common.' She paused, taking a step closer to whisper. 'Our fathers both were executed for treason and we are both close cousins to royalty.' She paused and I remember being entirely captivated by the liveliness in her eyes and the delicacy of her features. 'And I believe your mother, like mine, is a duchess who has wed beneath her.'

'She married her groom,' I said, smiling, surprising myself, for I hated to be reminded of this fact.

'My stepfather was once our steward.' Juno laughed at this as if there was not a care in the world that could touch her, and I felt a churn in my belly, akin to that when a lad you like comes courting. 'Indeed, our lives are so alike it would be almost impossible for us not to become either the greatest of friends or the greatest of enemies. And,' she added, pressing her mouth right to my ear, 'I believe the happy accident of our physical similarity might give rise to some pleasurable mischief.'

I was instantly enchanted – to find a soul equally driven by mischief as myself was indeed a stimulating thought. I held out my hand then, but instead of taking it in the usual way she grabbed my wrist, lifting my palm up to hers, and pressing them together, matching up the tips of our fingers, saying, 'Look, identical!'

'Identical,' I repeated, as if I had no words of my own.

'My friends call me Juno.'

'And your enemies?'

'I know not, and nor do I care,' was her answer. And so our friendship was sealed.

Now that hand lies limp against the rumpled linen bedclothes and I am devastated by the thought that the other me, my perfect double, may not last this night.

April 1558
Hampton Court
Mary

A swift trills above. I look up and catch it with my eye, a sharp black W up high in the blue, announcing spring. I have watched the back of the lad carrying my litter for the best part of four days now; it is straight and strong and muscular. I imagine my own shape and ask myself what lads like him think when they see me. Pity, I suppose, or disgust; it is always one or the other. This one was so very kind, helping me efficiently up into the seat, arranging the cushions for me, avoiding my eye carefully, embarrassed, probably, by my oddness. But then as he picked up the shafts he turned and threw me a wide, sunny smile. Perhaps he was pleased by the small size of the load that he was to carry all the way to Hampton Court from Beaumanor, for though I have passed my thirteenth birthday I am still no larger than I was three years ago.

There are marks on the wall at Beaumanor, in Maman's garderobe, where she measured Peggy and me – 'As a memory,' she said. Peggy was leaving for Elizabeth's household at Hatfield. At five foot, Peggy had grown a good dozen inches taller than I, and needed a set of new gowns, for she could not be seen in Elizabeth's entourage with her hems skimming her ankles. I have had a letter since from her describing life there, 'all the grandeur of court and much gaiety that suits not my quiet disposition, and her maids are unkind'. Elizabeth, she says, 'largely ignores me', and is a 'force of nature', which conjures up an image in my mind of her atop a great mountain stirring up the winds.

The litter rolls about. The journey seems endless; my body aches and if I don't keep my gaze fixed ahead I find myself beset with nausea. I watch the round chestnut rump of Levina's horse, which moves at a rolling gait behind the pair of grooms, up ahead for our protection. Beyond them all I catch a first glimpse of the red turrets and chimneys of Hampton Court, feeling a twist of unease bore into me at the thought of being near the Queen again. I wonder if I will be able to keep up the façade of the devout Catholic girl under her scrutiny, remembering what occurred the last time I was at court. Nothing came of it, but the fear lingers. And I am called back to court for the first time in three years. Maman had successfully managed to keep me away and I thought myself happily forgotten. But the Queen had unexpectedly expressed a need for me in the absence of my sister, who is nursing Juno Seymour, so Levina came to Beaumanor to deliver some portraits and accompany me back. As we left, Maman wore a painted smile, but it didn't fool me.

'Nearly there, Mary,' calls Levina, turning in her saddle and pointing towards the palace. Her horse shakes its bridle and snorts. She has a leather bag strapped tightly across her shoulder, which she touches repeatedly, as if to ensure that it is still there, and I wonder what precious item it contains that merits so much care.

The guards wave us through and we clatter into Base Court, a place I remember brimming with life. But today it is empty and the clop of our horses' hooves against the cobbles echoes about the walls. Levina dismounts, handing her horse to a groom. A porter offers to carry her bag, taking the strap, but she snatches it back, too quickly, hugging it to her body.

I am helped out of the litter, lifted by the armpits and deposited on the ground. I thank the lads, offering each of them a penny, and follow Levina into the gloom of the building, up the stone steps to the great hall. There is no one there either, save for a couple of scullions stoking the fire and a few kitchen staff clearing away the remains of dinner.

'Where is everyone?' I ask. 'It is like a morgue in here.'

'Many have had the influenza and others, like your sister, are sent to nurse them,' Levina replies. 'Most . . . ,' she lowers her voice and pauses as a page trots past, 'most are glad of an excuse to get away.'

My fear begins to take hold. She must read my expression for she says brightly, 'We shall continue with your portrait while you are here. It will provide a pleasant distraction.' We move on into the gallery, towards the Queen's rooms. 'I should warn you,' she says, whispering, 'you will find the Queen quite diminished. She has not been well.' I nod in response. 'She still believes herself with child, though she is not, so if she says anything to you about it, agree and smile. That is the best way.'

A group of councillors are leaving as we arrive at the Queen's rooms, amongst them Uncle Arundel, who asks after Maman and her husband. He says the name Stokes with his mouth pursed in distaste. Maman wouldn't give two figs for his disapproval; she used to say Arundel was 'insufferably arrogant and not particularly gifted'. The men pad off down the gallery and an usher I do not recognize announces us.

It is true, the Queen is frail, thinner than ever, her skin papery and lined, her eyes puffed up. Susan Clarencieux and Frideswide Sturley are next to her and there are one or two ladies in the window alcove; that is all. Even Jane Dormer is absent. Susan glances up from her sewing with a haunted look and nods in our direction.

'Our little Mary Grey,' says the Queen, opening her arms out, coming to life suddenly. 'We *are* pleased to have you back.' She pats her knee and I am obliged to clamber up on to it as I used to, I am a young woman though now, thirteen years old. I feel, beneath my fear, the old residue of hate rise up in me, like smoke from a greenwood fire. 'What news have you of your dear Maman?'

I swallow my feelings and begin to tell her of life at Beaumanor and Maman's happiness and that though she was with child a few months ago she lost it early and is quite recovered now. The Queen looks wistful, placing a hand on her own belly. I fear for a moment she might cry, and worry that I have reminded her of something she would rather forget. But Cardinal Pole is announced then and her attention is turned.

The Cardinal hobbles towards us on a stick; he seems to have aged a decade in these last three years. The Queen shoos away the other women but I am left abandoned on the royal lap, wondering about the way my life goes in circles like a pattern at the border of a tapestry. The Cardinal collapses into the seat beside us with a great wheezing sigh, taking the Queen's hand in his.

'We suppose, Cardinal, that our Privy Council has pressed you to discuss the naming of our heir.' Her voice is low, so as not to be overheard, though neither of them seems to have considered *my* ears. I may as well be a wooden puppet. 'They think you best placed to prise it out of us, no?'

'Madam –' he begins to speak but she talks over him.

'Will it be *our* sister, who it seems has half of England in the palm of her heretic hand, or *her* sister' – she taps me on the head – 'the daughter of a traitor? Or would you prefer that Scottish cousin, who is wed to France?'

I am struck now by the Queen's frailty. It had not occurred to me before that her time on this earth is drawing to a close. She is not so old but she is so very sunken-eyed and wraith-like. Though Maman has talked often of the perilous position my sister could find herself in were she named as heir, particularly now Elizabeth's popularity is so great, it is only in this moment that I begin to understand the true danger of the situation – that history may well be on the brink of repeating itself. I want to say something, but can think of nothing. What would Jane say? *We must not question God's plan for us.*

'Madam,' the Cardinal says once more. 'It is not the question of the succession that I come to you about. It is Bonner. He has planned to burn a dozen heretics at Smithfield on the morrow.'

The Queen's face lights up. 'England will be cleansed further.' She shakes the Cardinal's hand up and down in what I can only suppose is excitement. 'We will yet be saved, Cardinal. We will yet be saved.'

'I fear the people, madam. There have been riots in the city and I am afraid that this . . .' He pauses. 'Such a public occasion, and so many of them.' He stops and wipes the flat of a palm over his eyes slowly, as if they are sore. 'It might set off something that cannot be quelled. The people – your people, madam – are full of anger.'

'No!' The Queen's eyes are wide open now and the fire in the hearth is reflected in them, giving her a saturnine look that sends a shiver through me. 'We shall not pardon them, if that is what you are after, Cardinal. We shall start wondering if *you* are not a heretic yourself. There have been rumours . . .' She leaves this hanging, and there is an uncomfortable silence between them. I can't help but be glad her suspicion is aimed towards him rather than me on this occasion.

'Madam,' he says eventually, in a voice so full of pain he seems on the brink of tears, '*my* beliefs are not in doubt, I assure you of that. I cleave to the Catholic faith; it has been my life's work.'

'*You* shall not stand in the way of England's salvation, Cardinal. The more witnesses to the burnings, the better. England will be purged of sin and it will please God then to give us an heir. We thank God for Bonner every day. *He* is the only one of our churchmen who has any mettle.'

I can see that the Cardinal wants to add something but the Queen has half turned away from him and is running her fingers over the wisps of hair that have escaped my hood. He looks stricken. The Queen starts humming; it is a psalm but she cannot quite manage to find the right key. Eventually the Cardinal gets down on one knee, kissing her hand before taking his leave. While they were talking I had noticed some kind of disturbance on the other side of the chamber, the few ladies gathered in a circle over something. Now Susan Clarencieux breaks out of the huddle and approaches.

'Your Highness,' her face is grim. 'I am afraid Forget-me-not has . . . He has –'

'Spit it out, Susan,' says the Queen.

'He is dead, Your Highness. Poisoned.'

'Oh!' says the Queen quietly, looking down at her hands, which are knotted together. 'Poisoned? How so?'

'There are fragments of nightshade root amongst his seed.'

'We were given that bird near on thirty years ago,' she says, slumping in her chair. 'Someone must hate us greatly.'

All *I* can think is that it was not much of an existence. Thirty years incarcerated in a cage and carted from palace to palace, with just that gilded prison to scratch about in and only the art of mimicry to amuse itself – a life akin to one of Dante's circles of Hell.

Susan nudges me off the Queen's lap and then, sliding in beside her, holds her, like a child, rocking back and forth, while she sobs. I wonder how it is she can be so very grief-stricken over the poor parrot and yet able to condemn so many to the flames with such fervour. Her faith seems to have made her quite mad. I go over to where Levina is making arrangements for the parrot to be removed.

'Come,' she says to me, as the sad little carcass is carried off by one of the pages. 'There is a chamber set aside for me here where the light is good and I can make some sketches of you.'

Levina

The April light falls over Mary's black dress, revealing unexpected colours. As with the plumage of a jackdaw, iridescent hints of blue and purple slide across the surface of the inky satin. Levina and Mary have been silent for some time, lost in their own thoughts. Levina is sure her things have been searched since she left for Beaumanor. She can tell from the pattern of dust on the floor and a sense that things have been minutely shifted. Thankfully, she had the foresight to take the latest set of papers with her. She touches her hand to the satchel she wears, reassured to feel the rolled shape beneath the leather – more accounts and images of terrible events committed in the name of the Catholic Church, a seemingly endless catalogue of horror. Her mind buzzes with thoughts of how she will find a way to get them to the courier. They cannot stay here at the palace, it is too dangerous; people are watching her.

Mary moves slightly and the light catches her differently. Levina's sketch refuses to take shape. Her head is too full of thoughts. She wonders how George and Marcus are faring in Bruges, remembering the argument she had had with her husband the night before they left. It was a month ago; he had reserved a passage for the three of them and sprung it on her.

'You are my wife. You are subject to me!' he had shouted, when she complained that he had no right. She simply refused to go and they had slung angry insults at each other until George stormed out with the words, 'How could you put a family of traitors before your own?'

Those words have echoed about her head ever since and she has swung between fury and understanding. She didn't sleep and heard him return in the dead of night, finding him, in the morning, sprawled unconscious across his bed, fully clothed and stinking of ale.

She had tried to make amends as they were leaving, but George wouldn't look at her. She remembers his back turned in the doorway as she embraced Marcus, feeling that painful pull of separation a mother knows when a child leaves, but glad, all the same, he was leaving for a safer place. Taking his arm, she walked with him into the yard. George then swung himself on to his mare, kicked her into a trot and left, without so much as a farewell. Riven with doubt, Levina had written that evening a long letter of heartfelt apology. He has not yet replied, though she consoles herself with the knowledge that because of the war there are delays to traffic across the Channel. But a place has hollowed out inside her, filled now with regret.

The house in Ludgate felt cavernous and empty without them and she rattled around like a pea in a pan. Byrne breathed down her neck, ensuring she was at Mass, dropping in at the house when she least expected it, looking over at her in church with that unsettling smile.

'Where did you say your husband had gone?' Byrne had asked her at their last encounter. 'Geneva?'

'It is Bruges, where we are from.' Levina knew he was fishing. Geneva is where the papers end up.

'Why do you not join him? A woman without a man's protection is at risk.' He elongated the 's' sound as if emitting poisoned gas into the air.

'I remain to serve Her Majesty,' she'd replied, forcing a smile on to her face.

He seemed satisfied with that and had suggested then that they pray together. She felt a moment's reprieve from the constant worry, but only a moment. She has forgotten what it is like to live without fear, and is glad to be recalled to court. Even though it is grim at the palace, at least she doesn't spend her nights listening to every shout in the street and each creak of the beams, imagining Bonner's men coming to take her to Newgate, or worse. But now she is certain someone has been searching amongst her things here, so nowhere feels safe.

Mary shifts again, saying, 'Veena, how long do you suppose I will have to stay at court?'

'We cannot know, dear. Though I'm sure when your sister is back you will be given leave to return to your mother.'

'And will Katherine be named as heir?'

'I hope not, Mary,' she replies, wishing she could reassure

the girl, but the truth is that nobody knows and the hope is that the shadow of her father's treason will save her.

They are quiet again for a while and her thoughts continue to tumble about in the silence – if she could only lose herself in her work. She has an idea of how she wants to compose this portrait but the proportions seem wrong and she cannot manage to convey the thoughtfulness of Mary's disposition and the look she wears. What *is* that look? It is not in her eyes alone, it is in the set of her jaw, in her posture, but Levina cannot depict it. She puts her charcoal down with a sigh and takes a new sheet of paper.

'Have you painted the Queen often?' asks Mary.

'Once or twice.'

'And do you paint her as she is or . . . or as she would wish to be?'

'I suppose my attempt is to be faithful to the essence of her. But I fear if I showed her as she is, so frail, so emaciated –' Levina stops herself from admitting that she dares not show the Queen as she truly is.

They are silent again and Mary seems deep in thought, as if she has a clock's complicated workings whirring in her head. Eventually an idea appears to rise to Mary's surface. 'I would like you to draw me as I truly am – my crookedness, my ugliness – I want you to show it, for anything else would not be me.'

'You are sure?' asks Levina, suddenly understanding what it is she is not capturing in the image before her – the truth.

'Never more so.' Mary seems excited, her eyes bright. 'If I were to remove my over-gown, you could better see me.' She begins to unhook the front of her gown, peeling it from her shoulders and then unlacing her stiff stomacher and untying the tapes that attach her sleeves, tugging them undone, until she is standing in just her white linen shift with her clothes in a pile about her feet. But she is still fumbling beneath her shift, eventually pulling out a garment, some kind of truss, and flinging it to the corner of the room.

Levina sketches the scene, the lines of charcoal suddenly coming to life beneath her fingers, the contents of her leather bag temporarily forgotten. 'Perfect, you are perfect,' she mutters, almost to herself.

'No one has called me that before.'

There is no hint of self-pity in her, or if there is she hides it well. Levina sketches on, indulging in the malformations of the girl's shape, working out how the parts of her hang together beneath her shift, imagining her spine. It makes her think of the painting of Adam and Eve's banishment from Paradise on the wall of the church her family used to attend when she was a child. How she had remarked that Eve's breasts were high, hard mounds, nothing like her mother's heavy lolling globes. Now she thinks about it, that long-forgotten artist, a man of the church, perhaps, had likely never seen an undressed woman. It makes her want to draw Mary naked. She smiles at the thought, for Mary is already skimming along the boundaries of decency by offering herself up thus, and she knows these images will never be shown.

'Here, Mary,' she says, getting up and moving to the vast chimneypiece. 'Try standing here, that I may show your smallness as it truly is.'

Mary crosses the chamber, stopping to take a look at the pile of sketches. 'Oh, Veena!'

Levina looks over to her, worried that she finds the images disturbing, but she is engrossed, holding the drawings up to the light the better to take them in. Eventually she moves over to the hearth. 'How is this?' She places one hand on the stone upright and turns her body away, looking back over her shoulder, then with her free hand she loosens the ties at her throat, allowing her shift to drop down, exposing her shoulders and spine. There are deep red creases where the truss has left its mark, making it seem as if she has been lashed.

'Yes,' says Levina, feeling herself in the grip of something exciting. 'This is our picture.' She rummages amongst her things for the inkbottle, finding it, lining up her brushes, taking a sheet of vellum. An animal scent lingers on it. She pegs it to her easel and begins to imagine, with a flickering thrill, the lines she will draw on its virgin surface.

'You know they have never allowed me a mirror. They think that by obscuring the truth from me I will be better off.' Mary pauses. 'It is not the case. Their intentions are good, but –'

'You mean your parents, your sisters?'

Mary nods. 'They sought to protect me from reality.' She pauses again, seeming deep in thought, before saying, 'I too have the feelings of a young woman. I sometimes see a lad and wonder what it would be like to . . . There is a scribe in Maman's house: Percy. I sometimes wonder what it might be like. He doesn't notice me.'

Levina says nothing, allows Mary to talk, feeling the privilege of being trusted with her innermost thoughts.

'I have been reading Plato – his *Symposium*. Have you read it?'

'I have not.' Levina feels a little ashamed that this young girl is versed in Plato when she has failed, in near on forty years, to read the ancients.

'It is all about love. There is an idea in it, that in our true state we were once like wheels, two heads, four arms, four legs, spinning across the earth, and that somehow we became split and are destined to seek out the other half of ourselves. It is silly, of course, but a little like the story of Man's fall, is it not?'

Levina nods and smiles, then is surprised at the force with which Mary says, 'Do you suppose there is the misshapen half of a wheel somewhere in the world to match me?'

Levina is touched to the heart but doesn't know how to reply, can think only of meaningless, comforting words, so remains silent and Mary continues. 'They all think I bear my cross like a saint. But I don't – I sometimes hate God for what He made me.'

'It is your right to feel angry, Mary, even with God.' Levina finds her voice at last. 'But you are worth a thousand of those ordinary pretty girls.'

'Ordinary prettiness is a thing I shall never know. And don't say it –' She holds up a hand. 'That I am beautiful on the inside.'

'Patronize you with platitudes? That I would not do.'

'I know.' Her voice has softened. 'You are the only one I feel I can be honest with.'

'There is honesty in *this*.' Levina taps at her drawing. 'Despite the fact that no one else will ever see it.'

They fall into a deep silence, she in the thrall of what is before her, in the image taking shape on the page. Now she sees the truth of that look Mary wears – it is more than just a stoic mask; it is filled with tightly censored anger and passion. She absorbs herself in the mechanics of her craft, holding out a brush at arm's length, measuring what she sees, making minuscule marks on the vellum, looking until she sees the things that are not at first apparent, the relationship between the parts of the figure before her, the empty space around her.

After a while Mary says, 'Thank you, Veena, for this . . . For doing this.' She stops and a smile dances over her lips. 'The truth is so very important. Do you not think?'

'It is all there is.' Levina remembers now, quite vividly, the dwarf's corpse at the morgue in Bruges. She can hear her father's voice guiding her, as she sketched the odd proportions over and over again until he was satisfied she had learned the lesson – that nothing is as you suppose it to be. It strikes her that she is still learning that lesson.

She sees Mary with new eyes: her permanent shrug, as if she is seen through a flaw in a pane of glass; her round eyes with their grave seriousness hiding that passionate rage; her hands, fragile as butterflies; the particular tone of her dark chestnut hair that carries with it the memory of her dead sister, Frances too, the three of them so alike really – so unlike Katherine, for Katherine is entirely her father's daughter.

She stops herself from being dragged away by her thoughts, bringing her attention back to what lies before her, how the light sculpts the planes of Mary's face, how the edge of her blurs into the shadow behind. Levina, entirely captivated by what she sees, works almost in a trance – the chink of her brush in the bottle, the metallic tang of the ink, the eager pat of her heart – now finding the composition that eluded her, barely aware that the day is fading. She stands back eventually to survey her work, then, taking her most delicate three-haired squirrel brush, adds the finest details, fronds of hair, a stitched pattern of ivy on Mary's shift, the perfect discs of her small fingernails.

'If I am ever to be a great artist,' says Levina, 'then it will be you, Mary, who has made me so.'

'Who would have thought?' Mary exclaims with a wry laugh. 'The runt inspiring such greatness.'

'Runt,' says Levina. 'That is a harsh word.'

'But it is the truth.'

The chapel bell rings out announcing Mass, interrupting them. The two women respond without thinking. Levina pulls her apron off and reaches for her hood, tying it beneath her chin, then drapes a cloth over her easel, careful not to smudge the drying ink. When she turns back to Mary she realizes to her horror that the girl has pulled out the roll of papers from her satchel.

'What are these that you have been guarding so closely?' she asks, unfurling them, her eyes moving over them. The colour drops from her face. 'Why do you have such things? You risk your life with them.'

The hinges of the door squeal slightly as it is pushed ajar. 'Is someone within?' calls a man's voice.

'What is your business?' asks Mary.

'We are ordered to search these chambers, My Lady.'

The two women swap a look of alarm. Levina swallows.

'Enter not!' cries Mary, with authoritative firmness. 'I am unclothed.' She shoves the papers inside her shift and pulls on her truss over them, tying its tapes, then steps into her kirtle, hitching it on to her shoulders.

When Mary looks up Levina shakes her head but the girl nods defiantly, saying, loud enough to be heard beyond the door, 'Would you kindly pass me my stomacher and gown, Mistress Teerlinc.'

Levina does so, helping to fit her into her clothes, burying the drawings beneath the layers.

'You may enter now,' Mary calls out.

Two men appear. One Levina recognizes from the courtyard earlier. He had been a little too eager to take her satchel off her, which had roused her suspicion. The other she has never seen.

'Come, Mistress Teerlinc, let us leave these men to their duties, or we will be late for Mass.'

At this Mary glides from the chamber. Levina, at her side, feels like an infant in the face of such courage, scolding herself inwardly, horrified that she has been so careless with her charge's safety. Mary only betrays her fear once they have reached the far end of the corridor, with a deep expulsion of air.

It is not only in the colour of her hair and the features of her face that she resembles her sister Jane, thinks Levina.

May 1558
Hanworth Manor
Katherine

I have my Juno back. It is six weeks since I sat with her that night, when none thought she would survive; it seems longer, but now the colour is returning to her cheeks. Here at Hanworth the days stretch out with little to do, save stroll by the lake with the dogs when the weather is fine, though Juno still cannot walk far. The Duchess has allowed me only two of my dogs here, the rest of them, with Hercules, are at Beaumanor. I am glad to have Stim and Stan to keep me company in the long hours when Juno is resting and I ride out with them in the park where they chase rabbits and bark at the deer, generally making a nuisance of themselves. I find ways to occupy myself, there is music and a relatively handsome dance master who comes twice a week, but I am restless for the bustle of court where there is always scandal of one kind or another to swap.

Here it is the nights, though, that are the best times, when we are tightly curtained in bed, snuggled together for warmth and Juno and I explore each other's bodies, taking it in turns to pretend we are boys. Sometimes, in the half-light when I see the silver blonde of her hair and the curve of her cheek, I imagine she is me and I her. I run the tip of my tongue along her neck, tasting the salt tang of her skin, and nuzzle into her, enveloping myself in her particular scent, rose water and something beneath it that reminds me of the sea, feeling the firm grip of her hand on my thigh and hearing only the mingling sound of our breath. I never imagined such pleasure was possible.

Juno, bundled up in furs though the weather is clement, holds my arm as we stroll in the gardens. I mimic Mistress Poyntz, firing orders like arrows, to draw a laugh out of her. It is washing me through with joy to hear that laugh once more, but the effort of it provokes a fit of coughing and we have to stop on a bench that she may recover her breath.

'Shall I send for a drink of hot lemon for you?' I ask, rubbing her shoulders.

'I should like that,' she replies, with a limp smile.

I run to the house to find Mister Glynne, Juno's manservant, and make my request. On my way back out I bump into the Duchess in the hall.

'Katherine,' she snaps. 'Walk!' she commands me as if I were a wayward mare.

'Yes, My Lady,' I mutter, stopping before her and bobbing in a curtsy.

'And straighten your hood.'

'Have you seen what a beautiful day it is, My Lady?' I say, by way of ameliorating the atmosphere.

'Juno insists on your continued presence, but let's not pretend we are friends, Katherine. The sooner you are back at court, the better.' She purses her lips and glides off like a ship into the Thames, before I have time to form a sufficiently clever response. Since the night of Juno's crisis, when I observed the other side of her, she has treated me with increasing contempt. I suppose she regrets the fact that she allowed me a glimpse of her weakness and would rather not be reminded of it by my continued presence. I may be slight and small but I have thick skin and if she thinks she can penetrate it with her sharp tongue, she has another think coming.

As I am crossing the moat, I notice a pair of riders in the distance and stand for a moment watching them as they come up the drive, still too far off for me to make out their features. I can see, though, that their horses are good ones, not like the winded hack that the Duchess has set aside for me to go out on, so I deduce these horsemen must be noble. One of the mounts seems to be a handful, skipping about and tossing its head, but its rider is well seated. Something is keeping me on the steps watching them. Perhaps it is the idea of male company to break up the boredom that has ignited a little thrill in me.

I run back to Juno, calling, 'There are visitors.'

'What sort?' she asks.

'Male, I'm sure of it.'

'Oh, not Uncle Richard, I hope. Mother said he's been threatening to come. I'm warning you, he's a terrible bore, and don't get caught alone with him. He has wayward hands.' She slides her own hand around my throat and down towards my breast, with a giggle.

I laugh too but I feel a dip of disappointment. I had allowed my imagination to run away with me for a moment, conjuring up the possibility of some harmless flirtation in this barren place. Juno snatches her hand back as a page approaches holding the toddy, handing it over with a bow.

'That's better,' she says, taking a sip.

Stan spots a squirrel, chasing it across the grass and yelping in excitement. It scales the nearest tree and Stan waits at the bottom in a frenzy of high-pitched barking with Stim now joining in the din. I try to call them back to no avail.

'Lets walk a little and they will follow us,' suggests Juno, draining her cup.

'You are sure you're not too –'

'Look,' she interrupts, standing and opening her arms up. 'The sun is out and at last I feel almost human. I am well enough. Don't worry.' She holds out a hand to me and as I stand she places a kiss on my cheek. 'You have been such a good friend. I am ever in your debt, Kitty, for the way you have cared for me these last weeks. You are the sweetest, kindest friend in the whole world – and the most entertaining,' she adds, with a smile.

'No, you are,' I say, slipping my arm through hers and moving off in the direction of the lake, both dogs at last falling obediently into line.

'No, *you* are.'

'No, *you* are.'

'There is only one thing for it, then. We are both the *most* entertaining, the *most* sweet, the *most* kind girls in the –'

'World,' we say in unison.

'In the universe, I'd say,' comes a voice from behind. We turn together.

'You!' cries Juno, freeing herself from my grip and running into the arms of a mud-spattered young man.

'You will dirty your dress,' he says, laughing, spinning her around. 'I thought you were at death's door, Juno. I came to sit vigil.'

'I was, I was,' she laughs. 'But I am better now. Much better, and all the more so for seeing you.'

'So I see.' He holds her shoulders and stands back, appraising her. 'Though it is hard to see you properly inside all those furs. You look like a fat old countess.'

They are both laughing now and I find I am piqued that it is Juno in the arms of this man and not me. But mostly I am cross that she hasn't ever told me about him. I thought we confided everything to each other. I think of all the secrets I told her about Harry Herbert, allowing a little pool of resentment to form, and pretend to amuse myself throwing sticks for the dogs as I watch the two of them cavorting from the side of my eye.

'Juno, you are forgetting your manners,' the man says then, waving his arm in my direction. 'Are you not going to introduce me to your exquisite companion?'

My mind is awhirr – exquisite, indeed. He is looking at me intently from beneath a straw-coloured cowlick of hair with a pair of bright eyes. I meet his gaze and then allow myself to brazenly look him up and down. He is filthy dirty; his hose, once white, are quite black with saddle grease and his habit is covered in mud, there are even spots of it on his face. His fingernails too are grubby as a blacksmith's, but I can't help the idea slipping into my head of those filthy hands getting under my skirts.

'I'm sorry, you are right. How rude I am.' Juno is quite breathless with the excitement of it all. 'Ned, this is my dear, dear friend Lady Katherine Grey.'

'Lady Katherine.' He bows. 'I feel I should get down on my knee.' From the tone of his voice it is abundantly clear that he has no intention of doing such a thing.

'Don't be silly, Ned,' says Juno.

'I believe we have met before, Lady Katherine.' I rack my brains to think where, for I surely would have remembered meeting such a fine specimen. 'But you were only seven at the time,' he continues, 'and I was all of eight. You were as pretty then as you are now.'

'Is that so?' I say, glancing towards Juno, who I am surprised to find smiling rather than scowling at her beau – her *secret* beau – paying compliments to me.

'Kitty,' she says, 'this is my brother, Edward, who should be Duke of Somerset or at the very least Earl of Hertford – everyone refers to you as Hertford rather than Seymour anyway, don't they, Ned? Were it not for that monster Northumberland . . .'

Everything falls into place.

'He ousted our father,' seethes Juno, for my benefit I suppose, though I know the story well. 'Had him sent to the Tower; Mother too. Took his place as Protector.' She is counting off each point on her fingers.

'Never mind all that,' he interrupts his sister, who continues listing the injustices Northumberland visited on the Seymours.

'Had Father executed as a traitor; confiscated our lands . . .'

Hertford has fastened his gaze on to me. I now see the likeness; he has Juno's perfect bow-shaped mouth, her oval face, her fair colouring – they are peas in a pod.

'You didn't come with Uncle Richard, did you?' Juno exclaims with an exaggerated scowl.

'Not likely!' he replies, finally looking away. 'I came with John Thynne.'

'John Thynne! The father or the son?'

'The son.'

'I shall be glad to see him.'

It is I now who can hardly tear my eyes away from the pair of them as they talk.

'Shall we seek him out?'

'Where is he, then?' asks Juno, linking arms with her brother and indicating with a nod that he should take my arm too, which he does, and firmly, pulling me close so I can smell the sweat and the horse on him.

'He is in the stables seeing to his mare that is lame.'

'Juno,' I say, 'are you sure it is prudent to be out for so

long? Shouldn't we perhaps go inside and your brother can bring this John Thynne to see us in our chambers later?' I do have Juno's health on my mind, but really what I want is an excuse to get out of the plain everyday gown that is beneath my cloak, and put on something more becoming.

Our bedchamber is in the old part of the house above the medieval hall and must have been the solar once, for it is roomy enough for a vast tester bed, which is curtained off, separating out a spacious area that serves as a privy chamber. As soon as we are there I fling off my gown and hood and rummage through my things for my pale blue satin, deciding to leave my head bare to better show off my hair.

'Can I borrow your cochineal?' I ask Juno, picking up the little pot of crimson-stained goose grease. I balance the looking glass on the window sill for the best of the light, and rub some on to my cheeks. 'What do you think?' I face Juno for her approval.

'You look like you have a fever. Wipe some off.'

I take a handkerchief and do as she suggests. 'Better?'

'Much.' She smiles at me as if she knows something I don't. 'Is this for my brother?'

'Maybe,' I say, unable to conceal my smirk.

She claps her hands together. 'This is perfect, Kitty. I hadn't dared hope.'

'You mean you had thought such a thing and never mentioned it?'

'Perhaps.'

'You won't say anything, will you? Promise me,' I say, helping her off with her hood and wrapping her fine wool shawl about her throat, placing a firm kiss on her lips. She takes hold of me behind the neck and holds me tight, slipping her tongue into my mouth.

'Is this a sin, Kitty?' she whispers, letting go of me.

'Nothing that nice could not be a sin,' I reply.

'You're not to run off with my brother and forget me altogether, Kitty Grey.' Though she says this lightly, there is a discordant note in her tone.

'That wouldn't be possible. I am too fond of you.' I stroke her cheek. 'I mean it.'

'I hope Mother will not make a match for me miles away. She *was* talking to the Percys in Yorkshire, but the boy died or it fell through for some reason. Imagine me there. It is so far.'

'I couldn't bear it,' I say, suddenly feeling the drag of the world upon us. We will both be married before long. I want time to stop and keep us here together. 'Some of this?' I hold out the jar of cochineal.

'I think not,' she says.

'So this John Thynne isn't likely to take your fancy, then?'

'Not for all the gold in the Vatican.'

'Really? What is wrong with him?'

'He is the son of Father's old steward; I have known him too long. Besides . . .'

'Besides what?'

'Oh, you shall see. Pass the cards over; we can play primero while we wait for them.'

We settle into the game, snapping the cards down and picking them up with quick fingers and in silence. As we have no coins we have raided the carton of seed pearls as wagers and I am accumulating quite a stock. I may be better at spending coins than counting them, and I have never beaten her at chess, but I can give clever Juno a run for her money at primero. I do not have my usual focus, though, with one ear listening out for footsteps on the stairs. When I hear them my heart makes a little jump. It is only the chandler with new candles, but as he is moving about the room with his taper the door is flung open and in stride Hertford and a man I can only presume is John Thynne.

The thing that is most instantly noticeable about John Thynne is that he is not at all thin; and the first thought that strikes me is that it is no wonder his mare is lame, having had to carry such a great lump about on her back. Just as I am about to nudge Juno and whisper as much to her I stop myself, feeling mean for thinking so uncharitably about a man who cannot help the way God made him. But Hertford, standing tall and lean beside his friend, is only rendered all the more comely by comparison. He is dressed quite plainly in dark wool with a black rabbit collar, as if he has not gone to much trouble to impress, and I like him the more for it.

'Lady Jane,' Thynne is saying. 'And Lady Margaret, how –'

'No, Thynne,' interrupts Hertford with a little laugh and a flourish of his fingers, 'this is not my sister, Margaret; may I present Lady Katherine Grey.'

'I . . . I am so very sorry, Lady Katherine, Your . . . er, Your . . .' He is clearly flustered, stuttering slightly and dithering. He drops on to his knee and, looking at his feet, sweeps his cap from his head, holding it in trembling hands.

'"Lady Katherine" is entirely adequate, Mister Thynne. I am not named the Queen's heir yet,' I say. 'And it is likely I never shall be.'

Juno and her brother are smirking and I try not to look at them for fear of succumbing to the giggles.

'Can you forgive me, My Lady?' he pleads. 'You look so much like a Seymour I was quite fooled.' His jowls wobble as he speaks, but he has such an apologetic hangdog expression I find myself quite charmed.

'You are forgiven,' I say. 'I shall take it as a compliment.'

'Get on your feet, man,' says Hertford. 'There's no need to stand on ceremony here, is there, Lady Katherine?'

Poor Thynne looks utterly mortified, so I say, 'I am touched,' and give him a smile before changing the subject. 'We were playing primero.'

'Primero,' says Hertford. 'Who is winning?'

'Kitty has the upper hand, as usual,' says Juno.

'So you have a talent for cards, do you, Lady Katherine?'

'I would not call it a talent,' I say, barely meeting his gaze. I notice that he seems to approve of my sky-blue satin and rouged cheeks, for he does not seem able to take his eyes off me, which was, after all, the aim.

'Was your journey a long one, Mister Thynne?' I ask, offering my shoulder to Hertford as I turn to his friend.

'It was most arduous,' he says. 'But what rewards at its end, to have such delightful company.'

'Do you play?' I ask, ignoring the compliment, waving the pack of cards. 'It is better with more people.'

Two stools are pulled up to the table and we play a few hands before Thynne takes his leave to check on his mare, whereupon Juno announces that she is exhausted and must lie down. I have a suspicion that this a conspiracy to ensure that Hertford is left alone with me, or more or less alone, for Juno has retreated only as far as our curtained-off bedchamber.

Hertford scuttles his stool closer to mine, closer than is proper. I busy myself sorting the cards and scooping the seed pearls back into their carton without looking at him.

'My mother has warned me to keep away from you,' he says quietly. 'She says you are trouble and that our family has had more than its fair share of trouble.'

'Did she indeed?' I shift myself away from him and try to keep my composure, but I am affronted that the Duchess should say such a thing.

'But I told her I would make my own opinion.'

'Did you now?' I look him directly in the eye with no hint

of a smile. I want to ask him what other slanders the Duchess has heaped upon me. 'And don't you think you should take your mother's advice seriously?' I am doing my best to seem nonchalant, not to let it show that my heart is hammering. But all I can think about is what those bow-shaped lips, so akin to Juno's, might feel like pressed against mine.

'A mother's advice has its place, but . . . ,' he says, leaning towards me as if to take my hand. There is a little residue of dirt beneath his fingernails that raises an ineffable tender feeling in me, but I ignore his gesture, turning away, rising and moving towards the window. It has started raining and I watch the drops chase each other down the panes. I can feel him move up behind me. 'Trouble is not necessarily a *bad* thing.'

He has me with that; it is the sort of thing that I myself might have said.

'And who are you to say what a bad thing is or is not?' I reply, still not turning round to him.

'Touché!' I can see, reflected in the glass, that he makes a little stabbing gesture with his finger and steps minutely closer. 'Were you . . . are you not Harry Herbert's girl?' he murmurs. I can smell soap but cannot help thinking of him so filthy earlier, carrying the stench of sweat and horse. I want to lean back into him, allow him to take me in his arms, but I step away.

'We *were* married,' I say without any explanation. After all, everyone at court knows the story of my annulment; he would have had to have been hidden under a stone not to have heard about it.

'I am not fond of the Herberts,' he says with a scowl, seeming to forget altogether that he is wooing. 'I begged Pembroke's help when Northumberland was trying to oust my father. He was the only one with enough power to have done anything. He refused me, the b—' He slaps a fist hard against his thigh, to prevent himself uttering an oath in front of a lady, I suppose, and looks away out of the window.

'I know what it is like to lose a father on the block,' I say, for I can see plainly, in the rigid set of his shoulders, that the pain of the memory still haunts him, as mine does me. He turns, looking towards me with a puzzled expression, as if he'd forgotten momentarily that I was here.

'Yes,' he says, then his posture relaxes once more and he smiles. 'So!' he then adds, hesitating, moving a step closer to me. 'Do you still love him?' As he speaks, the mirror I had balanced on the window sill earlier slides and falls to the floor, shattering.

We both drop on our knees to gather the pieces, carefully placing them on the sill. A smear of red appears on the floor and, opening my hand, I see that my finger is cut. We both stare as the berry of red swells, then slips down to my palm. I do not feel it. Hertford then lifts my finger to his mouth and sucks the blood away. An unbidden gasp escapes me and I snatch my hand back. He looks at the floor, as if ashamed, and holds out a handkerchief, still not looking at me. I take it, binding my finger tightly.

'Do you still love him?' he repeats.

I collect myself. 'You are forgetting your manners, sir, in asking such an intimate question of me.' I hold his eyes with mine and I think I can see that something is ignited in them – he is a fish on a hook, my fish. My finger has begun to throb. Sir Edward Seymour, Ned, Somerset, Hertford, whatever it is he wants to call himself, will be mine. As I think of it, the place between my legs feels hot with longing, but I quash the thought. 'You had better leave.' I say firmly. 'It is not correct for us to go unchaperoned.'

'Very well,' he says, turning and meeting my eye as he exits. 'But will you stay at Hanworth awhile?'

'The Queen will want me back soon. There is no doubt of that. And now Juno is mended . . .'

'Stay a little. You can always find an excuse.'

'Perhaps I like it at court,' I say, but I know I shall stay a few days at least.

November 1558
Beaumanor
Mary

I wake disorientated to a loud banging. The maid sits upright on the truckle with a little cry of 'Lady Mary, what is it?'

I climb down from the bed and fumble in the darkness for a candle, finding the nub of last night's and lighting it from the embers that are still alive in the fire.

I can hear the girl's teeth chattering, though whether from fear or cold I cannot say. 'Wrap yourself,' I tell her, throwing her a gown. The banging starts up once more. It is someone at the door.

We tiptoe to the head of the stairs and watch the steward, drunk with sleep and brandishing a torch, shuffle towards the entrance.

'Have patience, whoever you may be!' he calls.

Maman appears beside us, bleary-eyed, saying, 'It can only be bad news at this time of night.' Stokes takes the stairs two at a time, brushing past the grumbling steward.

'It is I, Katherine,' comes a voice from beyond the door. 'I am with Levina and Juno. Let us in.' We all rush down as Stokes draws back the vast bolt and it swings open.

'*Chérie!*' cries Maman, drawing my sister to her. 'What has happened to bring you here at this hour?'

'The Queen . . .' begins Levina.

‘She is gone?’ says Maman. Katherine and Juno slump, exhausted, on to the settle.

‘No, but I think it will not be long,’ replies Levina.

‘She collapsed in the watching chamber. Her fingernails were purple. Susan Clarencieux was beside herself, wailing and moaning.’ Katherine’s voice has an urgency to it and her face is hollowed by exhaustion. They must have ridden hard to get here.

‘The council didn’t know whether they were coming or going and half the court has left for Hatfield,’ says Juno.

‘To Elizabeth?’ I ask.

‘Yes, Mouse, to Elizabeth. And let us hope to Heaven she is named. Given the exodus in her direction, it seems to be what most desire.’ Maman has begun to help the girls out of their cloaks and I am thinking once more of the dreadful possibility of history repeating itself. The whole country is beloved of Elizabeth; God forbid that Katherine be named, for it would cause the lid to fly off Pandora’s box. We must all be thinking it, for the tension in the room could be pierced through with an arrow.

‘You are frozen,’ Maman says to Katherine, rubbing her hands to warm them.

‘We left without permission,’ says Levina. ‘I feared for this one’s safety.’ She places a firm arm about my sister’s shoulders.

‘You did right, Veena. It is a risk should she rally, but who knows what chaos might ensue if she goes without naming an heir. Kitty would be . . .’ She doesn’t finish her sentence but asks, ‘Has she named anyone?’

Stokes has found a few flames in the great hearth and tipped on some kindling. It flares up, throwing warmth and light into the room. I had not thought of the possibility of the Queen not naming *anyone*.

'She had not when we left.' I can't help the feeling that is surging through me – it is not exactly happiness, it is much more complicated than that, and is mixed with fear for my sister, but I am glad if the Queen is dying. It feels something like revenge, I suppose. 'She was repeating over and over,' continues Levina, '"No boys, not a single boy, if there were a boy I would name him. All I have to choose from are girls."'

'Did she hint at anything?' Stokes asks.

'Not really. And I thought it best to get Katherine away rather than wait and see.'

'You did right,' says Maman again. We are silent for what seems like an age until Maman says, 'Up to bed, girls.'

'The cart is following on with our things,' says Katherine. 'My dogs.' She looks so young in this moment, asking for her pets, as if barely out of infanthood. 'Will you let them in with us when they are here?'

We mount the stairs slowly, leaving Maman, Stokes and Levina by the fire. There must be things they want to discuss without our hearing. Once in our chamber Peggy and I help my sister and Juno out of their clothes, which I only now see are filthy from the journey. The maid takes the truckle and the three of us clamber into the tester, but I am beyond sleep, so I sit up for a while watching Katherine and Juno slumbering in each other's arms in a way that is so natural, so comfortable. I, who can hardly even bear to hold hands for longer than a moment, cannot imagine such proximity.

The thoughts whirring about my head are keeping me wide awake, so I slip from the chamber and crouch on the landing to listen to the talk downstairs.

Levina is speaking of some man Byrne and how he has been 'closing in' on her. I wonder if it has anything to do with the drawings I found that day. Terrible images of people being burned alive, so vivid I could almost hear their screams. I sat through Mass with the paper next to my skin, as if they were love letters, their rough touch reminding me of how much I loathed the faith that would sanction such things. Levina came with me later to the river. We wrapped them around stones, flung them in and watched them sink.

'Do you think Katherine in such great danger?' It is Stokes who asks this.

'I think it unlikely. Things are changed,' says Levina. 'It is not like –'

'Remember Jane,' says Maman.

I am trying to remember a time when we were not afraid. I think back, far back to Bradgate, and remember the summer when I learned to milk a cow – my small fingers on the warm, bulging udder. If I close my eyes I can get a sense of the joy of that first thin spurt of warm milk. How old was I then – seven, eight? I am not sure, but those days are like my Paradise before the Fall.

Katherine has been here for several days now and she is not herself. She sits with her feet tucked up, hands wrapped across her body, staring blankly out of the window. She will not leave Juno's side, clinging to her as if she were the sole piece of floating wood in a stormy ocean. Juno flicks through a book of woodcuts, trying her best to distract Katherine, pointing out images of mythological beasts, to no avail.

'Where is your brother?' Katherine whispers to her. 'Why does he not come?'

'He cannot, Kitty. He must remain at court for the good of our family, and for Mother. You know that,' she replies.

It is early morning and we are gathered in Maman's rooms – a collection of wan faces and dark-ringed eyes: none of us has slept much these last days. Maman and Levina sit huddled together close to the hearth, talking in low voices.

'You never know what happens when a monarch passes,' Maman keeps repeating.

I remember when my cousin, the young King Edward, died and our whole family was in a state of excited frenzy, for Jane was to be made queen. I was left at Bradgate alone with my nurse, trying to understand why it had never been mentioned when we were growing up that Jane would one day succeed. I did not understand then the significance of the threads of blood attaching families together – that a measure of Tudor blood can put you on the throne, whether you want it or not. I know more now.

I move to the window seat, next to my sister, looking out; the park is a shimmering landscape of frost, the leaves all encased in icy fronds, the lawns crisply furred. Beyond is the lake, shrouded in mist, and the sky behind as white as the ground. It will be advent soon and we will be eating salted fish for weeks. A grave Christmas it will be this year. A lone deer scrapes at the hard ground with a hoof, sniffing the place to see if there is anything edible there. It is the only live thing in the whole landscape, though there is a trail of tiny, three-pronged footprints along the outside sill, evidence of at least a single bird. I remind myself to scatter some seed.

I feel Katherine tense slightly beside me, kneeling up a little, like a dog pricking its ears. I follow her gaze and can see a vague shadow moving slowly towards the house through the morning fog. It is a lone rider.

'Someone is here,' I say. 'One of the messengers, perhaps, or a visitor.' And Maman sends out the steward to greet him. We gather at the window to watch the man dismount, trying to catch a glimpse of his face.

'Hertford,' whispers Katherine, and I see a little glimmer of her old self.

The man is wrapped in a voluminous cape and has his back to us; it is impossible to tell who he is.

'I don't think so, Kitty,' says Juno. 'I would recognize the horse.'

I feel Katherine droop once more, and we watch as the steward greets him, seeing then that it is one of the messengers.

'News,' says Maman as we watch the steward walk slowly back towards the door with a paper in his hands. We sit in silence listening to the bang as the great door shuts and the rasp of the bolt being thrust back into place; the steward's footsteps echo on the stairs as he mounts them, seeming to take an age; the door to the chamber complains with a creak as he enters.

Maman takes the letter from him, inspects the seal, saying, 'The palace,' before turning away from us all as she tears it open, scattering red shards of wax and unfolding the thick parchment, holding it to the light. 'She has named Elizabeth.' She sighs deeply, as if to expel a month's worth of breath. 'Thank God.'

Then with a burst of laughter she tugs her rosary from her girdle so hard she breaks the string, scattering the beads. They sound like heavy rain as they fall on to the floorboards.

'We won't be needing those.' She grabs both Levina's hands and they spin together in a circle; Juno is clapping and laughing too and Kitty's dogs are caught up in it all, scampering about and barking, adding to the din.

I have never met Elizabeth, but she is someone people talk of often, so I am aware of her intelligence, she is well known for it. Though Maman always said Jane was better learned than she, and I hear that she is not a beauty, but is striking in such a way that you think her so: this is what Katherine has said of her, anyway. Peggy has told me snippets in her letters and I remember the comment she made: *a force of nature*. Is that a good thing, I wonder, but judging by Maman's response to the news, it surely is. And Maman knew Elizabeth as a girl, so she should know.

Juno rips off her rosary too now, flinging it towards the skirting, where Stan grabs hold of it, shaking it as if it is a rat he's caught. Am I the only one to notice Katherine slumped in the window seat with her face in her hands? I sit myself next to her.

'*You* didn't want to be named, surely?' I ask.

'Of course not,' she replies, slightly choked, as if she might be holding off tears. 'I should make a useless queen . . . Imagine. They'd have my head off in days.' A tart little laugh escapes with this. And we are both silent for a moment; I am thinking of Jane, of course, and I suppose she must be too.

'So you are safe,' I say after a while, briefly taking her hand in mine. It is cold and feels as fragile as the dead goldfinch one of the cats left in my bedchamber this morning.

'But Elizabeth loathes me. I have managed to make an enemy of her already and I barely know her.'

'Then don't go back to court,' I say.

'Do you not know me at all, Mary? I'd shrivel up and die stuck out in this place.' She sidles from the chamber with a scowl.

Maman hasn't noticed that anything is wrong; she, Levina and Juno have their heads together, planning a feast for this evening.

'Syllabub,' says Levina.

'Oooh yes,' Juno replies. 'And comfits.'

'And marchpane, lots of it,' adds Maman, calling the steward over to fetch the cook. But just then there is a rap at the door and one of the pages enters, standing before us red-faced, looking at his knotted hands. I can hear a peal of church bells and then another further off.

'What is it, Alfred?' Maman asks. 'Have you something to tell us?' More bells add to the sound, closer this time; it must be the church in the village.

'Yes, My Lady.' It seems that he is having trouble getting the words out and we all watch him wring his hands, until eventually he mumbles with a blush, 'Word from London. The Queen is dead, God rest her soul.' Another messenger must have arrived with word, on the tail of the first. Alfred makes the sign of the cross and I wonder momentarily if he is one of the true Catholics, or if he is just so accustomed to the gesture, as we all are now, that it has become second nature.

'*Mon Dieu!*' exclaims Maman. 'So it is over.'

We are all silent. This news has been ten days in the coming.

'Thank the Lord,' murmurs Levina. 'There will be no more burnings.'

'Mary and I were girls together, you know . . .' Maman stops, as if thinking back to the past. 'I feel not a drop of sadness, not after Jane. How power corrupts.' She flops into a chair, resting her chin on her upturned palm. 'And all those souls . . .' She doesn't finish, but each one of us knows she is talking of the burnings.

The page is standing twisting his cap in his hands. 'Oh, Alfred,' says Maman, suddenly remembering he is there. 'You had better get the chaplain to ring the bells.'

'My Lady, there is something else,' he mumbles, looking at his feet.

'Yes?' says Maman.

'Cardinal Pole . . . he is gone too.'

'The Cardinal? On the same day?'

'That is what I have been told to announce, My Lady.'

'How odd,' says Maman, shaking her head. 'I suppose they shall be together, then. Thank you, Alfred; off you go and see that the bells are rung.'

I am wondering where they will be together, the Queen and the Cardinal, if they will be in the burning fires of Hell for rejecting the new faith, or if they will be in purgatory because that is what they believe in. I try to imagine a world where the truth is what you believe in most.

Alfred turns on his heel with a mumbled, 'Yes, My Lady,' glad to get away, I should think.

'Where is Kitty?' bursts out Juno, breaking the silence.

'She was upset. I think you should look for her,' I say.

'Why did you not tell me?' Juno seems genuinely concerned as she scoops up Katherine's favourite dog and leaves the room.

'What will you do, Veena?' Maman is asking. 'Will George and Marcus return now? You *shall* stay in England?'

'England is my home really, Frances,' she replies. 'I am settled here; *and* the court is my living. Elizabeth knows me well enough from the days we were together in Katherine Parr's household.'

'It may well work to your advantage,' says Maman.

'Indeed,' she replies. 'Cecil has already sounded me out to see if I intend to remain at court.'

'I am glad of that,' says Maman. 'I could not bear to lose you, Veena. I suppose Cecil will be her chief advisor.'

'Doubtless,' says Levina.

'He is some kind of cousin of mine. Well, only distantly, by marriage. He used to work for the Seymours, you know.'

'It'll be to their advantage too, then.'

'I'm glad I will not be called on to go to court,' says Maman. 'My days of all that are over, *finis*. I have Stokes now, who has brought me to a better place.' The two women share a smile.

'And Mary.' She looks over to me, meeting my eyes. '*You* would not want to be at court, would you, Mouse?'

'No, Maman,' I reply. I imagine the peaceful life we will lead here at Beaumanor or even at Bradgate. 'Do you think Bradgate will be returned to us, now things are different?'

'It is unlikely.' I can see that it is something Maman doesn't want to talk of. I conjure up Bradgate in my mind, mapping out its corridors, walking through the great rooms. Jane is there, indelibly in my memory, reading at the window seat, strolling in the park, kneeling in the chapel, and I feel the chill of sadness creep beneath my skin.

'What is that look?' asks Maman.

'Nothing,' I say, forcing my smile to return. 'Nothing would please me more than to stay wherever *you* are, Maman. You know I am happiest away from court.'

'We must try and persuade Katherine to remain with us,' she says. 'Though I suppose she will have to sit vigil. She is one of the Queen's women, after all.'

'She will not like that,' says Levina, then adding, 'Are you aware of the Hertford boy?'

'Juno's brother? There is always one boy or another with Katherine.'

'I believe it is quite serious.'

'I suppose if it comes to it,' says Maman thoughtfully, 'he wouldn't make a *bad* match. He has a good enough pedigree. Do you know him, Veena?'

'Seen him about. Very like his sister – you might even think them twins, though I believe they are not.'

'I like *her*. So if he is anything like his sister in temperament, all will be well.'

'He has a reputation for ambition,' Levina adds.

'A dose of ambition is a necessary thing for a boy,' Maman says, 'particularly one such as he, whose family has taken a fall. But it is something to remain aware of nonetheless. After all, Katherine is no common-or-garden girl. I wouldn't want her falling into some kind of marriage trap with a suitor who merely wants to hoist himself up.' Maman seems to be thinking aloud. 'That Tudor blood of ours can be more a curse than a blessing. Though Hertford is high enough up already, has a little royal blood of his own, and I'm sure Elizabeth will grant him back his titles. She always had a soft spot for that family.'

Levina emits a cynical burst of laughter, with Maman joining in, and I sense there is a subtext that I am not party to. '*I* should have to suffer the mother if they married. She is a poisonous creature, completely insupportable – we used to call her Stanhope, which she loathed.'

'I hear she is much mellowed these days,' adds Levina.

'Married her steward, didn't she? That must have brought her down a peg or two.' They both laugh at this. 'Indeed, haven't we all come down in the world? Well, perhaps not you, Veena.'

Watching the two of them gossiping happily, I realize that I have never seen Maman so content. A warm feeling floods through me, for I am part of it.

III
Queen Elizabeth

January 1559
The Tower of London
Katherine

It was bad enough having to spend night after night on my knees in the chapel at St James's, with the Queen's dead body and the smell of the embalmers' unguents making my eyes smart. We were supposed to pray for the Queen's soul, so she will not be long in purgatory – though according to Maman there is no such place, and now the Queen is gone we no longer have to pretend there is. But nonetheless I was there and it was my duty to pray, along with the Queen's other ladies. It put the shivers up me, being at such close proximity to a dead person. I had to concentrate very hard to keep my mind from thinking about what happens when we are gone. Just the thought of it makes me want to shut my eyes, press my fingers into my ears, hum a happy tune and pretend there is no such thing as death.

The chapel was cold as a grave and when we were not praying for the Queen's soul, we had to make-believe that a wooden figurine, all got up in Her Majesty's clothes, was the Queen herself. We had to serve food to it, curtsy to it, dress it, wash it, as if it were really she, and even sing psalms to it. Then there was the Queen's interminable funeral, with the corpse in its box and the doll sitting beside it wearing the crown on its wooden head.

That was bad, but believe it or not, this is worse. I have

been herded with a great crowd of courtiers into the keep at the Tower, to celebrate the new Queen's state entry into London. It is so cold I can no longer feel my feet and flurries of snow are blowing about my cheeks, making them sting. I have on my very best emerald-green gown but no one can see it, for I am wrapped up against the weather and dare not even open my cloak an inch to show my jewelled forepart, for fear of freezing to death.

It would be more bearable if Juno were with me, but she has been called as one of Elizabeth's ladies, so I never see her any more as she is so busy with her duties in the privy chamber, where I am no longer admitted. And when Juno is done with the Queen she cannot stay awake long enough to listen to the events of my day, which are so few and so dull as to hardly merit recounting. She is in the White Tower now, preparing to take her place at the front of the procession; her brother is there too. I have barely seen him either. Even Maman is not here. Surely if *she* were here we would be taking our rightful place as the Queen's closest royal cousins. But Maman is ailing, though I suspect she feigns it so she can stay away, and Mary wasn't even invited. So I stand jostled amongst strangers here in the shadow of the Tower. Thoughts of Father and Jane mill about my head: I wonder if they once trod on the place where I now stand, if it is the spot where Jane lost her life five years past. Which window did Father look out of imagining his escape, and did he think of me when pondering his death?

I push those thoughts away, for I can feel tears nudging at the back of my eyes. The crowd surges and I am drawn back with it, my silk-slippered foot landing in a puddle of icy water. I suppose the Queen has come out and the procession will begin, but I can see nothing of it above the heads. I try and imagine Juno in her new scarlet livery. Who partners her? Does she wish it were me?

'Her hair is like spun copper,' cries someone. They must mean the Queen. It is true, her hair *is* beautiful and I suppose she wears it loose for the best effect. I would, if it were I processing into London to accept the crown. I know what she is wearing, for it was Juno and I who took Mary Tudor's coronation gown off the wooden figurine and delivered it to the seamstress to be altered for her sister.

I can just about see the top of the canopied litter in which she sits. Behind her Robert Dudley, who is my brother-in-law, for what it's worth, swings on to his horse. Once mounted, his chiselled face and curled dark locks are easily visible above the heads. He has a look of triumph about him, an arrogance, as if he is party to something of which no one else is aware, but then all the Dudleys are like that. I remember Guildford the day he married Jane – the day I married Harry Herbert – he had the same expression on his face; that father of theirs wore it then too. They all look as if the world is theirs for the taking. The thought flits through my mind that were I still married to Harry Herbert, I would be up there in the Queen's train. Dudley's horse tosses its head. It is no wonder, given the splendid look of him, that Elizabeth has made Robert Dudley her Master of Horse. They are filled to bursting with ambition, those Dudleys.

I am pushed with the crowd towards the Tower's wall and there find a step from where I find I have a better view; I can see a white palfrey, the Queen's, I suppose. Dudley has it on a halter, its bridle oiled to a sheen, its mane crimped. And I catch a glimpse of Elizabeth herself; she looks at Dudley, her eyes spending longer than they should wandering up and down the length of him – I know that look; it speaks of desire. There is a sea of scarlet – all the pages and grooms who are helping the Queen's ladies on to their horses. Thirty-nine ladies. I know this for everyone has been talking of it; it is a vast number – and *I* am not one of them. I question how it will be arranged with an uneven number, whether there will be a trio or a single at the back. Up they swing on to their red velvet saddles and come into line behind Dudley. I spot Juno and wave but she doesn't see me; I am invisible in the crowds.

Once the riders have set off behind the Queen's litter, the rest of us are herded into a line of chariots. Mine at least is furnished with a cushion, for there are some who must jiggle on the cobbles with nothing to sit on but a plank of wood. It takes an age but we follow on eventually, passing by the whooping crowds, people lining the streets, leaning out of windows, perched atop walls, to catch a glimpse of the new Queen.

'She has picked up a baby and kissed it upon the cheek,' squeals Lady Something-or-other, who is next to me. None of us can see anything at all, not Lady Something-or-other, nor her plump daughter, nor the elderly man opposite, whose beard is so dense his mouth cannot be seen. We are all relying on word being passed back down the train. 'She has shaken the hand of a tailor and accepted a spray of rosemary from a supplicant.' Lady Something-or-other is beside herself.

'Immodestly familiar,' mumbles the bearded man. Perhaps he would like the old Queen back. Judging by the jubilant throng, no one else would. Amongst the crowds and hubbub I have never felt so lonely and I wish Mary were with me, for at least with Mary I feel less sorry for myself.

'To the Lord Mayor, she said that she would gladly spill her own blood for the safety of us all,' someone calls out from in front.

'I never thought to see the day.' It is Lady Something-or-other, who is now dabbing at her eyes with a square of lawn.

Her daughter, who is seated on my other side, looks at her hands or out at the crowds, anywhere but towards her mother.

I am barely aware of it all, for I am trying to see if I can catch sight of Hertford somewhere in the melee. He had found me yesterday, in Juno's chambers, which is where I have been sleeping, for I no longer have my own rooms at court.

'I have been granted back my title,' he announced. 'I am truly Earl of Hertford once more, Kitty.' He was bursting with it and I wanted to be happy, but somehow I felt that his rise was dependent on my fall, and that he would soon tire of me since I had lost my position. What use is even a thousand pints of Tudor blood if you are not admitted further than the public chambers at the palace?

'I am happy for you.' I tried to fix a smile on my face but then he said that 'our *thing*' – yes that is what he called it, not 'our love', not even 'our fondness for each other' but 'our *thing*' – must be kept secret from Elizabeth.

'It was hardly a "*thing*",' I had replied. 'That makes it sound so . . . so much more than it was.' I was using all my strength to feign nonchalance, deliberately using the past tense for something that was so very urgently, burningly, present. I was churning with the fact that since I had become a nobody – just the out-of-favour daughter of an executed traitor – he had lost interest. All he had wanted was to hitch himself to a girl brimming with royal blood and improve his position – but now that girl has lost her lustre.

As we trundle at the back of the snow-blown procession, I allow myself to think of the moments Hertford and I had last summer. We had trysts in the garden pavilion at Hanworth and the orchard at Whitehall or the occasional hour in my rooms at court when the servants were at Mass, when I would lie in his arms and listen to him whisper, 'I know what it is, Kitty, to lose a beloved father so brutally. I understand you more than anyone ever could, for I have lived what you have lived. We are like one person.' And then we would kiss away the pain of it. 'You and I, Kitty, we were meant to be.' Half a year for love to bloom and now it is nothing but a '*thing*', its petals all dropped.

Most likely he knows he can climb the court ladder better without me. Perhaps all those words of his were empty. Perhaps he thought me loose enough to be charmed into giving him a free tumble. I have begun to wonder if Juno has told him of the things she and I have done to each other under the covers at night – no, not Juno, she would never say. But then I think of something I have not considered before, that Juno might be jealous – that what had seemed like a good idea to her in the first place had perhaps turned out a source of regret.

'It was really nothing more than a passing fancy,' I had said, as careless as you like. I thought I saw a little stab of sorrow in his eyes, which had been the intention. But then I couldn't bear it and pressed my lips full to his, slipping my tongue in, pushing and sliding until I felt the belly fizz of desire. But as he responded I shoved him away, saying, 'Harry Herbert sent me a rose. Look, isn't it a beauty. It is silk, of course, for even a magician couldn't get their hands on a real rose in January.'

It is true – Harry Herbert did send me a silk rose. It was in reply to my letter in which I told him that it was impossible for us to be together. He replied with a poem about a thorned rose, enclosing the flower with it. And though I love him not, I have it pinned to my stomacher in the place where I would put a jewel or a silk flower from Hertford, if he had chosen to give me one, which he did not. So it is not a '*thing*' after all – it is a '*nothing*', and I am a '*nobody*'. But still, even brought so low as I am, I cannot bring myself to go to Sheen Priory down the Thames, where Maman and Mary are installed.

One of the horses in the procession up ahead is lame and we are asked to squeeze up to accommodate its rider in our chariot. I am already tightly packed in between Lady Something-or-other and her daughter and have a headache from the constant squeals of pleasure at each and every ribbon that has been hung out, and each and every jongleur that so much as tosses a ball in the air, and my feet are wet and frozen. But to my delight I find Jane Dormer climbing into our conveyance – at last a familiar face. Lady Something-or-other's daughter is shunted to the seat opposite and Jane crams in next to me. The last time I saw Jane was in the abbey at the Queen's funeral Mass; since then she has married Feria.

'Must I call you Countess now?' I ask, teasing her, thankful for a moment's respite from my brooding. 'So, what is he like? What is *it* like?' I am so full of questions for my newly wed friend I can barely contain myself.

Jane blushes, shushing me with an embarrassed smile and saying under her breath, 'He is nice.'

'Nice?' I say, and she nods, but it is clear she will not offer up the secrets of her marriage bed. I think of him, Feria, how safe she must feel in his arms, for he is a proper man, not a pup like Hertford. 'And Durham House?'

'It is a lively place indeed, Kitty. I am glad to be away from the palace now that . . .' She pauses. 'You know.' I suppose she means now that the old Queen is gone, for Jane was like a daughter to her.

'And will you leave for Spain?'

'Not just yet. My husband' – she says the word with a further blush – 'has to continue as envoy here. Though,' she drops her voice, 'he likes not the new one.' By this I suppose she must mean Elizabeth. 'But you, Katherine? Why are you not with everybody?'

'Since you have been under the plummet with your new husband,' I say this in a whisper, so as not to embarrass her further, 'I have found myself demoted to the presence chamber. It would seem that "the new one" likes not me.'

'But that is not possible, you are her highest-ranking cousin.' She stops to watch a pageant as we pass. 'Oh no . . . That is . . .' A sorry-looking boy is sat upon a barren mound with a dead tree at its top, and beside him is a gorgeously dressed fellow in a lush green landscape with a cluster of pretty shepherdesses about him who are reciting something that we cannot hear above the crowd.

'The implication is clear,' she says. I have rarely heard Jane Dormer so angry, but I'm not quite sure what she means. I suppose it is a metaphor for something. 'Pastures green.' She is furious. 'It is not fair to depict the old Queen's reign thus. It lacks respect.'

Now I understand the meaning of the dumb-show, I think there may be some truth in it – these last years have been so full of fear and famine, it is no wonder people are hoping for something better. It is said that Elizabeth intends to not condemn anyone for their faith, and that must surely be a good thing. I don't say what I am thinking, for it would upset Jane, given her closeness to the old Queen. I suppose if you are very fond of someone you may be too close to see their flaws.

'But, Katherine,' Jane continues, when we have passed the Cheapside pageant, 'what will you do? Will you remain at court?'

'I suppose so. Juno Seymour will let me share her lodgings.'

'But . . .' she begins, then stops and we sit in silence, with the roar of the crowd all about us, and Lady Something-or-other still whooping with delight – 'See how the people love our new Queen' – at every turn.

Eventually we arrive at Westminster and are discharged from our chariot into the courtyard to join the crowd. Jane disappears to find her husband and I am unsure where to put myself, so used am I to being told where to be and what to do; I almost miss bossy Mistress Poyntz barking orders at me. I wonder if I have a chance of finding Levina, who would happily take me under her wing, but she has been busy preparing scenes for a masque and must be somewhere overseeing things. The mass of courtiers is now in a dither of excitement, for the great doors have swung open. I am heaved along with the throng that is trying to get a glimpse of the new Queen and her bejewelled entourage. I manage to break away and weave a path towards the western arch, near the stables.

As I enter the gloom of the archway, glad to be alone at last, a hand grabs my wrist. I gasp, my heart pounding like a smith's hammer, imagining myself ravaged by some drunken wastrel that tags along with the court, or worse.

'Kitty,' says a breathy voice, which I can only assume is attached to the hand.

My heart slows; my legs lose their strength. 'Hertford,' I whisper.

His lips are on mine in the dark, he is pressing me up against the wall, holding both my wrists above my head, one leg thrust between mine, pushing at me until I lose all sense of myself. My head is spinning; all I want to do is take him to Juno's rooms and offer up every last iota of myself to him. But then I remember the '*thing*' and I am gripped by the thought that he has come for his free tumble with his loose Kitty.

Twisting my face away from his, I say, 'Off me, Hertford.' His grip loosens and I duck away, out of his hold.

'But Kitty!' He follows me a few paces but I am running away from him in my wet slippers. Pieces of my heart are breaking off and fall in my wake.

'Leave me be,' I call back into the darkness.

'But . . .'

I am out of breath when I get to Juno's chambers and collapse on to the floor beside the fire. Then the tears come and I curse myself for being such a baby, but the truth is I am frightened of the feelings Hertford has aroused in me. I fear I cannot control them, and if I cannot control them then God alone knows to what depths I might be dragged. Then it strikes me that this, this terrible sensation, this feeling of being about to fall, this precipice edge, must be love itself, and that what I felt for Harry Herbert, the pale cousin of it, must have been something else. I would give anything for that warm, safe feeling back, and to not be in the thrall of this other uncontrollable thing.

I stab at the dying fire with the poker and throw on a log, watching the blaze catch, spitting blue from the bark, sending little sparks up the chimney. Only now do I feel my exhaustion and, pulling a cushion off the bed, I let my head sink into it, too tired even to remove my damp cloak. I allow myself to drift off in the warmth but, much as I try to banish them, thoughts of Hertford seep in at the edges of my awareness, disturbing my dreams.

Fingers stroke my cheek; a soft voice whispers, 'Kitty.' I half open my eyes. It is he. I shake myself out of sleep; sit up abruptly to see that it is not Hertford at all but Juno, who is lighting candles in the wall sconces with the long taper, infusing the room with a yellow glow. 'What are you doing sleeping in your cape on the floor?' she is saying.

'I was so tired, Juno, and . . .' I am unsure of how to

explain the confusion of feelings that churns in me.

'Come, let's get you into the bed.' She helps me up and starts to undress me, unlacing my sleeves and my kirtle so I can slide out of them and into a clean shift. She too wriggles out of her over-gown. 'Here, can you unknot this? It is too tightly tied.' She is struggling to reach her own laces. I tease the knot loose with my fingers and she heaves a sigh of relief as I lift the stiff garment away from her. She pulls her hood off her head, wincing as a few hairs catch themselves in one of the jewels. The wires have left marks on her temples. Her beauty surprises me suddenly, as if I am seeing her for the first time.

'Let me do your hair,' I say, starting to unravel her plaits. Then I take up the comb and draw it slowly through her pale tresses, carefully so as not to pull at the knots.

We are silent for some time, but she breaks it saying, 'Kitty, I have missed you.'

I drop my forehead on to her waterfall of hair. 'I too,' I whisper. 'I cannot bear things the way they are. I never see you and then when I do, you are too tired to . . . Are you jealous, Juno? Is that why?'

'Jealous, of what?' Her voice is so gentle, so reassuring, so lacking in guile.

'Of my, my . . .' I don't know what to call it, so I use Hertford's cursed word. 'My *thing* with your brother.'

'Oh, Kitty, that.' She turns round to face me and seems on the brink of laughter. 'How could I be jealous of *that*? I never imagined I could keep you for myself and my brother is the next best thing.' How I envy Juno her clarity, the way she makes sense of the world. We may be alike on the outside but beneath the skin we are fish and fowl, Juno and I. 'Anyway, you appear to have lost interest in him.'

'Mmmm,' I murmur, unable to express my turmoil, for if

I put it into words I fear it will have an even greater power over me.

'Did you see her today?'

'The Queen? Barely more than a glimpse. I was too far back.'

'Poor Kitty,' she strokes my cheek. 'She will come round, I'm sure. I can tell you this, I have never seen such a dress.' She makes shapes in the air with her hands in an attempt to describe it. 'More than twenty yards of gold and silver cloth, overlaid with gilded lace and trimmed with ermine.'

'Not the old Queen's robe?'

'No, that is for tomorrow – the coronation.'

'The coronation,' I echo, feeling that my humiliation will be endless, that I will be stuck in some far corner of the abbey, out of sight, and I cannot bear it – the idea of being so invisible – just want to forget it all.

'I don't think I could stand it here, Juno, if it weren't for you, and . . .' I pause as the truth of my feelings strikes me. 'I am afraid, Juno. What if she finds some reason to clap me in the Tower like . . . Like my sister?'

'No!' says Juno, but we both know that anyone as close to the throne as I, who find themselves out of favour, can just as easily then find themselves going downriver accompanied by an armed guard. 'You could go, after the festivities. Join your mother and sister. They are at Sheen Priory now, are they not?'

'They are. Elizabeth shoved out the prior and gave it to Maman. Seems she will do anything for Maman, save reinstate me. I think Maman wanted to be closer to me. Beaumanor is so far.'

'Sheen is just a short way upriver.'

'Even so.' How can I go there and leave Hertford here? My heart would break. 'I did see *him* though. Dudley,' I say to change the subject.

'How could you not, he is larger than life,' giggles Juno. She brings her face close to mine. 'Do you think they are doing it?'

'Have you heard such a thing?' The air is suddenly thick with gossip.

'No,' she says. 'But when you see them together it seems inevitable.'

'Maybe they are,' I say. 'Maybe they sneak off out riding and . . .'

'Perhaps they use her nether place, that she may remain a virgin.'

'Juno! Such filth, out of so pretty a mouth.' But when I look at her mouth I see Hertford's. 'Here,' I say, pulling her down on to the bed. Her hair falls across my face; it smells of rose water. I take a strand of it, hold it next to mine and cannot tell them apart. I nuzzle into her neck, breathing her in, then I face her and bring my eye to hers and we allow our butterfly lashes to touch and flutter together.

March 1559
Whitehall
Levina

Levina stands in a window alcove scrutinizing the planes of the Queen's face. The Queen is seated in the best of the light, leafing through a sheaf of papers. They are from Foxe in Geneva, printed copies of Levina's drawings – images of the burnings. How things have changed. But then, everything is different, Bonner and Byrne have melted away and the palace is transformed. Gone are the solemn silent chambers; now the place echoes with music and mirth, as all the new favourites dance about the young Queen. And the fear – well, that is always lurking somewhere at court, but for the time being no one is sure what exactly to be afraid of.

The place is full of new faces: Elizabeth's old companion Kat Astley, whom they say is like a mother to her, is by the hearth. Beside her are Lady Knollys, Dorothy Stafford and Blanche Parry, sewing and talking quietly amongst themselves. At the far end of the room, lined up before the new Italian dance master, are the maids of the chamber. Little hair-lipped Peggy Willoughby and plain Frances Meautas are like two daisies amongst a display of lilies. Juno stands beside Lettice Knollys, a brace of beauties, and next to them a pair of pretty Howard girls. The new Queen has surrounded herself with old friends and cousins – the Howards and the Knollys are cousins on her mother's side.

They watch the dance master demonstrate the steps to the accompaniment of a fey boy, with long hair and cow-eyes, on the lute. Katherine should be in that line-up – of course she should be, by rights she is Elizabeth's heir. But Elizabeth, it would seem, has held on to the vindictiveness she had as a girl, for poor Katherine has no longer the right to go beyond the presence chamber. Clearly the Queen doesn't want competition from a girl who exceeds her in beauty and, according to some, has an equal claim to the throne.

Levina fears for Katherine. The girl has a hollow look about her and seems on the brink of decline. She refuses to go and join her mother and sister at Sheen, despite its proximity. Levina has started a painting of her, as a reason to keep her close. But much of her time is taken up with crafting miniatures for Elizabeth's favourites, who all want little likenesses of themselves to give to each other and hang from their girdles, or slip beneath their pillows. There is a great fashion for such things these days and more's the better for

Levina, for it is her living, and today she is painting the Queen herself.

Her brush is poised but she has not yet made a mark on the card. It is the ace of hearts. Elizabeth had asked for that one in particular and Levina wondered, as she carefully adhered the thin skin of vellum to the reverse, whose pillow it would end up under – very likely Dudley's. She had primed it with a dun pink, very pale, and she has chosen well, for the Queen's skin seems, in this light at least, to match it. She has a high, slightly feverish, rosy flush to her cheeks, which Levina suspects may not be naturally hers.

Levina wants to convey that look Elizabeth has, as if she has seen everything and become immune. She wants, too, to show that her turbulent history has not etched itself on the smooth lines of her face – but it is there in the wide-set eyes, which, if you look hard enough, reveal a profound sadness beneath their surface.

The Queen calls over a cup-bearer with an almost imperceptible twitch of her hand.

'We are thirsty,' she says to the boy, who has a hot blush rising up his neck and on to his face. 'Mistress Teerlinc, will you drink with us? Bring us something cool. Anything will suffice, as long as it is cool.'

Levina finds herself now looking at the Queen's hands. They are fine and long-fingered – musician's hands. A memory pops into her head of Elizabeth playing the virginals as a girl, full of zest, wanting to be better than everyone else. She always was. Hero stretches at Levina's feet, yawning and turning in a circle before resettling in a puddle of sun.

'I remember your dog. He was a puppy when you painted me last. He took a disliking to me.' Elizabeth leans down to him, her hand outstretched. He emits a low grumble and swivels his eyes to watch her. She laughs. 'You never did like me, did you, boy?' Ignoring his bared fangs she begins to ruffle his ears as if he is an amenable little spaniel. Hero, entirely seduced, gazes at her like a lovesick youth. 'Do you remember how he used to growl at me?'

'Indeed I do, madam,' Levina replies, remarking how she slips easily between the singular and plural of the personal pronoun. Not like her sister, who insisted on the plural even amongst her closest ladies, as if clinging on to her status for dear God. 'It is many years since I painted Your Majesty. Much has happened since.'

'Mmmm,' says the Queen, with pursed lips that hint of disapproval, or perhaps suggest they have stumbled into conversational territory that is off limits. Levina wonders if she too is remembering the affair with Thomas Seymour, a decade ago, that nearly brought her down. Most women wouldn't have survived the scandal – he was Katherine Parr's husband, her own stepfather, or as good as. But Elizabeth manages to shake off infamy as water runs off grease. Seymour lost his head and took the secret of it to his grave. Perhaps it is best Elizabeth doesn't remember that Levina was there at the time.

Elizabeth holds out her palm for Hero to lick the salt taste from it, saying, 'All the ones who seem the most fierce are soft as you like underneath. It's the others one must beware of.'

Levina asks herself if she means anything by it.

'They all want me wed,' she says out of the blue. 'Look at Cecil.' She rhymes Cecil with thistle. 'He is desperate to come and display his stack of little portraits to me. All my suitors . . .' She nudges her head towards Cecil, who, it is true, is hovering, itching to approach. But the Queen doesn't meet his eye and whispers, with a little smirk, 'I shall pretend I have not noticed he waits.'

‘I imagine it is hard, with so many suitors,’ says Levina.

‘Wed one, and upset another. Look how my sister fared with her marriage. She lost the love of her people. And she lost Calais fighting her husband’s war; that was the worst of it. Us women . . . ,’ she begins, pausing to look about her. ‘You are wed, Mistress Teerlinc, and you are a woman of the world – a woman with her own life. How does the institution suit you?’

Levina is thinking of George. He has been so distant since his return and his resentment of her work continues to bubble beneath the surface of him. ‘It has its complications.’

‘Yes. But then to not feel what it is to birth a child.’ She seems to drift off, the sadness in her eyes intensifying. Levina begins to paint, now seeing the image form as if it is not the product of her own hand, but guided by some other invisible ministration over which she has no control.

‘It is a powerful lure, a share in the throne of England.’

‘Indeed, madam.’

Elizabeth drops her eyes back to the drawings in her lap and after some time says, ‘This one, it is Jane Grey, is it not?’

Levina glances over, assaulted suddenly with the image of the girl blindly seeking the block, the crimson spurt of blood. It is so vivid it makes her flinch. ‘It is, yes,’ she replies, careful to keep her tone neutral. It wouldn’t do to make a display of her affiliations.

‘Awful business. I knew her quite well. Pious girl.’ Levina is trying to see from her expression what she means by this, but she is opaque. ‘You are close to her mother, I believe.’

‘I am. We are old friends.’ Levina wonders where this is going.

‘I am fond of Frances, too. She is my cousin. But that daughter, Katherine.’ Her mouth turns down momentarily in distaste. ‘So like her father. He was the real traitor in that family. They were all coloured by him. A weak man, Henry

Grey.' She involuntarily places a hand on her neck. 'And the other sister, the crookback, what is she like?'

'Mary, she is uncommonly clever, madam, and quiet – quite biddable.'

'Biddable, well she would have to be, I suppose. If she is as deformed as they say, then she will have to work all the more hard to be good, if only to convince everyone she is not the Devil's work.' She lets out a little huff of laughter that Levina interprets as ironic. 'But if she is clever, then she will know that, won't she?'

'Lady Katherine is biddable too, in her own way.' Levina thinks it worth at least an attempt to change the Queen's opinion of Katherine.

'I'd not call her that; she is nothing but trouble – trouble of the worst kind.' She waves for Cecil to approach now. 'I'm afraid I must deal with this, Mistress Teerlinc.'

Levina begins to clear her things, asking herself what Elizabeth meant by 'the worst kind' and watching as Cecil begins to produce miniatures that are cached about his person, like a conjurer. 'This,' he is saying, waving one under Elizabeth's nose, 'is the Archduke Karl.'

'The Habsburg, Cecil?' she scowls. 'You think to counter that Scottish cousin of ours, who seeks to claim *our* throne for the French, by matching us with a Habsburg?'

'She means the Scottish Queen Mary who is wed to the French Dauphin,' whispers Mistress St Low, who has seated herself beside Levina.

'It is true, France would fight to put that Scottish girl on the English throne,' Levina replies. She imagines Europe as a great game of chess with two queens still in play.

'Erik of Sweden.' Cecil is proffering another portrait.

Elizabeth snatches it and seems on the brink of laughter. 'He is a little more comely, this one.'

'I think, Your Highness, with all respect . . .' Cecil begins.

But Elizabeth interrupts. 'We are jesting, Cecil, jesting.'

Cecil can barely conceal his impatience. 'Saxony and Holstein both have made suits,' he says.

'Show me,' she demands, holding out a hand.

'There are no portraits as yet.' Cecil is clearly at the edge of exasperation.

'You cannot expect us to make a match without so much as a likeness. Perhaps we shall have none of them.'

Cecil titters politely as if she has made a joke. Levina thinks it is less of a joke than it appears, though it *is* unthinkable that a queen would rule without a king. Though less unthinkable perhaps with this particular queen, muses Levina – unprecedented certainly.

There is a commotion at the far end of the chamber, the doors are flung open and an usher steps forward with a bow. 'Lord Robert Dudley,' he announces. The Queen lights up like a firework and Levina notices Cecil's lips purse in disapproval. How she would like to paint *this* scene – two men on the rise, pulling themselves up on the skirts of their Queen. Cecil circles his eyes, like a frog watching a fly. His domed forehead gives him the look of a scholar and the russet beard falls to two points – a look that was fashionable a few years ago. Levina wonders if it is deliberately done in order to make him seem as if he cares not for shallow things like fashion. But who couldn't notice the fine fabric of his gown, expensively black, so black it swallows the light, and the gilded aiglets that sprout from the seams, or the crisp white furls of linen at his throat, or the delicate tooling on his shoes – all so very discreet.

But the whole room watches the other man.

Mistress St Low leans in to murmur, 'This is the one she *wants* to wed.'

'He is wed already,' Levina replies.

Dudley, in contrast to Cecil, bathes in conspicuous splendour; there is nothing discreet about *him*. His doublet is fashioned from cloth-of-silver, slashed and notched and jewelled and laid over white satin, with a high collar in the Spanish style. His cape, which is scarlet and short, and edged with gold braiding, swings from one shoulder as he swaggers across the chamber on long legs clad in inky stockings. He wears a slight smirk on his handsome face. Levina remembers him not so long ago in a doublet that once belonged to his father, restyled – it was full of mended rents – and hose worn so thin at the heels his skin was visible in places. Robert Dudley has been spending his new salary as Master of Horse, a thousand marks, it is said, and that is before the perquisites.

He has asked that Levina paint him, but she has heard rumours that, despite the thousand marks, he is one of those who pays his dues only when absolutely necessary, and suspects that he will make some excuse: it pleases him not; the likeness is not good; the colours are wrong. So she has bought some time by saying she must first paint the Queen.

He bows before Elizabeth, removing his cap, allowing his curls to swing forward, then flicking them back to expose his eyes – an affectation, surely, for his hair is quite magnificent, dark with highlights of red ochre, falling in ripples. His eyes are an unusual shade of indigo, not unlike that which Holbein favoured as a background for some of his portraits. This is a man who is clearly aware of his best features.

'Your Majesty,' he says, raising his eyebrows, as if she is a servant maid he has been bedding.

The Queen looks down her long nose at him silently, in an attempt at imperiousness, but the little upturn at her mouth's corners gives her away.

'I just passed Katherine Grey in the presence chamber,' he says. 'I don't know why you keep her hidden away out there. She is a little jewel. Surely the Queen must have all the finest jewels in her crown.'

Levina keeps her eyes down but her ears are pricked.

'Her,' says Elizabeth. 'We do not find her . . .' She pauses. 'Personable.'

'I am surprised,' says Dudley. 'She seems friendly enough to me.'

'To you? Well, she would be. Why is it everyone seems to want us to favour that doxy?' Elizabeth's mouth is set in a sneer, which makes her, for a brief moment, quite ugly.

He looks at her and, pointing an index finger at the roof, as Christ points to Heaven in so many Italian paintings, mouths the word '*Jealous*'.

And then she leans in, cupping a hand to Dudley's ear, a gesture that seems somehow more intimate even than a kiss, and whispers something. Cecil looks as if he's been sucking on a lemon as he shifts uncomfortably from one foot to the other.

Dudley pulls back with a conspiratorial smile. 'No!'

Elizabeth nods, clearly satisfied with his response, then turns to Cecil, saying, 'Anything else?'

'I think not, madam,' he replies with an obsequious crouch, before turning to leave.

'There is something,' she says, as if she has lost her thread flirting with Dudley and is just remembering her responsibilities. 'You have not shown us all the correspondence. Things are passing through without our eye.'

'Madam, just inconsequential affairs. Things Your Majesty need not trouble yourself with. Petty suits and suchlike.'

'Cecil.' She places a hand firmly on his black sleeve and lowers her voice. 'Let us make ourselves plain. *All* correspondence is to be authorized by us.' He shuffles his hands as if about to deal a deck of cards but says nothing, though it is clear he would like to speak. Levina watches him. He knows Elizabeth well enough. She always had a formidable authority; even as a ten-year-old you wouldn't have wanted to contradict her unless you were absolutely sure of yourself.

'Clear?' she says with a granite smile.

He nods and walks slowly away from her backwards, head bent like a monk at prayer. Dudley watches him, his mouth downturned.

'Shall we dance?' says Elizabeth, transformed in an instant, back to the coquette. She glides over the room as if on wheels, stopping to look at Levina's likeness, discussing with her some little details she would like and fussing over Hero once more.

Dudley hovers, watching her like a bird of prey. The dance master stands to the side awaiting instructions, his lutenist perched on his stool, and the entire room watches the Queen as she pets the dog and converses with the humble artist, casually, as if she is a nobody passing the time of day with some family member or other.

Then she turns, saying, 'What are you all waiting for? Into the presence chamber.'

Her ladies start to scurry, gathering up their bits and pieces, waiting then for Elizabeth to make the first move, that they may follow her through the door. Levina tucks her papers away, wishing she could slide off discreetly but her time is not her own these days. She can feel Hero's wet nose against the back of her hand as she stands waiting to slip into the Queen's wake with the others.

The doors open, exposing a hubbub of activity in the outer room, and as the Queen walks in everyone drops to their knees. Levina spots Katherine in the far corner, crouched down like the others, but not in respect of the Queen; she is tying a blue ribbon about the neck of her spaniel, Stan. Once Elizabeth has circled a little and established her territory, Levina sidles over to the girl. The two dogs sniff out a greeting, Stan rolling on to his back, baring a pink belly, allowing the bigger hound to sniff him thoroughly. More musicians have gathered and they begin to play a gavotte.

'I cannot stand it,' hisses Katherine.

'Why don't you join the dancers? You dance so beautifully. Perhaps then she will change her mind.'

'Or the opposite. If I had a crookback like Mary or a club foot, she might be more inclined.'

Levina ignores the bitter comment. 'You could write to her, a heartfelt letter, and send a gift.'

'I think not. Maman keeps suggesting that but . . .'

'But what?'

'I will not grovel, Veena. I may be afraid, afraid of what she might do to me, and I am aware that my reason seems petty, but I am her cousin and she should treat me as such, without me eating the floor strewings in order that she do so. Look how Lady Knollys is in the fold, and I am at least as close a cousin as she, though far *better* bred. Perhaps I am proud, but this whole place is constructed on pride, is it not – pride, and things being in the right order. I was not raised to fold at the first sign of trouble.'

She is right, thinks Levina. 'But things can't remain the way they are with you twiddling your thumbs in the wilderness waiting for her to capitulate.' She sees for the first time the resilience in this girl and that, for all her silliness and shallowness, she is as much a Grey as the others.

'Well, she won't change her mind, I suppose, will she?'

The dance master is singing out instructions in heavily accented French: *Doublez à droite*; *pieds joints*; *petit saut*, he claps out the time. There is a thud as the dancers all jump and land together. Elizabeth laughs. Dudley's eyes follow her.

Marquez pied gauche croisé; *marquez pied droit croisé*; *à grève droite croisée et petit saut*; the feet thud to the floor once more. The ladies' dresses move like ringing bells. Katherine watches Juno and twists her gloves in her hands. *Pieds joints*; *capriole*; they all fling themselves into the air and try to cross their feet, once forward and once back, before landing. Only Elizabeth can do it; the others stumble and giggle as they meet the floor awkwardly.

'Jane Dormer has invited me to stay at Durham House. I think I shall go. At least I will be away from here without being stuck out at Sheen,' says Katherine, still watching Juno, who is red-cheeked from effort.

'I think it a good idea,' says Levina. 'You will at least be safe there. Though the Queen will not like it.'

'That may be so,' she replies with a little smirk, then Levina notices her eyes catch something across the room. Hertford has arrived, with a group of young men, and the Queen is making a great fuss of him, laughing loudly at something he says, while Dudley looks on unsmiling. Katherine turns away, gazing out of the window.

'*Et puis la volte*,' calls the dance master. Upon which Dudley takes his opportunity to pull the Queen to the centre of the room, taking both her hands and forcing her attention back on to him.

'We are quite tired out,' she says. 'We have had enough dancing for today.' She moves to the door, with the room on its knees once more, save for Mary Sidney, Kat Astley and Lady Knollys, who follow her out. Levina is struck once more at the difference in these bright-clad ladies and the old Queen's dismal companions. Then Elizabeth turns briefly.

'Dudley, come.' She beckons him like a dog, and he too falls into step behind the women.

Juno peels herself away from the dancers, who are circling, now partnered by Hertford and his friends. She approaches, grabbing Katherine's hand and tugging her into the centre of the chamber, ignoring her pleas to be left alone, delivering her to Hertford, who is wearing a smile like the cat who got the skin of the fish. Katherine looks coldly beyond his shoulder, holding up her hand to his. They begin to move through the steps of the dance, she still refusing to meet his eye as he grasps the base of her stomacher to lift her.

As they circle the other way Levina notices that they have struck up a conversation, but then the partners are swapped and Hertford is dancing with his sister. Katherine is being twirled and lifted by another lad, all smiles now. Levina is struck then by the similarity of the three of them, Katherine, Hertford and Juno, that they could all be siblings, wondering why she has never noticed it before.

'They make a fine picture, do they not?' It is Mistress St Low. 'My girls, dancing with such gallants. I imagine you are itching to get your paints out.'

'A fine picture indeed,' replies Levina, thinking how unlike her predecessor she is. Mistress Poyntz would have been fussing around, eagle-eyed, watching that the boys were not letting their hands wander. Mistress St Low is talking on about the recent festivities, complimenting Levina on the scenery she designed for the masque on the eve of the coronation, dissecting the parts each of her girls played, how they carried themselves. What a shame it is, thinks Levina, that Katherine is not in this woman's care, for she would surely thrive.

Katherine is dancing once more with Hertford; his face looks thundery and he is shaking his head as she says something. Then he breaks out of the circle and storms away with his sister in pursuit. Katherine pretends nothing has happened and takes up Juno's abandoned partner with a skip. She finishes the dance before dipping in a little curtsy to the boy, who has clearly, judging by the besotted look on his face, fallen under her spell.

'I must say, Lady Katherine, you are a wonderfully graceful dancer. My girls could all learn a trick or two from you,' says Mistress St Low as Katherine joins them.

She smiles, saying, 'I thank you kindly.'

'It is a shame you don't get much opportunity.'

'Yes,' she replies with her sweetest smile. The woman, like the boy on the dance floor, is clearly in her thrall.

'What was that about, with Hertford?' asks Levina in a low voice, when Mistress St Low has moved away.

'He is angry that I'm going to Durham House. Thinks I will be matched with a Spaniard before the week is out.'

April 1559
Durham House
Katherine

'I was married in this spot exactly,' I say to Jane Dormer.

From the instant I walked into Durham House on the Strand, my mind was flooded with memories of the day, six years ago, that I was wed alongside my sister Jane, and Katherine Dudley too, all of us in borrowed dresses, so hastily had it been organized. It was all part of Northumberland's plan; I suppose he wanted to attach his family firmly to ours before the King died. If *I* was upset that day, my nurse was more so.

'Twelve is too young, even for a noble girl,' she said, and argued with Maman over the fact that I was to go without her to live under the Herberts' roof at Baynard's Castle. Maman said it was for the best, but I found her weeping in her bedchamber the night before, though she tried to disguise it by insisting they were tears of joy.

'You mean wed to Harry Herbert?' asks Jane Dormer, though she knows as well as I that I have only had one wedding.

I nod. 'I thought myself truly in love with Harry Herbert.'

The chapel smells sweet, the incense seems to have got into the very stones, and I have a vision of my sister murmuring out her vows in a cloud of perfumed smoke, Guildford Dudley taking her right hand and she snatching it back, pressing it up against her left in prayer, eyes firmly shut. *I* could not pull my gaze away from Harry Herbert, who even though he had been dragged from his sick bed to be married to me seemed, with his jade eyes and dark hair, the most beautiful boy I had ever seen.

'But you have forgotten him now?' Jane Dormer says this with a curiosity in her voice that she can't conceal, and I ask myself what it is she is trying to tease out of me.

'Completely,' I say.

'And what of Hertford – didn't he ask permission to court you once?'

'That was a while ago before . . .' I mean to say, 'before the old Queen's death', but stop myself for the sake of her feelings. 'He is forgotten too.'

I wonder if there is an inkling on my surface, of the devastation inside me that Hertford has caused – it is like a battlefield in there. I suppose not, for she says, 'That is good.'

I want to ask her what she means by that; this is not the kind of intimate conversation I am used to having when girls talk of love. Perhaps Jane Dormer is unaccustomed to such banter. Her mind seems to have drifted though, and she is gazing at an image of the Virgin in the window. The sun casts a blue glow through the stained glass over her pale skin. She genuflects and kneels at the prayer stand, closing her eyes, thumbing through her rosary. I follow her lead, out of politeness more than anything, and expect she is praying for *my* sorry soul. I am glad I thought to wear my rosary out of courtesy for my Catholic hosts. It feels unfamiliar under my fingers; I have lost the habit these last few months. My eyes wander; there is a haunting image, set near the Virgin, of a woman in nun's garb, a saint I suppose; her cheeks are hollow, her wrists thin as twigs, but she has the enraptured look of a maiden in love.

Jane opens her eyes and starts to rise with some difficulty, leaning hard on the lip of the stand, as she is great with child. I take her elbow, helping her to her feet.

'My baby moved as I was praying,' she whispers with a beatific look. 'God has this infant in His sights.' Then she grabs my hand, slipping it beneath her over-gown, to the round drum of her belly. 'It moves again.'

I feel a ripple beneath my fingers. 'Oh!' I say, only then fully understanding it as an actual living creature in there, then thinking that it must come out too. 'Are you afraid?'

'Not one bit,' she smiles. 'She is watching.' She raises her eyes to the stained-glass Virgin. 'And if God chooses to take one of us, or both,' she genuflects once more, 'well, that is His will.'

I nod, wondering how one gets to believe with such conviction, and am reminded again of my dead sister whose beliefs, though quite different from Jane Dormer's, were equally strong. And a silly thought strikes me, that perhaps the name Jane itself carries with it a conviction, an ability to believe. But then I remember Juno, who is more like me and believes in what she sees about her, in the things she can feel beneath her fingers. It is not that I don't ever think of God, it is just that thinking of God leads to thoughts of death and I can't hold on to the idea of not being here in this body of mine, without turning sick with fear.

'I am glad to see that you have not abandoned the true faith,' she says, touching her index finger to my rosary, 'as so many others have.'

I smile, glad she can't tell that I only wear it out of politeness.

'It is an exodus,' she adds with a sigh.

'Who is that?' I ask, pointing to the image of the enraptured nun, thinking it best to talk of something else.

'It is Katherine of Siena. You must know her. God rendered her unable to eat anything but the sacrament, so she was purified entirely by the time she came to His side.'

'Oh yes,' I reply, as if I am remembering Katherine of Siena, when I have never heard of this woman who starved herself in the name of Christ. We did not learn of the saints in our household. 'Katherine of Siena.'

'Perhaps she watches over you – you have her name, after all.'

'I think she must,' I say, although I know I am not named after this starved nun, but after Katherine Howard, who was Queen when I was born and lost her head soon after, for taking a lover. They say she haunts the long corridor at Hampton Court. I wonder which Katherine is watching me.

As we leave the chapel we find Feria in the hall, just back from court. He is pacing up and down with an angry furrow running between his brows. A page scurries behind him with a stack of papers.

'*Esta mujer*,' he is saying, '*será mi muerto*.'

'*Mi estimable esposo*,' says Jane, and just as I am asking myself how I shall manage in this house without a word of Spanish, she adds, 'In my tongue, please, My Lord.'

'Excuse me,' he says in thickly accented English and appearing surprised, as if he has only just noticed my presence. 'I am forgetting myself. Lady Katherine, you are the most welcome.' He takes my hand and squeezes it, bringing it to his lips. 'Most welcome. I apologize for – what in English, Jane, *genio*?'

'Your temper, My Lord.'

'Yes, yes, my temper. I have been with the Queen.' He says 'the Queen' as if it is some kind of jest, only one that is not supposed to be funny. 'She refuse to consider the Archduke without to see him in the –' He seeks the word.

'The flesh?' says Jane.

'The flesh,' he repeats. 'It is no possible that the Archduke display himself like, like horse at auction. It is not dignity.' Feria's hands are both fisted and his eyes are angry. 'He is the son of the Emperor and she, she is . . . *Nada más de una bastarda.*' He starts to pace again. 'And this Dudley. All say she wish to marry him when he is wed already, with wife no one has seen, who is sick, they say. Sick or, or . . . *Envenenado.*'

'*Querido*,' whispers Jane softly, taking one of his clenched hands and unfurling the fingers one by one. It strikes me that they look more like father and daughter than husband and wife. 'You must not say such things. Dudley may be' – she searches for the right word – 'he may not be ideal. But he wouldn't poison his wife with all of the court watching him.' She threads her fingers through his. 'Gómez, *querido*, our baby was moving again today.'

It is as if he melts. '*Mi ángel.*' He places his hand on her belly, a smile breaking over him, Elizabeth forgotten entirely, me forgotten too; they are in their own private world.

I look on, imagining someone speaking to me with such tenderness, remembering the occasions when Hertford and I weren't urgently tugging at each other's clothes. Those moments when I rested my head in the crook of his arm and he whispered things like, 'My own sweet darling, my precious jewel, there is nothing, no one, more dear to me than you, my love.' The feeling seeps through my body as if I am dipped in warm water, and with it a longing is dragged up from the root of me. But then I remember the '*thing*' and draw in a sharp cold breath to dispel those thoughts.

'We shall make splendid match for you, My Lady.' I am jogged back to the present, realizing that it is me whom Feria addresses. 'Spanish royalty, we have some fine young men, full of good blood, Habsburg blood.'

'I am in your hands, My Lord,' I paint on a smile and imagine for an instant a pair of Spanish hands about my person. His smell would be different, like the spices that are delivered in earthenware jars to the kitchens, and he will be a man like Feria, not a boy. His hair will be dark and his skin swarthy, his chin rough. But Hertford's flaxen hair substitutes itself in my mind, his pale gold skin, his smooth hands, greedy for me. I hear his voice: *My own sweet darling, my precious jewel.*

'Promise it, My Lady, you will consider no proposals of marriage without first to me consulting.' Feria's face is hard to read but it is clear he means this, and I wonder for a moment why he should care so much whom I marry. But of course I am full of Tudor blood and he is the Emperor's envoy, the confidant of Felipe of Spain. That is the reason – I may not be clever like my sisters, but I know my own worth in the marriage market. And why not marry Spanish royalty? I would have the protection of the greatest family in Europe, and I am not wanted here, not by Elizabeth and not by Hertford. I am glad now of my polite pretence at Catholicism, for it means these people will take me under their wing. The thought reassures me, makes me feel safe.

'Yes,' adds Jane as if reading my mind. 'We will take care

of you now. You are in good hands, Katherine. We will see that you make an illustrious match.'

A memory flits through me of Father saying the very same thing, 'I will find you an illustrious match, my pretty little Kitty; just you wait and see what fine specimens I shall line up for you to choose from.'

But when it came to it, there was no choice – not for me, nor Jane. I crush the thought of my sister and offer Feria a smile. 'That would please me greatly, My Lord.'

May 1559
Ludgate
Levina

'How many queens have you painted, Veena?' In one hand George holds an unfinished limning of Elizabeth and on his other he counts with his fingers. 'Katherine Parr, Queen Mary, Queen Elizabeth, did you paint Katherine Howard too? Let's not forget the kings, King Edward, you did paint a likeness of him, did you not? And how many duchesses?'

Levina cannot tell if he is praising her or criticizing her. 'Enough,' she says. 'We would not have so many fine things about us, no glass in the windows, were it not for –'

'I am proud of you, Veena, couldn't be more proud.' But she can sense something in him. Since he returned from Bruges he has been different, more distant, distracted, as if he is just playing lip service to their marriage. He is holding up a sketch of Katherine Grey now. 'This one is a vision.' He seems quite mesmerized by what is nothing more than a quick line drawing. Levina thinks it is probably Katherine's beauty rather than her own talent as an artist that he is drawn to.

'You know who that is?'

It is airless in the room so she opens the window, allowing the hubbub of the street in: a slop bucket is emptied with a warning cry, then a splash; a dog barks; someone whistles a tune; snippets of conversation, all drift in with the breeze. She notices a cart off-loading trunks at the Carruths' house. The shutters have been opened. They must have returned from abroad. Hero swings his slender forepaws up on to the sill to look out, barking back at the dog. 'Shhh, boy,' she says, rubbing his cheek, noticing how his muzzle has become white with age and experiencing a brief moment of sadness at the thought that he won't be with her always. 'Down from there.' He obeys her and trots over to his bed, his claws clicking on the flagstones.

'Of course I know who she is. You have been drawing those Grey girls since they were children,' George says. 'I know all about Lady Katherine Grey and her demotion.' He sounds prickly and Levina can't understand why he is talking about this. 'You think we know nothing in the guards' quarters, Veena?'

'But I didn't say that. I don't think you know nothing . . .'

He doesn't let her finish. 'The gossip reaches there too and besides, standing silently at the door with a halberd we often hear more than we should.'

She forgets that he is at court almost as much as she, his presence, in his guard's uniform, is so discreet. She always likes to think that he is not infected, as she is, by the poisonous goings-on there, that he doesn't know or care who anyone is.

Pulling off her coif and beginning to untie a plait that is pulled too tight, she starts to speak. 'There is something . . .' she begins, but changes her mind, stopping. There *is* something, a piece of information, she is party to, that she doesn't know what to do with; but George is annoyed with her, annoyed for being reminded of her link to the Greys – 'the bane of his life', or so he likes to call it. 'Tell me what Marcus recounts in his letter,' she says to change the subject. Her son's letter must have arrived while she was out at Durham House, for it lies on the table, the seal broken.

George picks it up, unfolding it. 'He has been in Florence and was much impressed with the statue of David. You know the artist, Marcus doesn't say. I forget his name.'

'Michelangelo, you mean.'

'Yes, him. And he has been studying with a man called Vasari, who has taken him on in his studio.'

'But that is wonderful news, George. Vasari. To think of it, our son studying with a great artist. Why didn't you tell me?'

'I *am* telling you.'

'You are,' she laughs.

'And more lately he was in Rome; he says the Colosseum is like nothing he has seen before.'

'Let me look.' She snatches the letter, scanning down the page. The sight of her son's hand makes her feel tender. 'He says the food is so good he's growing fat, and has had to have a tailor let out his doublets. He could do with a bit more meat on him.' When she thinks of her son, her boy, seeing the world, becoming a man, she feels she might burst with pride, but the piece of information she holds still prods at her. 'We should think of a match for him, George.'

'I suppose we should. But let him live a little first.' He shuts the window. 'It is not so warm, Veena.'

She realizes, with a shiver, he is right and pulls her shawl over her shoulders. He straightens it for her and kisses her on the top of her head, as if he is her father, saying, 'What about a game of chess before we retire? It's a long time since we played.'

Levina takes the board down from the shelf, blowing a layer of dust from its surface and tipping the pieces out from the cloth bag. She then begins to arrange them on the small table by the window to make the most of the evening light, while George fetches two chairs. She calls the servant girl to bring them some ale and a plate of sweetmeats and they settle into their game in silence.

It is a familiar ritual and each has an idea of what the other's next move will be. Levina's worry keeps on prodding at her, like a dog that wants something, but she is unsure whether she can discuss it with her husband. She trusts him, but isn't sure whether he would understand. They play on, barely aware of the fading light, quietly shifting the wooden pieces about the board, but she is distracted and George is winning.

'I am concerned, George,' she says, finally feeling she must unburden herself whether he understands or not. But the maid comes in to light the candles just at that moment. She says nothing, watching the girl move slowly about the room with her taper. When she is done she asks if she should light the fire.

'Yes,' says George.

'No,' says Levina simultaneously. Her worry is pressing up to her and she can't speak while the girl is here. 'I shall see to it.' She gets up and begins to tie on an apron. 'There's no need for you to wait up for us.'

The girl leaves and Levina drags the creaking log basket towards her as she crouches by the fire. 'We are running low on kindling.' She carefully sets the logs in a pyramid shape, stuffing the last of the kindling in the space beneath them, getting to work on the tinder.

'Send the servant out for a flame,' he says.

'This will be quicker.' She scuffs the flint over the firesteel to no avail. 'I am worried about Katherine Grey,' she says, without looking up at him.

'Oh, Veena, n-n-not this again.'

'No, George.' Levina has not heard his stutter in weeks, can't bear that she is visiting difficulty on him once more. 'This time I need you to listen to me. It is serious.' She looks up at him now, meeting his eye directly.

There must be something he sees in her expression, for he says, 'Go on; you have my ear.' He moves to crouch over the hearth next to her, taking the flint out of her hand, finding a spark almost immediately. The charcloth takes flame.

'I fear she may be unwittingly at the centre of some kind of plot.' She is whispering now.

'What do you mean?' What kind of plot? How do you know this?' The flame catches on the kindling, flaring up, reflecting brightly on their faces.

'I overheard something the Spanish ambassador was discussing with Feria when I visited Katherine at Durham House today.' Her mind conjures up an image of the place, palatial and ancient with a vast and badly conceived painting of the Annunciation in the chapel. The perspective was wrong, making the Virgin seem ill proportioned and the angel awkward. The place was teeming with people, Catholic nobles mainly. Levina counted four Dormers, three Jerninghams, Susan Clarencieux and the prior recently turfed out of Sheen Priory to make way for Frances.

'What does *he* think of *you* being here?' she had whispered to Katherine, catching her alone for a moment.

'They all think me rejected by Maman for adhering to the old faith,' she had replied, with a small shrug. Given the conversation Levina had overheard earlier, this alarmed her all the more and she had been about to warn Katherine, tell her she was in danger. But they were whisked off by a cluster of women to look at the gardens and never had even an instant alone thereafter. What would she have said, anyway?

'Why is the girl at Durham House and not at court or with her family?' asks George. She can feel his exasperation beneath the veneer of sympathy.

'You may well ask.' But it is clear to Levina why she is there, for she is treated like a princess, everyone kowtowing, falling over themselves to do things for her. Though she is but a faded version of the girl she was; the impression Levina had that afternoon was of a candle almost down to its nub, its flame shrinking – and Katherine had always burned so brightly.

'They were talking of smuggling her out of the country,' she continues, and has George's full attention now. 'They think to wed her to one of the Spanish Habsburgs without Elizabeth's knowledge. There is a plan to moor several small boats in the Thames. To whisk her away.' She had heard this when she first arrived, while awaiting Katherine's arrival in an anteroom. Feria and the ambassador can't have known she was there for they spoke quite clearly.

'Oh,' George says. 'And you are sure she is not party to it?'

'I truly think not. But it seems the Ferias have taken her into the fold and – well, they could use her ultimately to oust Elizabeth, particularly if she *were* a Habsburg bride.'

'Why would they seek to do that? Why should Spain care so much?'

'King Felipe fears – and I heard them say this quite clearly – he fears that the King of France will invade England in the name of his daughter-in-law, the Scottish Queen, and put *her* on the throne.'

'Mary of Scotland,' he says. 'I see. Felipe would be on the run if France got a foothold here. Veena, you can't get involved in all this. These politics. It is too dangerous.' He has his hand on her shoulder, squeezing it, as if to emphasize his words. The fire is hot against her skin, too hot. She moves back to the chessboard, with George following.

'Perhaps, but I should warn the girl. She's got herself into something she doesn't understand.'

'I suppose you could say something to her. But Veena, I mean it, if you aren't careful you might find yourself at the wrong end of a poniard, Spanish *or* French. Or even English, for that matter.' He brings both hands up and spreads them over his face, as if he is washing. Levina notices that he looks old; the years of fear have taken their toll on him. Marcus's letter is lying on the table beside the chessboard; she tries to think of her son, take her mind off this other thing, but can't.

'All I will do is warn her,' she replies. 'I won't even say a word to Frances.'

'Not to anyone.' George takes her hand briefly. 'I've had enough of this, Veena.' He stands. 'We can finish the game tomorrow. I think I will retire.'

'I'll join you.' She gets up, suddenly feeling exhausted and wondering if she too looks as old as her husband. She supposes she must, she will be forty next year, after all.

'I shall sleep alone tonight.'

She feels a dip of disappointment. He has not visited her chamber since his return from Bruges.

Levina perches in one of the wherries that convey all and sundry back and forth across the Thames. Her satchel of painting materials is stashed beneath the bench; she hopes the boat is watertight and there is no bilge at the bottom to soak her parchment but it all seems dry enough about her feet. She had to pay the waterman a penny on top of the fare to get him to stop at the steps near Durham House, for he was intending to cross over to Lambeth rather than run upriver, but the tide is whisking them up at a fair speed and he seems merry enough, whistling a ditty as he rows.

It is a fine day with a warm breeze and not too much of a stench rising from the water. A family of ducks floats past, a string of fluffy ducklings gliding after their mother, who occasionally dips down under the water. A small boy, sitting on his father's lap, coos with delight, trying to reach out to them with a fat little hand. Two women, each one with a vast basket, are chatting happily about the Queen and whom she will choose as a husband. There is a sense of optimism in the air, has been since Elizabeth came to the throne. But Levina feels weighed down by the things she knows, wonders if it will ever end, this intrigue, this almost permanent sense of dread at the back of things. It makes her question why she remains at court at all now Katherine is no longer there; but it is where she makes her living and they have got used to the finer things of life now, she and George, and how else would Marcus be travelling the Continent, getting an education?

The boat draws up to the steps and the waterman helps Levina out with a smile. She stands for a moment watching as the craft moves off across the river, girding herself for her visit to Durham House. She has brought her painting equipment with her as an excuse to be there and hopes it might give her the opportunity for a moment alone with Katherine. She can offer to make a quick sketch of Jane Dormer too, perhaps. People are always willing to have their likeness drawn, even girls like Jane Dormer who are not in the least bit vain.

There is a Spaniard at the river entrance who greets her in broken English, opening the door and calling an usher to fetch the mistress of the house. She waits in the empty hall, wondering where everyone is. There is an iron clock that rasps and clicks. Levina paces, inspecting the carvings, gruesome depictions of Hell in the most part, but beautifully crafted all the same. After some time Katherine arrives alone.

'Veena,' she says. 'Twice in as many days! The Countess is at prayer. She won't be long, I am sure.'

'Perhaps I can draw you while we wait,' Levina says, and then dropping her voice to a whisper, 'It is you I came to see; there is something I must tell you, in confidence. Where can we go?'

'The light is best in the gardens I think, and the weather is fine,' Katherine replies, catching on. She has a knack for intrigue, though usually for her it is of the romantic kind. She leads the way out, telling an usher to let the Countess know where they are when her prayers are done.

They find a spot with a view of the river and Katherine sits on a stone bench while Levina sets up her things, pinning a fresh sheet of parchment on to her board. The light is too strong really, and Katherine's face is carved harshly with shadow, but it is the quiet setting that meets Levina's purpose.

'Have the Count and Countess mentioned a marriage for you, Katherine?' she asks, trying to make it seem innocuous.

'They talk of almost nothing else. They would match me with a Spaniard, a Habsburg, Veena. What think you to that?' Katherine has a smug little beam on her face.

'I think,' Levina lowers her voice, 'that you need to beware.'

'I think not, Veena. The Ferias are so kind to me; they only mean me well, not like Elizabeth. Besides, the Count is leaving tomorrow for the Continent. He has business with the Emperor. And I feel sure he will be making arrangements for me also.'

'Katherine,' Levina says firmly. 'Remember what happened to your sister.' She is wondering if it is a good thing or not that Feria is leaving.

'My sister Jane?' The girl looks crushed, as if she is collapsing in on herself. 'And Father.'

Levina nods. She can see Jane Dormer approaching, crossing the garden, waving. She waves back. Katherine turns to see who it is.

'What do you mean?' she hisses.

'Do not think to wed anyone without the Queen's say-so. Do not think you are so well protected here,' Levina whispers. Then Jane Dormer is upon them.

'Mistress Teerlinc,' she says, taking Levina's hand with a smile. Levina half rises. 'No, don't let me disturb you at your sketching. I should like to watch though.'

'Of course. And perhaps I could draw you also,' says Levina.

'I should like that – whilst I am great with child. It will make a pleasant memory.' She perches beside Levina. 'So what were you discussing so intently? You looked quite . . .' she pauses, looking from Katherine to Levina and back. 'Quite in cahoots.'

'We were talking of the Queen's planned summer progress. She has expressed a desire for Lady Katherine to join her retinue.' Levina had thought that the progress might be a good way to get Katherine away from Durham House. Frances could write and ask Elizabeth. She wouldn't refuse that, and it would be a small triumph for the Queen over the Ferias – to get her cousin back from their clutches. But a thought pops into Levina's head: *Out of the frying pan and into the fire.*

'Ah,' Jane Dormer says, pausing, twisting a bracelet round and round her wrist. 'And does that please you, Katherine?'

'There are more pleasant things I can think of. But if the Queen commands it, then I shan't be able to refuse.'

'True,' says Jane Dormer.

'Look,' exclaims Levina, pointing at the river, relieved by the distraction. 'There goes Dudley's barge. Look how it is festooned.' She is thinking perhaps it is better that Katherine is kept in the dark, given her perverse desire to so often do what is most ill advised. She will ensure the girl is called on progress and that will be that, for the moment at least. Perhaps Katherine can visit her mother at Sheen too; Frances could send word she is ailing with a letter saying Katherine is forgiven in matters of faith, then it will seem all the more genuine. Levina can imagine Jane Dormer reading the letter, saying, 'But you *must* visit her, Katherine dear, if she is ailing.' There is no need to frighten her out of her wits. Levina's mind whirrs; there is much arranging to be done.

'Good gracious,' says Jane Dormer. 'I have never seen a barge so draped and decorated.'

'Eighteen oarsmen!' cries Katherine.

That thousand marks will be all spent before the month is out, thinks Levina.

'That man is a disgrace,' says Jane Dormer. 'I know it is ungodly to be critical thus, but . . .' She doesn't finish. The whole country would agree with her about Dudley.

August 1559
Nonsuch Palace
Katherine

My beloved Kitty,

It seems an age since we were together a month past at Sheen. Your visit was all too brief. It was a happy few days indeed, though not entirely so for you I fear, dear sister, as you were ridden with melancholy that was, as ever, well hidden beneath your ebullient surface. I know you too well, Kitty, and it pains me to witness your sorrow, however expertly you try to hide it. It is my greatest hope that things go better for you now and that the Queen is treating you a little more kindly. Maman tells me you are still lacking the proper privileges of your rank. I know what Jane would have advised you: to remain stoic and remember God has His plan for us. I keep her book, it is your book really, under my pillow. It is a source of great succour, giving me the feeling that our sorely missed sister is close. I think often of her and wonder if you do also. There are roses blooming in the gardens here at Sheen, which remind me of her. Do you recall her fondness for white roses? I daily cut a few stems to put in my chamber and delight in their scent.

I long for you to join us here. Sheen is such a pleasant place and not so far flung as Beaumanor. The river slinks by as a constant reminder that you are somewhere along it, though now, I remind myself, you are on progress and I know not where this letter may find you. The land here is lush and green and wild flowers speckle the pasture. It makes for good walking and though this place is too quiet for your tastes, I should like to walk with you here sometime soon. I am most content watching the fowl nesting by the river and waiting for their eggs to hatch, witnessing God's hand at work in nature. I saw two kingfishers at battle yesterday. It is astonishing how fierce the little creatures can be, the one holding the other beneath the water by the beak. Nature's brutality is sometimes surprising but then man, who should know better and is guided by the Lord, is capable of worse. I do wonder what separates us from the beasts, beyond our faith.

A heron fishes most days on the stretch of river that is visible from my chambers. All these birds remind me of poor old Forget-me-not. Do you remember him, Kitty? I suppose him free now to fly where he will. My favourite heifer calved last week, with twins – quite a miracle. Both survived and are thriving. I will not bore you further with my bumpkin matters, but how I should like to share these simple pleasures with my own dear sister.

Mistress Teerlinc was with us last week, but is I believe back at court again now, and may well be with you already. She left a drawing she had made of you, a fine one indeed. Maman has pinned it to her bed hangings. Maman has not been so well of late, but seems recovered now and Stokes is the model of a husband, fully doting.

I am told that Jane Dormer, or the Countess of Feria as she is now, has left for the Low Countries to join her husband. I know you are fond of her, Kitty, and that you have sought refuge with the Ferias of late, but I have to say I am glad she is gone. I know of the marriage they have been trying to broker for you and I cannot say strongly enough that it makes me uneasy. However thoughtful Jane Dormer is, Kitty, her faith is what defines her, her faith and her husband, and it is a faith you do not share, so be careful. It would displease the Queen greatly to find you had made a match such as they wish, or for that matter any unsanctioned match. Do not be seduced into thinking Feria cares for your well-being; he sees a political advantage in you and might well go to any lengths to achieve it.

I do not seek to alarm you, dear sister, nor do I believe you to be unaware of all these things, but I am reassured now the situation with France has changed. With the French threat diminished the Emperor, who we must not forget has Feria in his pocket, is less inclined to gain a foothold here, but . . .

I tear Mary's letter into tiny pieces and hold my hand above my head, allowing the breeze to take the fragments, watching them scatter like cherry blossom.

'What are you doing?' asks Juno, who is seated on a rock above the river pool, her legs dangling over the edge. We slipped away from the others; on progress there is so much happening, it is not so difficult to escape unseen. The day is so glorious it seemed a sin to stay inside, unpacking the Queen's things.

'My baby sister has started telling me what to do.' I watch

the fragments of paper twirl and flutter down to the water below.

'What does she say?'

'She is warning me against a Spanish match. Everyone seeks to warn me.' I am wondering when it was my little sister made herself so aware of state affairs.

'She is right, and you know it.'

'Don't *you* start telling me what to do, as well. I am not so stupid as to be entirely unaware of my value.'

'I know you are not stupid,' she laughs, lying back and opening her arms out as if to invite me to lie down with her. 'I am so very glad to have you back, Kitty.'

I take off my shoes and stockings, feeling the warm stone beneath my bare feet, and peel off my outer garments and my coif, allowing my hair to fall about my shoulders. 'I wish I were just an ordinary girl, free to wed where she pleases.' I move to the lip of the rock, looking down into the green pool, imagining the coolness of the water.

'My brother arrives today,' she says.

'Your brother.' I try to keep the excitement from my voice. 'Your brother has ill used me.'

'He wants to see you. Says he pines for you.'

'Before I left he certainly didn't behave like a person with . . .' I hesitate, 'with feelings.'

'He feared you would make a Spanish match.'

'Not that again! Everyone seems to fear that. I have had enough of other people's misplaced concern.'

'Kitty, don't be bitter. We have each other.' She stands now, joining me at the edge.

'Jump with me. Prove your love,' I say.

'Kitty, no. You don't know what is down there. The water may be foul. There may be hidden rocks.' She has taken hold of my wrist and is pulling me back.

'Are you scared?'

'I am not a fool.'

I shake her off and jump, feeling the rush of air all about me. The thrill of it catches in my throat, making me squeal with glee, and then the cold surprise of the water. I am breathless with wet laughter.

I watch Hertford from the side of my eye. He is sitting beside Juno some way up the table. I am down beyond the salt as usual – I have become quite used to being snubbed by Elizabeth. His hair is shorter and he is wearing a notched satin doublet I haven't seen before. There is not much of interest to eat at this end of the table and there is a squawking band of musicians right behind me that would be enough to put anyone off their food; but I find I can barely eat a morsel as it is. I put this down to the fact of Hertford, and his becoming new hairstyle, at the other end of the table, and the fact that he is sitting next to pretty Mary Howard, who has engaged him in deep conversation.

When he entered the hall he passed me, making a little bow. I responded with a vague curtsy, but my heart was thudding so hard I thought it might disturb the ladies reading at the far end of the chamber. He has tried to catch my eye several times and, though I am all a-wobble inside, I have assiduously resisted meeting his gaze.

'What have you to say of the new French King, Lady Katherine? I hear he is but fifteen years of age.' My neighbour is trying to make conversation but I am not really listening.

'I do not have much of an opinion on the matter,' I reply.

'It is said his wife is a great beauty.'

'Mary of Scotland? I have never seen her.' I smile and tilt my head, as if I am stupid. Life is easier that way.

'She claims the English throne is hers.'

'Well she will never have it,' says a man opposite. 'Not now her father-in-law is dead and she has only her milksop husband to fight on her behalf.'

They talk about how the old French king died, going into the greatest detail about the splinter that gouged his eye and worked its way to his brain, and how he was in agony for weeks. I am watching the servers parade some great culinary gargoyle up and down for people to gasp at – the back end of some kind of large fowl and the front end of a pig. Even mythology couldn't conjure up something that ugly and I am quite relieved that none of it will end up this far down the table. Uncle Arundel, who is our host, is seated up beside the Queen and is oohing and ahhing loudly, making a great fuss over it all. Elizabeth looks unimpressed but nods slightly in acknowledgement before turning to peruse a juggler who has picked up three crystal glasses and is about to throw them into the air. Arundel looks furious behind his smile, doubtless thinking of his best Italian crystal. I cannot keep myself from glancing towards Hertford, who is now sharing a joke with Mary Howard. Oh how they are laughing.

'Who are you looking at?' asks Levina, seated on my other side. She notices everything, says it is her artist's eye that makes her see things others don't. More like she is spying for Maman, making sure I behave.

'Nobody,' I say, but despite pursing my lips tightly, my smile can't be hidden.

'Nobody Hertford?' she says, making me laugh. 'He is a fine enough fellow,' she adds.

'You think so?' I pretend indifference, but Levina knows me better, sometimes better than I know myself.

'Would you like me to talk to your mother about him?' she asks quietly, so the people around us can't hear – anyway, they are all transfixed by the juggler, waiting agog for the sound of crystal shattering against stone.

'There is nothing to say.'

'I could talk to her anyway.'

'As you wish,' I concede, as if I care not a jot.

Hertford is whispering something to Juno. Then they both look at me, he only momentarily, before casting his eyes back to his food, Juno giving a little flutter of a wave. I smile at her, feeling Levina's artist eye on me. The '*thing*' hovers in my mind, making me unsure how to be, but the tug of Hertford is impossible to deny. I have always known exactly how to behave, exactly how to have them all, boys and men alike, eating out of my palm; but now a flood of contradictory feelings has befuddled me.

A marchpane facsimile of Nonsuch is being carried up to the top table now, and the hall erupts with applause. Even the Queen is impressed, for every detail is there, down to the elaborate Italianate carvings and the stone lions perched on the turrets, bearing flags. Uncle Arundel looks as smug as if he'd made the thing with his own hands. Juno and I made some subtleties yesterday. Levina had helped us make plaster moulds of the fruits we picked in the Nonsuch orchards: pears, peaches, pippins and apricots, rare as diamonds – but nothing is too rare for Arundel's gardens. We pressed the sugar paste into them, turning out perfect white shapes. Then we concocted paints of beetroot and carrot and the juice of green grasses. Under Levina's direction, the white shapes transformed into counterfeit fruits so convincing you could hardly tell them apart from the real thing. It was a long time since I'd made sugar fancies, back at Bradgate, when life was different. Maman had shown us how to carefully heat the sugar in an earthenware pot set over a few coals, and then shape the warm paste into all manner of fanciful things.

Now our platter of pretend fruits is being offered to the Queen, who acknowledges Juno with a smile. Everyone knows of her sweet tooth. She picks out an apricot, turns it over in her hand, appraising it with raised eyebrows, then seeks me out, making a little nod of acknowledgement in my direction. Unless I am imagining it, the corners of her mouth lift slightly into something that could be construed as a half-smile. Levina gives me a nudge with her foot. I stand and bob in a curtsy. The Queen seems satisfied. Perhaps she is relenting a little, but my head is too full of Hertford to think of what it might mean.

The Queen eventually takes her leave, to a great fanfare, followed out by Dudley; and Arundel; and Cecil; and Norfolk; and all the privy chamber ladies; and the twenty or so others who have her favour, Juno and Hertford amongst them – but not me. Directly after go the musicians and a string of servers with the sugar subtleties. Our display of sweet fruits is taken with the rest of the platters, all loaded with colourful fancies in towering piles, and carried out to the banqueting hall in the gardens.

I am abandoned while the boards are cleared away about me. Those who are not invited to the banqueting hall mill around in groups but none approach me. My rank makes them uncomfortable. Just as I am starting to wish myself back under the wing of the Ferias, a page appears before me.

'Lady Katherine Grey,' he is saying.

'That is I,' I reply, thinking that he must have some bad news from Maman or Mary – news that one of them is ailing, or worse. But he has a mild look on his face that does not seem to spell disaster.

'The Queen requests your presence, My Lady.'

'*My* presence?' I repeat, wondering if my ears don't need cleaning.

'Yes, My Lady,' he says. 'I shall accompany you to her.'

I nod, unusually lost for words, and follow him, meek as anything, out through the gardens to the banqueting hall. It has been draped in great sheets of white cotton and lit by clever contraptions that cast shadows of Roman gods and goddesses over the walls. An usher announces me, and a few turn my way. Juno is across the room with Hertford, whose look I take care to avoid. I drop into a deep curtsy before Elizabeth, who, after leaving me on my knees longer than is strictly necessary, bids me stand and beckons me closer.

'We are considering admitting you to the privy chamber.' Her smile is an icy rictus and she drops her voice further, adding in a hiss, 'A privilege you hardly merit, Lady Katherine.' I can sense everyone craning in, trying to get the gist of what is said.

'I know not how to express my gratitude, Your Majesty –' I begin, but she interrupts.

'Just *thinking* about it, mind; it is not done yet. We shall see.'

So she is toying with me. She likes to play those kind of games, games that show her strength, like when she left poor Jane Dormer, so great with child she could barely stand, waiting an hour on her feet for an audience. The Spanish were beside themselves with rage; it nearly caused a diplomatic incident. Juno said it was punishment for the Ferias getting their clutches on me. I wonder if Jane Dormer has birthed her baby yet.

I offer the Queen a suitably humble thank-you and she dismisses me, shooing me off with a flick of her wrist. I back away, careful to keep my eyes low, but despite my show of grovelling, I feel elated. It is as if I have at last been dealt a good card from the pack – a royal card – when lately I have had only the most miserable of hands – twos and threes at best. I hear Kat Astley mutter something in disapproval but I don't care what Kat Astley thinks of me, favourite or not; I have dealt with worse women than her. I can see people about the room asking each other what was said to me.

A small platter is thrust into my hand. 'Turn it over,' says Margaret Audley, Norfolk's new duchess, whom I find myself standing beside. 'See what inscription you have been given.' She is showing me the underside of her plate, where some words are inscribed in Latin.

'*Moribus et forma conciliandus amor*,' I stumble out, wishing, not for the first time, that I had concentrated more at my Latin studies instead of gazing out of the window at Father's pages practising their archery.

Fortunately Margaret Audley translates it herself, 'Love is conciliated, won by manners and beauty.'

'The Queen thinks highly of you,' I say. In the corner of my eye I am watching Hertford talking to Frances Meautas.

'It would appear so,' she says. 'Though there is discord between my husband and that *creature* of hers.' She holds her feather fan close to her mouth to mask her words from others. I can only suppose that by '*creature*' she means Dudley. 'Norfolk,' she continues, 'is of the mind that the upstart stands in the way of a proper royal marriage. My husband supports the Habsburg suit. What is your mind?'

'I would agree with that,' I say. To be honest I haven't given much thought to whom the Queen will marry, though it seems to be all anyone wants to talk about; but it does remind me of my own 'illustrious match' and Mary's letter of warning.

'Show me yours,' she says. For an instant I don't know what she means and I hesitate, until she takes my plate from my hand, turning it over, reading, '*Amicos tuos prope et inimicos tuos propius tene.*' The Latin is, of course, meaningless to me.

'But that is not a Roman saying,' she continues. 'It is supposed to have a Roman theme. That is Machiavelli, isn't it? Or perhaps one of the Romans said it first. But it can't be for *you* – not that. You must have the wrong one.' Then, looking beyond my shoulder, she adds, 'Norfolk beckons. Will you excuse me, Lady Katherine; my husband does not like to be kept waiting,' leaving me none the wiser.

I seek out Juno, showing her the inscription. 'What does it say?' But her face crumples as she reads it and she shakes her head slightly. 'What does it say?'

'Keep your friends close . . .' she begins.

'. . . and your enemies closer,' I whisper. 'Oh don't look so worried, Juno.' I put an arm about her shoulders. 'We all know there is no love lost between Elizabeth and me. But she *has* intimated that she may reinstate me to the privy chamber. Though it is highly likely she is merely toying with me.'

'So that is what she was saying. This is good news indeed, Kitty.' She smiles, though only fleetingly. 'But "enemy", that is a strong word.'

'It is only a game, Juno. She is warning me to behave, that is all.' But I am wondering if the Queen has somehow got wind of my 'illustrious marriage', and that she is playing with me before she pounces. I push that thought away and watch as a whisper travels through the room – hands cupped to ears, eyebrows raised. 'What are they saying?' I ask Lettice Knollys to my right, who has just heard it from Frances Meautas.

'Dudley's inscription said, *Audax ad omnia femina . . .*'

'In English, Lettice,' I say. 'Please.'

'A woman who loves or hates will dare everything.' She giggles. 'Would you believe it? And,' she adds in a conspiratorial tone, 'they say Dudley's wife has a malady in one of her breasts and they are waiting –'

'I *have* heard it,' I say before she can finish.

I cannot bear the thought of poor Amy Dudley and her malady, with her husband and Elizabeth just waiting for her to be dead so that they can marry. People have said *I* am cruel – Harry Herbert has said it, and he was not the first – but I could never be cruel like that.

The musicians start up a galliard, just a pipe and a drum initially. Dudley offers his hand to the Queen, who surprises everyone by accepting. Across from where I stand Norfolk and Cecil exchange a look, as Dudley leads Elizabeth to the centre of the room where we have all crowded back to make space. They begin to move through the steps, eyes locked. He struts like a cock in a henhouse, in his pinked silver doublet and sleek black stockings, with a smirk on his face. I see the way his hands take ownership of her body, slipping behind her neck, stroking her cheek, tight about her waist – everyone must see, for he makes no effort to hide it, seeming not to care that the Queen appears loose – apparently she cares little either. Cecil is stone-faced.

I still have half an eye on Hertford, watching him speak to Norfolk; they are chinking their cups together as if celebrating something. Then he makes for the door. My stomach drops with disappointment as if it is suddenly filled with pebbles. People are joining Dudley and the Queen to dance now, and Juno pulls at my hand but I am rooted to the spot by the weight in my gut, not daring to ask her where her brother might have gone. I suppose it is to some romantic assignation under the stars in the Nonsuch gardens.

'Will you not dance?' she asks.

I shake my head, for I fear if I say anything in this moment I will lose my composure altogether.

'*Now*, they must be lovers,' she whispers, nodding in the direction of the Queen and her prancing partner.

'The Virgin Queen,' I say, attempting to compose myself, behave normally.

'Nether hole!' she breathes. We both snort with laughter, and for a brief moment my belly is lighter.

I feel a tug on my sleeve. I turn, and there is Hertford.

'But –' I start, wondering how it is he has reappeared so suddenly beside me, like a genie out of a lamp.

'Come outside,' he says so quietly I barely hear it. I feel my insides melting. Juno is dancing with the Norwich boy, laughing as he lifts her in the air.

'What for?' It is all I can do not to fall into his arms.

'To talk.'

'To talk? Do you think me a fool?'

'No, Kitty, I mean it.' Then he leans in, whispering, 'Just to talk to my precious Kitty.'

And my self-control is altogether lost, as if I am atop a bolting horse. I allow myself to be led out through the gardens, where the lake shines as if the moon has fallen to earth. There is hardly a breath of air and the music from the banqueting hall trickles out into the still night. He has hold of my hand; I dare not look at him in case I was mistaken and it is some other lad who has tempted me out into the dark with him. But I *do* look and see his dear, dear profile beside me, and I can barely resist the urge to reach out and touch his skin to see if he is real. We sit on a bench beside a willow and listen in silence to the frogs croaking out their night chorus.

'I have missed you so very much,' he says eventually, mumbling into his collar. 'It was as if –' He stops and I fancy I can hear the whirr of his thoughts. 'It was as if I were torn to pieces, as if my whole world were fragmenting. All the time you were at Durham House I feared . . . I feared . . .' He cannot seem to finish.

'Feared what?' It is all I can do to stop my own feelings from gushing out of me.

'All the rumours . . .' He hesitates; then blurts out, 'I feared you would marry another.'

'But I did not,' I say.

'Thank God, Kitty. Thank God.'

'You did not behave as you should have.' I attempt to sound stern.

'You are right, my precious. I put my standing at court over my love for you. I thought I could harness my feelings but' – he squeezes my hand and I feel quite sick with desire – 'I could not. I would rather die, than feel that I had not your favour.'

'Elizabeth must not know.' I remark the irony; that it is I now who insists upon secrecy. My mind interrupts me with the thought of the 'illustrious marriage', but I push it away. There is no need to think of any of that now, and besides, the Ferias are away. 'I am hanging by a thread with Elizabeth. If she were to think –'

'I know,' he interrupts. 'I would not put you at risk, my sweet. I shall not breathe a word.'

'Only to Juno,' I say. I am on the brink of telling him of my hopes of promotion to the privy chamber, but I stop myself. I would rather he loved me knowing I am not favoured by the Queen. But neither do I mention the inscription on my plate, for it is true what Juno said: 'enemy' is a strong word, and I fear scaring him off.

'Only to Juno,' he echoes. I feel his arm slide over my shoulder and I nestle into him as he strokes my hair. I believe I have not felt so content, so safe, since Father used to take me in his arms and squeeze me in a bear hug, whispering that

I was his favourite and tickling me with his whiskers. 'I would wed you tomorrow, Kitty Grey,' he whispers.

And I would wed you; I don't say it, but I think it. Then we are upon each other, unlacing, untying, unhooking, with urgent fingers desperate to press skin against skin. In my mind sits the thought that were I to marry him, Juno would be my sister-in-law. His mouth seeks mine. I sink into his kiss as if it is the first I have ever had; and then, lifting my disarrayed skirts, I climb to sit astride him, not caring that my bare knees are rubbing against the rough stone of the bench. As he fumbles with his laces I slip my hand around his neck, where I can feel the soft bristle of his newly shorn hair, and beneath it the throb of his pulse.

'Just to talk?' he breathes in my ear.

'We *are* talking, aren't we?'

November 1559
Sheen Priory
Mary

I read to Maman from Katherine's letter. 'I am reinstated to the privy chamber. The Queen has relented at last.'

Maman brings her palms together as if thanking God. 'I never thought it possible. I must say, Mouse, it is a great relief . . . a good sign. *Tu crois que c'est un bon signe*?' Maman's voice is a croak, despite her levity at Katherine's news. She has been unwell these last weeks and can't seem to shake off her malady. We are both sitting as close as we can to the hearth without getting burned, and Maman is wrapped in furs. The weather is the worst kind, both bitter and damp with a freezing drizzle that prevents us from taking the air. The summer birds have gone to warmer climes and the winter arrivals have begun. Last week I came upon a flock of redwings picking berries at the edge of the woods – predicting the long, cold evenings ahead.

'I *do* think it a good sign, Maman. It shall keep her out of Feria's clutches and evade that secret marriage he was trying to broker.'

'God only knows what mischief was behind that.'

'Is there more news of it?' I ask. 'Has Levina heard anything more?'

'No, *Dieu merci*. Feria remains on the Continent. The French are less of a threat these days. But you can never tell what those Spaniards are likely to spring. I heard they had a boat moored on the Thames to smuggle her off under darkness.'

'They truly planned to snatch her away?'

'As rumour would have it. But that won't happen while she's under the Queen's nose.'

'I sometimes wonder if she isn't attracted to the danger of it all.'

'As an infant she was always the one to do the very thing she was warned against. I used to despair of her, Mouse. Not like you; you were good as gold, or Jane . . .'

'I wish she would come here, Maman. She would be safe here.'

'You know Katherine.' Maman exhales loudly. 'She can't bear the quiet.'

I read on: 'The Queen called me up to her, in front of everyone in the privy chamber and said, "Lady Katherine, your privileges are restored," and then she warned me to be on my best behaviour, which I have been, I assure you, Maman. She has been most unusually pleasant to me.'

'Good news indeed. But you never know with Elizabeth.'

'She asks that her dogs and the monkey be sent to her.'

They have been here with us, causing havoc. They chew up the carpets, gnaw at the bed legs and, in the case of Hercules, steal foodstuffs from the stores. Maman had the monkey banished to the stables. I couldn't bear to see him cuffed and chained, which was the alternative.

'Oh Mouse,' Maman had said. 'You cannot even bear to see a monkey's freedom curtailed.'

At least in the stables he has the run of the place, and the lads like to play with him, so his life is not so dull. I have become quite attached to one of the spaniels, Echo, who sleeps on my bed and has taken to following me about like a little shadow. I will write to my sister and ask if she may stay at Sheen with me.

Katherine tells, in minute detail, which of the Queen's ladies have the most beautiful dresses, what fabrics they are made of, what colours, which furs they are trimmed in, how fine their embroidery, and who has new jewels, which stones, set how, worn in which way. She has news of Peggy, too, who is to be married to one of the Arundel cousins early next year. 'Peggy is bursting with excitement at the idea of her wedding,' Katherine writes.

Peggy has written to me herself of it, how it goes a little way to assuage her grief for her brother who died quite suddenly in the summer. I am glad for her and, if I search my heart, there is a part of it that thinks: if Peggy can marry then there is hope for me. But a harelip doesn't hinder the birthing of healthy infants. Marriage and women are for breeding, after all. What use is a woman who likely cannot carry a child, I ask myself, but I try not to dwell on my deformities. Jane always said it was my challenge – that I would become a better person for it, closer to God. If she were still with us, she would have produced some nieces and nephews. I sometimes imagine

I can hear the whoop and giggle of children about the house.

Katherine also tells at length of the gossip about the Queen's preoccupation with Robert Dudley. 'She has given him rooms next to hers. Kat Astley is beside herself and Cecil is apoplectic. Erik of Sweden's envoy threatens to leave court in high dudgeon and the Habsburg ambassador is sulking,' she says. But we already know, here in Sheen, of Dudley's goings-on, and of his poor sick wife – all the tongues in England are wagging on it.

'Elizabeth is like Homer's Penelope with all her suitors,' Maman says dryly. 'I am thankful not to be a part of that any longer. And glad that neither are you, Mouse.'

'I am cut of the wrong cloth for court life.'

'There were times, *quand j'étais jeune* . . .' She seems to drift off in thought. 'There were times, Mouse, when it was quite wonderful. When your father was courting me.'

'Did you love Father once?' I ask. I know well that by the time he met his death she loved him no longer, that she blamed him, his ambition – and his foolishness – for what happened to Jane.

'It was not a great passion, like some you hear of. But I liked him well enough. He was dashing and comely and given to grand gestures. When one is young those things seem to have importance.' She looks at me, then adds, 'I suppose you are not so shallow, Mary. You have a different view of things, always have. Even very young, your thoughts were – *comment dire?* – so profound.'

'Perhaps that is the impression I give,' I say. 'Because it is always assumed that I am not vain and shallow. But truthfully, Maman, I *have* had thoughts, thoughts of romance, like any girl my age. My shape only makes me different on the outside.' I am thinking of the scribe Percy, who served Maman once. He stirred something in me. Percy is long gone and never looked twice my way as it was. 'But it is true, I am not like my sister.'

'Yes, Katherine, she is governed by her emotions – bless her. She is her father's daughter through and through.'

'Maman?' I ask.

'Yes, dear?'

'Why, if you have been so worried for Katherine, did you not strive to remain at court yourself to keep an eye on her?'

'Do you mean why did I marry your stepfather?'

'In a way I suppose I do mean that.'

'Chances for happiness are few in life, Mouse. Sometimes they must be grabbed with both hands. I truly believed that Katherine would join us eventually.' She pauses. 'Once her wild oats were sown.'

'I think Kitty's wild oats will never be quite sown.'

She laughs at this, but it provokes a painful fit of retching that has her groaning and gasping for breath. I settle her and stoke the fire to keep the chamber warm. 'And the other things, the package and . . . that?' She points to another letter that arrived from court with Katherine's. 'What is that one?'

I tear it open, reading it. 'It is Peggy. She has leave from court and would like to come to Sheen.'

'Poor girl, she must be feeling the loss of her brother. It is harder when death comes to the young. Do you remember him?'

'Only vaguely. I was very young when he was with us at Bradgate.'

'Anyway, I am happy for her betrothal, and I am glad she's coming to us here. Will you reply to her, Mouse?'

I am glad too, at the thought of having my close companion here with me. There is always a variety of cousins and suchlike about the place, but none I am fond of as I am fond of Peggy with her easy straightforwardness.

'And the package,' I say. 'Shall I open it?'

'Let me see.' She holds out her hand for the parcel. 'It is from Veena.' The delight in her voice is palpable. She unwraps it. 'Look, it is Foxe's book. In Latin. Did you know it was Veena who smuggled documents to Foxe for this book?' I remember the roll of papers I concealed beneath my clothes that day. It seems long ago now, the old Queen's reign, though it is only a single year. Maman is shuffling through the pages searching for something, finding it, holding it out to me. 'Look, Mary.'

I glance, instantly recognizing the familiar words, words etched on my heart: *It shall teach you to live and learn you to die*. A shiver runs through me with the idea that little by little I will forget her and all that will be left is words.

'I miss her, Maman.'

A knock at the door interrupts our silent separate thoughts of Jane. It is one of the pages.

'You have a visit from the Earl of Hertford, My Lady,' he says, unable to hide the concern from his face on seeing Maman so very grey with fatigue.

'Young Ned Hertford,' she exclaims, sitting up a little. 'I suppose he has come to ask if he can court Katherine. Send him in.' The page leaves; I straighten Maman's wrap and stroke her hair beneath her hood. 'That would put a stop to Feria's schemings, if Katherine were to marry *him*.' She stops speaking as the door swings open and Hertford enters, pulling off his cap and bowing deeply.

He is a fine-looking fellow with pale curls and apricot skin that looks smooth as a girl's. His elegant boots are spattered a little from the road and the tip of his nose is red from riding in the bitter weather. Maman shifts in her seat with a wince. 'My Lord Hertford,' she says, 'how glad you must be to have your name back.'

'I am most happy, My Lady.'

'This is Katherine's sister, Lady Mary,' she says, taking my hand and bringing it into her lap.

He turns my way, saying, 'It is a true delight to know any sister of Lady Katherine's.'

Smooth words indeed, I am thinking. I explore his expression for disdain or disgust, not finding it there, not even in the smallest way. Perhaps Katherine has warned him about me, prepared him for my strange form. Anyway, prepared or not, he flashes me a warm smile and seats himself on the bench before us, as Maman has indicated.

'So?' says Maman, who has a little colour back in her cheeks.

'Um . . . I . . . I . . .' The boy is lost for words, and I like him all the more for it.

'Are you trying to ask me if you may court my daughter?'

'I am, My Lady.' He smiles again, seeming relieved to not have to explain himself, and I can see what my sister sees in him. He is so very much like her.

'I assume you are aware that Lady Katherine is no ordinary girl.' Maman has made herself sound quite stern, but she carries a hint of a smile, though Hertford is so nervous it is unlikely he has seen it.

'I am, My Lady. And I hope you do not find me wanting. I was first cousin to the last King Edward, and on my mother's side we are descended from –'

'The third Edward,' Maman interrupts. 'Yes, I know all about you and the royal line you come from. I knew your father very well – and your mother. How does she fare? She is at Hanworth, I am told?'

'She is, yes, and in good health too, My Lady.'

'And what is *her* opinion of your intention to court my daughter?'

He picks at a thread on his doublet, pulling a brilliant clean away. 'She . . . she is not yet aware of it.'

'Ah, so you think she will disapprove?'

'I suppose . . .' He pauses, twiddling the bright bead in his fingers. 'I suppose so, My Lady.'

'Well, never mind,' says Maman, who is smiling fully now. '*I* do approve. But I should like to have my daughter's opinion on it. You may only court her if she wishes it herself.'

'Oh she does, My Lady.'

'I should like it from the source, as it were. So when you return to court you shall bid her come and see me, and if she wishes it, then she is yours. I assume the Queen doesn't know, either?'

'She does not.'

'I imagine she's too caught up with her own affairs to notice if someone has set his eye upon one of her ladies.'

We all know she means Dudley when she says 'affairs'.

'We shall worry about the Queen when the time comes,' continues Maman. 'I shall approach her myself. I knew her well as a girl. But you must be discreet in the meantime – we wouldn't want any trouble.'

Hertford throws himself at her feet, taking both her hands in his. It is a gesture rather too dramatic for the occasion, but quite charming nonetheless. 'Do you believe she will grant us permission?'

He is like a boy in a poem begging for the hand of his love. How Katherine must delight in his overblown ways.

'I am confident that all will be well,' says Maman. 'But I suggest you try and persuade as many as you can on the council to your way of thinking; only those you trust, mind. That will help.'

'I shall do so, My Lady. Anything.'

'And tell Lady Katherine she can collect her pets when she comes. Unless you want to take them back for her.'

It is less than a week after Hertford's visit that Katherine arrives, and, with her, dearest Peggy. Katherine was unable to hide her shock on seeing Maman, who has gone into a decline and has a look of unbearable frailty about her. I fear for her greatly – she can hardly manage even the lightest of broths, and is so weak she struggles to leave her bed. Stokes is a rock; he has sat up with her night after night; he administers her tinctures and holds her hand, reading to distract her while she is being bled and cupped. But the Doctor makes a glum companion when he visits and we know it is only a matter of time. He says it is a stoppage of the spleen and gives her physic for the pain, which at times is so bad she screams out like a woman birthing. She has begun to recount stories from the past, the days at Bradgate, and talks much of Jane, how she put us all to shame with her learning. And she talks of regret. It is as if she has gone back into the past and means to stay there.

I try to imagine a world without her, but it is like trying to think of the sea without salt. It is said that there is a sea in the Holy Land so full of salt that you can never drown in it. Maman is that sea to me; she has held me up, kept me buoyant, and I wonder if I can float alone. When I think of our family, so shrunken, a little seed of fear sows itself in my core – it will be just Katherine and me, with nobody to stand between Elizabeth and us. There is no doubt that I shall be called back to court, as a ward of the Queen, I suppose.

I watch Katherine talking to Maman. She is describing a masque in which she played one of the muses. I admire the way she can be so light, so entertaining, and watch Maman's muted pleasure on hearing Katherine's stories. I wonder why it is that I feel too freighted with grief to distract Maman from her woes with pretty tales.

'I was Terpsichore,' Katherine says, jumping up and dancing a few steps, to demonstrate her part. 'And Margaret Audley was Erato, which was the best part, and poor Peggy got Clio. You had to recite an endless tract about the history of England, didn't you?'

'But I enjoyed being Clio,' pipes up Peggy, who is beside me, twisting skeins of embroidery thread.

'I should have liked to have seen it,' says Maman. There is a little life back in her bearing – it has lifted her spirits to see Katherine.

I had met Katherine and Peggy down at the door when they arrived and had warned them of Maman's condition.

'She will get better, I know it,' Katherine had said.

'No, Kitty,' I told her. 'We must prepare ourselves.'

'Mary, you are always the pessimist.'

I had left it at that. Perhaps it is easier for her to believe that things will always improve.

Maman is smiling as she watches Katherine dance, and Katherine hums as she trips lightly about the chamber. My sister is full of life, as if her seams will burst with it. I am heartened to see Maman's smile and it makes me think I have been a rather gloomy companion for her. I resolve to brighten up, to take a leaf from my sister's book and make Maman's last days full of joy.

'Come and sit, Kitty, you are making me giddy,' says Maman, patting the bed. Katherine climbs up beside her and drops a kiss on to her forehead. It is an oddly inverted gesture, as if she is the mother and Maman the child.

'Do you want to ask about Hertford?' Katherine says.

'He was here, as you know.'

'I *do* want to wed him, Maman, truly I do.'

Stokes peeps round the door. 'Would I be interrupting, Franny dear, if I sat with you ladies?'

'Not in the least,' Maman says, and I can see the fondness she has for my stepfather written in her eyes. He sits on her other side.

'*Venez ici*, Mouse, Peggy,' Maman says. 'This bed has room enough for us all. See, we fit like puppies in a basket,' she adds as we settle beside them. A small part of me has the wish that she would depart this life right now, in this moment, for she seems so very content to have her family all about her. I cannot bear the thought of her creaking slowly, excruciatingly, towards her end. 'Now, we were talking about Hertford.'

'He is . . . He is . . .' Katherine cannot formulate her words. 'He is perfect, Maman.'

As she says this, I notice Peggy purse her lips and minutely shake her head, but no one else sees it – Peggy herself is probably unaware, but I mean to find out what her misgivings are when we are alone.

'The Queen must give permission,' says Stokes. 'That is vital. I'm not having you getting into deep water, Katherine.'

'Deep water,' she repeats thoughtfully. 'No.'

I can't help myself from thinking that the idea of deep water has a grave allure for Katherine.

'Elizabeth is more artful than her sister,' says Maman. 'I knew her as a girl. Knew things about her she would rather I didn't.'

'Perhaps if you wrote to her, Franny?'

'Yes,' Maman says. 'It is unlikely she would refuse *me*. I shall remind her of the days we were together in Katherine Parr's house, that should spur her on to give you her blessing.'

Stokes snorts out a small dry laugh at this, and I look in turn to Peggy and Katherine, who seem equally confused by what is being said – or what is not quite being said. It would appear though, that Maman has some influence over the Queen.

'Yes, I shall write to her. That will do the trick. And Kitty . . .' She turns to my sister. '*Pas de bêtises!* No naughtiness!' We all laugh at this and I want to keep the moment for ever, preserve it like bottled summer fruits. 'Now tell me,' she says when our mirth has died down, 'how it goes with Levina at court. I hear her limnings are in great demand.'

'They are, Maman,' says Katherine. 'She has painted just about everyone. And the Queen more times than I have fingers on both my hands. She pictured you, didn't she, Peggy?'

'She did.' Peggy is fumbling in a pouch attached to her girdle and pulls out a small package. 'This is for you.'

She hands it to Maman, who passes it to me, saying, 'I'm afraid my fingers are not so very nimble lately. Would you open it for me, Mouse?'

I pull off the wrapping and there is a tiny portrait of Peggy. Maman smiles, taking it. 'Peggy, that is so thoughtful. I am grateful, my dear.'

'You have been as good as a mother to me,' says Peggy, unable to hide the crack in her voice. Suddenly the atmosphere in the chamber is heavy, unbearably so, too heavy for any of us to speak.

Eventually Maman says, in a wilting voice, 'I think I will have a little sleep now.'

I can see the dull glow of morning creep through the gap in the hangings – despite the draught, I like to leave them open a hand's width, so if I wake in the night I can look out. From my window here at Sheen, there is a particularly bright star I can always see on clear nights, framed at the exact centre of one of the windowpanes. It is a constant, and if I fix my mind on it, it steadies those night thoughts that tend to whirl out of control. I imagine in my more fanciful moments that that star is Jane, looking down on me.

I feel Echo's wet nose against my fingers, nuzzling, wanting me to stroke her. Peggy sleeps quietly beside me, and Katherine, on her other side, has one arm flung out above her head, making a dark shape against the white pillow. They are both good sleepers, unlike me. I am kept awake more often than not by the unanswerable questions, the whys and wherefores of the world, things that are most easily answered by faith. But there is a part of me that does not tend to seek the easy way to answer things; I want an explanation for everything that does not require the leap of imagination that God asks of us.

Then I remember Peggy's little scowl yesterday and a pebble of doubt about my sister's marriage plans drops into my thoughts. I had asked Peggy what she truly thought of Hertford when we were abed last night, before Katherine had joined us.

'Do you not think he is . . .' She had hesitated, twiddling at her necklace. 'I don't know. He seems . . .' She had never finished, for Katherine came in then and the subject had been firmly changed to what she would wear for her wedding. I tried to be enthusiastic but I couldn't shake Peggy's doubts out of my head.

I am aware that my pessimism has taken hold. Contradictory thoughts spill over one another. The fact cannot be ignored that anyone hitching themselves to my sister could find themselves nicely placed. It may be a risk but then the greatest risk produces the greatest reward – Hertford will know that as well as anyone. Strictly speaking, according to the old King's will, Katherine is Elizabeth's heir, even if the Queen refuses to acknowledge it. I think of the stuttering

Hertford I met the other day. Surely there is true affection there? But it is expected of a boy like him to gain back lost ground for his family. I suppose he carries all their hopes on his shoulders. The Seymours took a tumble during Edward's reign, it is well known. I was very small then but I remember all the talk of it, Hertford's father, the Duke of Somerset, going to the block and the Duchess festering in the Tower. My trickle of thoughts becomes a gush as I am engulfed with memories of my dead sister. The Seymours are not the only ones to have taken a tumble.

I clamber down from the bed with Echo in my arms, taking care not to wake Katherine and Peggy, fumbling for my gown. It is bitterly cold, so cold my head feels tightly compressed, as if I am a fledgling that has outgrown its egg. I poke about in the hearth to see if any embers are still alive, finding a few hopeful glowing flecks. I take a handful of kindling, placing it carefully and blowing gently to bring it back to life. One by one the embers extinguish themselves. I am not much given to superstition, but I cannot help thinking that it is a sign, and I am gripped with the fear that Maman is gone.

I rush to her chamber, Echo in my wake. There is a sliver of orange light beneath the door. My throat is clogged and I picture the physician, called urgently in the night, standing over her like a shadow in the early-morning gloom. I open it stealthily, entering, meeting a wall of warmth and light. There is a blazing fire and Maman is sitting up in bed with Stokes beside her. They don't notice me for they are both laughing at something in a book Stokes is holding up. I feel, all of a sudden, silly for my fears and my pessimism. Katherine was right; Maman has rallied.

'Maman!' bursts out of me. They both look up from the book, flushed with mirth and health, and I run over, scrambling up on to the high bed. 'You are better.'

'I *am* my sweet, *beaucoup mieux*. And it is thanks to your gentle care. You both have brought me back to life.'

I think that this is only partly true. It is the visit from Katherine that has lifted her spirits – and the idea of the forthcoming wedding. When I think about it, I suppose she must have worried herself sick over Katherine. And now she is to wed the Hertford boy, Maman will see to it that they have permission, and he will keep her out of harm's way. I have become so used to worrying about my sister I find problems where there are none.

Maman turns to Stokes. 'I find I am quite ravenous. Do you suppose there is anyone awake in the kitchens?'

Stokes seems unable to wipe the happiness off his face. 'I shall go and investigate, my dear Franny,' he says. 'What would you like? A caudle, something that will slip down easily?'

'As a matter of fact,' she says with a smirk, 'what I really have a fancy for is cake.'

It charges me with joy to hear such a thing.

Stokes leaves with the words: 'Then cake you shall have, My Lady.'

'I think I shall start on my letter to the Queen. Mouse, would you find my writing box for me? I believe it is over there, by the window.' I do as she asks, pulling back the bed hangings to allow the thin November light to get to her, and bring over the candelabrum, putting it as close as I can without setting fire to the drapes. 'I shall begin with a reminiscence of our times together in Katherine Parr's household.' She stops, seeming deep in thought, running the feathered end of the quill over her lower lip.

'What happened there?' I ask.

'Oh goodness, Mouse. I don't know that . . .' She hesitates. 'Let us just say Elizabeth compromised herself and I am sure it is something she would rather that people forget.'

'Maman, you missed your calling as a diplomat.'

'Perhaps not.' A vague smile passes over her mouth. 'Being the Duchess of Suffolk has called for my diplomatic skills quite often enough.'

'But I would like to know, Maman. You always say it: knowledge is power. Maybe one day it will be useful for me to know the secrets of the Queen's youth.'

She looks at me with a wry smile. 'If I tell you, then you must swear never to inform Katherine. She does not have your talent for discretion.'

I nod solemnly. 'I swear it, Maman.'

'Very well, I shall tell you. The scandal occurred when Elizabeth was about fourteen years –'

'My own age,' I interrupt.

'Goodness, yes. How time passes.' She strokes the side of my face with a papery finger. 'It was an indiscretion involving Thomas Seymour.' She pauses, then adds, as if she has just realized it, 'He was young Hertford's uncle. He was married to the dowager queen at the time, Katherine Parr.'

'Who was your dear friend, was she not?'

'We *were* close, it is true, and your sister Jane was in her household at the time. I happened to be visiting her when Elizabeth was sent away for the sake of her virtue.'

'Her *virtue*?' I cannot believe what I am hearing.

'Yes. She was carrying on with the Seymour fellow in a most unseemly manner. I happened upon them once in each other's arms, though I said nothing. I didn't want to stir the waters. But soon enough they were discovered.'

'Yet his wife was her hostess?' Everything I have known about Elizabeth shifts in my mind, rearranging itself to accommodate this new information. I can see why she wouldn't want Maman talking too freely of this.

'Her hostess and her stepmother. Imagine! No one ever

thought Elizabeth would be Queen then, of course. Things have a way of turning out how you least expect.'

'And was she –'

'I have said enough. Do not push me further. Just remember, she is not someone to be entirely trusted.'

Maman dips the quill, beginning to write, her spidery hand marking the paper like a line of black-stitch.

Stokes returns, pushing the door open with his foot. He has a platter piled up with all kinds of delicious things, cake amongst them. The letter is set aside.

It feels like a celebration, some kind of midnight feasting, as we gorge ourselves on cake and sip on thick sweet caudle on a dark November morning, serenaded by the robins and redwings singing in the dawn.

December 1559
Sheen Priory
Levina

Levina rummages in her chest for her best black fustian gown. She pulls it out, holding it up by the shoulders, noticing that the moths have got at it, wondering if she has time to get someone to darn it. It must have been packed damp, for it is badly creased and smells slightly of mildew and there is a faint whitish tide mark above the hem too, which she hopes can be got out with a stiff brush. She bundles it up and begins to make her way to the laundry to see if someone there can do something with it before tomorrow. Tomorrow is Frances's funeral.

The thought that Frances is no more makes a knot tighten in Levina's gut, a knot of grief that will never be unpicked. Levina has not been easily befriended by women; it isn't that she is not respected, but she is regarded with suspicion by most, who cannot fully understand her profession as a painter – and she is a foreigner, after all. But Frances was different; they had their shared faith, yes, but more than that, it was a simple rare affinity they had that defied explanation. Sometimes friendship appears from nowhere, like an exotic flower that seeds unexpectedly, and that was the case with Frances. From the first time she visited Bradgate to paint the family an easy bond was forged. Levina wishes more than anything that she'd had the chance to say a proper goodbye.

The messenger had come to Whitehall with the news and Levina had left immediately, with the Queen's blessing. Elizabeth always had respect for Frances, in spite of her choice to marry beneath her, or perhaps because of it. The short journey by boat to Sheen seemed to take an age. She barely noticed the bitter, driving rain – she was numb already. She remembers, on arrival, the lonely black silhouette of Mary standing on the pier, surrounded by the naked November trees, watching the barge approach. As the boat pulled up Mary had taken her hand without a word, just a little shake of the head and a downward turn of her eyes, and they had run into the house and up the stairs, still in silence. Only when they reached the door of Frances's bedchamber did Mary speak.

'She slipped out of consciousness an hour ago.'

Levina could see blotches on the girl's pale skin where she had been crying. But she wasn't crying then, and pulled herself up to her full height, opening the door and saying, as if all was as it should be, 'Maman, Veena is here.'

Frances lay propped up on pillows, her head dipped to one side, cheeks sunken, her lips blue-tinged and hanging open slightly, with a thin trail of saliva trickling from one corner. Levina took out her handkerchief and tenderly wiped it away, only then fully understanding, with a twist of sorrow, that her friend was barely there. She stroked her cheek, feeling the clammy chill of her skin, only just able to hold back her own tears. She had been almost unaware of the other people in the chamber, until Stokes spoke up.

'They say the hearing is the last thing to go,' he said. 'Speak to her, Veena, she will hear you.'

She looked up to see him standing at the foot of the bed beside the chaplain, with his arm around Katherine's shoulders. The girl seemed stricken, staring into space, glassy eyed, a piece of paper hanging limply from her fingers. Peggy Willoughby hovered, half-hidden behind the bed hangings; she lost her brother too not so long ago, and now this, poor child, thought Levina.

'Frances, dear,' she started, but then couldn't think of what to say. She wanted to talk of fond memories but all she could think of was Jane and that horrific, windblown morning at the Tower. 'You will be with her soon.'

Mary ran a cloth over her mother's brow and Levina thought she could see a slight twitching behind her eyelids, a small sign of life. How do they know the hearing is the last thing to go? she wanted to ask. Then it came to her, an epiphany – the one thing Frances would want to hear. She moved close, close enough to see the empty little puncture in her friend's ear where an earring once hung, the sight of it forcing a wave of grief over her, and said, 'I will look after your girls – I promised it before and I promise it now – see they come to no harm.'

It may have been her imagination but she had the impression of something like an exhalation, as if that was the moment Frances chose to leave them. Stokes lay on the bed beside her and took her in his arms, succumbing to great heaving, choking sobs. The girls were grey with shock and Katherine all but collapsed into Levina's arms.

That had been two weeks ago. Levina has stayed at Sheen since, and tomorrow Frances's body will be taken by river to Westminster, where she will be accorded full honours, a state funeral at the abbey – so Elizabeth is happy to recognize her cousin's status in death, when she is no longer a threat. Poor Stokes is so grief-stricken he barely functions and Levina has taken over the smooth running of things, preferring to keep busy.

She knocks gently at the door to the girls' chamber, opening it ajar. They are all on the bed, poring over what appears to be a letter.

'Do you have your dresses prepared for tomorrow?' she asks. 'I am taking mine to the laundry. Can I take anything for you?'

'The maid has seen to our clothes,' says Mary. 'But thank you, Veena.'

'What is that?' Levina asks, pointing to the letter. 'Condolences?'

'No,' says Mary. 'It is a letter. Well a half-letter, really. From Maman to the Queen.'

'What does it say?'

'She was to write and request permission for my marriage,' says Katherine. 'But she has barely written three lines, preamble and reminiscences. Nothing about my wedding. Nothing.'

'Hertford will be here soon, dear,' Levina says, stroking the girl's head. She feels stiff and brittle like a dried flower. 'I'm sure he will have good news for you.'

'He has had nothing from the council,' she replies. 'I *hate* them all, every last one of them, and I hate *her* more.' She gets up and walks to the window. 'He says they want to wait for *her* to decide about *her* marriage.' She bangs her small fists down on the sill so hard she winces. '*Elizabeth* can't bear the idea of anyone else being married if she is not. They won't even broach it. Maman was right; she *is* more artful than her sister. I want my Maman back.' She is sobbing now.

Levina goes to stand next to her, rubbing a palm over the black satin that covers her upper back. She can feel the bones beneath, bird's bones. 'Katherine, we will all do everything we can. You are grieving now; everything is bound to seem all the more hopeless. I overheard Cecil talking the other day. It seems he might take your part. No doubt *he* believes you deserve the respect of the next in line. Cecil is a distant cousin of yours, isn't he?'

'Next in line! I don't want *that*. Look what happened to . . .' She looks for a brief moment like a terrified little girl. 'Even *I* know Cecil can't be trusted.'

She is right, Levina thinks: there is something inestimably dark about Cecil. 'Fret not,' Levina says. 'Elizabeth will birth her own heirs. And Cecil's favour cannot do you harm.'

Katherine has stopped listening. She is pressing her face right up to the uneven windowpanes, looking out at something.

'It's him,' she cries, coming to life. Turning, wiping her eyes on her sleeve and rummaging amongst a stack of clothes, finding a fur-lined cloak, flinging it about her shoulders, searching for something else, apparently not finding it and rushing from the chamber.

'Your shoes, Katherine,' Levina calls after her. 'You cannot go out barefoot in December or we will be burying you next.' But she is gone and in a moment can be seen running at full pelt across the garden, the cloak flying out behind her like wings. She arrives at the pier before the barge has moored and jumps up and down waving, as if she is a little girl. They are all watching her from the window, Peggy, Mary and Levina. There is something infectious about her joy, and God knows, thinks Levina, we all need a little joy at the moment – something to get us through tomorrow, when that barefoot girl down there needs to hold herself together enough to stand as chief mourner.

'Juno is with him,' says Peggy.

'So she is. That will cheer her up doubly,' Levina says.

Hertford is standing in his boat now, swaying about, and the craft looks fit to capsize. His sister is tugging him by the hand in what appears to be an attempt to get him to sit down, as the poor oarsmen are struggling to keep the vessel upright. The moment it touches the pier, Hertford is out and Katherine is off the ground and in his arms. It is a sight to behold. Juno is helped out and she too is subsumed into the huddle. When they have done with their embrace, Hertford scoops Katherine up and carries her back to the house with Juno beside them.

Once she has delivered her dress to the laundry, Levina joins them all where they have gathered about the hearth with Stokes, who seems a little renewed. They are passing around cups of hot, spiced wine and Levina is reminded that it will be Christmas before long. It has been a full year since Elizabeth came to the throne.

'Cheer us up, Hertford,' says Stokes. 'Give us news from court.'

'The thing everyone is talking about is Mary of Scotland. Somehow the Queen discovered that she had quartered the English arms with her husband's French ones.'

'So she claims the English throne. That is a bold gesture. The little Frog king doesn't plan an invasion, does he?' laughs Stokes. 'How old is he, fourteen?'

'It seems unlikely,' says Hertford. 'But Mary Stuart's Guise uncles might, on behalf of Scotland. The Queen is beside herself with rage.'

'Not surprising,' says Katherine. Her face is flushed from the wine and she slurs a little.

'The Privy Council are hot under their collars,' adds Hertford.

'I can imagine.'

'And as for Dudley . . .'

'Yes,' adds Juno, 'Dudley and Norfolk almost came to fisticuffs the other day and it is rumoured a fellow has gone to the Tower for attempted murder.'

'Of Dudley?' asks Stokes.

'Yes, Dudley. People are wondering if he'll last till Christmas. Cecil loathes him as much as Norfolk does. But the Queen –'

'Can't keep her hands off him,' interrupts Juno.

'If she would only hurry up and decide who she will wed, then . . .' Katherine doesn't finish and silence falls for a moment.

Hearing of court makes Levina glad to have been away from it for a couple of weeks, though the reason for her being here is such a distressing one. Frances's absence follows her about like a shadow.

'Oh,' says Juno, breaking the hush. 'I forgot to give you this.' She passes Katherine a letter. 'From the Spanish embassy.'

'What do *they* want?' says Hertford.

'Who cares?' chirps Katherine, draining her cup and holding it out for a refill. She puts the letter in her lap and swigs from her cup again. Hertford shares a smile with his sister.

'But on a lighter note,' Hertford says, 'the Queen is showing favour to your dear mother with a full state funeral. I think it may well be the moment, after the proceedings of course, to present the Queen with the letter. Don't you?'

The room falls silent. Levina looks at Hertford anew,

seeing the youth and ambition bursting from him, wondering if this boy doesn't have an ulterior motive after all. Everybody knows that any son he produced in wedlock with Katherine would have a greater claim to the throne than all those royal girls put together. But no, she reminds herself of the passionate greeting she witnessed from the window earlier – if that is not a man in love then she doesn't know what is.

'It was what your mother wanted.' Doubt creeps into Hertford's tone. He continues, trying to fill the uneasy silence. 'It would be a fitting –'

'There is no letter,' states Stokes, stopping him in mid-flow.

'What do you mean?' snaps Hertford. 'What do you mean, no letter?' His eyes flit back and forth, and it is as if all his assurance has deserted him.

Stokes tactfully asks if Hertford will join him in taking the dogs out, slapping an arm across the young man's shoulders, leading him from the room and whistling for the little pack to follow.

Levina sees the other letter has slipped unnoticed from Katherine's lap.

'Let's go up,' slurs Katherine, draining the dregs from her cup once more, and tugging Juno's sleeve. They get up, Katherine stumbling slightly and leaning heavily on her friend.

'Keep an eye on her,' Levina whispers to Juno. 'She is a little the worse for wear.'

Mary and Peggy both look wan with sorrow and fatigue, and Levina doesn't know how they will cope with the funeral. 'Why don't I ask the kitchen to send you something to sup on in your chamber? Then you can rest. Tomorrow will be a long day.'

Mary hangs back as the others leave the room.

'What is it, Mary?' asks Veena.

'Must I go to court? Can I not stay here with Stokes?'

'I'm afraid you must, Mary. The Queen has commanded it.' The girl slumps miserably and Levina's first instinct is to wrap her arms about her, feeling a surge of maternal love, but she stops herself, remembering that Mary can't stand to be touched. '*I* will be there, and Peggy too. And Katherine. You will be amongst friends and family, at least. But you can't defy the Queen.' It seems that Elizabeth wants to keep a close eye on her cousins.

When they are gone Levina picks up the forgotten letter, hesitating before ripping open the seal. It is from Jane Dormer: . . . *We are making progress, dear Katherine, with plans for a match. Don Carlos is the son of King Felipe, he is yet young but he would be a fitting husband for a woman of your stature . . .*

Levina screws the paper up and flings it on the fire without thinking. It was inevitable, she supposes, that Feria would turn back to Katherine now the French are looking troublesome once more. She can see it all now. The Spaniard would counter Mary of Scotland and the French king's claim by marrying his own son off to Katherine Grey, would he? She has an image of Cecil rubbing his waxy hands together at such an idea, and a shiver of fear runs through her. Suddenly Hertford, whatever his motive, seems by far the better proposition. But love and ambition make uneasy bedfellows. She feels the weight of responsibility hanging heavily over her, and fears she will struggle to keep these girls out of harm's way without Frances in the background.

IV

Kitty and Mouse

September 1560
Hampton Court
Mary

'Where did those come from, Lady Katherine?' says Kat Astley, pointing to the decorated gloves that my sister is unwrapping. I am in a corner of the presence chamber sewing with Peggy and Mistress St Low, who has dropped off and is snoring slightly. Mistress St Low is charged to take care of the Queen's maids, myself included. She is a solid, motherly sort and kindly enough, but she cannot begin to fill the great chasm of emptiness that was carved out of me when Maman died. Maman has been gone almost a year now. Our family is shrunk to a meagre two; it is a sorry excuse for a tribe. I watch Katherine on the far side of the chamber with Juno and Kat Astley, whom I have spent the last year assiduously trying to avoid. Of all the ladies, she is closest to the Queen and does not seem fond of us Greys.

'I don't know, Mistress Astley,' Katherine says. 'The package was handed me by one of the pages.' I can tell she is trying to sound respectful, but a sliver of insolence lies beneath her words. She cannot help it. 'A gift for Her Majesty, the messenger said.'

'Here! Show me.' Kat Astley beckons her sharply with a hand. 'Is there a letter?'

'I haven't seen one.' Katherine begins to burrow amongst

the wrapping, eventually pulling out a fold of paper, which is snatched smartly from her.

'But the treaty with France and Scotland was signed weeks ago and Marie of Guise is dead,' says Juno.

I suppose she means there is no longer a need to be suspicious of offerings for the Queen. For months we have been burning gifts – candied fruits, jewelled gloves, scented handkerchiefs, finely tooled books of poems, and gallons of exotic perfumes have been given to the pages to pour down the jakes – ever since the rumour came of the Guise plot to poison Elizabeth.

'You can never be too careful,' says Kat Astley, reading something written on the note but not sharing it. 'Put them on the hearth.'

'But there is no fire,' says Katherine with a little smirk. Kat Astley looks towards the empty fireplace with her lips drawn tight like a leather pouch.

'Give them to me.' She holds out her hand, but then seems flustered, snatching it back. 'No don't give them to me. Wrap them up again and *then* give them to me.'

'So you don't mind *Lady Katherine* risking herself on poisoned gloves, but not you,' says Juno, taking one of the offending objects and waving it close to the woman's horrified face.

I swap a look with Peggy; she raises her eyes to the ceiling. We both know it doesn't do to cross Kat Astley. But a part of me admires Juno's gall – she will say anything to anyone.

'Lady Jane, kindly desist.' Juno drops the glove to the floor. Kat Astley looks like thunder.

'Just leave them,' says Juno, taking my sister by the hand. 'We will be late anyway.'

'She's right,' says Katherine. 'You wouldn't want to make us late for the Queen's hunting party now.'

The woman is purple with rage.

'Where is your sister?' she calls out. 'I need her to help finish stitching the ornamental –'

'I am here, Mistress Astley,' I say. Peggy shifts, arching her back like a cat, with a little groan; she will be leaving court for her lying-in before long. I cannot bear the thought of her departure. Katherine comes over to me and plants a kiss on my cheek. She smells faintly of lemons and I wonder if it is the vestiges of Hertford's pomade. They have been trysting in secret – but there are no secrets my sister can keep from me. 'We *are* working on the ornamental birds.' I hold up my embroidery as evidence.

'So you are,' says Kat Astley.

'Your stitching is beautifully intricate, Mouse,' Katherine says. 'I almost think that finch there might fly away by itself. You are doubtless the deftest needlewoman at court.' Kat Astley scowls. She believes the accolade belongs to her, as Katherine well knows.

'No one would disagree with that,' adds Juno, taking my sister's hand and marching towards the doors.

As she tentatively picks up the offending gloves, protecting her hand with a piece of the wrapping, I hear Kat Astley mutter, 'To think, she has been made a Lady of the Bedchamber – whatever next.' She has made no bones about her disapproval of the fact that the Queen seems to be warming to my sister and has bestowed this further privilege on her.

A pair of lovebirds twitters in a cage beside me, egg-yolk yellow with blushing faces – they were a gift from Dudley to the Queen. 'I'm surprised she didn't make us burn those too,' I whisper to Peggy, who brings a hand to her mouth to disguise her snort of laughter. I scoop up a little of the bird seed, pouring it through the bars, and am tempted to open their prison and set them free. I wonder if they know there is a better life than the one they have.

The far doors are opened and the Queen sweeps in, dressed in her riding habit, with a collection of councillors. I remember once hearing a group of courtiers described as a threat – a threat of courtiers, how very apt. Mistress St Low starts out of her nap in response to a poke from Kat Astley and we drop into curtsies, but the Queen is deep in conversation with Cecil and doesn't look our way. Eventually, Kat Astley, who is bustling about seeming to be busy, indicates silently for us to continue with our stitching.

'You *must* make her sign it,' the Queen is saying. 'If she won't, it is a sure indication that she continues to believe she has a claim on *our* throne. Peace treaty or not, it means Scotland remains our enemy. All that good work you did will be undone, Cecil.'

I suppose they are talking of the Scottish Queen, who is proving stubborn in her belief that the English throne belongs to her.

'Your Majesty, I have done all I am able. We must not forget she is an . . .' Cecil pauses. 'She cannot be *made* to do it.'

'Yes, yes, an anointed Queen. Oh come, Cecil.' The Queen's tone is sardonic. 'You have a few tricks up your sleeve, we are sure.'

I am thinking about how it must be to feel your heels snapped at perpetually as hers are, how hard it must make you.

'Will you stop clucking around,' she says, giving Kat Astley, who is making an attempt to tie the Queen's riding hat on, a little shove and snatching the hat, tying it on herself. 'Now to my Master of Horse.' She says this with one eye on Cecil, who looks suitably disapproving. Everybody knows he cannot stand Dudley. A part of me admires the way she has these men dancing back and forth. She knows exactly what she is doing, is quite the puppet master, and has none of the self-doubt her sister had.

'And, Your Majesty,' says Cecil diffidently, 'the coinage –'

'Yes, yes,' she interrupts. 'Have Northumberland arrange it.'

'It is an expensive measure, Your –'

'The coinage of England stands for our reputation. It is our face on it, not yours. We will not have our face on such debased coin. What kind of message is that for the world?'

Cecil shrinks slightly and there is a general nodding of assent amongst the councillors as they move on through the chamber. When they are gone, quiet descends and I am content at the thought of an entire day of calm, for most have joined the hunting party. I crave solitude greatly and there is so very little to be found, these days, even at night, for us maids are crammed in a single chamber together like salted fish packed tight in a barrel. I long for the peace of my bedchamber at Sheen and being able to lose myself in a book without it being snatched off me and thrown about, which is a great game for some.

Katherine

The courtyard is high with the stench of fresh horse dung and alive with people. Grooms are running to and fro, bringing last-minute necessaries, tightening girth-straps, lengthening stirrups, helping riders mount their horses. Dudley is trotting back and forth on a skittish black Barbary named Bellaface, barking out orders, assigning horses.

'Is Delicate ready for Her Majesty?' he calls out to one of the grooms. 'Quarters chequered?'

'Aye, M'lud.'

'Hooves oiled?'

'Aye, M'lud.

'Mane plaited?'

'Aye, M'lud, and beribboned.'

'Whiskers trimmed?'

'Aye, M'lud, I never did see a mare look so fine.'

'Bring her out, then, so I can look at her.' The boy scurries off. Though there are at least two dozen senior grooms to do his bidding, Dudley always likes to inspect the Queen's mount himself. I watch him for a moment. He cuts a fine figure and the way he handles the difficult Bellaface is impressive, making little clicking sounds to calm him and giving him a long rein, when others might make him more nervous by pulling his mouth back. He catches me looking.

'Like what you see?' he asks.

'I like your horse.'

He laughs. 'I have given you Gentle today, Lady Katherine.'

'Truly?' I ask. Gentle is one of his favourites and I have become unused to such preference.

'Indeed,' he says with a grin. 'Her Majesty made a point of asking that you be given one of the better horses.' I can see Gentle being led over now. He is a chestnut gelding with a sweet temperament and a white star between his eyes.

'I am honoured,' I say, scratching Gentle on his star. He flares his nostrils in pleasure and huffs out a billow of hot breath towards my neck. I stroke the velvet-soft tip of his nose and place a kiss there.

'Got one for me?' quips Dudley.

'Don't be silly,' I say. Dudley is always like this with me when the Queen is not about. It is harmless, his flirting, just a sign he is on my side. Or that is what I suppose. I wonder if this new favour I have with Elizabeth isn't something to do with *his* influence. There has even been talk of her adopting me; not to my face, but people tell me things and what is discussed in the council meetings leaks out one way or another. It would appeal to Cecil, I'm sure, to have the succession secured in such a way, he is kin of some sort, after all. Perhaps it was *his* suggestion. Juno thinks Cecil champions me. She says it is because he would do anything to prevent Mary of Scotland getting her Catholic backside on the throne of England. I flatten a twisted strap on Gentle's bridle.

'Let him have his head,' Dudley says. 'And go easy on the whip. He won't need much encouragement.' He wheels round and leaves me with the groom, who helps me mount.

Juno is up as well and pointing out her two brothers across the yard. 'Let's join them.'

We nudge our horses forward to where Hertford and his younger brother Henry are sharing a stirrup cup. Just the sight of Hertford makes my insides churn, and I am awash with thoughts of our snatched moments alone together – a glorious year of secret trysts.

'We shall be accompanied by the finest beauties of the entire court,' says Henry, by way of a greeting.

'I wouldn't say that too loudly,' I quip. 'There is someone who wouldn't appreciate it.'

As if on cue, the Queen appears. Dudley helps her mount, as is his duty – he is the only man with the right to touch the Queen's body – and it shows on his face each time he does it, as if he has taken ownership of her. She signals for him to fall in beside her as she picks up the pace, trotting out through the arch. The rest of us urge our horses on to keep up. Hertford is beside me, our legs pressed together in the crowd; he allows his hand to brush mine. The thrill is as fresh as it was that first evening at Hanworth when I was pretending I did not care a fig for him. I smile to myself, remembering. Our eyes meet, he winks, I blow him a kiss, not caring who sees. Our so-called secret is quite well known, amongst our friends at least, but the Queen is sufficiently preoccupied with her own passion that she seems entirely blind to ours.

Uncle Arundel has sidled up beside Juno. He is wearing the most inappropriately over-embellished doublet, with a swinging cape fringed in gold, and looks as if he is off to a banquet rather than out hunting.

'Lady Jane,' he says. 'Would you do me the honour of allowing me to ride with you?'

'My Lord,' she replies, 'I have promised Lady Katherine that I shall accompany *her*.'

'Then I shall escort you both.' Juno and I exchange a look and I try not to laugh. Hertford and Henry *are* laughing.

'Arise, Sir January,' whispers Hertford to his brother, but not so quiet that *I* can't hear it. Arundel has made no secret of the fact that he wants Juno's hand and since he is nearly fifty and she only nineteen we have dubbed her Lady May and he Sir January. He has given her a miniature of himself dressed as a Roman emperor with all his hair miraculously and abundantly returned to his head and all the creases ironed from his skin. It is not one of Levina's; *she* wouldn't take flattery to such lengths.

'You find something amusing, My Lords?' This is directed at Hertford and Henry, who are red-faced with laughter. 'You think me an old fool like the one in Chaucer's tale, do you?'

Both boys look abashed and Hertford begins to form an apology, but Arundel continues.

'You should be careful where you throw your insults, Hertford. You may need my influence one day.'

'They meant no harm, Uncle,' I say in my softest voice, touching a hand to his sleeve. 'They are only envious of your . . .' I am about to say manliness but stop myself, for it occurs to me that it might be interpreted as an extension of the jest. 'Riches and command.'

'Ha!' he puffs, seeming satisfied, mumbling 'riches and command' under his breath, with something that resembles a smile, and flicking his crop over his horse's quarters.

Once out in the open we all break into a canter. I give Gentle his head, as Dudley bid me, and feel the strength of him, his exhilaration. The horses' hooves against the hard summer ground make the sound of a thousand drummers, and I am gripped with excitement, urging Gentle on to a gallop, feeling pleasure and laughter bubbling up in my throat. The Queen is far ahead with Dudley, who struggles to keep with her and her pack of deerhounds streaking beside her. One picks up a scent with an ebullient yelp and Elizabeth yells, 'Hoy!' further picking up speed.

Hertford is beside me on his roan mare. I watch how the muscles of his legs ripple as they grip at her flanks. I look behind to see Juno and Henry coming up.

'I see you have shaken off Sir January,' I call out, above the thunder.

'His horse was lame, he had to call for another.'

'Seems God is on your side, Sister,' cries Hertford, causing us all to laugh.

The countryside is parched; most of the crops have been harvested now, leaving dry stubble with stacks of hay punctuating the view. The river is a silver ribbon in the distance. The hounds circle back towards it. The Queen, riding, as ever, like a demon, turns and shouts something to Dudley, who is a length behind her. The wind has detached my hair from its ties, I can feel it flying out behind me and my breath is quick with effort, but Gentle still has plenty of go in him. We are approaching a spinney. The Queen and Dudley have slowed to a canter and the hounds are baying about the edge of the trees. The buck must have taken cover in there.

'Find him! In you go,' cries Dudley, urging on the hounds,

who disappear into the undergrowth. All the riders have crowded about the edge of the copse, hoping for an early kill.

'This is your moment,' says Juno, tapping my arm. 'Slip away before the beast breaks cover.' She calls to her manservant, 'Mister Glynne, would you accompany Lady Katherine back to the palace?'

Hertford catches my eye, drawing up beside me. 'You go first, my sweet,' he whispers. 'I'll follow on in a few minutes and meet you in Juno's rooms.' He points vaguely in the direction of the palace. There is a hullabaloo from within the spinney; the buck must be at bay in there and I feel a moment of regret for the animal, there in the dark, surrounded.

On my return I meet Uncle Arundel on his fresh mount. I tell him I am suffering from a slight ague and point to where he can find the rest of the field.

'Glad to see you have someone to accompany you,' he says, indicating in the general direction of Mister Glynne. 'Would you like me to come and seek out my physician for you?'

'My sister will be there and Mistress Astley; they will take care of me. I have more need of rest than a physician, I think. Don't miss the hunt on my account, Uncle.' He looks relieved not to have to play the chivalrous role.

'If you are certain.'

'I am, Uncle.' I urge Gentle into a sedate walk, only increasing my pace when Arundel is out of sight. I hope he will not also come upon Hertford heading the same way as I. I imagine the big tester bed in Juno's rooms, sinking into it, with Hertford's lean arms clutched about me. But beneath my eagerness I feel something else. I am tired of the subterfuge, of having to always take care not to find myself with child. I have had enough of remembering the stinging vinegar-soaked ball of wool, the tinctures of rue and Queen Anne's lace, of the worry each month that my courses will not come. And Elizabeth may be entwined in her own affairs but things have a way of getting out. I long to spend a whole night in his arms, but I know a single night would not be enough. I am twenty now and should by rights be wed. But there is not a soul who would dare broach the idea of the match with Elizabeth. Perhaps *I* will approach her. If no one else has the stomach, then why not me?

When I get to Juno's chamber I am surprised to find Hertford is already waiting for me, stretched out on the bed with his doublet undone and his boots flung on to the floor.

'What kept you?' he says. He doesn't return my smile and is holding something in his fist that I cannot see.

'How did you get here so fast?' I press the door shut behind my back, leaning against it. I can see a few twists of golden hair where he has loosened the lacing of his linen shirt.

'I saw Arundel with you and skirted round, not to be spotted.' He looks me up and down in silence. 'What is this?' He waves a small silver relic box containing a phial of rust-coloured liquid, supposed to be the blood of St Francis. 'Been flirting with popish superstitions?'

'It is nothing. Just a gift from the Spanish ambassador,' I say.

'What does he imagine you are going to do with this?' His jaw clenches and he flings the little box at the far wall. It opens and the phial shatters, creating a small dark puddle on the floor.

'I don't know. People give me presents all the time. You know what those Spaniards are like about their relics.' What I do not tell him is that Jane Dormer has written, more than once, talking anew of the Spanish match.

'Bolt the door,' he barks. I do as he bids, sliding the bar over its fixing. 'I will not have you accept things like that. Send it back.'

'It is broken. I cannot. Besides, I do not welcome such tokens. You know that.'

'I'm not completely blind, Kitty,' he says, scowling. 'I know there are some who would have you wed to Spain.'

'But I will not marry Spain. I will marry Hertford,' I say, and watch the spite fall away from him.

'Now come here.' His voice is a growl. 'The colour of your riding habit doesn't suit you; I think it needs to be removed.'

I wake to an urgent rapping, momentarily confused. The late-afternoon sun is blazing in through the window and for a moment I wonder where I am. The rapping starts up again. I sit up in an attempt to wake myself, and see Hertford's naked body sprawled beside me. My mouth curls into an involuntary smile.

'It is Juno. Let me in.' I crawl from the bed, wrap myself in a blanket and undo the bolt, opening the door. 'You took your time,' she says, slipping into the chamber, and on seeing her brother she adds, 'Cover yourself, Ned.' He rummages about for his trunk hose, pulling them on, and sits on the edge of the bed rubbing his eyes with his fists. I sit beside him and bring my nose to his shoulder, breathing in his scent – he smells of me – my mind drifting back to the intimacies of an hour ago.

'What is it, Sister; is something wrong?'

It is only then that I notice the look of contained panic in Juno's eyes.

'Something has happened,' she says. We are both looking at her, waiting for her to continue. 'Dudley's wife is dead.'

'Everyone expected that, she had a malady of the breast,' says Hertford.

'No. I mean yes, but . . .' She stops, as if trying to work out how to put it. 'She was killed and it was made to look like an accident.'

'Oh,' I sigh, thinking of poor Amy Dudley, whom I have never met but often thought of, with her husband dancing about the Queen constantly and she never seen but always whispered about.

'I suppose people think it done by Dudley's order?' says Hertford.

'Most, yes. An investigation has been launched. Dudley has left the palace and the Queen will admit no one, save Lady Knollys, Kat Astley and Cecil, of course.'

'How did it happen?' I ask.

'I know only what I have heard, but it is on everyone's lips. Amy Dudley sent the entire household at Cumnor Place off to the village fair this morning and when they returned they found her with a broken neck at the bottom of some steps.'

'So it could easily have been an accident,' says Hertford.

'Just a pair of stairs – how can you break your neck falling down a pair of stairs?'

'True,' he replies.

I cannot stop thinking about the poor woman and her miserable life, wondering if she is not better off dead, imagining what it must have been like to be her, knowing the Queen wished her gone so she could have her husband for herself. But I am also thinking of myself, as usual, and that Amy Dudley's suspicious death has thwarted my plans to petition the Queen with my request to wed.

'Do you think she took her own life?' I ask.

'Some have said it. But most are calling it murder.'

'She can't marry Dudley now,' I say. 'Not now people think him a murderer.'

'You are right, Kitty,' says Hertford. 'They will never be able to marry without seeming guilty. *Cecil* is the one who gains most from this affair. He would have done anything to prevent the Queen from marrying Dudley.'

'Are you saying it is Cecil's doing?' asks Juno, clapping a hand over her mouth as if to censor herself.

'I am not saying anything and neither must you,' he says. 'Cecil is not one to cross.' He gets up and begins to dress himself before leaving with a warning: 'Go carefully. We don't know what the outcome of all this might be. Who knows if the Queen will survive this scandal.'

Juno and I dress hastily and go to the presence chamber, which has been laid out for supper. Mary is there, looking white as a winding cloth. Indeed, everyone seems horrified by the news and we all sit down to eat, just the Queen's ladies, no one else, in virtual silence. The Queen herself doesn't make an appearance but Kat Astley comes out, haggard with worry, carrying each of her sixty years on her face. She asks one of the servers to prepare a platter of food, which she takes in herself, without ceremony, coming back out for a flagon of ale, closing the door behind her without a word.

I remember the gloves from this morning, thinking of all the fears we had that someone would try to poison Elizabeth and in the end it is poor Amy Dudley who has met an untimely death. They say her marriage to Dudley was a love match, that they cared deeply for each other and that he married her against his father's wishes. You only do that when it is love. That makes me think of Harry Herbert and I feel a pang of sadness, for I truly believed I loved him and then it was gone, like the pop of a bubble, and I wonder if that is how Dudley's love for Amy went, all in one go. I resolve that

I will never stop loving Hertford, that *our* bubble will never burst – just the thought of it makes me feel sick to the stomach and, worse, the thought of Hertford's love for me popping to nothing.

Mary seems exhausted, black rings circling her eyes, and Mistress St Low suggests I take her to settle her in the maids' chamber. She doesn't speak as we walk the length of the corridor, only saying as I open the door, 'Empty, thank goodness. I can have the bed to myself for a few minutes.'

Once Mary is out of her things, I help her into bed and we lie alongside each other, little fingers interlinked. 'I wish Veena was here,' she says.

'She will be back before long.'

'I wonder what her home is like.'

'She lives at Ludgate, doesn't she?' I realize that it has never occurred to me to think about Levina's real life, away from court.

'She has a husband and a son,' says Mary.

'I didn't know.'

'Yes, Marcus is her son. He is away on the Continent and her husband, George, is in the Queen's guard.'

I berate myself internally for not knowing any of this when Levina is such a dear friend to us, for not asking, for being so wrapped up in my own affairs that I forget to think about anyone else.

'Do you miss Maman?' I ask.

'Of course I do.'

'I do too,' I say, not even realizing quite how much until the words are uttered. It is as if the two of us are floating unmoored on a small raft in the ocean with not a parent or sibling to our names. 'Thank God for Veena,' I add.

'If you marry Hertford,' she says quietly, 'do you think you will set up house somewhere and I can live there with you?

With you and the dogs and Hercules, and Veena can visit and you will have little ones that I shall help care for. We would be like a proper family again, Kitty. I could create a fine library there for you, and people shall come from far and wide to seek out our rare volumes.' She sounds as if she is telling a story.

'*When* I marry him,' I reply, but it all seems so very intangible, so very far off, for the two of us are stuck here at court, at the Queen's pleasure. It is a kind of prison when I think of it. And now there is this scandal and all is on the brink of shifting once more, so yet again my dream of marriage seems to slip further and further away. 'I will do my very best to make it happen, Mouse.'

October 1560
Greenwich
Mary

A group of us are gathered close in about the hearth, sewing, encircled by the yellow glow of candles. Levina and Mistress St Low are talking quietly across the room. I am glad to have Levina back at court, for I felt quite lost without her. Katherine is nowhere to be seen and I am wondering where she has got to, for she hasn't appeared since dinner at midday. Though it is barely four of the clock, autumn sits gloomily over the palace. I hear the unmistakable honk of geese flying over and turn towards the window, but cannot see them. That is a sure sign that autumn is almost gone. Daylight has become a rare commodity and I can sense the edges of winter, the dismal stretch of cold dark months that awaits us. I dread the day it becomes too cold to walk out, for a stroll in the gardens is the only solitude I have. I remain raw with grief for Maman, as if I have been flayed, and pine for the glorious simplicity of my old life. Those precious moments of quiet give me the chance to think of her.

There is barely a moment alone at court and I am herded about with this bunch of spiteful maids, who, when they are not gossiping about Dudley's misadventures, talk only of whom they will marry, or who has caught their eye, or which one they have kissed or which they want to, ad nauseam. I turned fifteen this year, marriageable age – now there is an irony. But at least I have Juno and my sister to defend me, though Katherine is more often slunk off with Hertford, whenever the Queen's back is turned.

Cecil parades through the outer chamber with his entourage, ignoring the bustling petitioners and their attempts to gain his attention. His eyes flit about, giving the impression that he misses nothing, and there is something about his exquisitely tailored black damask, with its careful embroidery and the quietly expensive touches of gold here and there – a buckle, a ring, a row of buttons – that makes him seem dissembling. Since Dudley's banishment he has taken on the look of a dog triumphantly marking out its territory, which belies the discretion of his garb.

We all look up from our stitching to watch him pass, but he doesn't look at us until he is at the far end of the room, almost at the entrance to the privy chamber. Only then does he turn briefly and cast his eyes over us women slowly, as if taking a head count, before disappearing through the door. I imagine a puff of smoke left behind him. He is one of the few the Queen will see since the scandal broke with Dudley. No one is permitted to talk of it, but they do, speculating in corners as to who might have been behind this murder. For there is no doubt, in my mind, that it was murder, although the official word is 'accident'. Cecil's men are left waiting outside, leaning against the wainscoting, appraising the women in the room, talking in hushed voices. One flashes a wink at Lettice Knollys, who is seated next to me.

'Who's that?' Juno asks her in a whisper.

'Oh, him. He used to work for my father.'

'And,' says Juno, 'why was he winking at you?'

Lettice, who bears a striking likeness to the Queen, though in my opinion is a good deal more beautiful, taps the side of her aquiline nose with her forefinger and raises a single eyebrow.

'Lettice Knollys,' says Juno.

'Actually, he is a good source of gossip.' She smiles conspiratorially. 'He told me something that Mary of Scotland said.' Lettice leans in and all the women follow suit. 'She said that the Queen of England is about to marry her horse keeper, who has murdered his wife to make way for her.'

'What, publicly? Is the Queen aware she said that?' asks Frances Meautas.

'If not, she will be soon,' says Juno.

'She will be incensed at such a slight,' says Frances.

'The Scottish Queen is only saying what half the court thinks,' I mutter, more loudly than I realize, as Frances turns to me with a face bitter as dandelion greens.

'*You* may be thinking it but I am not, Mary Grey.' She makes a stabbing motion towards me with a pointed finger.

'Of course I'm not thinking it,' I say sharply. 'Dudley is not so much of a fool as to have his wife murdered, knowing that the suspicion would fall on him.'

Frances exhales loudly, turning her nose to the ceiling. 'It is wrong for another Queen to say such a thing publicly, even in jest.'

Lizzie Mansfield, who is relatively new to court and has

adhered herself to Frances Meautas, throws me a look that would freeze Hell over. I make myself hold her gaze until she looks away. I am learning how to negotiate this place.

'I'm sick of hearing about that business,' says Frances. 'No one has talked of anything else since it happened. Besides, this place is dull indeed without Dudley about. Do you think we will ever have any music or dancing again?' She sighs dramatically.

'Not if Cecil has anything to do with it,' says Juno. 'I believe he comes out in a rash if he gets too close to anyone who is enjoying themselves.' This provokes some muffled laughter.

'Dancing,' I utter, though I do not mean to say it out loud. I am thinking of a time long ago, when I learned a few steps.

'What do *you* care about dancing?' spits Lizzie. 'You can barely walk in a straight line as it is.' She looks around the group for support, catching Frances's eye, exchanging a little nod with her and a couple of the others.

In an instant my hand flies out, needle pinched between thumb and forefinger, making sharp contact with Lizzie's bare wrist.

'Ow!' squeals Lizzie like a stuck pig, snatching back her hand and bringing her wrist to her mouth.

Frances makes an indignant gasp. 'You *can't* do that.' She places a protective arm around Lizzie, who has now descended into outraged sobbing.

My head is spinning with what I have just done; I have shocked even myself, for I usually keep such a tight grip on my anger. Shaped as I am, people expect me to be doubly virtuous as proof I am not the Devil's issue. But it is as if a little demon has colonized my heart, for I am enjoying Lizzie's anguish and I can see I have allies in Juno and Lettice, who are holding their needlework up to their faces to cover their mirth.

'What's going on?' says Mistress St Low, approaching us.

'She pricked me with her needle,' Lizzie squeals, pointing at me.

'It was an accident,' announces Juno. 'Wasn't it, Lettice?'

'It was,' adds Lettice.

'I am truly most sorry, Lizzie dear,' I say. 'I took fright when a log fell in the fire. I was jolted.' I am quite surprised at the ease with which the falsehood slips out of me. I like it more than I should.

'Try and be more careful,' Mistress St Low says.

'But . . .' sobs Lizzie.

'She has apologized, Lizzie, and no one ever died of a little prick.'

Lettice emits a burst of laughter, trying to disguise it as a sneeze.

'Bless you!' says Juno, pressing her lips hard together, presumably to stop herself from laughing too.

I hope it will put a stop to Frances and Lizzie's constant taunting. It is a triumph of sorts and I can feel a little warm swelling in my chest. It occurs to me that Jane would have been horrified by what I have just done. I can feel her disapproval tapping at me and I think of Peggy too. I am glad she wasn't here to see it. I can imagine the look on her face. She is not so full of pent-up anger as I seem to be.

She birthed her baby boy last month. The Queen refused me leave to visit her, but I write daily and thank the Lord she survived her lying-in, for many do not. I reach for the blue thread, unwinding a length, and snip it off, sucking the end of it to thread my needle. The blue is for a row of small parakeets that Levina designed as the border of some hangings for the Queen. I am reminded of poor Forget-me-not and wonder how it happened that my life became like his, scratching about in a gilded cage, repeating the ends of people's sentences, feeling once more a surge of that anger.

Levina comes to sit beside me, sliding along the settle away from the others, drawing me along with her. She unrolls a new design across my lap – more exotic birds for the Queen's bed. 'They are beautiful,' I say. And they are, flying over the paper with their bright plumage. I lean my head back to the wall, closing my eyes for a moment, enjoying the blackness. How I wish I could install myself at Ludgate with Levina and her husband, but my sister and I can barely sneeze without the Queen's say-so, and she is keeping us uncomfortably close these days.

'Where is Katherine?' Levina asks quietly.

'With Hertford, I suppose.'

'I worry about that. If the Queen gets wind of it – or worse, if she finds herself with child.'

'I know. I worry for her too.' I suddenly feel so very tired – tired of always having those close to me stalked by danger. 'I wish Kitty could . . .' I stop, unsure of what I mean to say.

'Could . . . ?'

'Just be herself.'

The door to the privy chamber swings open and Cecil reappears, setting the petitioners twitching once more, gathering his entourage about him; talking to them in a low voice. At that moment Katherine bursts into the chamber out of breath, with Echo in her arms and two of the other dogs trotting behind. She is quite dishevelled, her coif at an angle, her hair falling out of its ties, and there is a line of worry running vertically between her brows.

'Lady Katherine,' says Cecil, turning to her. 'Where have you been?' There is a threat hidden beneath his steady voice that makes my insides shrink slightly.

It is as if Katherine draws herself together with an intake

of breath and, standing as tall as is possible for someone of her slight stature, she says, 'I have had some trouble with my pet monkey, My Lord. Hercules bit one of the pages – drew blood. I had to deal with it.' She smiles disarmingly at the man and hugs Echo more tightly to her. So that is where I developed my talent for fibbing – of course, Katherine is the expert in that art.

Cecil nods slowly, revealing nothing, and then leaves, disappearing like a shadow, entourage in his wake.

Katherine collapses on to the bench beside us, puffing out a sigh, setting Echo on to her lap and whispering, 'It's not what you think.'

'What's the matter, dear?' asks Levina, leaning across me to stroke the back of her hand.

'He's disappeared.' I can see now that she is trying to blink back tears. 'We were to meet at the river gate and he didn't come.'

'I'm sure there is a simple explanation,' says Levina.

'There is.' I see a flash of anger run through her. 'I saw Harry Herbert in the long gallery. He told me that Cecil had warned Hertford off me.'

'But Harry Herbert,' I say. 'He may be making mischief. He must be jealous, surely?'

'I don't know.' She drops her face into her cupped palms.

From the side of my eye I notice Frances Meautas pull something out from beneath her dress; it is a letter. 'If you're looking for Hertford,' she says with a sly smile, 'he is gone to his house at Canon Row.'

'How would *you* know that?' Katherine snaps.

'He sent me this.' She hands over the fold of paper with a moue of triumph.

Katherine takes it, opening it eagerly. 'A poem! *He* sent *you* a poem?' She cannot quite disguise the fault in her voice and holds the offending paper between her thumb and forefinger away from her body. I catch sight of the title: 'The Long Love That in My Thought Doth Harbour'. It is one of Wyatt's, they are quite the fashion at the moment.

Frances snatches it back, folding it carefully and tucking it once more next to her heart. All the while she looks directly at Katherine, and I am wondering how it is possible that Hertford could want to send a poem to a girl who has the allure of a turnip. I could understand were it Lettice, but Frances Meautas doesn't even have charm or kindness on her side. Juno has moved over to where we are now and is standing between Katherine and Frances, who turns back to Lizzie Mansfield, whispering something in her ear, provoking giggles. I am glad for that needle, would happily do it again.

'Did you know about this?' Levina asks Juno.

'Of course not,' she whispers. 'I haven't seen my brother for a couple of days. I would have said something.' She looks almost as upset as Katherine. 'Come on, Kitty. Let's go to my rooms. It is too dark for sewing now, anyway.' She holds her hand out, Katherine takes it and they leave together in silence.

I find them later in Juno's rooms. Katherine had given in to her tears if the redness of her eyes is anything to go by. But she seems to have pulled herself together and the two of them are playing primero on the bed, using pebbles as wagers.

'Juno told me about how you stuck Lizzie Mansfield with a needle,' is the first thing my sister says, looking over at me. 'Well done, Mouse! She had that coming.'

But I do not want to think about my anger and the extent to which it pleased me to vent it in such a way.

'Will you play, Mary?' asks Juno. 'It is much more fun with three.'

We settle into the game, flicking out the cards and laying our wagers silently. All the while I am thinking of the times I have comforted Katherine's broken heart and I ask myself how it is love makes such fools of people. I suppose I am saved from that at least. I am reminded of Plato's wheels, split in two, seeking their other halves, and find I am wondering once more if there is such another half for me, but I squash the thought – it can lead nowhere.

'You should write to him,' says Juno, and I suppose she means to Hertford. 'Tell him he will lose you. I don't believe for an instant he has fallen for Frances Meautas.'

'But what should I say?'

Juno slides off the bed and fumbles about beneath a pile of detritus on the table, finding paper, quill and ink, placing it in front of Katherine, saying, 'Tell him what you think of him.'

The game abandoned, Katherine begins to write, reading phrases out loud as she goes: 'You are not what I thought. I shall have forgotten you by the time you regret your actions. My love is dead. Vex not for my future, Hertford, for more fine men are after my hand than you could ever imagine. There is an illustrious marriage in the offing for your sweet Kitty . . .'

'Do you not think you go too far?' I say. 'Is it not better to say nothing?'

'Mouse, you do not understand these things. I know what makes a man turn his attentions back to a woman. A little jealousy will not hurt him.'

A knock at the door reveals Lettice Knollys. 'You will never believe who is back,' she says, barely able to hold in her excitement. 'Dudley!'

'Thank goodness for that,' says Juno. 'Perhaps now we shall have some entertainments again.'

'He is already making preparations for three days of feasting and a tilt.'

Juno gives a whoop of delight and claps her hands.

'And . . .' Lettice adds, 'she means to make him an earl.'

'Do you suppose she is ennobling the man in order to wed him, after all?' poses Juno.

'It seems hard to believe, given the scandal,' I say. 'But you can never tell what she's up to.'

'True,' replies Lettice. 'You should have seen Cecil's face. Like vinegar.' She nudges Katherine, who is still scribbling away at her letter.

'She plays those two men off against one another with expert ease,' I say.

'Oh, and, I put a frog in Frances Meautas's bed,' says Lettice. To which Juno starts up a round of applause.

'Poor frog,' says Katherine.

November 1560
Westminster
Levina

The sky is exploding. Levina stands in the door of the workshop watching as the Queen's accession day fireworks burst in golden cascades. She ventures a little way further down towards the river, where she can clearly see the flotilla of barges bobbing on molten-metal water. With each blast and fountain of fire the crowd cries out in amazement, necks craned as the sparks fall silently in the aftermath. She watches the way the brilliance kisses the edge of things, momentarily flooding them with light in the darkness. Were she to paint a picture of Hell, then this would be her palette. Her mind conjures up an image of Bosch's Hell that she saw once long ago. There was no beauty it in, just grotesque distortions, perpetual pain and fear.

She thinks about the girls down there at the core of the inferno, on the Queen's barge, and wonders to what extent she can truly protect them as she promised their dying mother. Her memory of Frances surprises her with its clarity and the well of feeling that accompanies it brings the faint twinge of threatening tears. Frances had warned her about Elizabeth, but Levina hadn't needed warning, she knows the woman well enough. The Queen has been in good humour of late, now Dudley is cleared of suspicion – publicly, anyway. He prances about as before, basking in her favour. He will never shake off the whiff of scandal, though; it is stuck to him as egg tempera adheres to old church walls. But the Queen's mood can change on a pinhead – in that respect she is truly her father's daughter.

Levina returns to the workshop where an army of artisans, during the daylight hours, has been painting scenery for a grand masque. As she is taking a torch from the sconce she notices the vast shape of Keyes, the Sergeant Porter, all six and something feet of him, across the courtyard, checking that the doors are bolted. She waves to him, calling out that she will collect her things before she leaves.

'Don't tarry, I might lock you in by mistake,' he jokes.

'How is your wife?' she asks, remembering Mistress Keyes has not been well of late.

'She will mend, I'm sure.'

She notices how his shoulders slump a little as he says this.

'I'm sure,' she echoes, as he moves away to continue his rounds.

Levina enters the workshop, holding up her torch to inspect the images. It is a woodland scene, festooned trees with deer loitering, a centaur here and there peeping from behind the vegetation. The maids of the chamber all have costumes of nymphs and dyads, which were fitted and altered this afternoon, the seamstresses, with mouths full of pins, gathering waists, stitching darts, lifting hems, while the girls tested each other on their lines of poetry.

She hears a sound, deep in the shadows – heavy breath, as if someone is hiding in the dark – and feels her skin prickle, her stomach shrink. She puts a hand out to the wall, hoping for reassuring solidity, but what she finds is a makeshift piece of scenery that sways against her touch. Her breath quivers, too loud. Pull yourself together, she says inwardly, holding her torch forward, throwing some light into the gloom. The door slams shut behind her, making her jump. Was it Keyes, thinking her gone already? She listens for the sound of the bolt being shot, about to shout out that she is here, but then from behind, she feels a light touch on her shoulder.

Gasping, she turns, brandishing the torch, ready to use it as a weapon, seeing only then the mess of black curls that belongs to the Hilliard boy. He is the son of a goldsmith, a friend of Foxe, recently back from exile in Geneva, who has been helping paint scenery.

'You!' she says.

'Mistress Teerlinc, beg pardon if I scared you.'

But, she is thinking, he intended to scare, shutting the door, not calling out to her that he was there. She manoeuvres herself around him to get to the door, relieved to find it unlocked, pushing it wide.

'What are you doing?'

'I fell asleep.'

'You'll catch your death sleeping in this place. You don't even have a blanket.' Perhaps it is true, she disturbed his sleep and the wind slammed the door. But there is something about the way he is smiling that makes her uneasy. Perhaps he enjoys scaring people – there are boys like that.

'I know,' he replies. 'But I became carried away . . .' The

light has fallen across a painted area behind him. Levina moves in to better inspect it. It is a group of satyrs in animated conversation. The detail is astonishing, each face with its own characteristics and, she notices, each resembling a member of the Privy Council: there is Arundel pulled up to his full height, hands on hips, speechifying but paunchy about the girth, and there is Cecil, smooth, darkly furred, his curved horns polished to a sheen but with a slyness about the eyes, and holding his white stick of office as if it is a weapon.

'This is most excellent work, Nicholas,' Levina says, moving closer to see the detail, silently admonishing herself for letting her imagination get the better of her. This is just a boy with a passion for painting that has kept him here long after all the others have left. 'What age are you?' She touches the back of his hand. It is icy.

'I am fourteen.'

'Well, you have a rare talent for one so young. And I will not risk you catching a chill and have it wasted. Gather your belongings and you can ride with me to Ludgate. Where do you reside?' She feels silly for having been so afraid.

'I am a page at the Bodleys, Mistress Teerlinc, at Cheapside.'

'And Richard Bodley allows you to offer your talents as a painter for the Queen? I see.'

'He says it pleases him to serve Her Majesty in any way he can.'

'Well, Cheapside is only the other side of the cathedral from Ludgate. I shall have my man accompany you home. Mister Bodley must be missing you at this hour.'

She notices that the festivities have moved inside as they leave the palace. Keyes waves, bidding them a safe journey from the steps, and the sound of music fades as they head east, allowing their eyes to adjust to the darkness. There is a stream of folk heading back home from the riverbanks where they had gathered to watch the fireworks, and a few carry torches, making the occasional splash of yellow light in the gloom. Levina is feeling the uninterrupted hours of work and, thinking of her bed, would like to speed up but the horses have to wind their way carefully between the walkers and there are children and dogs scurrying willy-nilly about their feet.

From time to time her groom shouts out, 'Hoy there! Mind your backs.' Nicholas is mounted pillion behind him, clutching on to his leather bag of painter's equipment as if it is the most precious thing he owns – which it probably is. Levina remembers her first satchel of materials, given her by her father; she can't have been much more than twelve. Her sister Gerte teased her, for she slept with it on her pillow so that when she woke in the night she could bury her nose and breathe in the glorious chalky scent of the crushed pigments and the sharp tang of the gum arabic. Those odours still remind her of her father and the memory sends a wave of longing through her, even after so many years.

'Mistress Teerlinc?' the boy asks tentatively.

'What is it, Nicholas?' She thinks he sounds worried about something; he's probably imagining Richard Bodley's anger at his lateness.

'I was wondering . . .' he pauses, then says, 'Never mind.'

'No, what is it you want to say?' Levina's curiosity is aroused.

'I would like . . . Would you ever consider teaching me the art of limning? I find I am quite drawn to making miniature likenesses.' It seems now he has started he cannot stop. 'Father intends for me to become a gold-worker, as he is. I am to be apprenticed to the Queen's goldsmith soon, and though I like working in metal, and I have an eye for a fine setting, and it is a good trade, and I do not want to defy my parents, but I am so very drawn to portraiture.' He takes a gulp of air.

'What is it that draws you so?' asks Levina.

'It is the closest I can imagine to seeing into men's souls.'

'I will write to your father.' Levina is thinking of those satyrs, the way he had invested so much character into them, the delicacy of the brush strokes. She feels quite excited at the thought of passing her skills on, as her father did for her. This boy shows such promise. 'You certainly are suited to the skill. Perhaps we can come to some kind of arrangement with your father and Mister Bodley.' She is thinking as she speaks; he could help her prepare the cards for painting, gum the vellum, paint the carnation, even fill in the fine details on the clothing. She laughs silently at herself for being so frightened earlier – this boy is no threat, but she has become used to suspicion.

Besides, she misses Marcus, now he has settled in Rome. His most recent letter announced his hopes to wed a girl out there. His letters have been full of her, 'Letitzia', this and 'Letitzia' that, and she had felt that emotion mothers feel when they must let go of their sons and hand them over to another woman – in this case a stranger. It is a jealousy of sorts. She had always imagined he would return home and marry one of the daughters of the families now crowding back into London from exile abroad. George and she had discussed the possibility of ordering Marcus home, forcing him to break with this 'Letitzia'. But neither of them had the heart.

'I shall be forever in your debt,' Nicholas says, half looking at her but not quite able to meet her eye. Embarrassed, probably, she supposes, now he has asked a favour.

'I can't promise you anything just yet. Your father must be in agreement.' She finds herself hoping that the father will prove willing, and is already imagining the things she will teach him, already thinking about where the boy will bed down at Ludgate. In a flash of wayward imagination she thinks of Katherine and Mary housed with them too – quite the family. She slaps that thought down, aware of how far-fetched it is. But she is left with the residue of worry for those girls, poor Mary's difficulties in settling at court, the viciousness of most of the women there. And Katherine – there have been more noises from Spain. She cannot get the thought out of her mind of the old plan to smuggle Katherine out of the country and into the arms of one of the Spanish princes. She wonders if that plan has been reignited, now the French are rattling their swords once more. And then there is Hertford blowing hot and cold – it is such a mess and the poor child tangled up in it all.

The crowds have thinned now, so they pick up their pace until they are inside the city walls and the streets become too narrow and winding to keep up their trot. Soon they reach the Ludgate house and she asks the groom to take Nicholas back to Cheapside. There is a faint glimmer of candlelight beyond the window and she hopes it is George in there and not just the serving maid tidying before bed. She tries to remember his schedule of duty, whether he is on guard late this week or not. Dismounting, she leads her horse through the arch to the stable at the back, hearing George calling out to her.

'Is that you, Veena?'

'It is.' She will have a word with George about the boy, he knows the boy's father well enough. At moments such as this she feels the fortune of her marriage. Where most women barely tolerate their husbands after so many years, she finds herself more fond of him now than she ever was as a girl. She is suddenly struck by sadness, thinking of all the time they have spent apart, her at court, chasing commissions and never here for him to come home to. It is no wonder he has been so distant of late. She will make amends.

November 1560
Whitehall
Katherine

'He is here,' says Juno, who has her nose pressed up to the window. She taps on the glass and waves. We hear the door bang shut at the bottom of the stairs.

'I don't know if this is wise,' I say.

'Since when have you ever done what is wise, Kitty? You, of all I know, are folly's friend and I love you all the more for it. See him just this once, if only because he is my own dear brother.'

Juno knows as well as I do that it is impossible for me to refuse this visit, and as I hear his footsteps mount the stairs my chest tightens, making me short of breath. I wonder for an instant where the old Katherine has gone: the one who jumped from the high rock into the river pool, thrilled by the danger; the one who had them all eating from the palm of her hand, who never felt unsure over a lad. The door opens with a slow creak; there he is and I am weak at the sight of him. He is holding what appears to be some kind of package, his face shot through with worry. My dogs cluster round him in greeting, but I hold Stan tightly in my arms as an ally, despite his wriggling and whimpering – my dogs are as fond of Hertford as I, it would seem.

'Ned,' Juno cries running into his embrace. He looks at me

over her shoulder with the irresistible air of an abandoned puppy, forehead creased, hangdog eyes.

'My Lord Hertford,' I say, trying to contain myself, to keep things formal, to not give away anything of the tempest that rages in me. But I feel pulled to him by a great force that I fear I will not be able to resist. 'This *is* a surprise.'

He produces a green apple from beneath his cape and, unsheathing his pocket knife, slices it, handing a piece to Hercules, who is cuffed on the window sill.

'Treats for the monkey, Brother,' says Juno. 'Have you brought something for us too?' She indicates the parcel he is holding. 'Have you sweets in there?'

'Not sweets, no,' he replies, kneeling down on the floor and unwrapping the package as we watch on, puzzled. He produces what appears to be a handful of mutton ribs, and Stan, getting a whiff, wriggles out of my grip to join the frenzy at Hertford's side. He makes them all first sit and then each perform their little trick, rolling over, begging, offering a paw. It touches me that he remembers which of my pets best performs what, and I feel I might melt away watching this scene.

When the dogs have all scattered to the corners of the room to chew at their bones, Hertford remains on his knees, looking up at me wistfully. 'For goodness' sake, Hertford, get off the floor,' I say, pretending sternness.

'Kitty,' he breathes, 'I thought I had lost you.'

'What's to say you have not?' I move away from him towards the hearth, happy to regain a little of my old self. Juno is seated there with her arms tightly crossed, rubbing at her shoulders. Since the influenza struck her down she has remained particularly susceptible to the cold and falls ill easily. I take one of the furs, covering her with it, and poke the fire until it flares up. She reaches out to take my hand and we watch the flames in silence for a moment.

'Perhaps,' says Juno to her brother, squeezing her fingers around mine in a gesture of solidarity, 'you could explain your behaviour – why you left Hampton Court without so much as a word.'

I still can't look his way but I can feel his eyes on the back of me.

'It was Cecil,' he says. 'He had words.' I turn now to look directly at him.

'Words?'

'He cornered me in the stables, stood by cracking his knuckles as one of his henchmen had me by the throat up against the wall. Said if I didn't leave you be, he felt sure some kind of accident would befall me. Ordered me away from court. Said it was the Queen's wish. I had no choice, Kitty, since it was the Queen who sent me away.'

'That is not "words",' says Juno. 'That is an out-and-out threat. I thought Cecil was on Kitty's side.'

'He does the Queen's bidding,' I say. 'Not mine.'

'Yes,' she says. 'Cecil is on Cecil's side, first and foremost.'

Hertford holds out his hands for me to take and I hesitate, engulfed by the feeling that if I touch him now, feel his skin against mine, there will be no return. So I keep hold of Juno and reach out with my free hand to stroke his sleeve instead. 'You tremble,' I whisper.

'So the Queen has ordered you from court. Is it not too dangerous for you to be here now?' asks Juno.

'I *had* to come. I thought I would lose you, Kitty. Your letter –' He stumbles over his words. 'You seemed set on a Spanish match. I couldn't have borne it.'

I feel my heart begin to unfurl, then I remember. 'And Frances Meautas?' As I say her name I have an image of her brandishing that poem as if it were a crown she'd captured on a battlefield.

'Yes, what *of* Frances Meautas?' adds Juno.

'I don't know.' He collapses on to the seat beside his sister, leaving me still standing, not knowing where to put myself. Touching Juno's hand, he says, 'Cold,' beginning to rub it between his palms. This tender gesture makes my heart lurch.

'You haven't explained yourself,' she says.

'I thought to convince Cecil that I had given you up,' he replies. 'And I knew Frances Meautas wouldn't be able to keep quiet about it, that it would be around the palace within hours.'

'You were right about that,' I say, unsure whether to believe him. 'But Frances Meautas!'

'I thought you would know, Kitty,' he says, 'that I would never court such a girl. Thought you would divine that something was up.'

'A note would have been better,' says Juno in a clipped voice. 'So Cecil fully terrified you, then,' she adds, softly now. He is nodding slowly when we hear the lower door opening and shutting. We look at each other. 'Glynne or the chandler,' she whispers. 'Or the lad with more firewood. You'd better hide, Ned. Get behind the hangings.' He slides behind the bed curtains just as the door swings open. It is Lettice Knollys.

'I thought I'd find you in here,' she says. 'You've missed all the entertainment.'

'What entertainment?' I ask.

'There was a fight. Pembroke's men and Dudley's.'

'Was anyone hurt?' asks Juno.

'Several black eyes and a few bloody noses; nothing serious, but the Queen is beside herself with rage, what with Cecil's servants refusing to lift their caps as Dudley passed the other day.' Lettice is clearly enjoying the opportunity to gossip. 'She bawled at Cecil and though the door was closed you could hear every word. She ordered him to fall into line and offer Dudley the respect he deserved. You could have heard a pin drop in the privy chamber.'

From the corner of my eye I notice Stim sniffing about the hangings where Hertford is hidden, I whistle him back but he stubbornly refuses.

'Anyway,' continues Lettice. 'You were missed and I was sent to find you. You'd better think of a good excuse.' She makes a slicing gesture across her neck. 'Astley is in a fine temper.'

'Tell her I was caught short with women's matters and that Juno was helping me change. We will be along in a moment.'

'Don't tarry or I shall be in trouble too.' She makes for the door.

From the window I watch her walk across the yard below and enter the door to the Queen's apartments; only then do I go to Hertford's hiding place. I pull the curtain aside with the words, 'She's gone.'

He grabs my wrist, and before I understand what he is doing I realize I am wearing a ring set with a pointed diamond. 'What is this?'

'With this ring I promise myself to you, Kitty. Juno, will you bear witness?' He looks over at his sister, who is smiling as if it is she who has been proposed to.

'Oh, Ned,' she says. 'What about Cecil?'

'I will speak to Cecil myself, if necessary.' I hear the splinter of doubt beneath his words but pretend to myself I have not. '*He* would not want Kitty wed to Spain any more than I do.'

'What if I don't accept?' I say.

'Then I shall be the most miserable man alive.'

I can hardly bear to look at the forlorn face he wears.

'Of course I accept.'

At last I allow him to wrap his arms about me and, closing my eyes, I nestle my nose into his neck to catch his scent. I am thinking that this could send the pair of us to the Tower and I am standing over the river pool once more, throwing myself into the air, charged up with the thrill of it.

'As soon as you can find a way to leave court, come to me at Canon Row. We shall be wed there. Juno will let me know of it.'

'And the Queen?' I say.

'She will come round; besides, Kitty, she favours you these days. And since Dudley is back in her orbit her mood is bound to lift. With Dudley on the rise once more, Cecil will be going down. You heard what Lettice said; he is out of favour.' He seems now buoyed up with confidence, his doubt disappeared entirely.

'Yes,' says Juno 'and you are the Queen's closest cousin.'

'Don't,' I say sharply, thinking suddenly of my sister Jane.

'We must go, before someone else comes looking for us.' Then Juno turns to her brother, saying, 'Can you get out without being seen?'

'You go,' he says, pressing his mouth to mine briefly and I am flying through the air again. 'I shall protect you, Kitty,' he whispers. 'I will not let any harm come to you.' And then, as I peel away from him he draws me back, taking my ring finger. 'Better this is not on show, here.' He unclasps a fine chain from about his neck and, slipping the ring on to it, fastens it at my nape, then helps me tuck it away beneath my stomacher. His hand lingers a moment on my breast and he meets my eyes with a half-lidded look that makes a flower of heat blossom in me.

'Hurry,' says Juno, tugging at my hand. 'God speed, Ned, I shall contact you at Canon Row when the time comes.'

As Juno and I rush towards the Queen's rooms, a sense of

calm settles over me, as if everything is at last falling into place. I would rather risk everything and be married to Hertford than see him wed to another. Besides, things have a way of working themselves out and Elizabeth may like her power games, but she is not bloodthirsty as her sister was – she has not ordered a single execution yet.

'Do not tell your sister of this,' says Juno.

'But why? I can trust Mouse.'

'It might visit danger on her.'

'I suppose you are right.' My secret gives me a stirring feeling, as if I have a pouch of saltpetre upon my person and must take the greatest care not to pass too close to a flame.

We slip into the privy chamber quietly, making our excuses. Mistress St Low clucks about, asking if I have everything I need. I keep up the charade with a grateful but appropriately wan smile and hold my hand to my lower belly. I notice Frances Meautas and Lizzie Mansfield whispering, thick as thieves, in the corner and glancing over at me. I throw them a smile and a wave, touching my fingers to the chain about my neck, physical proof of my secret. Frances seems wrong-footed by my friendliness, half-smiling back with a puzzled expression. I wonder if she still has that poem tucked under her dress and if she awaits another from the man who will be *my* husband.

I sit beside Mary, who is alone at the window with a book. But the Queen, who is sitting in the warmest part of the room listening to Lady Knollys recite poetry, looks over, beckoning the pair of us to her with a smile.

She pats the stool beside her with the words, 'Come and sit with us, girls. Lady Knollys is reading from Wyatt's poems. I am particularly fond of them.'

I settle on to the stool and Mary takes a cushion at my feet. I can see the tension in the set of my sister's jaw; we are both unused to this friendly treatment from the Queen and I remind myself to take care of what I say.

'We are all cousins here, are we not?' she says with uncharacteristic warmth.

'That is true,' says Lady Knollys.

'My Boleyn cousins and my Tudor cousins,' she says.

But I am thinking that, if there is any truth in the rumour, we are all Tudors, for it is said that Lady Knollys's mother, Mary Boleyn, was the mistress of the eighth Henry before he moved on to her sister, Anne, and that Lady Knollys was his natural daughter. I wouldn't know anything about that but it is true both she and Lettice have a Tudor look about them.

'Call Lettice over,' the Queen exclaims. 'We would be surrounded by our close family.'

Lady Knollys catches her daughter's eye and Lettice peels away from the group of women sewing in the corner, bobbing in a curtsy and settling down next to Mary.

'Ah yes, family,' sighs the Queen. 'We should have Mistress Teerlinc paint a set of limnings for us before you leave to wed Devereux, Lettice.'

'You are to wed?' I whisper, feeling a wave of elation. If the Queen has given permission for Lettice to wed, it is a sign that her aversion for marriage amongst her ladies must be on the wane. There is hope for me, then.

'I have had news of another plot of late,' says the Queen. 'It appears now that Huntingdon would see himself on my throne. Seems to think a dribble of Plantagenet blood is enough. There is always *someone* who would like to take my place. See, ladies, how our family needs to stand united.' She then turns to Lady Knollys, calm as a millpond, as if there were no plots or fights or poisoned gloves or any worries at all, saying, 'You didn't quite finish reading the poem.'

'From the beginning?' Lady Knollys asks, lifting the book,

which is bound in embroidered velvet worn thin in places by the fingers that have held it.

'No just the end – it is the part I like best.'

Lady Knollys begins to recite in a voice that is clear, like clean water:

And graven with diamonds in letters plain
There is written, her fair neck round about:
Noli me tangere, for Caesar's I am,
And wild for to hold, though I seem tame.

There is a moment's silence before the Queen speaks. 'That was written for my mother. Wyatt was in love with her before she married my father.'

'It is beautiful indeed,' I say.

'He found himself in the Tower for his love. Did you know that?' It is a question that seems directed at me, for the Queen has locked her dark eyes on to mine, but she does not mean for me to reply as she continues immediately. '*He* escaped execution, unlike the others.' There is an unmistakable sadness in her voice. 'We have all lost those close to us.'

I wonder if this is her attempt to forge a bond with Mary and me, to bring us back truly into the fold, for we have all lost a parent to the axe. I allow myself to imagine that we may be forgiven the accident of our Tudor blood, indeed that it may even be thought of as fortunate, and another spark of hope is ignited in me for my wedding. I touch the chain at my neck once more, to remind myself of the ring nestling against my hidden skin, feeling the memory of Hertford's warm hand resting there.

'What terrible times those must have been.' It is Mary who says this, and I am struck, as ever, by how she always seems to be thinking of the way others might be feeling – so unlike me, who always first thinks of myself.

'Yes,' the Queen replies. 'But I do not have the memory of it. I was but an infant at the time.' I only notice now that she has been using the first person singular rather than the plural – another sign of her desire for intimacy, I feel sure of it.

'Still,' says Mary. 'A great loss such as that leaves its scar, even on the young.'

'What age are you now, Mary?' she asks.

'I am fifteen.'

'You have depth for one so young.' She stretches out to run a hand over Mary's hunched shoulders. It is a rare fond gesture, and I am the only one to see Mary flinch slightly. She hates to be touched as much as she ever did. 'Just as well no one will want to wed you, Mary,' continues the Queen. 'Men do not like wives who think too deeply on things.' She appears amused, seeming entirely unaware of her cruelty, and I have to stop myself from jumping to my sister's defence.

But Mary doesn't need my help, for she replies, 'A clever woman knows how to appear shallow.'

Both the Queen and Lady Knollys burst into laughter at this. They are not laughing *at* her, this is clear – they are impressed. I exchange a look with Lettice, filled with pride for my little sister.

'Depth *and* sense,' says Lady Knollys, her mirth subsiding.

'If you weren't so well-born, Mary, I should appoint you my fool.' It is the Queen who says this. I am not sure whether it is an insult or a compliment.

'Shame then for my birth, as it would be an uncommon honour to be the Queen's fool,' quips Mary.

'But your birth makes you my cousin. Do you not think it better to be the Queen's cousin than the Queen's fool?'

'The opportunity to serve my Queen is all I ask.'

Elizabeth seems satisfied with this as she pats Mary on the

shoulders, saying, 'It would seem you have inherited the Tudor intelligence.'

It is only now that I notice a page hovering with a sheaf of papers in his hand. Lady Knollys bids him pass them over, which he does with a bow, fumbling simultaneously to remove his cap. The Queen takes the documents, beginning to shuffle through them, and the page is dismissed.

'Can you guess what these are?' the Queen asks, tapping a paper. 'The patent for Dudley's earldom. I intend to give him Leicester. A few noses will be put out of joint by this.' Her face gives nothing away, except for her eyes, which glimmer like faceted gems. 'What think you to that?'

She is directing her question to me. I wish I were as sharp-witted as my sister and could come up with some clever repartee about Cecil, for that is surely the primary nose she refers to, but all I say is, 'My Lord Dudley is wholly deserving.' She seems moderately satisfied with this as she nods in agreement. But what I am thinking of is that once Dudley is made Earl of Leicester the Queen will wed him – after all, Leicester is a title usually reserved for the sons of royalty. That will displace Cecil's nose sufficiently far as to render his threats to Hertford entirely empty. Then the Queen will be happy to see me married, I feel sure of it.

We sit silently as she looks through the rest of her papers. One appears to grab her attention. She holds it up, reads it through again with a smile threatening the edges of her mouth. 'Seems that young upstart François is ailing, and it is serious.' I suppose she talks of the King of France. 'Perhaps my Scottish cousin will not be the French Queen much longer, then.' She sits back in her chair with a satisfied sigh. 'It would please me greatly to no longer have the French waiting to jump into my grave. They think me weak for being a woman. Let them think that.'

'Indeed,' says Lady Knollys.

I am wondering if it might not be such a bad idea to capitalize on the Queen's good humour and simply ask her for permission to marry, but something Juno said earlier echoes in my mind.

'Ask permission and have it refused, yet wed anyway,' she had said, 'and it is a far greater misdemeanour – to flout a direct command – than if you simply marry having asked nothing.' She is right of course.

December 1560
Whitehall
Mary

'Would you be so kind as to direct me to the Sergeant Porter's lodge?' I ask one of the pages milling about in their room off the watching chamber.

'It is something of a walk,' he replies. 'Are you sure you can manage . . .' He stops, looking me up and down, as if he has never seen such a creature, and is surprised I can speak his language.

'I may be hunched about the shoulders but my legs work perfectly,' I say a little too brusquely. It was only an attempt at kindness on his part but I am as tired of pity as I am of spite, and I no longer care if I offend.

He leads the way to the Westminster watergate and up a set of steps tightly spiralled like the inside of a sea shell, knocking on the door at the top. A muffled voice bids us enter and I find myself staring up at the towering shape of the Sergeant Porter. I have seen him often from a distance at the palace gates but up so close in this small space he seems inhumanly tall, and my first thought is to wonder how he negotiates that cramped stairway. He is gruffly bearded and also, I notice only then, pink about the eyes as if he might have been weeping.

'Lady Mary,' he says, bending into an awkward bow. I ask myself how he knows me, but I suppose I am well known as the Queen's crooked cousin – certainly I would never be mistaken for someone else.

'You are Keyes, the Sergeant Porter?' I don't know why I ask, as I know very well who he is, but I feel awkward in the face of the sadness he is clearly taking pains to hide.

'I am he, My Lady. How can I be of service?' I am sure of it now, in the wet glottal sound of his voice, that this man has staunched back tears, and I ask myself what kind of misery could reduce such a man thus.

The page is loitering on the landing, his nose pressed up to the window, from where there is a view of the river and the passing boats.

'Mistress Astley bid me deliver this. "Directly into your hands," she said.' I hand over a sealed fold of paper. 'It is from the Queen, though I am not privy to what it contains.' It is likely something to do with Dudley's investiture, which is to take place today. Perhaps the Queen expects trouble and wants Keyes to be extra vigilant.

He opens it and begins to read, and really I should take my leave but something moves me in the sight of this man's misery.

'Mister Keyes, what has upset you so?' I ask quietly, so the page cannot hear.

'It is nothing, My Lady.' But a tear slides down the side of his nose, incongruous on a man such as he.

'It is not nothing. You can tell me. It may help to share your woes.'

'My-my wife is ailing,' he stammers. 'And my duties here

keep me from her.' He pulls out a handkerchief, blowing his nose noisily.

Watching him I am reminded a little of Stokes, who is also a burly man much given to uxoriousness. 'Does she have a servant, or someone to care for her; do you have children, daughters?'

He nods in reply. 'My eldest is with her now.'

'Then I am sure your wife would rather you did your duty to the Queen. It would vex her the more, I think, if you did not.'

'Perhaps you are right, My Lady. I am sorry to have made such a spectacle of myself.'

'There is no need to be sorry, Keyes, and I am sure she will rally.' As I say it I feel disingenuous – it is nothing but a platitude, after all.

Once back out in the courtyard I hand the page a purse of coin, instructing him to visit the apothecary for some physic that I list for him and also some comforts and foodstuffs, telling him to find the whereabouts of Keyes's wife and deliver them to her. I find myself deeply touched by this man's situation, perhaps because he reminds me so of my stepfather, and in turn I am led to think of dear Maman, for whom he grieved so deeply. Maman is gone a full year now; that is a year spent at court. I must not allow myself to think of her, for I fear my fastenings shall begin to break and I will be in tears like Keyes.

I find my way to the watching chamber, where Juno and Katherine are practising scales with the singing master nearby. By rights they should not be in so public a space, but the Queen is with her councillors in the privy chamber as the council chamber is being decorated. Levina, brush in hand, stares intently at Lettice, who sits on a stool in the window embrasure making the most of the morning light. Levina has a boy assistant today who cannot help but keep glancing over at Katherine, as if he has never seen such a creature – and perhaps he never has. All my life I have seen boys respond in such a way to my sister, and it amuses me to watch him quite befuddled in the face of her beauty. He is invisible to her, though, despite his raven curls and bright eyes. And in turn I am invisible to him, despite the fact that Levina makes a fuss of introducing him to me as her pupil. He removes his cap but looks over my shoulder at my sister.

As we are all dressed in our finery for Dudley's investiture, Levina is adding the finishing touches to the set of portraits that the Queen had commissioned. The Queen has been curiously forthcoming towards us Greys of late. Since our exchange the other day she has requested that my sister and I accompany her quite often when she eats in her privy chamber, and I am expected to perform witty verbal acrobatics for her amusement. She has even decided that she wants me to accompany her out riding and has had Dudley procure a miniature pony for that purpose. Sygnet is the kind of docile animal on which children are taught to ride, and gives me no trouble. There are benefits to the Queen's favour, for it means that those who torment me for their sport have realized that it is in their interests to be kind to me, in public at least. But it has also caused some jealousy, which is not something I am accustomed to, as my sister is.

I settle nearby, unable to rid myself of the image of Keyes stifling his sorrow. A great gruff man such as he, who is charged with the safety of all within the walls of the palace, so brimming with kindness, is incongruous in this place, where such gentle qualities are not held in high esteem. I saw in him a glimpse of kindred spirit, though perhaps it was my imagination, that he too, with his beloved wife, would do better leading a more simple life away from court. I take out a letter from Peggy that I have already reread several times. With capable fingers Levina stirs some vivid blue in an empty mussel shell and the paint smell wafts over to me: sharp resin and chalky pigment. She occasionally asks the boy to do this and that, 'Move the easel a foot towards the window, would you; pass me the gold leaf; add a little cadmium to a measure of resin.'

The boy notices me watching him and I swiftly drop my eyes back to Peggy's letter. *I have been churched*, she writes, *and the baby thrives with the wet nurse.* But she says her husband is taciturn and she wishes I were there, for sometimes she doesn't know how to behave with him, whether to fuss over him or to leave him alone. Nothing she does seems to please him, or so she says – poor Peggy. I miss her too and hope she will be back at court before long and not obliged to stay in the country with that husband of hers. I wonder if motherhood has altered her and am struck by a momentary sadness that I will never know what it is like to birth an infant, to create a life. But I soon shake off my mawkishness, allowing myself to imagine one day being aunt to the brood that my sister will surely produce.

The Queen's yellow lovebirds chatter in their cage that hangs in the window. I think perhaps it is a worse torture for them to have a view of what they are missing – the expanse of open sky above the river where a cluster of gulls wheels – than to have no view at all. Yesterday at dusk I watched a flock of starlings dip and dive out there, making a great dark cloud in the sky, in constant motion. They formed shape after shape, each in silent communion, separate yet moving as one, and I tried to imagine what kind of sensation it must be to feel the rush of air beneath outstretched wings. I look out now at the December morning, muffled with cloud, the little boats struggling upriver against the tide. Perhaps it will snow and there will be a morning's excitement, throwing snowballs, making snow-angels, faces bright with cold. But then will come the slush and the icy flap of drenched hems about the ankles and the bitter air and chilblains.

'Mouse, Mary, are you dreaming?' My sister's voice seeps into my thoughts. Her light touch on my shoulder brings me back. 'Will you accompany us on the virginals?'

'But what of the portraits?'

'I do not need you for the moment,' Levina says.

A pair of fat cushions is procured and they are placed one above the other on the instrument's stool. I am balanced on the top of that, just high enough to reach the keys. I catch the boy watching on with an amused smile. He looks as if he would laugh outright were he not in such company. I suppose he thinks I resemble a performing monkey. The girls cluster round so he is out of my line of sight. '"Poor Bird"?' I ask, my fingers hovering over the keys.

'Not that one, it is much too gloomy,' says Juno.

'"Old Woman"?' suggests Lettice.

'Yes,' says Juno. 'In rounds.'

I begin to play and Katherine sings the first line.

'There was an old woman who lived under a hill.'

The others join her:

'Fa la la, la la la la la la,

'If she's not dead she lives there still,

'Fa la lo, fa la lo, fa la la la la la lo;

'A jolly young man came riding by.'

I notice Harry Herbert walk past, slowing his pace to take in the scene, and fancy I can detect a look of longing for my sister in those green eyes of his. I know that look well. Now we are so conspicuously in the Queen's favour it is likely Pembroke will change his tune about their marriage. But I cannot forget that slap the brute gave her. I calculate when it was, counting back in my head: six years ago. I remember as if it were yesterday, the red mark on Katherine's cheek. She deserves better than a bully for a father-in-law. I pick up the speed until my fingers ache with it and the words jumble up, crowding into one another, which makes us fall about with laughter.

'I am ready for you, Kitty,' says Levina, who stands before her easel, gesturing for Katherine to take the stool facing the window.

Katherine perches herself prettily, larking about, pouting, batting her lashes and sticking her tongue out for our amusement. Levina's helper cannot drag his gaze from her; he flushes beetroot when he sees I have noticed him staring, shuffling round to Levina's other side, pretending to be busy arranging the pigments from light to dark.

'I fancy Her Majesty would not appreciate a portrait of you with your tongue stuck out,' Levina says, but she is smiling too. We are all drawn to Katherine's irrepressible sense of fun, but I am particularly happy she appears to have overcome her heartbreak so soon, and I suppose this exuberance is a sign that her desire has alighted elsewhere.

Levina straightens Katherine's ruff and smooths her hair back under her coif with a smile, then adjusts her necklaces. 'What is this?' she asks, pulling out something on a chain from Katherine's stomacher. I cannot see what it is but the curious expression on Levina's face makes me wonder.

'Nothing!' Katherine replies firmly, tucking it back under her dress and closing the conversation.

As Levina paints I watch the comings and goings. People are beginning to congregate for Dudley's investiture and the watching chamber is filled with groups of finely clad courtiers loitering about, playing cards or dice, laying down wagers they cannot afford to lose, gossiping, assessing each other.

A messenger, blue-lipped with cold, passes through and is stopped by the pair of guards at the privy chamber door.

'Important news from France,' he states, proffering a letter that one of them casts his eyes over before nodding to his colleague. Lady Knollys is called to the door, and she too reads the letter before beckoning the messenger into the chamber.

'What do you think it is?' I ask.

'French news, perhaps Mary of Scotland has insulted the Queen again,' says Lettice. 'I shall ask Mother when she reappears.'

When Levina is finished with Katherine, it is my turn. I sit quietly, watching her quick fingers work. She stops after a while, approaching to show me my likeness, and I am surprised, for she doesn't usually like sitters to see her unfinished work. On a bed of brilliant blue lies my face, which though lacking in detail is surely the me I see from time to time in my sister's looking glass. My round brown eyes beneath a high brow, my pursed heart lips, my high-necked gown with the sleeves puffed. But it is not me, for there is no hint of my true shape, no twist or hunch to my shoulders or awkwardness in the set of my neck. I look at Levina, questioning, remembering the sketches she made of me in my shift all that time ago.

'I know,' she says. 'The Queen has requested it thus. I'm sorry.' I wonder for a moment how the Queen might have put it: *Make her look normal, Mistress Teerlinc*, perhaps.

'I know we must all do as we are told in this place.' Saying it out loud makes me long for my freedom all the more. I sit and she paints on in silence. The starched edge of my ruff begins to irritate the skin of my cheeks. The boy is sketching something, one of the other girls, I suppose, for he flicks his eyes their way every now and again.

The privy chamber doors open and Lettice is on her feet in an instant, talking to her mother in the entrance. The messenger walks out clutching a purse full of coin – he must have brought news that pleased the Queen. Lettice glides back to us, sitting herself down on the window seat, absently pulling her betrothal ring on and off her finger.

'So?' inquires Juno.

'The King of France is dead,' Lettice announces. We are silent and I am trying to work out whether that is a good thing for England or not, concluding that it probably is, for it means that Mary of Scotland is no longer also mistress of France. It is a good thing for the Queen, certainly. I remember clearly how she reacted to news of the French king's illness.

'Those French kings do not last,' says Katherine with typical flippancy. 'He was only sixteen. How old is the brother?'

'The new king is ten,' says Lettice. 'Charles. And I am told to say that the Queen wishes to take a hunting trip on the morrow – to Eltham. She wants us all there.'

'Even me?' I ask.

'Especially you. Mother made a point of that.'

I notice Juno exchange a look with my sister; it is no more than the briefest meeting of eyes but there is something behind it that puzzles me, and I mean to ask Katherine about it later. But then the Lord Chamberlain arrives and we are hustled down to the great hall to witness Dudley's ceremony. Dudley himself is done up like a peacock in his finery, and one of his men carries the ermine cape and the coronet and all the other bits and pieces of earls' regalia. He gets on his knees before the Queen, who has an odd look of amusement on her face as if this is a game. In contrast, Cecil, across the room, surrounded by his black-clad clan, looks as if he has just drunk a flagon of rancid ale.

Dudley begins his speech, but I am not listening, for

Katherine is rocking back and forth, clutching at the side of her face, making a low moaning sound. I whisper to Lizzie Mansfield, who is standing between us, asking her to find out what is the matter, but she continues gazing forward as if I am not there at all. Then, to my horror, Katherine collapses to the floor. I jump to her aid, as do Juno and Lettice, one cradling her head, the other stroking her cheek, whispering, 'Kitty, Kitty, what ails you?' But Katherine has fainted clean away. Dudley drones on, apparently oblivious.

The Queen turns to Mistress St Low, indicating with a nod of the head that she should see to it. Mistress St Low quietly calls over a page, who scoops Katherine up and out of the room. Juno is sent to accompany her and another page is dispatched to find a physician. All this is done so fast that those on the other side of the chamber seem hardly aware of what has happened. I try to attract Levina's attention but she is far from me, focused on sketching the scene, and doesn't see. I am about to ask Mistress St Low if I may go too, but she is back in her place, and the ceremony continues as if nothing has occurred, leaving me worried out of my mind for the health of my sister.

When Dudley, who has remained on his knees all that time, has finished, the Queen gets to her feet and moves towards him, asking for the papers to be brought to her. She takes them, pinched between her finger and thumb, holding them away from her body as if she fears that the ink is still wet and might stain her dress. Her seal dangles on its ribbon from the papers, almost touching Dudley's upturned face.

'Cecil,' she says. 'Your penknife.'

The man scurries forward fumbling in his gown to produce a small blade, saying, 'Have your quills not been sharpened, Your Majesty? I shall see to it.'

'Just give me the knife,' she says. He hands it over, then

backs away from her, his eyes following a triangular path between Dudley, the papers in the Queen's left hand and the blade in her right.

The Queen then takes a step towards her favourite, offering him a cold smile.

'Lord Robert,' she announces with a slight toss of her head. 'Are we not a woman?'

'Your gracious Majesty is indeed the finest woman in the land,' he replies.

'And as a woman we have decided to exercise our prerogative to change our mind.'

The chamber shuffles and watches on in astonishment as she slashes the papers right through several times, shredding them. Finally, the seal falls with a crack, shattering on the floor. There is a collective intake of breath and Dudley looks as if he might not be able to contain his rage, but I notice that Cecil is struggling to keep a sly smile at bay.

'I think it not meet,' continues the Queen, 'to elevate one to the peerage who comes from three generations of traitors. If we cannot learn from history, then what?'

Dudley opens his mouth as if to say something, but the Queen lifts up a hand, palm forward, to stop him. 'We shall see you on the morrow at Eltham, Lord Robert. We trust you shall make arrangements for our finest horses.' She wears a smile, as if the whole thing has been some kind of elaborate joke, and as Dudley reverses his way out of the chamber I'm sure I hear someone hiss at him, as if he is the Devil in a masque.

'What was the meaning of all that?' I ask Levina, once we are out, filing along the gallery in a slow squash of people.

'I can only assume it is some kind of test for Dudley. She is just like her father; he loved to test those close to him. It was no game.'

'Kitty is taken ill. I must go to discover what ails her.'

Levina's voice is full of concern. 'The Queen has asked to see my sketches and I cannot keep her waiting, but you must send word to me at once if it is serious.'

When I get to Juno's chambers the physician is just leaving. The bed hangings are drawn and the room is lit only from the fire that blazes in the hearth. Juno takes me to one side, whispering, 'A badly infected tooth. She will not be able to leave for Eltham tomorrow.'

I open the hangings a little to see the shape of my sister's sleeping body, just able to make out her pale hair splayed out over the pillow. 'She has begged that I stay with her,' continues Juno. 'Would you kindly ask the Queen's permission that I may be excused the hunting trip, Mary?'

'Is it serious?' I ask.

'I think not,' she replies. 'But she must rest.'

Even so, as I go back to the Queen's chambers I have a knot of anxiety in me, once an infection is established it can spread and then . . . it doesn't bear thinking about.

The Queen is in a merry mood when I return, is quite bright-eyed, teasing Lettice about her imminent nuptials. But she turns to me without ceremony asking, 'How does your sister, Mary?'

'She is sleeping, madam. She has an infection in her tooth. The physician orders her to rest and Lady Jane begs to stay with her.' The Queen is nodding.

'Have they bled her?'

'I believe not.'

'It is wise when there is infection. I shall ask my physician to arrange it. And yes, Mary, you may convey to Lady Jane that she has permission to stay.'

'And I, Your Majesty; might I stay also?'

'And miss the amusements? That would be a shame. Leave

Lady Jane to tend your sister. It is only a toothache, not the plague.' She turns to Kat Astley, who is hovering near by. 'Ah, Kat. I want you to . . .'

Our conversation has been perfunctorily closed, so I sidle away, bobbing in a curtsy though the Queen is not looking at me.

In the anteroom are both Cecil and Dudley, each one surrounded by his men. Cecil's are ebullient and do not seek to hide it, whereas Dudley's are seething and silent in a huddle. Suddenly I understand the purpose of the Queen's antics: it is to divide and rule. She needs both men but cannot let either be more powerful than the other. I see, too, that she will never commit to wed Dudley; her power in Europe lies in her being able to play off France against Spain: just as she does with Cecil and Dudley, so she does with Europe. It demands high regard; a woman who knows her power lies in her vacillation.

One of Dudley's men strides over towards Cecil's crowd, his hand on the hilt of his sword. I move swiftly towards the door. I do not want to find myself at the centre of a violent squabble. Some harsh words are exchanged and Dudley's man is dragged aside by two of his friends. 'Leave it,' they are saying. 'He doesn't merit it.' The air is charged with rage. I slip away.

The morning is dull and bitterly cold. I can see the pattern of frost on the window and snuggle further into my blankets. Two of Katherine's dogs have curled themselves close, one in the crook of my knees and the other tucked into my belly. Due to Katherine's illness, I was given leave to sleep in Juno's rooms, on the truckle at the foot of the big bed that the two of them share. Since she was bled yesterday, my sister has seemed better, and the giggles and whispers emanating from the bed last night assuaged my fears for her health.

It occurs to me, remembering the look they exchanged yesterday, that the whole thing might have been a ruse to avoid the discomfort of a December trip to Eltham, which is not the most comfortable of the palaces. The Westminster bell sounds out six of the clock; I drag myself out from my warm cocoon of blankets, feeling the chill air through the thin fabric of my shift and raising my arms to stretch out the ache in my back. Peeking round the hangings, I spy Juno and Katherine sleeping soundly side by side. If I am honest, I am a little annoyed that they didn't include me in their ruse, for the idea of a day's ride through the biting cold and ending in that vast draughty old place pleases me not one bit. *Be stoic, Mary*, I imagine Jane telling me. At least I will not be expected to go out with the hunt, for my pony is too small to keep up the pace when the going is fast, and the Queen gets impatient if there are stragglers.

I am tempted to wake them and rub their noses in my misery but they look so very peaceful and angelic, and it would serve no purpose, so I make my way to the maids' room. There I find Mistress St Low in a flap, attempting to get everyone up and into their riding habits. All the gossip is of Dudley and his public humiliation – of what it might mean. I have come to see that favour shifts on the Queen's whim in this place and that it is impossible to anticipate the way the wind will blow even tomorrow.

'There was a scuffle over it,' says someone.

'Hardly surprising, putting him in his place in front of everyone like that,' says another.

'How will he ever be able to hold his head high?'

'Less of the tittle-tattle,' says Mistress St Low. 'It is none of our business.'

'Shows you can never count on the Queen's favour,' says Frances Meautas under her breath, clearly aiming her comment at me.

I ignore her, allowing the chatter to slide over me as I hastily shove the things I will need into my chest before the porters come to take the luggage.

'Why are *you* coming, anyway?' Frances asks me. 'I thought you didn't hunt.'

'The Queen likes her company,' says Lettice.

'The Queen likes her company,' mimics Frances.

'Better than a dullard like you.'

'What'll she do when you are wed, and not here to defend her?' says Frances, talking to Lettice but looking at me with narrowed eyes.

'I can look after myself perfectly well, Frances.'

'Yes, you are good with a needle, aren't you, Mary?' adds Lettice, with a wink, which sends Frances striding off to the other side of the room in a sulk.

Lettice and I help lace each other into our outfits.

'What of your sister?' she says. She is the only one to ask.

'She will live.'

'Was she feigning?'

'Let us say it is not as bad as it first appeared and the physician has worked his magic.'

Once down in the courtyard we find our mounts. Even bundled up in my fur-lined habit, I can feel the bite of the December wind. I manoeuvre Sygnet into a place that is sheltered, to wait for the Queen, feeling my fingers already burning with cold and wondering how I will bear the journey. When she eventually arrives, she is hand in hand with Dudley, sharing a joke, as if nothing had ever occurred. Everyone stares agog as he helps her up on to her horse, hands lingering about her waist, adjusting her girth-strap, lifting her skirts aside to better get at it. I watch the whispers circulate; nobody seems to know what to make of this happy scene. There is no sign of Cecil, but then he never joins the hunting parties, though there are a few of his men and one I recognize from yesterday when the trouble occurred. They are scrutinizing the scene, their eyes flitting between Dudley, the Queen and each other.

I am asking myself how a man such as Dudley has managed to swallow his pride and it occurs to me that perhaps he is truly fond of the Queen. They were childhood friends, after all, and he knows her well enough to be aware of her games, of whether she is testing him. If he does truly care for her, he would be the only one. All the rest feign fondness to garner a little power for themselves. There is much I do not understand when it comes to what goes on between a man and a woman, but I like to think I have a nose for genuine sentiment. Watching them I am reminded, as I often am, of Plato's divided beings, seeking the other part of themselves, and it strikes me that it must be lonely being Queen.

'Lady Mary.'

I turn to find Keyes standing beside me. 'Sergeant Porter,' I say. He has hold of Sygnet's bridle and is feeding him a nub of carrot from the flat of his palm. 'How does your wife; is she better?'

'She sent word to me of your kindness, My Lady. Says the physic has eased her greatly.'

'I am glad of that.' I can see from the corner of my eye a few of the maids sneering. They wonder, I suppose, why I give a man so low-ranking the time of day. Let them wonder; he is worth a dozen of them.

'I don't know how I shall ever thank you for your kindness.'

'I do not seek thanks,' I say. 'Your friendship is all I ask.' He begins to speak, but I continue. 'And do not mention rank. I care not for that.'

'It would be an honour to call you my friend.' He smiles then. It is the first time I have seen him do so, and he is quite transformed by it.

'Send my best wishes to your wife for a swift recovery.'

Dudley then vaults nimbly on to his mare; she fusses, rearing up, spinning about. He calms her with an impressive demonstration of horsemanship, while the Queen looks on approvingly. They then set off together, heading the train, looking for all the world as close as brother and sister.

December 1560
Whitehall
Katherine

'Kitty, wake up. Kitty.'

I open my eyes to a death-head looming; screaming in terror, no sound comes out of me. Then I am jerked awake, truly this time, emitting a sharp gasp, to find Juno leaning over me, gently shaking my shoulder.

'Don't fret, Kitty, it is nothing but a dream.'

My arm is tender and I open it up to find a bruise running from my inner forearm to the crook of my elbow, a flowering of purple and ochre, recalling in my confusion that I was bled yesterday. 'That physician was a butcher,' I say, only then remembering what day it is. Juno is breathless and effervescent, as if it is her own wedding day and not mine.

'Brave Kitty,' she is saying, placing a careful kiss upon the blemish.

I can't help but think of the blood drip, drip, dripping into the bowl, how bright it was. Captivated by the sight of it, I imagined that the bleeding was some kind of purification ritual for my wedding. It reminded me of how Jane Dormer liked to talk at length about Christ, in the way most girls talk of love. Her stories of nuns, young women who were visited nightly by Christ and fed off the blood from his wounds, were so vividly told they have stayed with me. I have that image of Katherine of Siena, all skin and bone and beatific smile, from the chapel at Durham House, seared on my memory. I thought of those nuns as I watched my own blood drip out of me. Our ruse had worked a little too well; Juno had sat me by the fire tightly swaddled like an infant, where I drank a toddy so hot it burned my tongue. By the time the physician arrived I was flushed with what convincingly appeared to be a fever.

'That is Tudor blood,' Juno had said, quite as fascinated by it as I, and then had leaned in close so the physician couldn't hear her whisper, 'When you wed my brother and make a child, it will mingle your Tudor blood and my Seymour blood.' Hearing her say it – 'make a child' – allowed the idea to take shape in my mind and I imagined holding an infant in my arms, making me go soft inside. 'We shall be sisters at last,' she had added.

'Did you get word to him?' I ask, fully awake now and suddenly afraid that Hertford may not be prepared, that perhaps we had made the whole thing up.

'Vex not, Kitty, it is all arranged.'

'I want things to stay as they are between us,' I say, weaving my fingers through hers, struck then with the fear that my wedding might irrevocably change our friendship, if that is what it is.

'Stop fretting.' She pulls back the hangings, adding, 'Sister,' with a little smile. Beyond the window the sky is thick and white as if it has a mind to snow. I feel for the ring about my neck.

'Put it on your finger,' Juno says, reaching out to unclasp the chain. 'Just for today.' And I am reminded that we will have to keep our wedding secret, which scrumples me up a little inside, spoiling my excitement.

'Do you think the Queen will disapprove?' My voice is small.

'I believe that when the time is right you shall tell her and she will be delighted. See how she favours you these days? And she has been worried that those Spaniards will wed you to one of theirs. She has intimated so, more than once. Anyway, you know all that.'

I push my fears down. It is true, Elizabeth has drawn me into the fold. Everyone supposes she means to name me as her successor but I prefer not to think of that. 'I shall be Countess of Hertford by this afternoon,' I say.

And Juno grabs both my shoulders looking into my eyes, laughing, 'I know!' Her laughter brings on a coughing fit. 'I can't seem to shake it off,' she splutters between bouts.

'Wrap up warmly, Juno. I won't have you risk your health on my account.'

We help each other dress. I change my gown three times, unable to decide which one to wear. I keep thinking of my other wedding, the borrowed gowns that were hastily adjusted, and my sister, nearly seven years gone, but I must not think of Jane now.

'He will not care what gown you have on, only how easily it comes off,' Juno says, teasing a laugh out of me. And then she makes me eat a slice of marchpane, though I have no appetite at all, and passes me a big black velvet cloak with a hood that covers me from head to toe, standing back to appraise me. 'You look like a mad monk,' she giggles.

I rummage amongst my things, finding Maman's best fox-lined cloak, draping it over her and tying it tightly about her throat. 'This will keep the cold off you.'

She smiles and slowly strokes my cheek with a faraway look that gives me an unexpected moment of sadness.

'Where are the animals?' I ask, only now realizing that they are not here.

'I gave them to Mister Glynne. Said you were ailing and needed quiet.'

It seems Juno has thought of everything. I wonder if this wedding would take place at all if it weren't for her.

Whitehall is hushed as a cathedral as we wind our way to the narrow staircase of the orchard entrance. Outside, our breath billows in the cold, and the wet grass soaks through our shoes and up our hems before we even reach the orchard wall. The espaliered fruit trees are lined up there, leafless, like lace against the white-grey sky. In the spring this place is a paradise of wild flowers but now it is dank and high with the rotten remains of autumn's windfalls and the mulch of dead leaves. At the far end is a little gate shrouded in overhanging evergreens; I reach it first and try the latch but it is locked. I look at Juno, feeling the first sensations of defeat, thinking momentarily that all this has been nothing but an extravagant game for our amusement, that there will be no wedding; perhaps Hertford isn't even aware of today's plan. She is shuffling about beneath her cloak, finally producing a key, whipping it out from her stomacher as if drawing a sword, and my disappointment dissolves.

'Juno!' I exclaim. 'How?'

'Don't ask,' she says, tapping the side of her nose, her eyes flashing, and my heart is back in my mouth once more.

The steps are dark with overgrown vegetation, narrow and perilously slippery. I cling on to the metal balustrade, which is so cold it burns my skin. In the rush I have forgotten my gloves. But my fear of falling is greater than my fear of frostbite, and besides, all my senses are dulled in the face of the anticipation that simmers in me. And then we are down and out on the river beach, a vast expanse of murky sand, punctuated here and there with some mysterious mound or other left exposed by the receding river. The breeze blows bitterly off the water and the damp hems of our skirts become heavily encrusted with filth and sand. I clutch the flapping edges of my cloak tightly about me, holding my hood to keep it from blowing off. Several boats pass but none seems to notice or care that we are there, two shapeless bundled figures picking their way along the bank. We could be anyone at a distance – picking cockles, searching for coins, taking the short cut to market – and there is certainly nothing of our outward appearance that might suggest that I am the Queen of England's close cousin heading for my secret wedding.

December 1560
Ludgate
Levina

Levina watches Nicholas work with the single-hair brush. He has made a copy of her limning of Katherine and has captured precisely her air of lightness, as if she might blow away in the wind like a dandelion clock. He has an uncommon gift for drawing eyes, makes them look directly out, like a challenge to the viewer. Katherine's eyes are cornflower blue and he has juxtaposed the weightless air of her with a solid directness of gaze that describes her perfectly. It is as if he knows her well, though he has only seen her the once; Levina remarked at the time how his eyes followed her. She has that effect on men, even older ones who should know better.

Nicholas strokes a minuscule touch of lead white on to each of her tiny black pupils, barely discernible, and then adds a flick to a frond of her hair, creating the impression of movement, making the whole thing come to life. The boy is developing a distinctive style, quite different from Levina's. Where she likes to create an impression, using exaggeration to emphasize a point and a blurring of edges, a softness, Nicholas's lines are defined to the finest detail with a precision that is almost mathematical. She imagines one day he might be a far more celebrated artist than she, for such verisimilitude and detail are becoming fashionable and are entirely lacking in her own work. She wonders if she is envious – perhaps. His style is certainly striking; there is no doubt of that.

She brings her focus back to her work, tipping out a measure each of russet and ochre, mixing them, stroking a little of the colour on to an offcut of vellum, holding it up to the light and trying to conjure in her mind's eye the exact hue of the Queen's hair, a kind of burnished copper. She shakes her head, not happy with the mixture, going back to the facial features. Levina has deliberately made the tiny queen appear young, quite innocent and wide-eyed, but she has given her, too, a hardness in the set of her jaw to suggest something of her strength of personality. There is no doubt Elizabeth is a fine-looking woman, handsome, rather than pretty. Levina recalls her first encounter with Elizabeth on her arrival in Katherine Parr's household; King Henry was on the throne and Elizabeth was barely older than Nicholas is now. She always had that air of supreme resilience, even as a girl. No one back then ever truly imagined that she, the younger daughter of a disgraced Queen, would one day be Queen herself.

Nicholas screws up his paper, tossing it into the log basket with the words, 'More kindling for you.'

'Why did you do that?' she asks.

'I can't get it right.' He cannot hide his annoyance.

'I thought you had something.'

'No, it lacked her capricious edge. I failed to convey whatever it was she was cooking up with that friend of hers. I could see it in the brightness of her eyes but couldn't render it.'

'Cooking up?'

'I noticed some shared secret.'

'Those two have always got some benign trouble on the go.' Levina is impressed by his astute summing-up of Katherine, but doesn't say it, for fear of his head swelling and that arrogant streak in him becoming insupportable.

'I can't get her quite right.'

'You are too much of a perfectionist.'

'Is perfectionism not at the heart of what we do, Mistress Teerlinc?'

Levina wonders if it is a veiled criticism. But she will not defend her loose style of painting to this tyro, however talented he may be. He has some way to go yet before he has perfected his art.

'Perhaps,' she says. 'Now help me clear all this away. I must return to Whitehall and make sure Lady Katherine is on the mend.'

'You are very close to the Grey girls,' he says.

'Yes,' she replies. 'Their mother was most dear to me.'

'Bodley says Lady Katherine will likely be named the Queen's successor. Is it true?'

'Heaven knows,' Levina says bluntly. 'I doubt it. The Queen will marry and spawn a string of heirs.'

'And what of that crooked girl?' He doesn't attempt to hide the disdain that lurks in the tone of his voice.

Levina feels her anger bubble up. 'I will not have Lady Mary referred to in such a way, Master Hilliard.' She firmly closes the conversation, turning away from him to re-cork her pigment jars and return them to the shelf. He seems chastened by her sharp change of mood, quietly rolling up his sleeves and setting to scrubbing the worktop.

Once the boy is gone Levina gathers her things, instructs the servant girl to change the bed linens and makes for the door, bumping into George arriving home from his night shift. 'Where are you off to?' His tone has a slight accusation in it.

'I won't be long,' she says. 'Just have a few errands to run.' She doesn't mention that she is going to the palace to visit Katherine, doesn't want to rile him. He won't like having to play underdog to the Grey girls yet again. She slides her hand into the folds of her gown, touching the hard shape of the phial of clove oil for Katherine's toothache.

'You smell of paints.'

'That is nothing novel,' she replies. 'Don't I always have the scent of the workshop on me?'

'You do, you do.' She still thinks she can sense an edge of annoyance but then he adds, 'Shall I walk with you a little, Veena?'

For a moment she feels him drawing close, softening inside.

'Take me as far as the river steps,' she says. 'I shall be glad of the company.'

They walk arm in arm, as they used to, with Hero tucking in beside them. He moves creakily, the lithe agility of his youth gone, which makes Levina think of all the time that has passed, calculating his age in her head; he must be thirteen at least. They stop to greet Henry Carruth, who is standing in his doorway watching the world go by, discussing the news: the new French king with his Medici mother who has put the Guise family in their place; Dudley's thwarted investiture; the restoration of the debased coinage. As they walk on, it strikes Levina that it is already two years since they lived in fear for their lives, with that monstrous Bonner breathing down their necks. How time speeds by. It is but a vague memory now, the dread of even leaving the house for all the rioting.

'We live in peaceful times, at last,' she says.

'And long may they continue,' George replies.

The houses are more densely packed down towards the river, like a mouth too full of teeth, the upper floors leaning in to each other, allowing little light to filter down to the street. In the gloom Hero has stopped, is growling at something, hackles up. They step closer, to discover that he is in a stand-off with a rat that appears to be defending a heap of rags. George grabs a brick from a stack next to a building site, lobbing it at the rat, who turns tail and disappears into the midden. Hero moves forward, burying his nose amongst the rags, whimpering, distressed about something. It is then that Levina sees, with a sharp intake of breath, a human hand drop on to the ground.

'Oh Lord!' she gasps as George turns the bundle over to find a face, once belonging to a young man, its nose quite eaten away by vermin.

'God rest his sorry soul,' says George. 'It's a while since we've seen one of these hereabouts. Not since the plague was last in the borough. You go on, dear; I shall see to this.'

On the wherry, she cannot get the image out of her head of that poor soul, pondering on the fact that he was someone's son, someone's brother. It makes her think of Marcus, out in Rome where the summers are longer, the winters milder and as a consequence they are more afflicted with the plague. She stops herself. Those thoughts don't do anyone any good – you could go quite mad with worry if you let your imagination run off. She looks out along the riverbank towards the turrets and banners of Whitehall Palace, rising up beyond the vast tracts of exposed sand that are scattered with river detritus. There is hardly a soul about, save for two women in the distance, bundled up against the biting wind, cloaks billowing, their ribbons flying up prettily as they pick their way along the shore. She registers something familiar in the posture of them, the impression of a physical intimacy that reminds her of Katherine and Juno. A few gulls circle noisily about a fish carcass and another wherry passes in the opposite direction, throwing up waves, making their boat rock and water splash over her skirts.

As they draw beside the Whitehall pier, Levina watches the women disappear up the Westminster steps, thinking she would like to make a painting of the scene, to capture the crisp quality of its winter palette and the black blowing shapes of their cloaks. She makes a mental image of it, storing it up for another time. Having paid the waterman and clambered from the boat, she makes her way into the palace, walking through the empty courtyard and in by the back stairs which lead to the women's chambers.

The place is deathly quiet. She knocks gently at the door to Juno's rooms, where Katherine is most often to be found, but no one answers so she pushes it open to find the hearth still smouldering and a mess of clothing scattered about, but no sign of either girl, nor any of Katherine's pets. All her instincts are telling her that something is amiss and her mind is flooded with images of the moment Katherine was taken ill, so publicly, and then of the two shapes she has just seen disappearing up the Westminster steps. Nicholas's words echo in her head, *cooking up*. What were they cooking up? She searches for clues, rummaging through the bundles of clothes and bedding, not knowing what she seeks. Her thoughts dither and her feeling of dread expands until it fills her. She opens a book of poems, finding written in it: *Ever yours, Hertford.* And then hastily scrawled as an afterthought in a different hue of ink, *soon your husband.* Levina is then struck by the memory of the ring Katherine was wearing on a chain. How she snatched it back when asked what it was. 'Nothing!' she had said, in a way that clearly meant the opposite. A question insinuates itself into her mind: has Katherine hatched a plan to wed the Hertford boy?

She rushes out, twisting and turning through the familiar corridors, taking the steps two at a time into the courtyard and almost running at full-tilt into the huge bulk of the Sergeant Porter.

'Oh Keyes, am I glad to see you,' she says. 'I'm searching for Lady Katherine Grey and her friend. Do you happen to have come upon them this morning?'

'You'll not find them here, Mistress Teerlinc. All the Queen's ladies are gone to Eltham, hunting.'

'But they remained behind, Lady Katherine was afflicted with a toothache.'

'Oh dear,' he says, rubbing his beard. 'Lady Mary made no mention of it when the retinue left. Now *she's* no ordinary creature.' The man pauses, seeming to think, and Levina prepares once more to defend Mary, feeling her anger begin to inflate: *creature*, indeed. 'She is uncommonly kind, so very unlike most of those noble maids. I mentioned the other day in passing that my wife was ailing and she sent a parcel of comforts for her.'

'That sounds like Lady Mary,' Levina says, surprised,

pleased to hear such a thing said about Mary who is usually the butt of so much disdain. But she is twitching with impatience. 'You haven't seen Lady Katherine?'

'She hasn't passed through here, nor at the watergates – I'd have been made aware of it.'

'Hertford? Have you seen *him*? Was *he* amongst the retinue?'

'Hertford hasn't been at court for some time, Mistress Teerlinc.'

She is trying to remember the name of the street where Hertford has his London house. She went there once to paint him. Is it Canon Row? she asks herself. 'I hope you will forgive my rudeness, Keyes, for I must track down those young women before trouble finds them.'

'Anything I can do . . .' he calls out, as she hurries off.

Once out of the gates, Levina follows the road towards Canon Row at a run, arriving there quite breathless and unable to remember which house is Hertford's. She paces up and down, panting heavily and clutching at the stitch in her side, seeking something to jog her memory and wondering, dreading, what it is she will find when she gets there. She then recognizes the lime tree by the door set back from the cobbled square at the front, and the particular style of herringbone brickwork that surrounds the windows of Hertford's residence.

She bangs hard on the door with a fist, but there is no answer. She peers in the window but the place seems empty, even of servants, no sign of a soul. Feeling foolish, she admonishes herself for letting her imagination run away with her. Hertford is more than likely at Hanworth with his mother, and the girls are surely gone for a stroll in the long gallery at the palace, oblivious to Levina's misplaced concern. She ought to be simply glad to know that Katherine is better and up and about, rather than running around like a madwoman letting suspicion take hold of her – that corpse has put her in a strange mood. But the niggling worry will not leave her and she bangs at the door again, so hard this time she bruises her knuckles.

December 1560
Canon Row
Katherine

There is a loud thudding at the door. I turn to Hertford. 'Who is it?' He doesn't reply, just shakes his head, purses his lips and squeezes my hand a little tighter.

'Where is everybody? Why doesn't your man answer it?' asks Juno.

'I sent the servants off for the day, to give us privacy,' says Hertford.

'Even Barnaby?'

'Everyone.'

The chaplain, who is a round sort of fellow in threadbare black worsted with a crude wooden cross strung from a pewter chain about his neck, is fidgeting as if he has somewhere else to be. I wonder where Juno and Hertford procured him. From amongst the dozens such as he passing through London these days, I suppose. He will be back from exile abroad and seeking a position, now his faith is no longer outlawed.

'Who is banging?' I ask again.

My anxiety must tell in my voice, as Hertford says, 'Fret not, Kitty. We cannot be seen from the street in these chambers.'

'You have thought of everything, Brother,' says Juno.

The racket subsides at last.

'Are we ready?' says Hertford, directing his words at the chaplain, who is shuffling through the pages of his prayer book, squinting through a magnifier.

'Ah, yes, My Lord.' He looks up at us, seeming to take a moment to focus, rubbing his eyes.

'Shall we kneel?' asks Hertford.

'If you wish, My Lord.'

As we get down on our knees, I try to think about God and the sanctity of marriage, but all I seem to have in my head are memories of my other wedding – the splendour of Durham House; the great assembly of nobles there to witness our nuptials; my dress, more lavish than any I had worn before or since. I must not think of Jane. I look down at my mud-splashed clothes, the sand clinging to my hems and the rings of dirt beneath my fingernails, but rather than feeling sad for it, a little laugh fizzes up in me. I lean in to Hertford's neck and whisper, 'I love you,' and he brings my hand up to his mouth, pressing a kiss on it. But then a thought spins into my head: *I love you too much.*

'Never too much, Kitty, when it comes to love,' he says, and it is only then that I realize I have spoken the words aloud. Despite his reassurances I am not so sure, for I feel as if I am slipping on ice and don't know if I will land on my behind or glide beautifully like a Dutch skater. I concentrate all my thoughts on the grip of his hand upon mine, the firmness of it, and my worry recedes a little.

The clamour at the front door resumes. We are silenced and stilled, not moving a muscle. I look at Hertford; he is clenching and unclenching his jaw. Juno begins to cough, trying to suppress it and turning red with the effort. Thankfully, the hammering abates once more.

'What ails you, Sister?' asks Hertford.

'It's nothing,' she says as the fit subsides.

The chaplain picks up his book again, flicking the pages, scrutinizing the words, then reading from it, fumbling to hold his magnifier and turn the page at the same time. He appears not to be very familiar with the marriage ceremony. I catch Juno's eye and we exchange a smile. If it were not my own wedding we would be sharing a giggle about this inept cleric.

We repeat the vows one after the other, and my heart feels as if it will burst from my breast and soar up to the sky. Hertford takes a pouch from beneath his doublet and hangs it in the air before me, as if I am a favourite puppy and it is a treat. He pulls open its neck, holding my hand palm up, tipping a ring out into it. It is made of five gold hoops interlinked, knotted and twisted about one another, like a vine.

'Read the inscription,' he whispers.

I look over at the chaplain, wondering if he allows such a thing in the middle of his ceremony. He nods his assent and I read the tiny lettering engraved about the shank.

As circles five, by art compact, show but one ring in sight,
So trust unites faithful minds, with knot of secret might.

'Oh,' I sigh, giddy with love, and Hertford is sliding it on to my finger, next to the pointed diamond, while repeating the chaplain's words.

And it is done. We are wed.

Hertford is suddenly businesslike, handing the man a purse and hustling him out of the door. He tells him he must leave by the rear of the building and that he is not to speak to a soul of what has occurred here this morning, which causes me to sink inside at the thought of what we have done. But that sinking feeling is no match for the other sensation that is gripping me as if I have sprouted wings and am flying through the air.

Once the chaplain has gone Hertford turns to me, pulling open his collar and flinging his cap aside so his hair escapes, tumbling about his face, and saying, 'There is just one more thing. This marriage needs consummating, Countess.'

He swings me up into his arms with a laugh and makes for the door. Juno smiles as we pass her, but a fleeting thought blows through me as I wonder if she doesn't wish for a husband herself – though she has always said not. 'I savour my freedom,' she has told me, more than once.

I am carried through to the bedchamber and flung upon the bed. 'Let us make an heir to the throne,' he murmurs, undoing the ribbons of my dress. But I do not want to hear that, so I listen only to the blood rushing in my ears and the urgent huffing and moaning we make. The smell of him, the proximity of him, the fact of him, is making me so light-headed I might float away.

March 1561
Whitehall
Mary

I almost bump right into Hertford as I arrive at Juno's rooms.

'Lady Mary,' he says, politely enough, removing his cap and dipping into a perfunctory bow. His eyes are a little shifty, refusing to meet mine. 'I was just leaving.'

'You are to be found here rather often, My Lord,' I say.

'They *are* my sister's rooms.'

'True enough.' It is not that I mind the man really – there are far worse. But Katherine is becoming careless about her assignations with him and people talk. I can't help wondering if the Queen has got wind of their secret flirtations. Perhaps she doesn't care much, such things carry on all the time at court, and besides she is most likely too preoccupied with Dudley to notice. 'Is my sister inside?'

'She is.' He twists the cap as if he is squeezing water from it and we stand in silence for a moment; I do not know what to say to him, save to tell him to leave Katherine alone, and he clearly has nothing to say to me. He nods, mumbling an excuse, placing the cap, all bent out of shape, back on his head, then passes me to take the steps down to the courtyard.

As I enter, the dogs lift their heads and come to greet me, dancing about my feet, tails waving. I rub Echo's ears and, looking up, find Katherine lying on the bed with her hands folded over her chest, like a corpse. She is utterly motionless, doesn't even react to the rumpus of the dogs' greeting, nor the door closing behind me with a thud, nor my footsteps as I cross the room towards her. My sole thought is that Hertford has killed her. The fear wells up, filling my throat. But as I near, I see her lashes flicker, causing relief to wash through me. I throw myself on to the bed beside her, plastering her with kisses, saying, 'Kitty, thank God!'

'Mouse! What are you doing?' She sits up, pushing me aside.

'I thought you were dead.'

'I wish I *were* dead,' she says, bringing both hands up to cover her face, like an infant who thinks it an effective way not to be seen.

'What has he done?' I know Hertford is the cause of this.

'Him? Nothing,' she says. '*Cecil* is sending him abroad – a tour of all the courts, state duties,' her voice is bitter as pith. 'So he can cavort with all the beauties Europe has to offer. I hear there are some fine French princesses, and that the Low Countries are packed full of noble fillies and as for the –'

I press my fingers over her mouth to stop her. 'Kitty, what is this? So he will be gone a few months. Then he will return. It is not the end of the world.' I am thinking it is a good thing if he is to go.

'You don't understand.' She looks away from me, at the embroidery on the hangings, then down at her hands and picks her nails. I wait in silence for her to explain. 'Cecil is making him go. He has no choice.'

'That is not so remarkable, Kitty, and isn't it an honour to be sent abroad on state business? We all must do as we are told. None of us has any choice, when it comes to –'

'But . . .' She grips my wrist as she adds in a low voice, 'I fear Cecil will do away with him, send a poisoner, once he is out of sight.' She looks at me with liquid eyes: they are filled to the brim with the kind of fear and sadness I am unused to seeing in my optimistic sister.

'You worry out of hand,' I say, taking out my kerchief and dabbing at her tears. 'I cannot think of a single reason as to why Cecil would want to do away with Hertford. It is part of a young man's education, is it not, visiting the courts abroad? How else will he get on in the world?'

'You don't understand.' She rips one of her fingernails down to the quick, drawing blood. 'Cecil threatened him before.' I take her hand in mine, bringing it into my lap so she can do no further damage. She looks surprised. She is not used to me holding her hand like this.

'I'm sure your worries are unfounded. Cecil is more concerned with the Queen and Dudley to care about what you and Hertford are or aren't up to. I'd wager that by the time he comes back you will have forgotten him anyway.' She snatches her hand back and I fear I have said the wrong thing, made it worse.

'He is my husband,' she utters. 'Since December.'

'You are *wed*?' I am astonished at this news, not so much because it surprises me that Katherine has been foolhardy enough to make a secret marriage, not even because she failed to confide the fact of it to me, but because I didn't notice something so momentous – I, who notice everything, missed all signs of my sister's clandestine wedding for three whole months. And I am angry, too, remembering how people have talked of Hertford's ambition, thinking his intentions can only have been to elevate himself; but then I have also witnessed some moments of real tenderness between them. For once, I do not know what to think, but one thing I do know is that the Queen will not be pleased. My stomach turns over at the thought. 'Since December?'

She nods and her eyes spill over once more.

'Why?' I cannot bring myself to understand why she should put herself at such great risk. She may play the silly girl, but *I* know Katherine is not such a fool.

'I love him, Mouse.'

I go to speak, to ask what truly is love to her who has professed it so often, but something in her expression forces understanding on me. Perhaps this is no transient passion like the others.

'And I had my slim chance of happiness, so I grasped it. Perhaps the Queen would never have given permission. I might have been forced to remain a maid in her service for ever. Juno thinks it worse by far to defy a specific denial of permission than –' She stops, gulps in a lungful of air and dispels it in a great sigh. 'He might have married another, Mouse.'

'Oh, Kitty,' I say. I don't mean it to sound like an admonishment. But of course I am thinking of what happened to Jane when she fell foul of another queen.

'"Oh, Kitty,"' she mimics. 'How could you possibly ever know what it is like to feel what I feel?'

I am stung. Of course I will never know what it is like. It is my destiny to do just the thing she risks her life to avoid, to remain in service to the Queen, a maid for ever.

'No possibility of love for deformed little Mary Grey.' I cannot hide my anger. 'No path out of this for *me*.' She flinches as if I have slapped her across the face. 'Has it not occurred to you that Hertford might be pursuing his own ends?'

'He is not. Don't ask me to tell you how I know. I just do. He is terrified, terrified of Cecil, and yet still –'

'He has much to gain.'

'And much to lose!'

She is right, of course. 'Who else knows of this?' I ask.

'Only Juno.'

'There must have been a churchman.'

'Just some wandering cleric, who is long gone. Oh, Mouse.' Her voice has turned small and hollow. 'What have I done?'

The blood from her fingernail has smudged on the satin of her dress. 'You are not . . . ?' I glance at her stomach, my sympathy taking hold once more.

'No!' She seems unsure, though. 'At least, I don't think so. I have bled of late but only sporadically.' She hesitates, turning her fingers around and about each other. 'And lightly.'

'Well, that is because you are so thin.' I take her wrist, and even *my* tiny finger and thumb can circle it, their tips meeting easily. 'Everybody knows if you do not eat properly your courses stop.' Katherine has never been a good eater – more goes to the dogs under the table than into her mouth.

'Yes,' she exhales, dropping her shoulders. 'I hadn't thought of that.'

'See,' I say, 'it is not as bad as you think.' Neither of us is reassured much, though. I am thinking, and surely she is too, about what the Queen will do if she discovers this unsanctioned marriage – if, or when. She is fiddling with something hanging from a chain about her neck and catches me looking.

'Here,' she shows me a pair of rings, one a pointed diamond, the other five knotted links.

'From him?' I lean forward to inspect them. They are both beautifully crafted, not some hastily designed fripperies. I grudgingly accept that Hertford's intentions are serious.

'You have been a fool,' I say. 'You should have waited.' I am only thinking of myself, watching my dream, the hope of making a home together, being a family, disintegrate. 'I am weary of your impetuosity, Kitty. You never think of what your actions might visit upon anyone else.' What I really mean is that she never thinks of me.

'But . . .' She seems completely forlorn, destroyed by my anger, and I feel bad now, for having shown it when she is so very vulnerable.

There is a noise below.

'The downstairs door,' she says, stuffing the rings back into her shift. We hear heavy footsteps mounting the stairs.

The door swings back and there is Hertford with Juno in his arms. She is more pale than I thought it was possible for a living human to be, and *his* face is utterly stricken. Katherine has leapt from the bed and is pulling back the covers, clearing a space. I stand aside to let Hertford pass and he places Juno's limp body carefully down on the sheets. Katherine covers her with the plummet and then a fur, which she bundles up about her throat.

'She is cold, Hertford. Icy!' Katherine's voice is thin as water.

'Stay with her,' he says. 'I will fetch the physician.'

Juno is motionless apart from her eyes, which occasionally half open and roll about, before closing again; and her breath is shallow, up in her throat, rasping horribly as if she cannot get enough air into her lungs to keep herself alive. I throw another log on the fire and stoke it, taking up a warming stone with the tongs, dropping it amongst the embers, not knowing what else to do while we wait interminably for the physician. The heavens have opened outside and we sit there in limbo with just the sound of the rain thrumming against the window.

I take the warmed stone from the fire and drop it in the long-handled pan, closing its lid carefully and sliding it into the bottom of the bed. Then I light a candle and climb up beside the two of them, drawing the hangings around us to keep the draught out. Katherine is singing quietly, but she is struggling to hold the tune and I see her wet cheeks shining in the candlelight, as if strewn with fragments of gold leaf.

'She has been coughing for months,' she whispers. 'I didn't think . . . I didn't think . . . I was too wrapped up in my own affairs. Oh God, Mouse. Perhaps if –'

I put my hand on her arm, interrupting her, 'Nothing could have prevented this, Kitty. She will get better; just you wait.'

But my words are hollow and Katherine knows it as well as I. Juno will not recover. We have all seen plenty at death's door; we know what death looks like.

'She was dancing yesterday.' Kitty's voice is now invested with hope. 'I partnered her for a pavane.'

I was there, watching them dance, and now I remember how weak Juno had looked, how exhausted and how she had had to stop, because a fit of coughing racked her thin body so badly I feared she might be rent in two.

'She was dancing yesterday,' I repeat. Struck at the way, even now Katherine is twenty and I am still but fifteen, when it comes to a crisis it is I who assumes the lead. It has been thus ever since Jane was taken.

The physician arrives at last and I open the bed curtains a little. He is a large, lugubrious fellow clutching a vast, stiff leather bag to his chest. Hertford hovers at his shoulder, with the wild look of an unbroken pony.

'Now what seems to be the problem?' the physician says, jowls wobbling like aspic as he speaks.

I want to shake him and shout, 'Not what *seems to be*, what *is*!' But I just look on while he stands umming and ahhing over Juno's motionless body.

I think I am the only one to notice the moment she stops breathing and the life drops away from her.

Katherine has taken hold of the doctor's sleeve and is begging him to save her friend, pleading desperately, and he is trying to shake her free. My heart is wrenched at the sight.

'Kitty,' I say, putting one hand either side of her face, forcing her to look at me. 'Kitty, she is gone.'

'No!' she cries. 'NO!'

Hertford is weeping too.

The physician is searching for a pulse, his fingers pressed to her neck, but pulls his hand away with a shake of the head and begins to witter about cause of death and calling for a chaplain. I wish he would leave us alone, and what use is a chaplain now, anyway?

Katherine has clambered back up beside Juno and is whispering to her as if she is still alive and they are sharing a secret in the usual way.

Hertford pulls himself together enough to ask the doctor if he can please leave us to our grief, hustling him and his big satchel out of the door, closing it behind him.

I turn back to the bed. Katherine has Juno by the shoulders and is shaking her. 'Come back,' she is whimpering. 'Come back, my love.'

It is a sight to break even the hardest heart.

She turns eventually to Hertford saying, 'You cannot leave me now.'

I watch him; his face is contorted with grief – I have never known a brother and sister so close. It dawns on me that Juno was the pivot upon which Katherine and Hertford's love for each other turned. He seems about to say something, but then I notice what I think to be fear in his eyes, and he appears to change his mind with an almost imperceptible shake of his head, simply stretching out a hand to silently stroke Katherine's upper back.

June 1561
Ludgate
Levina

The sky is dark and bruised with angry streaks of pink, and everything is still, as if God is holding His breath; even the birds are silent. Then the wind, a whisper at first touching the tops of the trees, gains strength, shutters beginning to bang, everyone scuttling for cover, waiting for the rain. Levina watches the distant lightning, brilliant forks illuminating everything, counting the beats until the thunder rumbles, assessing the distance – one beat to a league – the sound closing down on the light. Then it announces its arrival with a jagged slash that rends the sky overhead, making her skin prickle. A simultaneous boom of thunder sets Ellen, the new servant girl, off screaming and sends poor Hero scurrying to hide beneath the table.

She watches the rain pass to the south. But the wind continues its howling, punctuated occasionally by bursts of thunder. Levina, with the help of Ellen, closes and battens all the shutters, hoping the glass in the windows will survive. The poor girl is petrified, too scared to sleep, though nobody could sleep through this racket, and so they sit up together, Ellen huddled by the fire, rocking back and forth, singing a children's rhyme.

Levina takes a candle to the table and begins to sort through a pile of abandoned papers. There is correspondence to be answered, accounts to settle and suchlike. She has hardly looked at any of it since George left for Bruges near on a month ago to make arrangements for his father's will. She can barely remember the last time they sat together at this table, can barely remember the last tender moment they shared – her marriage has become neglected as a forgotten tomb. But, she tells herself, he loves her for the fact that she is not like other wives, that she has a profession, that she can afford to put glass panes in their windows. She knows, though, that the opposite may well be true – that he has grown to resent her for all those things, for all the time spent away from him pursuing her own life.

She picks up a pamphlet from a group of Puritans. They are not happy with the Queen's middle way; they think she should go further with Church reforms, come down harder on the Catholics. There was a time Levina would have agreed with them but there is little fight left in her, and she is happy simply to be able to practise her faith without fear of persecution. But it does make her think of all the risks she took in the old Queen's reign, all those drawings, the smuggled documents. An image – that sickening crimson spurt – appears in her mind as if it was yesterday and not, she realizes with a shock, upward of seven years ago.

A great crash out in the street causes Ellen to start with a gasp of fear.

'Fret not, dear,' says Levina, trying to soothe her. 'It's probably just one of the tavern signs blown loose. They are never properly fixed. Why don't you heat us a toddy – that will take your mind off it.'

The girl gets up and busies herself fixing a pan over the fire, and Levina goes back to her paperwork. Near the bottom of the pile she finds an unopened letter addressed to her husband. Something about it ignites her suspicion; a certain flourish to the hand that makes her think it is a woman's. She lifts it to her nose, sniffing. It smells of nothing in particular, there is no residue of perfume. The seal is smudged and unreadable. She places it back on the table and continues sifting through the rest of the papers. Ellen puts a steaming cup down on the table beside her and Levina asks her if she wouldn't mind sorting her paint jars, more to give her something to distract her than because the task is necessary. She sips on her drink, burning her mouth slightly. Her thoughts keep wandering back to the letter, niggling at her, her suspicions raised by those careful loops of an unrecognized female hand. Eventually, curiosity gets the better of her.

It is written in Dutch, which surprises her. She thinks for a moment that it must be from George's mother, supposing she might have sent it after he left for Bruges, not realizing he was already on his way there. But no, his mother wouldn't sign a letter, *Ever your true love, my heart is yours, Lotte.* She sinks back in her chair, now wishing she hadn't opened the thing; wishing that she didn't know about this Lotte and her feelings of longing, that she could return to the bliss of ignorance. So her husband has found comfort elsewhere; it is no surprise; she has taken George's love for granted. She wonders when this began, supposing it must have been going on since he went to Bruges in the old Queen's reign four years ago.

Anger prods at her: four years he has kept this secret. She thinks back, understanding now, his coldness, the air of distant respect. Her assumption had always been that he loved her so much more than she loved him, and all this time he loved another. She berates herself for her neglect of him, for all that time spent at court. Scrutinizing her feelings, she finds a little jealousy, a little anger, some guilt, but the prevailing sense is one of regret, that only now she has lost her marriage does she realize how very precious it was. She can feel an emptiness opening up inside her, as if she is mourning.

Without thinking, she takes a sheet of paper and uncorks the lid on the ink jar, sharpening a quill, beginning to pen a request to the Queen for permission leave court and travel to Bruges. She will not lose George without a fight and the Grey girls seem in no imminent danger now. Feria has stopped his scheming since the situation changed with France, and the Queen seems to be favouring her young cousins. She remembers her panic over Katherine a few months ago, how foolish she had been to imagine some secret marriage plot, and besides, Hertford is out of the country and will be for the best part of a year.

She thinks of her promise to Frances. She has done right by her friend; the girls are safe enough. Poor Katherine is mourning Juno. Levina cannot shake off the image of the girl's wan face at the funeral, as if all the joy had been knocked out of her and would never return. But she has her sister to comfort her. Levina is reminded of what she felt when Frances died, an intense, painful longing that has diminished over the months but will never leave her. Did she choose her friendship over her marriage? She supposes she did. It didn't feel like a choice at the time, not after the horror of Jane's death, but that is all in the past. Yes, she will leave as soon as she can get a passage, and hope there is a future to salvage for her and George.

Someone is banging at the door. 'It's Henry Carruth. Are you there?' comes the call.

'Just coming.' She opens up, feeling the heave of the wind against the door.

'St Paul's is struck,' he says. 'The spire is ablaze. We are watching from our rooftop. It is quite a sight. I thought you might like to see it. Will you join us?'

'The cathedral? Good Lord.' He is right, she *would* like to see this awful spectacle. 'I will bring my girl, if you don't mind. She is too afraid to stay alone.'

She grabs her wrap and, taking Ellen by the hand, follows Henry Carruth the few steps from her front door to his. They climb upstairs through the house, up and up until the final flight narrows to accommodate only a single person at a time. Once they are out of the trapdoor at the top they can see Anne Carruth standing with her children, a row of dark figures silhouetted against a sky which is flushed an angry carnelian red. She calls out a greeting and Levina joins them as they stand in stunned silence watching the blaze. Ellen grips Levina's hand tightly, trembling like a trapped animal. They can feel the heat on their faces. The flames are bright, licking up high above the spire, spilling out of the roof; it crackles loudly, spitting sparks like fireworks.

'This is God's work,' says Anne Carruth. 'He would have this place rid of Catholics for good.'

Levina nods, but she is thinking that the Catholics will have their own version of events – their God will be angry too. She is sure the Queen will find a way to make this event serve her own purposes. People, small dark shapes far below, have formed a line from the river, passing buckets, damping down the rest of the building to stop the flames spreading. But it is a futile task with a conflagration like this. She licks her finger, putting it up to the wind.

'It blows away from us,' she says. Then she thinks of all the souls living to the east, all the houses piled one atop the other; old houses built of wood and daub, toppling storeys added to accommodate burgeoning numbers crammed into them – that is London nowadays. Alice Carruth cries out as the great bells topple into the south tower with a terrible crash. She is a pretty girl and still remains unwed. Levina thinks of Marcus, wishing he were here and courting her still, and inevitably her mind turns, with a needle pierce of grief, to George, cosy in Bruges with his Lotte. The wind changes direction, towards them, causing a buzz of panic, but behind it comes the rain, torrents of it, sending them back inside, where they sit up about the hearth, drinking a hot brew and awaiting news that the fire is out.

Levina finds the hall empty when she comes down the following morning. Her mind is still ablaze with images of the fire, her imagination running wild with impressions that she would like to translate in paint. The storm has cleared the air and a shaft of sun streams in through the window, pooling on the floorboards. Levina can see that the room hasn't been swept properly and that the dust has collected in the corners. When she looks about she begins to notice that the furnishings are looking tattered and that the whole place has an unloved air about it. She hadn't noticed it until now, that she has neglected their home, neglected their marriage, neglected George. It is no wonder he has found a warm body elsewhere.

She remains resolved to go to Bruges, but in the cold light

of day doubts have sprung up about what such a journey could achieve. She had felt so sure last night that if she went to him he would return with her, for they are married in the eyes of God, after all. But now she fears he will not want to come back. What is here for him with Marcus gone and his love alighted on another? But nothing ventured, nothing gained – she will go.

July 1561
Greenwich
Katherine

'Lady Katherine, where are the Queen's linens? They need packing. Are they back from the laundry?' Kat Astley's voice is hammering at my head. We are preparing to leave on progress.

'I have not seen them, Mistress Astley.' She looks on with distaste as I pour some water out for my dogs, who pant listlessly in the heat. She does not approve of pets. I wave a fan at my face but all it does is churn the thick air about a little.

'Well find them!' she says.

Her bluntness echoes the Queen's. I am out of royal favour once more. I suspect the Queen has been told of a dalliance between Hertford and me, although in fairness I hardly sought to hide it. She cannot possibly know of my marriage, though, for only three living souls are aware of that aside from me. A flirtation alone, mentioned at the wrong time, would be enough to displease her, and there are plenty of vindictive spirits amongst the Queen's women. Mistress Astley speaks to me as if I am a common servant maid – I suppose she thinks the Queen's disfavour gives her the right.

There is no point complaining – no one to complain *to*. Even Levina has left for Bruges on some business or other, not that she could have done anything to help me. Of all the people I have ever held truly dear – and that is only seven – six-sevenths are gone: Father, Jane, Maman and Juno to Paradise, Hertford to God knows where and Levina to Bruges. If it were not for Mary I would be entirely unmoored.

Mary does her best to cheer me, but it is a hopeless task; my spirit is quite broken. The Queen sharpens her vicious wit on me in public, singling me out for a ruthless drubbing whenever she can.

'Songbird?' she had laughed when Cecil praised my singing yesterday. 'That caterwauling?' She has called me 'Lady Caterwaul' several times since. The Queen has a nose for fragility, likes nothing more than to crush it, and my weakness is written all over me. Grief for Juno has emptied me, and now Hertford is gone too. He left me with a kiss, four hundred crowns, a will that names me as the beneficiary and a promise that he will return immediately if it so happens that I find myself with child. I am bereft to the bone and plagued by a fear, twisting about in me, that he will not return, that something will happen to him. I curse Cecil for sending him abroad.

Cecil took me aside on the day of my husband's departure.

'This *friendship* you have developed with the Earl of Hertford. It needs to stop.' He smiled, exposing a row of teeth, big and yellow like slabs of limestone, and I wondered how much he knew. 'You are not any girl who can have entanglements here and there, Cousin. It would be wise to take *my* guidance on the matter.'

'Your guidance,' I said. 'Have you a match in mind for me?' I suppose I thought to throw him off the scent.

'I know there has been secret talk of a Spanish husband for you.'

'Where did you hear of such a thing?' I had all but forgotten my proposed 'illustrious match'.

'There is nothing I do not know about, Lady Katherine.'

'Is that so?' I was thinking that he did not know I was wed to Hertford and that gave me a misguided sense of triumph. For what use is a secret if you cannot lever something with it?

'If Feria contacts you, I want to know. Am I understood?'

I nodded, saying, 'He will not.'

'We are kin.' The word 'kin' was said as a chaplain might say the word 'sin'. Then he'd added, so quietly I wasn't sure I'd heard correctly, 'I am on *your* side, My Lady.' I wanted to ask what he meant by that.

'I sent away that pup you are sweet on for your own good,' he'd continued. 'And perhaps when the time comes . . . It is all a question of timing.'

I couldn't look at his eyes and kept my gaze fixed on the three warts decorating the side of his face.

'With the right wedding' – he wiped a clammy hand down my cheek – 'sanctioned by Her Majesty. Well, I don't like to say it, but the Scottish claim could be swept aside entirely.'

Then he chucked me under the chin as if I were an infant, saying, 'You look in fine fettle, Cousin. Never better, I'd say,' and turned tail, leaving me wondering what plans he was cooking up with Kitty Grey at their heart.

I am exhausted with all the wondering. Once I might have shaken it off, but I am not me any more. When the Queen prods me with a rapier quip I find that, rather than delivering the kind of witty riposte that would smooth my way back to favour, I struggle to hold back tears. And Elizabeth can smell weakness – it is carrion to her. The fearless girl who jumped into the river pool is no more. It is as if she were buried alive with Juno – indeed, that is the dream that visits me nightly. I twist the death's head ring I wear in her memory, bringing it to my lips for a kiss. It is cold, even in this heat – cold.

'We don't have all day.' Kat Astley's brusque voice cuts through my thoughts. 'And what on earth are you doing wearing that in this weather? Don't expect my sympathy if you suffer heat stroke.'

'I do not feel the heat,' I lie, wrapping my loose black gown about me. It is heavy and unbearably hot, but I will not take it off, and hope they all think I wear it in respect of Juno.

I make for the laundry, my dogs in my wake, glad of an excuse to get out of the privy chamber. In the dank lower corridor, where it is cool and there is no one about, I stop, leaning against the chill stone wall. I unlace my stomacher a little and hold my belly, feeling the unmistakable sensation, as if something is unfolding itself in there, a cat having a stretch. It is my baby.

I let the blissful feeling wash over me, obliterating my misery for barely a moment. But nothing can stave off thoughts of the pleading letters I have sent to Hertford and no reply, not a word, nothing. So much for his promise, he who was so enthralled by the prospect of making an infant with me. I can hear him whisper, 'An heir for England,' feel his breath against the skin of my neck as he spoke those words. My longing is unbearable as a stretch on the rack, a twist of the thumbscrews. *You are abandoned*, says a voice in my head. There lies a dark fear in me that I shall lose my mind altogether and end up with the lunatics in St Bethlehem.

Hearing footsteps, I wrap my loose gown about me once more, asking myself how it is possible that no one has noticed. Mary, who is the only soul to whom I have confided, tells me it does not show, that I look as though I have developed an appetite, that is all. Soon, though, it won't be hidden – the thought of that is a noose about my neck, whichever way I turn it tightens. I must not think of it, nor must I allow myself to believe Hertford has abandoned me. Can there be another reason for his silence? Do not think of it; do not think of it; do not think of it.

I walk on towards the laundry, taking a short cut through the stable yard, where I see Pembroke at a distance dismounting and handing his horse to one of the grooms. He sought me out not even a month ago and made the suggestion, in a roundabout way, that things might be 'rekindled' – that was the word he used – between Harry Herbert and me. 'You have the Queen's favour these days, I am told,' he had said. I was looking at his hands, big and ruddy, remembering him slapping me across the face, and was laughing inwardly to watch him fawn.

I was tempted tell him he was too late if he meant to use that favour to his advantage. 'Well, *your* tune has changed,' is what I said, not minding my manners, watching him hold back his anger at my impudence. He would have liked to slap me again, no doubt.

'Much has changed,' he said. 'Give it some thought. Write to Harry at Baynard's. He should like to hear from you.'

He sees me across the yard now, lifting his cap and nodding. If he knew I was with child and secretly married he would not be so eager to doff his cap. He must not have heard that I have fallen from favour with the Queen. He cannot know I am with child to a man who has disappeared, and that I am unable even to prove I am married, for the only witness is dead and the chaplain – well, God only knows where he has got to; I do not even know his name. Worse still, I have managed to misplace the will Hertford drew up before he left. *You are abandoned*, whispers the voice in my head. The air is so heavy I cannot breathe it in. I must not think of all those things.

I ignore Pembroke and, heedless of the Queen's linens, go to seek out Mary in the maids' quarters. She is alone when I find her, stripped to her shift, reading a book on the bed. I flop down beside her, asking, 'How did you get away?'

'Feigned a headache,' she replies. I unpeel my layers of clothing. 'A rare moment alone together,' she says, helping me out of my kirtle.

'I miss Juno's rooms,' I say.

'Yes.' She knows I mean it is Juno I miss.

I put my hands on my belly, stretching the fabric of my shift tight to show her my shape. 'It *is* nine months, isn't it?'

'From start to finish? I believe so.'

'But from when do you count it?' I try and think about when it might have been planted in me, but it could have been one of a thousand times.

Her reply is a shrug. 'No one has ever spoken of these things to me.'

'Nor to me. Perhaps you count from when you first feel it move. Could that be right?'

'Maybe.' She sounds doubtful.

'To think, Mouse, how I was armed to the hilt with information on how to not get myself with child, but had never thought to discover how it goes at the other end of things.'

'More's the pity you didn't take –'

I interrupt before she states the obvious. 'I am married, I had no need.'

Mary is disappointed in me; I can see it all over her. And she's no help, she knows even less than me. Moreover, there is not a soul I trust to ask.

'I'm only saying it is a shame you find yourself thus.' She

takes my hand, giving it a squeeze. 'I wish I could help, Kitty.'

I remember the old Queen and the muddle over her pregnancy. I have watched married ladies in the privy chamber grow large and then leave for their lying-in, returning a few months on, slender as girls again. But sometimes they don't return at all. That is another thing I must not think of.

I pull up my shift, exposing my bare belly. Yes it is round, but not vast. 'What say you, Mouse, pleasantly plump?'

She strokes her small hand over my skin. Her touch makes tears prick at the back of my eyes.

'This is my niece or nephew,' she murmurs.

'Stop daydreaming about becoming an aunt, and tell me if you think I can hide it still.'

'I think you might. You do not have the look of Mary Sidney when she left to have *her* baby.'

'How would you know what she looked like?'

'I helped her dress when she was too big even to fasten her shoes. I saw her in her shift when she had a month to go.'

'And she didn't look like this?'

'Not at all. Her belly was vast and tight as a drum.' She makes a round shape with her arms as if hugging an invisible person. 'But Kitty –' She doesn't say anything else but I know she is wondering what will become of me.

All the things I must not think of crowd back into my head. I cannot breathe and run to the window, flinging it wide, trying to take in gulps of air. The stone flags below are smooth and hard. I imagine my head cracking open against them, bursting like a melon.

I feel Mary's touch at my shoulder. 'When things are at their worst, I ask Jane for guidance.'

'Jane? Our *sister* Jane? What do you mean?' I am still thinking of those smooth hard flags below.

'Sometimes it is a comfort,' she says, leading me gently away from the window. 'I wonder to myself what Jane would do.'

'I know what she would say to me. She would point out that I have brought this upon myself through my own folly.'

'She would say you must accept God's plan.'

I am thinking, *What use is God's plan when this baby is growing inside me?* but I do not say so, cannot say it out loud.

July/August 1561
Essex/Suffolk
Mary

I am spent by the time we get to Lord Rich's house at Wanstead. My pony Sygnet may be docile but my bent body was not made for a whole day's riding. My back aches terribly, making it hard to walk when I dismount. A thrush is singing somewhere and I close my eyes for a moment, leaning against the wall to listen while Katherine retrieves her dogs from the luggage cart, letting them run about and do their business before we go inside. I fear greatly for her; she has barely said a word for the entire journey and seems more exhausted even than I, as if the light in her has been snuffed out. We slowly heave ourselves up the stairs; the dogs skipping behind, their claws clack-clacking on the stone.

As we get to the anteroom that has been set aside to serve as a privy chamber, a package arrives. It is brought by Henry Seymour, Hertford's brother.

'For Her Majesty,' he says, and I'm sure I see him wink at Katherine. 'From France.' It is a wooden crate about half a yard across and bound with twine.

'Here,' says Kat Astley in her usual brusque manner, 'give

it to me.' She takes the box and, ever cautious of foul play, inspects it minutely, sniffing it and asking Henry Seymour to lift it that she may scrutinize its underside. 'From France, you say, My Lord?'

'From my brother,' he replies. So that is what the wink was for. At last Hertford is in touch. I look at Katherine and see a bud of hope begin to open in her.

'Ah, the jewellery Her Majesty commissioned,' says Kat Astley. 'Why don't you open it, Lady Katherine, and relieve us all of our curiosity? You certainly need cheering up, that face of yours has been long as a yard of sackcloth for weeks.'

Katherine kneels on the floor beside the parcel and we all crowd round to watch her open it. Someone passes her a knife to cut the twine. Kat Astley is standing at a distance, peering over our heads as if it is full of gunpowder and might explode. My sister lifts the lid with a bright look and pulls out, one by one, a dozen packages. Each has a name attached and they are distributed amongst the ladies. With the largest of them taken, by Kat Astley, through to the Queen's bedchamber. We all tear them open, gleefully holding up the contents, each one a pair of gold bracelets. There is even a set for me, small like an infant's. I hold them up to the candlelight to better inspect the fine work of the French goldsmith, whose mark is stamped on the inside.

Katherine doesn't open hers, I notice, but tucks it beneath her skirts. I am so very eager to know what lies within it. A note announcing Hertford's imminent return, I suppose. I sincerely hope so, for that would mean the end of my poor sister's anguish is in sight, though there is still the hurdle of informing the Queen of the infant she carries. When Hertford comes back, he will explain and all will be well. With luck we shall all be given permission to stay away from court – that would be a blessing indeed.

'Kitty, dearest, would you accompany me to the house of easement,' I say, as an excuse to be alone with her.

'Of course, Sister,' she replies.

She is fit to burst with excitement, her cheeks are flushed and her eyes shining. We rush out down the corridor, not knowing quite where to go, for neither of us has been to this house before. We eventually happen upon a little music room where the candles have been lit beside a set of virginals.

Katherine holds the package to her face, breathing in its scent as if she might find something of him there, and then, smiling, fingers fumbling, rips the paper off it. Inside is a pair of bracelets, identical to all the others.

'Oh!' she says, her smile dropping away. She picks up the discarded wrapping, inspecting it to see if she has missed the letter which must surely be enclosed within. Finding nothing, she allows the bracelets to fall to the floor with a clatter and drops her face into her hands.

'I'm sure he was simply being cautious, in case it wasn't you who opened it. Do not despair, Henry Seymour must have a letter for you. Come, Kitty, let's seek him out.' She says nothing but rises and makes for the door, leaving the bracelets on the floor. I hand them to her. 'You must appear as normal. If you are not wearing them, people will wonder why.'

She holds out her hand like a child and I slip them on to her wrist. I collect up the wrapping and inspect it myself, looking carefully through each layer in case she has missed something. But she is right, there is no word from Hertford.

Henry Seymour is still amongst the Queen's ladies when we return, flirting with one of the maids. I take him aside, asking discreetly if he has anything else for my sister, but he shakes his head and opens both palms up to the ceiling, uttering 'nothing' with a look of apology.

I consider telling him of the situation, asking him to get word to his brother, for perhaps Katherine's letters have gone astray. But the more I think on it the more it seems impossible, for she has written several times and how could they all be lost? The more likely explanation is that Hertford has had a change of heart – he would not be the first to leave a girl in such a way. I decide it is best to say nothing, for the more who know it the more likely it is to get out. Though get out it will, eventually, whether we like it or not.

We travel from Wanstead to Havering, packing up, the Queen's bed dismantled, all her jewels carefully stored and given into the care of one of the guards. The poor yellow lovebirds, flagging in the heat, are fetched from the house and their cage hung from a hook on one of the carts to swing back and forth for another leg of the journey. It is the closest they will ever get to freedom. If I am bone tired from restless nights on itchy straw pallets, I cannot imagine how Katherine must feel. But she will not talk of it – she will not talk at all unless asked a direct question, and even then answers with a nod or shake of the head if she can. The Queen loves to travel, to be seen, relishes the crowds that line the road to catch a glimpse of their beloved monarch. They hold out little bouquets of wild flowers; pots of jam; sweetmeats; loaves that they can ill afford to give away; and occasionally a sick child is proffered in the hope that it will be cured of its ills by the Queen's touch.

We are like a party of splendid ghouls with our legions of servants and guards, our fine apparel and our faces wrapped against the dust and sun, just eyes peeping out. Most of the maids find it hard to suppress their excitement on progress, for we move about so much to unfamiliar places, which means they are less closely watched, giving more opportunities for romance. I am not so fond of plodding around the countryside in the blistering heat and, for the sake of my sanity, imagine myself back at Beaumanor, by the lake, reading or watching Aphrodite glide by. Sometimes I recite Latin verbs in my head to stop me thinking of the things I can do nothing about. *Amo*, *amas*, *amat*, *amamus*, *amatis*, *amant*. I watch Katherine, who rides beside me listlessly. She is glazed about the eyes and silent as a slab of marble. I have stopped asking Jane's council: her voice whispered from beyond the grave has nothing to say on this situation. It is beyond her experience.

In mid-July we come to Pyrgo, the house of my uncle Lord John Grey, who is my father's brother. Dudley has arrived with an army of servants, all in new green livery. He is back in splendid favour, the puzzling thwarted investiture seemingly forgotten. I suppose, given his dead brother was married to my dead sister, he is our brother-in-law. So perhaps here, surrounded by family of sorts, Katherine will find a way to petition Uncle John and Dudley for help. I can think of no better plan. We all dismount and shake the dust from our clothes in the courtyard. I suggest it to her in a whisper, as we are shown the way to the Queen's rooms.

'But Uncle John is so terrifying,' she replies.

'He is gruff,' I say. 'But he is family. And you are beginning to show. I heard Lizzie Mansfield remark how fat you'd become earlier. Kitty, you must say something.'

We are seated near Uncle John at dinner, and he is friendly enough, which gives me hope. But when the Queen arrives, she has Katherine moved further down the table, away from her. From that moment she may as well not exist, for Uncle John, who has read the situation for what it is, assiduously ignores his out-of-favour niece. He knows which side his bread is buttered. He must have half bankrupted himself to put on this display of hospitality and is not about to waste it. I watch him as I try to eat, ingratiating himself with Dudley and the Queen, a counterfeit smile spread over his face. I try to catch his attention, but he goes out of his way not to see me.

We leave Pyrgo and nothing has changed save for Katherine's belly, which seems to swell hourly. She keeps her loose gown about her even though the heat is intolerable. There is hardly a breath of air and I fear she will faint and fall from her horse into the road. Most of the ladies take turns to sit in one of the litters, which are shaded with canopies, or the new coach, when the Queen is not using it. But Katherine is determined to stay mounted and has set her jaw in a stubborn clench. Despite my own exhaustion I remain at her side, thankful for docile Sygnet who lumbers along giving me no trouble.

We spend a weekend at Ingatestone and then on to Beaulieu, near Chelmsford, where I am haunted by vague memories of my infanthood. We used to come and visit Cousin Mary here long before she was Queen. I remember the vaulted ceiling in the great hall and the particular incense smell of the chapel and an image comes to me of Maman with a beaming smile. Those were happy times, I suppose, but I barely remember them. I imagine a world in which Katherine and Hertford have set up house together and I am with them awaiting their firstborn. The thought makes me slack with sadness.

The weather becomes so close by the time we leave Beaulieu that we can only travel in the morning; by midday we need to find shade. All anyone talks of is the insupportable heat and how they have not slept a wink. My sister says nothing, though I know she lies awake tossing and turning every night, for I lie next to her. We can all feel a storm brewing – the air is thick with it. But we get past Felix Hall and on to

Colchester, where there is still no let-up, then on to St Osyth, watching the bank of angry cloud accumulate ahead of us as we ride. We have just dismounted and entered the house when the storm finally breaks with an almighty clap of thunder that has all the ladies squealing. Echo is petrified, trembling in my arms, and the other dogs are cowering behind the mountain of trunks that hold the Queen's effects. Katherine sits on the floor huddled with them – she looks as frightened as they are.

I watch from the window as jagged streaks of lightning slash the sky, illuminating the parklands, and I remember the recent storm that burned down the steeple of St Paul's. We passed the cathedral on the river a few days after it happened and saw the blackened stump where the spire used to soar up to the heavens. It was a sign, they all said – of what, each had their own idea. The rain comes at last, like a stampede of cattle over the roof, bringing with it a drop in temperature, a relief to us all. But the rain is torrential and falls for hours in relentless sheets, with water gushing everywhere, flooding the gardens, and the horses have to be moved from the stables for they are standing in six inches of water. Even inside the house the scullions have to run about with buckets to capture the leaks where the roof is letting in the rain.

Soon after we are on to Ipswich, a cooler ride, if a muddy one, and we are splattered up to the elbows. The Queen is in an ill temper, railing at everyone. Cecil, who joined our party at Colchester, circles round and about, trying to placate her constantly. She even snaps at Dudley, which is rare of late. She has taken umbrage with the number of married churchmen in the city. Though why, I do not know, since she is of the new faith which champions wedded clergy. But Elizabeth is a conundrum that can never quite be understood. We all keep out of her way if possible; only Kat Astley has the nerve to deal with her moods. I keep Katherine well away, making excuses for her when it is possible. There is no hiding her belly now and my greatest fear is that her infant surprises us here in Ipswich. We are not all lodged together; Katherine, myself, and a number of others, are thankfully billeted in a town house a short walk from the Queen's lodgings, which at least gives us some space to breathe.

It is the dead of night when I overhear whispers from across the chamber where we are all bedded down on pallets.

'She is fit to burst.' It is Frances Meautas's voice, I am sure, and even surer when I hear Lizzie Mansfield reply.

'Does she really think we can't see?'

'Whose do you think it is?'

'Hertford?'

'Herbert?'

'That Dudley page who stares at her all day, eyes on stalks?' I hear a muffled giggling. My anger brews.

'It could be any one of the fawning varlets about court.'

'She is not known for her modesty, is she?'

There is more giggling and a shushing that seems to come from Mistress St Low's direction. If there is anyone amongst the ladies who will be sympathetic to Katherine it is kindly Mistress St Low. She is steady as a rock in the sea, and I resolve to persuade my sister to talk to her on the morrow, for we have gone beyond the point of keeping this secret. I lie awake listening to Katherine shifting and groaning all night. The poor girl seems unable to find a comfortable position and no wonder, given the size of her.

The first of the birds are singing, when she heaves her body up and plods from the chamber to relieve herself. I follow her lumbering figure out and divulge my suggestion that she fall on the mercy of Mistress St Low. She is entirely spent of spirit and agrees to do so, knowing there is no choice in the matter. Back in the room, and once the other maids are up and gone to their duties, I contrive to leave the two of them alone together and I wait outside, expectantly, like a husband outside a birthing chamber. I am not kept waiting long before the door is flung open and Mistress St Low appears, utterly beside herself, distressed in a way that is completely out of character.

'I wish to God I had been left in ignorance,' she wails, rushing past me and down the stairs. 'This will visit trouble on us all.'

I find Katherine lying on her side, spectrally white and staring at the wall. Her dogs stand uncertainly beside her; Stan whimpers quietly, apparently aware that something is very wrong with his mistress.

'I'd be better off dead,' she says, repeating it several times as if in a trance.

'Kitty,' I say softly, taking a cloth, which I rinse in the ewer and wipe over her forehead. 'You *must* pull yourself together.' I help her to sit upright, turning over in my head all the possible actions she might take, rejecting them in turn, alighting eventually on one that at least makes sense. 'I think you should put your trust in Dudley; he is our brother-in-law, after all. He can approach the Queen on your behalf – you know how she is with *him*.'

'Dudley?' She is looking at me as if I have suggested she offer herself up to the Devil himself.

'If anyone can persuade the Queen to show you clemency, then it is he. And,' I add, as it occurs to me, 'when she discovers you are with child she may well think it best to finally wed Dudley and spawn an heir of her own. Remind him of that. His sympathy is guaranteed if it means he may get what he wants.'

I can't imagine why I have not thought of this before. I am

beginning to think if I had been born a man I would have made a serviceable politician.

After some coaxing, Katherine resolves to speak to Dudley before the day is out, and it is just as well, for when we get to prayers several of the maids are whispering behind their hands and glancing over their prayer books towards her. It has already spread far enough, and it won't be long before the entire Queen's retinue is aware of Katherine's secret, and Heaven only knows what calumny will be invented to add to the story with each retelling.

It is late afternoon when the guards come, as we finish supper and are filing out of the hall. Katherine had returned from Dudley's quarters earlier bright, optimistic even – a little of her old self returned – and I had dared to think her reprieved. But here they are, half a dozen of them in full guards' dress, red-faced and sweating in the heat, armed with halberds and one even with a musket.

One of them grabs her by the upper arm, no greeting. Everyone gawps. I find myself wishing, not for the first time, that Levina were here or stalwart Keyes, for moral support, but I alone must take her side.

'Lady Katherine is the Queen's cousin,' I say, pulling myself up as tall as I can. 'Treat her with some respect.'

My words must have some effect as the guard lets her go and, standing before her, unfolds a paper from which he reads the terms of her arrest.

The colour drops out of her face and I fear she will faint there on the cobbles, so I take her hand and lead her to the side of the courtyard where there is a bench. One of the guards tries to tell us to remain standing, but I give him a look of such ferocity he is silenced before the order is fully spoken.

‘Where are you taking her?’ I ask the guard with the musket, who appears to be in charge.

‘The Tower,’ he replies. I think I can hear regret in his voice, but perhaps I am imagining it. I ask myself if Katherine is thinking, as I am, of Jane and Father, and wondering why it is that all the roads in our family lead to that dreadful place.

‘I shall accompany her on the journey,’ I say. ‘She is with child and must be treated with care.’

‘I am instructed . . .’ he stops, and is unable to look me in the eye. Then he drops his official tone, saying quietly, ‘She is to come alone.’ He opens his palms at his sides and makes a small shrug, revealing a sliver of sympathy that gives me a pinch of hope that at least she will be well treated on the journey. He is acting on the Queen’s orders and has no choice. I feel a storm of rage gathering in me towards that woman who hasn’t an ounce of sympathy in her. It is as if time has collapsed and I am back on Mary Tudor’s lap, hearing that Jane is to be executed. They are not so different, those sister queens, their spirits both woven through with ruthlessness.

A small crowd has gathered to watch. They all know her; all the girls have helped her dress and they have sewn together, hunted together, shared jokes and trenchers of food, exchanged their secrets, but not a soul comes forward with a soothing word. Eventually it is Kat Astley who shoos them all away. I never thought I’d find a reason to be grateful for something *she* has done.

‘Do you have a litter prepared?’ I ask, and the man tells me there is one waiting in the outer yard. I can see clearly now from his expression that he is ashamed by this duty he must perform, arresting a young woman so burdened with child. He points through a nearby arch and I see that her litter at least has a canopy. I call out to one of the pages, asking that he fetch some pillows and blankets and her chest of belongings from our rooms. 'And the dogs, the monkey,' I say, glancing at the guard, who makes to speak but then seems to change his mind and nods his assent. If I cannot travel with her, then at least she shall have the comfort of her pets.

She still hasn't said a single word as she is bundled into the conveyance, just stares silently ahead, lifeless as a wax effigy.

'I will petition the Queen, Kitty,' I whisper, kissing her on both cheeks. She doesn't respond, seems to have disappeared inside herself, and it is with a leaden heart that I watch them heave her litter up and march off, with a cart trundling behind and more guards at the rear.

I go immediately to seek out Kat Astley. 'The Queen will not see you.' She is folding linens and doesn't look up as she speaks.

'I beg of you to ask her.' I try not to sound too pleading, too pathetic.

'Look, it brings me no pleasure to see her taken to that place in her condition. You think I am made of stone; well, I am not. I have already asked the Queen to allow you an audience but her answer was "no".' Kat looks at me now, must see how surprised I am at what she says, that she has taken the risk of raising the Queen's wrath in support of the disgraced Greys. 'The words she used were, "That girl is from a family of traitors and she has shown she cannot be trusted – like her father. Do not ask me again, Kat. I will not see her, nor the sister, so leave it be."'

'I see,' I reply, sitting down, feeling hollowed out by the whole thing, completely exhausted.

'She had a match in mind for your sister,' Kat says. 'The Earl of Arran, I believe it was.'

I simply shake my head. I do not know this man, but only suppose that with a name like Arran he is close to the

Scottish throne, another card in Elizabeth's pack. Elizabeth likes to win at cards.

'The Queen had talked privately to me of your sister's marriage prospects. She might not have been altogether against Hertford if the Arran thing hadn't come to pass.' She straightens her gown, pulling the sleeves tightly down over her wrists, adding, 'But it is too late now.'

She leaves the room and I am alone with the lovebirds, whose cage I open. 'Go on, fly off. You are free.' But they look at me from their perch, heads tilted to the side, and do not take the opportunity to escape, as I have so often imagined they would.

V
Lord Beauchamp

August 1561
The Tower of London
Katherine

It is a beautiful day – not hot, not cold, with white puffs of cloud in a jewel-bright sky. A day for lovers, I am thinking, for I am trying to forget that a whole company of guards is marching either side of me across the courtyard before the White Tower. I don't know why there need be so many of them. Do they truly believe I, who can barely lumber a few paces without the need to sit and catch my breath, would try to escape? I watch as a cart is unloaded of my effects, imagining this is an ordinary arrival, that I am merely visiting relatives in an unfamiliar place. A man struggles with my pets, Hercules wants to perch on his shoulder and he is having none of it, shouting angrily; I will my monkey to bite him. Echo has spotted me and has begun to howl. The sound is getting right inside my heart, churning it up.

'Steady, Echo,' I call out to her, trying to hide the tremor in my voice. 'We shall be together soon.'

I am shocked to see that Mistress St Low is here too, arrived with another consignment of guards. She is being taken inside and I think I am not supposed to have seen her, as I am swiftly moved along, out of sight. Poor woman; had I not confided in her, she wouldn't be here. I have a glimpse of the way my thoughtlessness, my desire to pursue pleasure at all costs, is like a pebble thrown into a pond, the ripples moving outwards. If I thought more of God it would all be different. But if I thought more of God I would not be me.

The Chapel of St Peter is opposite. Seeing it, realizing that Father and Jane are buried there, I fully understand the gravity of my situation. The thought of them beneath the earth – my handsome father food for worms – swells in my head, expanding until I feel my skull will break in two. My throat constricts; a surge of panic runs through me. What did Mary say about asking Jane for guidance? I remember something. Closing my eyes I try to calm my breath, slowly, in and out, slowly, in and out. I see Jane's face as clear as if she is standing before me. *I shall learn you to die*, she whispers. I question how I will manage to hold on to my sanity in this place, without Mary by my side.

I open my eyes to see a smiling, voluminously bearded man before me with a wriggling Echo in his arms, holding her out for me to take. I clasp her to me, reassured by the way she snuggles into the crook of my arm and laps at my hand with her tongue.

'Sir Edward Warner,' the man says, taking a bow and removing his cap to reveal a shiny pate – it is as if all the hair has fallen from his head and landed upon his chin. 'I thought your spaniel might be of solace to you, My Lady.' He reaches out and scratches Echo's ear. 'This is difficult, I know, and I am sorry to be your host under such circumstances. But it is my hope that you will be comfortable here at the very least, and that your stay will be a short one.'

I manage a smile, my panic receding. I make myself imagine it is not so bad after all. Then I realize the implication of what he has said and become agitated once more.

'There is a fine chamber in the Bell Tower,' he points across the green. 'You will be comfortable enough there, I believe.'

A question insinuates itself into my mind. 'Was . . .' I cannot say it. Warner, still smiling, waits for me to continue. 'Was my sister housed there?'

'I think not.' His smile has dissolved. 'But the Queen herself spent some months there.'

I suppose he is trying to reassure me that most who come here do not end on the block, and I find I *am* a little reassured. Perhaps it is his kindly demeanour; perhaps it is the relief from the terrible anxiety of recent weeks, when I could see no way to turn and my secret was sucking all the life from me. I wonder about Mary, if she spoke to the Queen on my behalf as she said she would. I wonder if she is to be brought for questioning like Mistress St Low, but Mary is clever enough to outfox her adversaries.

'Mistress St Low . . .' I begin.

'Yes, My Lady?'

'She was not party to any of this.' I point at my great belly. 'She only knew when I fell upon her mercy. She never tried to conceal anything from the Queen.' The words are tumbling out of me now. 'Please spare her from any anguish on my behalf. She is a good woman and truly loyal to Her Majesty.'

'She will be well treated, as will you, My Lady.'

'And Hertford?' I am suddenly gripped tightly about the breast with a longing for him. 'Will he come?'

'Herford has been sent for, My Lady. Now, shall we get you settled?' He takes my elbow firmly, I let Echo jump to the ground and we walk towards my lodgings. 'My wife is waiting there for you and the Queen has asked us to provide a servant girl, who I hope is to your liking.' Then he leans in to whisper, 'If not, then we shall find another.'

As we arrive at the doorway I can't help but take another look at the chapel and I know, for everyone does, that the scaffold is erected on the green before it when it is required. That is the exact spot where brave Jane met her death. I wonder if I would be so brave – I wonder if I will need to be. She whispers again – *I shall learn you to die.* I try to remember the exact words she wrote to me, but it is so long since I saw it. I can't even recall what became of that book.

Warner has to help me up the stairs, for I find myself faint. 'A lady in your condition,' he mutters, 'in this place. It is not right.'

The main room is spacious and round with small window recesses at regular intervals, offering views of the Thames. I can see a great effort has been made on my account as a bed with damask hangings has been put up, and in one of the window alcoves sits a red velvet chair, a pair of footstools and a purple cushion. Hercules is seated on the floor grooming himself, seeming quite at home.

I am greeted by Lady Warner, who says she supposes I would like to rest, 'But perhaps you should like to first see outside,' she adds, leading me out on to the parapet where there is a sizeable walkway that leads to another tower. 'The Beauchamp Tower,' she tells me, when I ask its name.

'Was it there that my sister was held?' I inquire, once more. I don't know why but I feel compelled to know. She looks at me. Her demeanour is a little timid; she is younger than her husband by a decade, I'd say, and has the kind of smooth skin you want to reach out and touch, like the fine vellum they use for bibles. I imagine her being scratched by that enormous beard.

She shakes her head. 'I think not. I am of the mind it was her husband who was held there, but I am not sure of it. I was not here at the time.'

'Guildford Dudley.' It is a long time since I spoke that

name. He died too. I remember when I first saw him at my wedding to Harry Herbert, how Jane could hardly bring herself to look at Guildford Dudley for all his handsomeness, and I couldn't take my eyes off my own groom. Thoughts of that first wedding bring back the other: dear Juno and that nameless chaplain, Hertford and I kneeling before him, fingers entangled, as someone banged urgently at the street door. I am assaulted with fragments of my husband: the smell of sweat and horse when he has been riding; his fingernails, black new-moons of dirt beneath them; the look in his eye when he wants me. With those impressions comes a rush of longing; whatever he has done or not done, I cannot help that feeling. It is love, I suppose, and I am in its grip. The past swirls about my head, Jane and Juno and Father all there with my love, but I push them away. I shall be all right here if I do not dwell on things. I must not think of absence or death or the dead; that is the rule for this place.

'Do you need rest?' inquires Lady Warner, making me realize I am speechless with fatigue and must look it. 'Lie down, My Lady. I have had Cook make a cold broth of cucumbers for you. It is what I liked when I was with child. I shall have the maidservant fetch it here. Her name is Nan; she is a sweet girl and will see to all your needs.' She settles me on to the bed and allows my dogs to clamber up beside me; she smells fresh, of cut grass.

I sink into the bed murmuring, 'Feathers.'

'Feathers indeed, My Lady. From my own cupboard. You deserve a feather bed in your condition.'

My eyes begin to well up, thinking of all those weeks on a thin straw pallet spread on the floor, and the constant fear night and day of my secret being discovered. Though I am in this place, a place of nightmares, now that my secret is out the fear has receded. They will not execute a woman with child, I reassure myself – but I must keep my thoughts in check.

I hear the key rasp in the lock and Nan goes to the door. It is Warner with another man, who bids her leave. I am sitting in the window combing the tangles out of Stan's coat. Warner has removed his cap, exposing his shiny pate, and the other man is shuffling in his wake wearing a sneer. He has a long pointed nose and an ill-fitting doublet and refuses to look me in the eye.

'May I introduce my deputy, My Lady?'

The man approaches, making a modest bow, lifting his cap a mere inch from his head and still not meeting my gaze. He holds a ledger carefully as if it is a gift from a lover.

'We have come to question you, My Lady.' There is the hint of an apology in Warner's voice. It strikes me that the Queen can't possibly be aware of the kindliness of my jailer; he would surely lose his post if she was.

'Please, Sir Edward,' I say, as if we are in the great watching chamber or some other illustrious setting. 'Be seated.' I indicate for him to take one of the footstools as I have only the single chair and it would not be proper for him to sit on my bed.

'I think I shall stand,' he says. The deputy, I can see, is wondering how he will make his notes in his ledger while remaining upright. I indicate another of the stools to him. He plants himself there, his knees reaching up beyond his elbows, giving him the look of a spider.

'I hope you don't find my manners lacking, that I remain seated,' I say. 'I find my condition makes standing rather arduous.'

We continue in this polite vein for a while, he asking if I have all I need for my comfort and suchlike, skirting about the real reason for his visit. But eventually he asks artlessly, 'Would you kindly tell me how you came to be with child, My Lady?'

I am tempted to deliver him a quip at this point – *You, a married man and a father yourself, must know well how I came to be with child* – but, though I am encouraged to see my spirit has not deserted me, I resist and say nothing.

'What are the circumstances of your wedding, if indeed there was a wedding, if indeed the Earl of Hertford *is* the father?'

I say nothing of my secret marriage, for I fear I might find myself in deeper water for it. I know I have told of it to Mistress St Low and to Dudley but that was not like this, with a man scribbling each word I utter in a ledger. Anything that is said in here, in the Tower, cannot be unsaid. The more I think of it the more I find myself tangled in it, and cannot tell if it is a worse crime to have dishonoured myself by getting an illegitimate child, or to have wed without the Queen's permission. The latter is treason, that much I know. So I say nothing of that winter's day at Canon Row; I do not tell of the fact that of the two witnesses, one is in Heaven and the other is – well, I know not where nor even who the other is – and I do not tell of Hertford's will, that named me and which I have already managed to misplace.

'The Queen believes you are not truly wed,' says Warner, adding to my confusion. Is he playing some kind of trick to force me to incriminate myself?

'Is that so?' I try to keep my voice steady but as I think of all the things that I do not say, my heart becomes heavier and heavier until I fear it will fall through the bottom of me. I am so afraid to say the wrong thing that I say nothing except, 'I trust Mistress St Low will not suffer on my account.'

'I am to question her myself.' It is the deputy who spits this out, scrutinizing me for any response.

'You shall discover that she knows nothing,' I say, narrowing my eyes at him. Then I turn to Warner. 'I shall wait until Hertford is here before I explain myself.'

'Oh dear,' is his reply. The deputy sighs loudly and closes his ledger with a slap, unfolding himself from the stool.

'But Hertford will come back,' I say. 'He will tell you everything you need to know.' I sound confident but I wonder, thinking of Hertford's long silence, if he has spirited himself away and will never be found.

'He has been recalled, My Lady.'

He makes for the door, rapping at it with the hilt of his sword. It is opened by Ball – that is the name I have given to my guard; the other one I have named Chain. I smile at him; he returns it briefly. I think Ball feels sorry for me. Warner too, though I believe his pity for me is smaller by far than is his fear of the Queen; but the deputy – it is clear as day what *he* thinks of me.

'You understand, My Lady, I shall have to question you again,' says Warner, as he departs.

'Indeed,' I reply. 'But my answers will always be the same.'

Later Lady Warner comes and sits with me, sewing clothes for my infant, little togs that touch my heart with their smallness. I imagine the baby who tosses and turns inside me, his miniature hands, miniature feet, miniature rosebud pout. When I picture him – for in my mind he has never been anything but a boy – his eyes are amber and his skin golden like his father's, and he has a soft, pale fuzz upon his head that I will kiss gently, breathing in his milky scent.

'You must love Hertford greatly,' Lady Warner says.

'I do.'

'Tell me of him. How was your wedding?'

I start to speak, but then stop, noticing the eagerness in her demeanour. Her husband has surely sent her to draw the truth out of me. 'Would you be kind and pass me the white thread, Lady Warner,' I say.

September 1561
Westminster
Mary

I look out at the Thames from Keyes's rooms above the watergate, thinking of Katherine downriver, glad to be near her once more. A hastily scrawled note was smuggled out to me yesterday. In it she described her lodgings and the parapet from which she watches the river traffic pass. She told me I was not to worry, that she was in good health, Hertford was on his way and all would be made right. So she has found her optimism once more. I feared greatly that she was sliding into insanity, that she might try to harm herself, or worse, but this letter has reassured me a little. It is something of a miracle, my sister's ability to hope for the best. But I cannot erase the forlorn look she wore leaving Ipswich under guard three weeks ago.

I left the court on its way to Hertford Castle, where the Queen was to receive the Scottish envoy. Peggy had sent word that she was returning to Whitehall, so I begged leave to join her and was surprised to have it granted. I could not have borne another hour in that company. The Queen appeared thin and worn and she would not look me in the eye; nor did she say anything, just dismissed me with a nod of the head. It was not an opportunity to plead Katherine's part.

She sent a consignment of guards – for my protection, or so I was told – and Dorothy Stafford, one of her inner circle, to accompany me. To spy on the traitor's sister, I suppose. But Dorothy is a gentle soul, beset by a crippling shyness, and though she is a good deal older than me, we found an unlikely affinity growing between us on the journey. Katherine was not mentioned, though she inhabited my thoughts and Dorothy's too, I think, for once, in the darkness of a bedchamber we shared along the route, she said, 'I do not agree with what has been done.' To say more than that, or to put a name to it, would have been folly.

The first person we encountered at the palace gates was Keyes and I cannot describe how my heavy heart was lifted on seeing him. His face was full of concern; he had clearly heard the news. I suppose the entire country has heard the news of Lady Katherine Grey's grave misdemeanour and her incarceration in the Tower. If I did not know it to be the truth, I would never believe that all my close family save Maman should end up in such a place. I pray night and day that Katherine will not meet the same fate as Jane and Father – it does not bear thinking of.

'I have been ordered to keep a close eye on you,' Keyes told me, as he helped me dismount. Upon which we shared a smile. Elizabeth cannot know of our friendship then, which means there remains a corner of my life that has avoided scrutiny. Keyes has propped me up like a pillar these last days and his modest rooms, a short walk from Whitehall, have become a refuge away from the vast echoing chambers of the Palace. There I can at least pretend, for an hour or so at a time, to have something like an ordinary existence.

We are gathered there in that lazy part of the afternoon when little occurs, glad that the court remains away and we have no duties to perform. Peggy and Dorothy are taking it in turn to read from a book of poems and Dorothy's brother Walter is strumming on a lute. It is a tune Katherine was particularly fond of, and the music conjures up a stream of memories from happier times. But when I think about it even the happiest times were shot through with one kind of sadness or another.

I am playing a game of chess with Keyes by the window, but I am not concentrating; I am watching the riverboats move back and forth on the murky swell and wondering about my sister.

'It is your move, My Lady,' says Keyes. I look at the board, exchanging a smile with him. There is little I can do to save myself at this point; I have not been concentrating and Keyes has my king at bay.

'The game is yours, Keyes,' I say. 'I am sorry not to have been a better opponent.'

'I say we play a round of primero,' suggests Peggy.

'Me too,' adds Walter, placing his lute on the table. 'Did you hear about Arundel losing near on a hundred guineas to the Queen at primero?'

'I did,' says Keyes. 'He stormed from the palace in a murderous temper, kicked a hole in one of the mounting blocks. I saw it myself.'

'He is not the only man to have lost such a sum to the Queen,' laughs Peggy. 'All us ladies know better than to find ourselves playing with her. She makes an appalling fuss if she loses – so they all feel obliged to let her win and then they are done for.'

'And find themselves on their stockinged knees begging for another estate from her, in order that they are able to pay their debts, I suppose,' says Walter, which even musters a laugh from me. They do their best to keep my spirits up.

We gather about the table and Keyes shuffles, flipping the cards about with the deftness of a juggler, despite the size of his hands. I watch his warm eyes dart about the company, occasionally meeting mine, feeling grateful that he welcomes us so freely to his rooms. Soon the court will return, we will be required to pass most of our waking hours in the privy chamber and I shall be in need of this sanctuary all the more.

We play swiftly and without speaking, save to call our suits or declare ourselves. Peggy, who has amassed a large heap of pennies, is eventually proclaimed victorious and we gather our things to leave. There is much to prepare for the Queen's arrival, but as we make to go Keyes holds me back, saying there is something he needs to tell me.

'In confidence,' he says. So I bid the others to go on ahead, never mind that it is not entirely correct for me, a maid, to be left alone with him. Nobody imagines there is the remotest risk that *my* virtue could be compromised.

'If I may be so bold, My Lady.' He seems doubtful, as if he fears he is overstepping his station, and I am reminded of Stokes, who had been such a kind husband to Maman. It is not the first time I have remarked a similarity, not a physical resemblance, though they are both big men; it is more a particular air they have in common, a surprising gentleness. 'It is about your sister.'

'Go on,' I say. I stand on a stool and we lean side by side on the window sill looking out. The afternoon sun falls in shafts across the water, transforming it from the murky depths of earlier into something of beauty, twinkling and light-struck.

'I have news of the Queen's interview with the Scottish ambassador.'

'What has that to do with Katherine?'

'The Queen has intimated – and I have this on good authority – that she may well not be averse to the Scottish Queen's claim. She falls well short of actually naming her as heir, but it takes the focus away from your sister.'

'How is it you know so much of all this?'

'It is my business to know. The security of this place depends upon it. I listen and I watch; and being a person of no consequence, few notice me. I may be large in size but I am quite inconspicuous.'

It strikes me that Keyes and I have something in common – the art of invisibility.

'I still don't see how this truly helps Katherine.'

'Without an heir of her body, the Queen will have to name a successor eventually; if she chooses Mary of Scotland, most of the Privy Council will unite on it. They so desire stability. And it will take the wind out of any plots that would see Lady Katherine on the throne. Your sister is fast becoming the reformers' cause.'

'The reformers' cause?' I repeat like a parrot. I had been so wrapped up with Katherine's pregnancy, her transgression, her sanity, fear of the Queen's wrath, all the immediate dangers, that of late I have forgotten to think about what else might be behind all this, or who might wish to take advantage. 'What do you know of that?'

He lowers his voice further still. 'I know the Queen suspects Cecil of being the puppet master behind your sister's wedding. Everyone knows Cecil would do anything to keep the Scottish Queen off the throne. That is why Lady Katherine is undergoing such a questioning.'

I hadn't thought they would question her, believing she had told them all they needed to know. But of course they would. It is more than I can bear to imagine my sister, huge with child, being interrogated in that place. I look down at the water below and my own dormant suspicions begin to waken; I try to think back, recall the facts, but all I can remember is Katherine running barefoot over the wet grass at Sheen to greet Hertford and Juno, he lifting her in his arms, the very image of love.

'It is a love match,' I say.

'But what it *is*, is less important than what it *seems*, My Lady.'

'Yes, of course.' I should know well enough that people are more swayed by how things appear than how they truly are. 'But I don't understand,' I say. 'I don't know what you think I can do to make a difference.'

'Lady Katherine is imprisoned because she has a legitimate claim to the throne and the Queen is well aware that if your sister births a son her own position could be under threat.'

I don't know why he is telling me what I already know only too well.

'Perhaps you could find the opportunity,' he continues, 'to provoke a discussion with the Queen about primogeniture. I believe she has a great respect for the notion.' He places a hand on the sill; mine looks tiny, a puppet's hand, beside it. 'Mary of Scotland may not have been in King Henry's succession,' he continues, 'but she *is* from the senior line of your family.'

'I know, I know.' It puts me in mind of that great family tree at Bradgate, its golden branches, the women hanging from them like fruits, ripe for the picking. 'But Mary of Scotland wasn't English-born, and she is Catholic. The Queen would never be convinced that *I*, of all people, would champion a Catholic.'

'That is neither here nor there, My Lady.' He brings his hands together now, as if in prayer. 'You would not be championing Catholicism, you would simply be on the side of tradition, the divine right – primogeniture being part of that.'

'To what ends?'

'It would serve to demonstrate your own lack of ambition and that could only be good for your sister . . . And yourself.' His logic is starting to make a certain sense.

'It is unlikely I will get the chance; the Queen can barely look at me, let alone give me her ear.' As I articulate this, it seems hopeless – everything hopeless.

'If you bide your time, My Lady, the opportunity may well arise.'

'Perhaps.' I shrug. 'Why do you do this for me, Keyes?'

'I don't want to see you come to harm,' is his reply. But I feel that there is something he is not saying, something beneath his words, something in the clumsy way he adds, 'You – your family doesn't – you don't deserve to have more . . .' He appears unable to finish, but eventually mumbles, 'More tragedy visited upon you.'

'Tragedy,' I say, as I leave the room. 'Us Greys are used to it.' I do not mean for my words to sound so full of bitterness – I do not want Keyes to think me bitter.

September 1561
The Tower of London
Katherine

Warner comes each day, his deputy always behind him like a shadow, and each day I say I have nothing more to tell him. This routine has gone on for a good three weeks now; time is measured in the swell of my belly. I feel Warner's frustration building as the deputy huffs and tuts in the background – I'm sure *he* would willingly use the rack on me. But they would not use coercion on a woman with child, of that I am sure. Lady Warner comes to sit with me each day too, but she only tried to tease the truth from me the once; we have never strayed into that territory again. So I sit and sew with her, or chat with Nan, always careful, even though Nan seems such an artless girl; or I stand on the parapet walkway, watching the riverboats pass. I do not let myself think of the future and I try not to dwell on the whereabouts of Hertford or what has become of him, for if my thoughts do stray to that place I know I shall never find a way to return.

But if I inspect the far reaches of my being, the quiet place behind my fears, I know my Hertford lives, that I am not abandoned. I can feel him drawing nearer as the moon pulls the tides. He will come and all will be explained and then we will be free – that is the only future I allow in my thoughts. Time creeps slowly here with so little to do and I wish I were more inclined to bookish pursuits like Mary. I try my hand at poetry, but find I have little talent for it, though happily Warner has procured me a lute. I play and sing with Nan, who has a high reedy voice that is not unpleasant.

I watch the river change colour through the day; sometimes it is rich and green and flat, sometimes choppy, the boats it carries at awkward angles, and in the early morning, when the cool sun is low, it is a length of silver satin. A few showers hail the approach of autumn; my belly has become stretched and round, the navel popped out. I wish I could show it to Mary, let her feel the hard curve of her nephew's heel shifting slightly, or the flutter of a little hand. I long for Mary almost as much as I long for Hertford and pray constantly for their safety – that we might all be reunited once more.

And then one morning, like any other, Ball pokes his head around my door, proffering a posy.

'Ball,' I say, in mock surprise, 'flowers for me? You are becoming quite the soft-heart these days.' I throw him one of my best smiles; I have developed quite a rapport with my two jailers who sometimes bring me sweetmeats and even snippets of information. I know from them that Mistress St Low has been released and is back with her family, which makes my heart a little less heavy.

Ball flushes red, glancing behind him to ensure we are alone, before he stammers, 'N-no, My Lady, these are from your husband.'

My head is full of fireworks. 'Hertford is here?'

'He is, My Lady. Arrived last evening, late.'

'Shall I see him?' We are whispering and I am prickling with excitement as I take the flowers, bringing them to my face, burying my nose in their scent.

'Sadly, no. Warner must verify your stories separately.'

'But where is he held?' I ask.

He says nothing, but inclines his head towards the Beauchamp Tower, which is clearly visible beyond the window. 'He will be there later. But *I* never told you so.'

I run my finger across my lips to demonstrate that they are sealed.

'And say the flowers are from me, if anyone asks.'

I nod. 'Why? . . . Why do you do this for me?' I have never had to ask this of a man before. I always knew why they would spring to do me service. Not now though, with my great belly and stuck in the Tower in disgrace.

He looks behind him, to verify once more that we are not overheard. 'Because I believe you are the Queen's rightful heir, My Lady. And I would not see that Catholic Scotswoman on our throne. I am not alone in this opinion.'

'Who else, then?'

'Others – I cannot say.' He stops and seems on the brink of naming someone. 'But you do not know this. And,' he adds, 'do not assume you can trust *anyone*.'

I run my finger over my lips again.

There is a shuffling on the stairs. It is Nan with a pile of clean linens.

'Thank you for the flowers, Ball, it is most kind,' I say. 'They remind me life goes on out there and that the fields are full of wild blooms.'

Nan smiles at me, saying, 'How lovely. I will fetch a jar for them and take the pets down to do their business.' She leaves the linens on the bed and then leaves me, hoisting the monkey on to her hip as if he is a baby and calling for the dogs to follow her. I hear the key crank as Ball turns it and I am alone with my posy.

Though there is no note with it, the flowers themselves are as good as a letter. The purple heartsease says 'you occupy my thoughts' and the sprinkled mist of baby's breath says 'everlasting love', as do the white anemones with their yellow pollen hearts. But the anemone tells me more than just a story of unfading love, it also stands for the truth, and the parchment circles of honesty need no explanation, the green fronds of chervil too: they all speak of sincerity. The message is as clear as if Hertford is in the chamber talking to me himself; he is telling me I can speak the truth, that he will do so too, and that our accounts will match. Something lifts away from my heart with that realization. I am lighter, as if there is more space for air in me. My baby shifts and I am spilling over with love. Bringing the flowers to my nose, I breathe in their bouquet again, finding something else there, something I had not noticed before: rosemary. Rosemary for remembrance, remembrance of Juno, and for a moment I imagine Juno's soul has found a new home for itself in the heart of my infant.

The sound of the lock brings me back from my thoughts. It is Nan with the pets. She arranges the flowers in a jar and goes to place it beside the bed. 'Not there, Nan,' I say. 'On the window sill.' I point to the window that looks out on the Beauchamp Tower, so if my dearest Hertford should look out when he is taken there, he will see that I have received his message. I can feel the excitement gathering in me at the thought of his proximity. It is as if the very air I am breathing contains fragments of him.

I move my chair to a position from which I have a clear view of the Beauchamp Tower, waiting until eventually I see the flicker of a candle within. I stand, holding my own light to make a silhouette of myself, willing him to seek me out, wondering if he knows I am here so close, no more than a dozen yards away. I do not see him, though, and Nan eventually urges me to go to bed, but my sleep is fitful and I am jolted awake by that dream of death again.

As soon as it is light I leave my bed, with Nan snoring on her pallet, and open the door to the walkway. The dogs run out in a frenzy, scaring the pigeons. I stand for a moment looking at the door to Hertford's prison – solid planks of oak weathered to grey, punctuated with black nails, just like mine. He is beyond that door. I am not abandoned. I notice Stan is whimpering, his nose pressed to the crack at the bottom, realizing with a thrill that he has caught Hertford's scent. I lumber over as fast as my great shape will allow and, without thinking, drop to the floor, bringing my own nose to the base of the door, imagining I too can catch a whiff of my love.

'Something wrong, My Lady?' It is Nan, standing in her nightgown, looking half asleep still and puzzled to see me sprawled thus.

'Oh no, Nan,' I reply. 'I dropped my ring and it seems to have fallen into the crack at the base of the door.' I surreptitiously slip the mourning ring from my finger, holding it aloft, calling out, 'Look here, I have it.'

And then I'm sure I hear it, 'My Kitty, my love,' from behind the door.

'Let me help you up,' says Nan. Who is now halfway towards me. I dare not reply to him, for fear that she will suspect something.

Stim has joined Stan now, and they are both scratching furiously at the wood and yelping, setting off the others in a great cacophony. Hertford will certainly know who his Tower neighbour is now, and just to be sure, I name the dogs loudly one by one, bidding them cease their noise. Nan takes my hand, helping me heave myself up to my feet; I allow her to conduct me back inside and it is all I can do to keep my excitement from spilling out of me.

It is not long before Warner, with his sly-eyed deputy, arrives for his daily visit and as ever he asks, 'Are you willing to tell me the story of your marriage, My Lady?'

He says it in such a way as to make it clear he knows my answer already. And so when I say, 'I *am*,' with a smile, he looks as if his eyes might pop out with surprise. And so I recount the day of my wedding, in great detail, repeating things when bid, so that the deputy may write it all carefully in his ledger.

My interrogation – for however kindly Warner may seem to be, that is what it is – continues for three days. All that time I feel the strings of my heart reaching out like a spider's filament, along the walkway, and into the chamber that houses my husband. I am asked the same questions over and over again, first by Warner and then by his deputy. The small details of things are reiterated differently by one or other of them to see if I will trip up and contradict myself. Between them, they pull the most intimate moments of my marriage out of me, as if to strip me naked and search my most secret pockets.

When Warner finally announces, 'That will be all, My Lady. We have what we need,' and they finally go to leave, I feel that a great weight is lifted from me, allowing my optimism to flood back.

Once Warner has left, the deputy lags behind, corking his inkhorn and taking a time to gather his things before making to go. Almost at the door, he turns to me, whispering, 'Your husband is here.'

'I do not believe you,' I reply, thinking it a trick. He looks directly at me with his bead eyes and I imagine, with a shiver, that he can see into the depths of my soul. 'I would know it in my heart if my husband were here,' I say. He is testing me, to see if I have wind of Hertford's presence, if we have communicated and made our stories tally.

'It is the truth.' He makes an attempt at a smile, but it is more grimace than anything and I notice his eye teeth are long and pointed, more like those of a hound.

'I doubt it,' I say, keeping the pretence.

'We have questioned him also. He told us almost exactly to the word what you have just recounted.' As he makes for the door, he adds, 'I champion you, My Lady.'

I feel I must have misheard such a thing coming from this ghoulish fellow and want to ask him what he means, but dare not. He slips a small pouch into my hand as he takes his leave, slinking off like a shadow, whispering something to Ball as he passes through the doorway.

When he has gone, I pull the neck of the pouch open to find a limning of my own Hertford, his face haloed in brilliant blue, a black-feathered cap set at an angle, a half-smile at the edges of his bow-shaped mouth. It is by Levina's hand; of that I am sure. Just to see his likeness there in my palm tugs at my heart unbearably.

Ball clears his throat to gain my attention. He has a wide grin upon his face that I don't fully understand until he says, 'You will find the door to the Beauchamp Tower is open today, My Lady, and your girl is occupied in the kitchens.' With that he locks me into my chamber.

I rush out on to the parapet and there, leaning against the wall as if he is just passing the time of day, stands Hertford. I remain in the doorway, suddenly feeling shy in the face of him. He too is motionless, gazing at me as if I am a stranger or someone returned from the grave.

'Kitty, it is you . . . look at you,' he says, now, at last, striding towards me. 'The size of you.' He comes to a halt and drops on to his knees, taking my hands in his, scattering kisses on them, then lifts his face. His eyes are full of tears.

'My love,' is all I can manage to say, for I too am choked with tears.

He has his hands on my belly now. 'Our infant. Oh, Kitty, this is the most wondrous sight. I feared it was one I might never set eyes upon.' He buries his head in my skirts sobbing and then, standing up, begins to laugh and I am awash with joy.

'Come to the bed,' I say. 'When I lie down he moves and you shall be able to feel him.'

We lie, side by side, holding hands, heads turned to each other, eyes interlocked. I open my gown, one hook at a time, and lift my underclothes so he can see the full extent of my vast belly, and taking his hand I place it where I can feel a shifting limb.

'He moves! Oh, Kitty, I never imagined.' He kisses the place where our infant kicks. 'Is it not an irony, given the name of my prison, that this son of ours will be Lord Beauchamp? Do you think he can hear me?'

'I like to think so. I have told him all about you.' I pause, for there are things I need to know, but I hesitate to spoil this wondrous moment. But now I have begun to think of those things I feel a great surge of anger rise up through my body that lifts me up on to my feet. 'You abandoned me,' I say, barely able to keep myself from shouting. 'You abandoned me!' Then, like a pan of milk, I boil over, punching and slapping and biting at him like a wild beast, crying out over and over again, 'You abandoned me! You abandoned me!' He doesn't move to defend himself or try to push me off but allows me to attack him, until I am entirely spent and collapse exhausted back on to the bed. He sits staring at the floor. 'Why did you not reply to my letters?' I say at last.

'I was a fool – a coward and a fool. I know you will never forgive me for leaving you in such a situation.' He slides off the bed and on to his knees, like a supplicant. 'I cannot forgive myself.'

'But you abandoned me.' I cannot think of anything else to say and we sit in silence for what seems an age. 'Why?' I murmur eventually.

He speaks, still looking at the floor as if too ashamed to meet my eyes. 'Cecil changed his tune; he told me that if I obeyed him, he would help our cause. But he said it would put you in grave danger if I made contact with you, told me of the Queen's spies, men who know the secrets of poison' – the words tumble out of him one on top of the other – 'and he reminded me that I had already lost one person close to me, that surely I didn't want to lose another.' His face screws up as he says this.

'What did he mean by that? Juno –' I stop, for I can't believe what it is I am saying. 'No, Juno was sick for months. She was never quite right since the influenza.'

'I truly feared for your safety, Kitty, and I stupidly believed Cecil would champion us with the Queen when the time was right.'

'Well he hasn't, has he?' I can still feel the anger roiling in me.

'I cannot expect your forgiveness but let me try and explain.' I nod minutely and turn my head away. 'I was terrified something would happen to you. Cecil's son, Thomas, was travelling with me, you see, and watched my every move. I made a great show of throwing your letters on the fire unopened, in front of him, to prove my obedience to his blasted father. I wondered why you wrote so often, feared something was amiss. But in the end, Kitty, I was nothing but a gutless coward.'

'What do you want me to say?' I ask, casting a stony look over him. 'You had the courage to wed me, but not to stand up to Cecil – twice.'

'Everything I have done was through fear of one kind or another, fear for myself, fear for you, fear of losing you to another. I am the worst kind of coward.' He says it again, spitting the word out this time. 'I have let myself be Cecil's puppet. I had no backbone, Kitty.' Then he stops, meets my gaze and, lowering his voice, says, 'I *did* think to abandon you, convinced myself you might fare better without me. But the idea of a life without you was unbearable. I couldn't do it, and had I known of this . . .' He touches a hand to my belly.

'I want to hate you, but find I cannot,' I whisper, unable to understand why all of a sudden I feel only the swell of love in me. 'I am glad you have been truthful.'

'I am so very ashamed,' he says, in a voice so filled with sorrow it would make even the hardest heart weep. 'How can you love a spineless recreant such as me?'

'I do love you, and I do forgive you.' I search myself for any residue of ill feeling at his treatment of me, but there is none – it is gone. 'This is Cecil's doing. That man –' I stop. There are no words to describe my loathing of Cecil.

'I am so very sorry, Kitty, that you have had to bear all this alone. You have never deserved . . . I'm sorry, I'm sorry . . .'

I stop his jumbled words with a kiss, and we lie together in each other's arms, eventually falling asleep – a deep and dreamless sleep, such as I haven't had in months.

We are woken to the sound of the key turning. It is Ball, warning us that Lady Warner is on her way up, so Hertford slips off across the walkway to his own chamber not a dozen yards away. It is as if we were simply an ordinary couple in our own house and I make a silent prayer of thanks for the safe return of my own dear husband.

'What is it you look at out there each evening?' asks Nan, when Lady Warner is gone and I am gazing out of the window.

'I like to see the lights on the river barges and imagine where they are going.'

'Do you think you will ever be allowed to leave this place?'

'If the Queen shows me mercy,' I say, but I wonder about that myself; each and every hour I wonder how this situation will end. Sometimes I dare imagine myself, with Hertford and our infant and Mary all together somewhere. Sometimes it is Canon Row, sometimes Beaumanor, sometimes just some nondescript place that is a setting for our family. Nan joins me at the window.

'Look,' I say. 'See that ship. Perhaps it hails from the Indies.' We watch the shadow of a vast craft moving like a ghost on the water, torches casting circles of yellow light on its deck, shadowy men moving about in the dark.

'I cannot imagine travelling so far,' she says. 'I have never left London in my life.'

'What, never?' I am suddenly struck by the difference in our lives. I hadn't thought to ask her about hers and I don't talk of mine, for fear of saying the wrong thing and it reaching the Queen's ears.

'Well, once I went to a fair up at Islington.' She says 'Islington' as if it is another country.

I, who have spent my twenty-one years travelling from one place to another, cannot imagine such a small life, where Islington seems as far as the stars. I think there can be no harm in describing some of the great royal palaces in which I have lived. I watch her eyes widen as I recount the banquets and festivities and how the court moves from place to place in a great train, with the most beautiful horses to be found and an army of liveried guards. 'Surely you have seen the royal progress pass through the streets or on the river barges?' I say.

'Oh, I have,' she replies. Her eyes are wide, as if the memory of it is as vivid as the real thing. 'At the coronation parade I was dressed as a shepherdess in the Cheapside pageant.'

'I remember that pageant.'

'So you must have seen me.' Nan's voice is breathy with excitement.

'And you me.' I return her smile, but I am thinking of the humiliation of sitting in the chariot at the rear end of the parade, when I should have been riding up near the Queen.

'Is something wrong?' she asks.

Then I feel it – a pain like a steel belt tightening about my belly. 'Oh, Nan,' I say. 'I think this infant is knocking at the door.'

I am engulfed with fear now, unable to imagine how it is possible for this baby to find its way out of me. Nan pales, as if someone has dropped a bag of flour over her head. 'Go and fetch Lady Warner,' I say, trying to control the quaver in my voice. 'And ask that she send for the midwife.'

As Nan leaves, I stand in the doorway. 'My baby is coming,' I say to Ball.

His face lights up. 'An infant is a blessing wherever it arrives in the world, My Lady, and this one may well be the next King of England.'

It is not that I have never thought it before, that I might one day be the mother of a king. It is just that I hadn't fully entertained it. But now I do. Why not? Stranger things have happened, and was Elizabeth herself not once incarcerated in this very room?

December 1561
Westminster
Levina

'I managed to see her, Mary.' The two women are in a corner of the great hall, heads together; Levina speaks in a low voice. 'One of her guards is an old colleague of my husband's and managed to get me in there for a brief hour. Pretended I was the midwife's woman, there to administer to the baby's colic.'

'How did you find her?'

'Surprisingly well. She is so very delighted with her little Lord Beauchamp she seems to forget where she is. And she is comfortably housed opposite her husband's prison. Told me the guards allowed him to visit her secretly from time to time.'

Levina had been horrified to hear of Katherine's imprisonment, and dismayed it had taken the news so long to reach her in Bruges. She had left immediately but had had to wait an interminable time for a crossing, as the weather was unseasonably stormy.

'So she has friends in there.'

'Warner and his wife are kind, she says, and there is a pair of guards who support her cause, as well as the lieutenant's deputy. But they have warned her to trust no one, not even her servant girl, Nan, who seemed entirely benign, I must say. I had to make a great show of mixing tinctures for the baby, until the girl left on an errand.'

'One wonders what kind of friends . . .' Mary looks thoughtful, worried. 'Whether they are political.'

'Yes, it would create all kinds of problems were she to become the focus of a serious cause.'

'And now she has a son. What do *you* think the Queen will do?'

'Impossible to say.' Levina doesn't repeat some of the things she has heard; the word 'execution' has been whispered about, but just because people say things, it doesn't mean they are true. It would seem the Queen is convinced that Katherine's marriage was part of a plot to overthrow her. 'What is her attitude with *you*, Mary?'

'I am kept at a distance,' Mary says, visibly drooping like a flower that wants for water.

'Katherine asked that I make you this. Said you would want an image of your nephew.' Levina slides something out from the folds of her gown, slipping it furtively into Mary's hand. Mary half opens her palm. In it is a limning of her sister with the infant Lord Beauchamp in her arms, strikingly like his mother. His little hand is tucked into her furred neckline – a touchingly intimate gesture – and hanging from Katherine's dress is a tiny limning of Hertford; it is a family portrait of sorts.

Mary gazes at the image for some time in silence and Levina thinks she might weep, for her face has a crumpled look about it.

'Did *you* give her that look of serenity or did you find her thus?' she asks eventually.

'She truly did wear an air of contentment.'

'Oh Kitty – ever buoyant,' says Mary. 'To think I have a nephew.'

'Keep the limning hidden.' Levina folds her own hand about Mary's so the tiny portrait is concealed. 'The last thing we want is the reformers getting hold of it and using it as an emblem for their cause. That would raise the Queen's hackles. There is already too much talk in the streets of this baby as Elizabeth's heir.'

'The Queen denies the boy's legitimacy. It would be for the best if he's deemed illegitimate in the law . . . Oh, I don't know, Veena. I just want them released from that place. I can't get Jane out of my head.'

'I know, I know.' Levina is thinking about how England has waited so long for a rightful male heir and now he has arrived, legitimate, of the blood, next in line according to the eighth Henry's decree, and the Queen does all she can to deny him. Levina has stopped trying to understand Elizabeth's actions. But the reformers have a strong voice and a stronger case and they will do anything to prevent the Catholic Mary of Scotland from being named.

She curses herself inwardly for having left, for not being here when she was most needed. She may have found a way to do something, but she knows really that it would have been futile. And her trip was all for nothing; George refused to return and now her promise to Frances is shattered. She cannot get Jane's fate out of her mind. History seems to repeat itself relentlessly and none of them can do anything to prevent it.

Dudley, dressed in gold, marches through the chamber with a pair of henchmen and a skewbald hound at his heels; the women curtsy as he passes. Levina is reminded, with a twinge of longing, of Hero who died in Bruges. She misses her faithful companion, but he was an old boy. Dudley has a new spring in his step. The rumour is that Cecil hangs by a thread, that the Queen suspects he had a part in Katherine's secret marriage, that it was a plot of Cecil's making. It certainly looks suspicious, the way the reformers are jumping on this infant as their cause, and Cecil is the one who least wants the Scottish Queen named. The Queen resolutely sticks to her middle way, refusing either faction the upper hand. Levina remembers the fears of Mary Tudor's reign. Then at least you knew your enemy, now it is impossible to tell who is on which side in a world where two lovesick young things, tying themselves together in secret, can be deemed a treasonous plot and put their very lives at risk. With Cecil's star waning, Dudley's is on the rise again; it is like some infernal see-saw.

'Smug devil,' whispers Mary, nudging her head in Dudley's direction. 'Still thinks himself in with a chance.'

'Would she wed him?' asks Levina.

'No. I think she will wed no one.'

'Truly?' Levina cannot imagine Elizabeth, that passionate girl she remembers, without a bedfellow.

'She will not share her power, I think.'

'You may be right.' Levina is impressed by Mary's astuteness.

'Stay awhile, Veena, I know Peggy should like to see you.'

'Peggy is back at court?' Levina is glad to hear this; at least it means Mary has a friend here.

'Arrived of late.'

'I should like to, but I must return home. I have been away so long and there is much that needs arranging. The servants have let the house fall into a terrible state.'

'Did your husband return with you?' asks Mary.

'Alas, no,' Levina replies, trying not to think of all that, of

George and his passion for this Lotte. He was cold in the face of Levina's impassioned pleas, refused to return with her and angry that she was returning for Katherine Grey's sake. It served as proof, he said, that his grievance was not unfounded. She had managed to resist pointing out that this absence of leave from his guard's duties, this affair of his, was all funded from the wages of her own labour, and that her income – their income – depended upon her alliances at court. Though how she managed to stay silent on that point is a mystery, for she was brimming with rage. Now she just misses him and considers taking up Mary's invitation to stay awhile, not returning to her empty house at Ludgate, without even Hero's company, but she must.

'I shall walk with you to the gates.'

The main entrance is crowded with an army of servants arriving with stacks of linens and plateware to set up the hall for dinner; some have begun moving the boards and benches to the centre of the room. The women decide to take the route through the privy chamber and as they pass, several of the ladies call out in greeting to Levina, saying how she has been missed. Mary hangs back by the window and Levina notices her strumming her fingers over the bars of a birdcage and remarks a certain shiftiness about her.

'What were you doing with the birdcage?' she asks, as they leave by the back corridor.

'I left the lovebirds' door unfastened,' she says. 'I can't bear to see them shut away like that. At least now they can fly about the palace for a while.'

Levina laughs, saying, 'You are a rebel at heart, Mary Grey.'

'It is my little game. I have seen those poor creatures dragged from pillar to post in that cage. Come summer I plan to set them free near an open window. What think you to that?'

'I think the poor creatures might end up fodder for the hawks if they don't succumb to the cold once winter arrives. They are very far from home, Mary.'

'Oh, I hadn't thought of that. The world is cruel for the little creatures.'

Levina wonders if Mary includes herself amongst those creatures.

'Ah well, at least they shall have a glimpse of freedom up amongst the beams of the great hall, until they are recaptured.'

In the base court they come across the Sergeant Porter, who stops them with a greeting. Levina is reminded that the last time she saw this man was the day she chased Katherine all the way to Hertford's house at Canon Row. How she had berated herself for her silliness on finding the place empty. She thought her imagination had run away with her, but it turned out her instincts were right, for that was the day Katherine married. She is reminded of the two windblown figures on the bleak stretch of winter sand, disappearing up the Westminster steps, wondering how things might have been different if she had managed somehow to prevent the wedding.

'What news of Mistress Keyes?'

'I am afraid to say she . . .' he stops, looks to the cobbles.

'Why did you say nothing, Keyes?' Mary has brought both hands up to her face in shock. 'Gone?'

He nods. 'You had so much else to worry about, My Lady.'

'But I am your friend.' She touches his arm briefly, something she rarely does, except to those who are particularly close. 'I am so very sorry. Is there anything I can do to –' She stops, looking him straight in the eye. 'You should have told me.' Mary seems filled with resignation as if she is only now realizing that nothing will bring back the dead. 'I am your friend, Keyes.'

Levina is struck by the way Mary always finds sympathy for the sufferings of others, even when her own are so great.

April 1562
Whitehall
Mary

I have a letter, smuggled out of the Tower. In it Katherine tells of my nephew – Beech, as she calls him; how well he suckles; how enchanting is his gummy smile. He has his first tooth, she says. He is seven months old already, and I wonder if he will have a mouth full of teeth before I know him, if I ever shall. The thought of it twists my heart out of shape.

She also writes of how, occasionally, the doors go unlocked, allowing her and Hertford to continue meeting. *So it is not as bad as you'd think, Mouse.* I am so very glad to know that her endless optimism remains alive and well in spite of everything. But then *she* isn't party to the rumours that find their way to my ears – all the gossip about what Elizabeth may or may not do with the disgraced couple. As support for the baby's claim grows, so the Queen's rage burgeons.

I snatch a moment alone to read it once more in the peace of Keyes's rooms, before I am needed in the privy chamber, and find myself gazing listlessly out across the water at the archbishop's palace. From here I had watched the barge transporting Katherine and Hertford upriver day after day in February, seeing them at a distance disembark at Lambeth Palace opposite, to testify before a Church Council. The object of this exercise, for the Queen, was to publicly prove their marriage to be void. In the absence of either poor Juno or the priest who conducted the nuptials, it was easy to give the Queen the verdict she wanted. My nephew is now officially deemed a bastard, though I know better. I am thankful I wasn't called to testify, for I couldn't have lied before all those bishops and would likely have ended up in the Tower myself for harbouring secrets – there is some advantage in seeming so insignificant, it seems.

I pray this judgment means my sister and her husband have shifted a step away from the executioner's block. I waited each day to catch a glimpse of dearest Katherine as she was taken inside for a further grilling. Seeing her small shape, rendered smaller by the accompaniment of guards, all a good foot taller than she and seeming taller still with their long halberds rising upwards, caused a lump to form in my throat – a lump that will not be dispelled.

I hear the door creak and turn to see Keyes, alone.

'There is something I must show you,' he says quietly, closing the door and pulling a limning out from beneath his doublet. I can only imagine that he wants to show me the likeness of a woman he is courting, to see if I approve; so I am surprised to see the image is of my sister holding her baby and that it is almost identical to the one I have hidden beneath my own stomacher. I take it and on closer inspection it is different, clearly a copy. Levina's likeness has a background of azure and this is dark, almost black; even Katherine's eyes are dark and not the cornflower blue they should be, and her hair is flame red rather than pale as summer straw. But it is certainly meant to depict her and little Lord Beauchamp; his tiny hand is tucked beneath her fur collar exactly as it is in my own portrait; Katherine's long fine hand sports the pair of rings I remember so well hanging from the chain about her neck; but the style of painting is wrong, it is too precise, it lacks Levina's looseness, the unmistakable character of her brushwork.

'This is not Mistress Teerlinc's work,' I say, taking my

miniature out from beneath my clothes and holding them together for him to see.

'No,' he says, 'When you see them side by side it is clearly a copy. I fear there are a number of them circulating amongst the reformers.'

'Where did you come upon it?'

'Dorothy Stafford passed it on to me. Said it belonged to one of her cousins. She was concerned, thought you should know. It would not do for the Queen to get wind of it.'

I feel a tightening about my guts. 'Can I take it?' I ask. 'I will show Levina. See if she knows how this came to be.' He nods and then seems to almost say something, but stops himself, his grey eyes swivelling towards the window and back to me again. 'What?' I say.

And he just says, 'Go carefully.'

When I arrive at the privy chamber the Queen has not appeared yet and, despite a group of musicians playing, I can hear a heated discussion going on beyond the door where the council are meeting. Spotting Levina alone sketching in a corner I join her, showing her the limning from Keyes, which she examines for some time, eventually saying quietly, 'Who has seen yours? It is the only one.'

I touch the place where the miniature sits invisibly beneath my dress. 'Not a soul, Veena; I wear it even when sleeping.'

'I don't understand.' Her face is etched with worry. 'This is a copy and there are too many similarities to make it coincidence. Someone has taken great care to make this appear to have come from my brush. The untrained eye would assume it so.' She studies the image once more. 'Look at the differences though, Mary. Her collar here is ermine, the fur of royalty, and the colour of their hair – not golden but flame red, as is Elizabeth's, as was her father's.' She lowers her voice further, though we can't be overheard where we are in the very corner of the chamber. 'The implication is clear, that this infant is of the royal line. The Tudor line. And look here, the limning Katherine wears pinned to her dress; it shows no face in it. Hertford has been erased altogether. I don't like this, Mary.'

'Keyes says there are a number circulating.'

'This is exactly what we didn't want to happen.' Levina folds her fist about the limning and slaps it into the palm of her other hand with an intake of breath. 'I know whose work this is.' She lowers her voice further still. 'He was about my workshop when I was putting the final touches on the original.'

'Hilliard?'

My disbelief must register in my voice for she replies, 'To think I trusted him. It could only be him, Mary; he has a fine hand for one so young *and* he comes from a family of staunch reformers.'

'As do we all,' I say. 'Perhaps he thinks he does us a service.'

'That's exactly the problem; everyone thinks it is what the Greys want. I suppose these images are circulated in every quarter by now.'

'It is only the Queen's opinion that matters, Veena. Not a single one of the Privy Council would keep Katherine in the Tower were it not the Queen's wish.'

I am aware of Frances Meautas watching us; she is trying to listen but must be too far off. I look up and hold her gaze.

'What? Have I a wen on my nose?' she says, thrusting her hands out either side in pretended innocence. She is too thick-witted to be much of a threat.

The doors are opened and the council members begin to file out behind the Queen, who breaks away from them, slumping into her chair and calling Lady Knollys over for a huddled conversation. Cecil hangs back, seeming in hope of a quiet word with her, but she waves him away with a dismissive hand and he skulks from the room.

'Where are our yellow birds?' she booms, pointing to the empty birdcage hanging in the window, the latch of which I discreetly loosened earlier. 'This must have happened at least a dozen times. Did we not ask for their cage to be properly secured?' Levina turns to me, raising her eyebrows minutely. I try to look guileless.

'Your Majesty's birds must be excessively clever to know how to operate the latch,' I say. The Queen gives me a blank, hard stare. 'In intelligence they clearly emulate their esteemed mistress.'

'We see your wit is sharp as ever, Lady Mary.' I detect a glimmer of the admiration she once had for my repartee.

I spot the pair of escapees perched up high, fluffing their feathers, hidden amongst the fixings of the wall hangings; no one else has noticed them. A frisson runs through me, as if it is I who is balancing there, gazing down upon the Queen and her ladies. Then, driven by the sudden inspiration of my vengeful demon, I sidle over to Kat Astley, whispering, 'Frances is the culprit. I saw her let them out.' I should be ashamed of such mendacity, but I am not. I cannot always be good-as-gold Mary.

A hubbub of excitement starts up in the corridor, distracting attention from the birds. A man I have never seen before enters, removing his cap to display a head of dark hair slicked to a sheen. His face is shiny with grease as if his pomade has run. He whispers something to Lady Knollys, which she conveys to the Queen, whose face breaks into a smile as she says, 'Send her in, then. We have been waiting for her.'

The man slides away, returning almost instantly accompanied by a female dwarf, who appears terrified, her eyes swivelling. Her hair is inky dark and pulled back from her high square forehead into a single plait, which reaches almost to the floor. She looks towards me, presumably as I am the sole person present of the same height as she. I smile and her mouth twitches with the promise that it might be returned, but I can see her hands are trembling and the smile never quite appears. 'May I present Ippolyta the Tartarian, Your Majesty?'

Lizzie Mansfield is gawping and, as Ippolyta makes an attempt at a deep curtsy, which is difficult given the shortness of her limbs, Frances Meautas lets off a snort of laughter that ripples out amongst the maids. Ippolyta's dress is unusual and I can only suppose it is Tartarian in style, the skirts cut high enough to expose a fat pair of calves, criss-crossed with red ribbons that attach a pair of pink dancing slippers. The man, still bowing and simpering, addresses the Queen.

'I have taught her a modicum of our language, Your Majesty, but she is not much given to learning . . . quite savage, really –'

'We are told she has a fine voice,' interrupts the Queen. 'Sing!'

The man begins to clap in a rhythm and Ippolyta, having taken a deep breath, puffing her small chest forward, begins to warble out a song in her own tongue, twisting the tune about the strange-sounding words. She seems to come to life with the music, a smile spreading itself over her face. It is true, her voice is finer than any I have heard, and all are captivated, seeming to forget her odd shape that had them staring with their mouths agape only moments ago. Even Frances Meautas is listening blissfully, her eyes tight shut.

When the song is finished Ippolyta curtsies awkwardly

again and the Queen begins to clap slowly, with the rest of us taking her lead. 'We shall have her sit beside us.' The Queen does not speak directly to Ippolyta but to her oleaginous keeper, who wears a smug look now. 'And, Lady Mary,' she turns to me, 'you will sit with us too. She will feel more at home that way.'

I doubt that the proximity of a crookbacked midget will make this poor dwarf feel more at home. It is likely that the unfortunate girl was torn unwillingly from the bosom of her faraway family, and brought here to this unfamiliar place to become a queen's plaything. But if there is a chance that my presence might alleviate her fears a little – I notice her hands are quivering once more now the song is finished – then I am happy to do so. Besides, it gives me an unexpected opportunity to converse with the Queen.

I sit beside Ippolyta, smiling stupidly, not quite knowing how to communicate. 'Your song was exquisite,' I say and she tilts her head to one side, shrugging slightly, making it clear she comprehends nothing. Then she picks up the dangling end of the Queen's girdle as a child might, examining the trinkets hanging there, a jewelled fan, a tiny prayer book, a limning of Dudley set in gold.

The room holds its breath, wondering how the Queen will react to the audacity of this girl who deigns to touch the royal garb. No one has yet worked out Ippolyta's position here, whether she is a kind of fool, in which case her behaviour is acceptable, or merely a curiosity, or even – and I laugh inwardly to think how some of the maids would react to it – a new maid of the chamber. For all we know she might be a princess in her own land. But the Queen laughs and chucks Ippolyta beneath the chin, saying, 'You are not the only one after our jewels,' and, turning to me adds pointedly, 'Is she, Mary?'

'No, Your Majesty.' My voice is barely more than a whisper; the implication is clear.

'What think *you* to your sister's behaviour? You have not exactly been vociferous in her defence.'

My throat is blocked and dry, as if I have ingested a length of linen. 'I think her foolish, madam.' I am being tested, scrutinized, but I will not let this woman get the better of me.

'She *is* a little fool if she thinks to get her rump on our throne.'

'If I may say so,' I clasp my hands together to prevent them shaking as I say this, 'I think her a fool for love, no more. She has not the wit to think beyond her own nose.'

The Queen huffs at this and I fear I may have overcooked my goose. Then she looks me directly in the eye, saying, 'And what do you think we should do with her, Mary?'

I am about to say that it is not my place to make decisions of such importance, but with a flash of insight I see my opportunity. 'I think, madam, that she is of little consequence, if one takes primogeniture as the basis for one's beliefs on the matter.'

'You would deny your family's ambitions in the name of primogeniture?'

She seems to inspect my very soul with those dark eyes of hers, but I continue. 'I think of the good of England before the good of my family, for one is but a small fragment of the other. I know well enough of the terrible bloodshed of the last century when the crown was passed from cousin to cousin and the direct line was denied . . . there was not an English soul untouched by suffering.' I cannot read the Queen's face; it is the blank one she wears to play cards – to win.

'But my Scottish cousin will not renounce her claim to my

throne. It seems she does not want to wait till I am gone. Would you have me favour such treachery?'

'She can dream,' I say, feeling bold as brass now. 'But she will never have the power to oust Your Majesty.'

The Queen stretches out her hand, and taking the frill of my collar between thumb and forefinger, rubbing them together, says quietly, 'Not stupid like your sister, are you, Mary?'

I force myself to look directly at her, to show her I am not afraid. She is smiling. 'Indeed, no,' I say.

'It is a pity you are not a man; we have sore need of someone like you on our council.' She laughs as she says this, has said things like it before. But then she adds, 'I believe you might be the single soul in this blighted place who understands the difficulty of being . . .' she pauses, eventually whispering, 'of being me,' before slumping backwards. 'You will never know what it is to bear a child.'

I wonder if she somehow knows she is destined to remain childless too.

'I will not,' I reply.

It is a moment of strange intimacy and I allow myself to imagine finding a way to persuade her to pardon my sister. But she thumps her hand down on the arm of her chair, causing Ippolyta to flinch, saying, 'And yet you are from traitor stock! Through and through.' There it is, the sting in her tail. I suppose she will hate me all the more for having allowed me a glimpse of her tender side.

Then she seems to gather herself, speaking loudly so the room can hear. 'Tell the dwarf we shall call her Linnet for her songbird voice, and Mary, find her some proper clothes; we cannot have her dressed in this manner, if she is not to be a laughing stock.'

I take Ippolyta by the hand, glad to get away, taking the

back steps as a shorter route to the maids' chambers, stumbling upon Levina and the Hilliard boy. She has cornered him where the stairs turn and is whispering angrily. They do not see us watching them.

'You have abused my trust, Nicholas, inveigled your way into my life, and you now seek to destroy those I care for. Shame on you.'

'But Mistress Teerlinc, with all respect, I support her cause.'

'You have no understanding of her plight, you . . . you imbecile.' She strikes him hard across the cheek. He turns his face away, only now seeing us, spitting a gob of bloody saliva on to the flags.

'Veena,' I say gently. She turns; anger has distorted her features, making her almost unrecognizable. 'Leave him be.'

She steps back, seeming shocked by her actions. He slides away, saying, 'I have nothing to apologize for.'

October 1562
The Tower of London
Katherine

I am playing peek-a-boo with little Beech on the bed; Hercules thinks he is playing too, but he understands the principles of the game even less than Beech and is getting bored already, gnawing at the bedpost. My husband is reading Mary's letter out loud one more time, before we throw it on the fire.

'"The bad news is that, with the Guise family causing such bloodshed against the Huguenots in France, the Queen has turned away from Mary of Scotland once more. She can't be seen to support such monstrous acts; the Scottish Queen is half Guise, after all."'

I am not really listening. I do not want more 'bad news'

and I couldn't care less what the Queen is or isn't doing, unless she means to set us free. I have lived a full year of my life in this place now and it is enough; the Queen has made her point.

'When was it that my sister got to such politicking?'

'This is good for our cause, Kitty,' Hertford is saying.

'Then why does Mary call it "bad news"?'

'She seems to think we are more likely to be freed if . . . Oh, never mind.' He sighs, dropping his arms to his sides in resignation.

'If what?'

'If we are not championed by the reformers; if we are not a threat.'

'She is right,' I say. 'Do you not dream of living somewhere quietly together?' I murmur, close in to his ear. There was a time I couldn't have borne the idea of living away from court but I find I am much changed by motherhood and love – and incarceration, I suppose. 'Imagine how happy we would be.' But a splinter of me is thinking, too, of the idea of being mother to the King. However much I reason it away it is still there, poking at my mind.

'We shall have more than that, Kitty,' he says.

'Perhaps.' I look at Beech's dimpled smile and the way he places his pudgy fingers over his eyes so he can peep between them. I grab his fat hand and pop it into my mouth to make him giggle. The sound is infectious.

'Come and sit with me,' I say. 'We have precious little time together. And we can do nothing to change things anyway. I want to feel you close. Look at your son. Is he not irresistible?'

'It is you that is irresistible.' His voice is husky with lust and he slips his hand into the front of my dress.

'My heart,' I laugh, 'you cannot.'

'I know, I know,' he says. 'But there is no harm in a kiss.' He runs his lips over my throat and then on to my mouth, gripping my hand with his. Beech complains, trying to unlace our fingers.

'He is jealous,' I say.

'*I* am the jealous one,' he replies. '*He* has you all the time. He sleeps with you every night. And I have to make do with an empty bed and a snatched hour with my own love, but once a month.'

'When we are released –'

'I love you, my sweet Kitty,' he interrupts.

'If you love me truly, then you should wish obscurity on me.'

Then I feel it, as if a tadpole is swimming in my belly, the new infant growing in there. I had known the minute the nausea set in this time, wondering how it was possible that I didn't know the time before. But to feel the quickening – there is the proof. 'Our baby moves.'

'Let me feel.' He presses his hands to my stomach but the little fellow has stopped his swimming. 'She will not be able to deny this one's legitimacy now that we have sworn our marriage before an entire council of clergy, even the Archbishop.'

'Who cares about all that? It is enough that I have you and baby Beech and this little stranger.' I point to my belly. I will not let myself dwell on the fact of where we all are, and I will not let myself think about the Queen.

The key scrapes in the lock and Hertford leaps from the bed, making for the parapet door, but it is only Ball.

'What is it?' I ask.

'There is news.' He seems excited, barely able to hold himself together.

'What sort of news?' says Hertford, moving towards him.

I feel my baby flutter again and I am spinning with joy, so much so I'm finding it hard to listen.

'The Queen is at death's door.'

Hertford says nothing, nor do I.

'Smallpox,' Ball adds.

Hertford walks over to him, slapping him on the back. 'Truly?'

'Truly.'

'Well, God just may be smiling on us. How bad is it?'

'They say she may not last the night.'

Hertford's grin is like the sun and I wonder if it is right to feel so pleased about the fact that the Queen is dying, if perhaps God might be angered. But I *am* pleased nonetheless.

'The servant is on her way up, My Lord,' adds Ball. 'You must be gone.'

I can hear Nan's footsteps clearly, before Ball closes the door and turns the lock.

'Kitty, our prayers have been answered.' Hertford takes hold of me, engulfing me in his arms.

'Will we be freed?' I ask, my voice muffled in the folds of his clothes.

'More than that,' he says, as he lets me go and makes for the door. His eyes are gleaming in a way I haven't seen before and he seems for a moment unfamiliar, a stranger, his features differently configured so I cannot quite recognize him. But then he blows me a kiss, eyes shut, lips pursed, palm up, and it is my sweet husband standing before me once more. Then he is gone; I am wrenched by his parting and pick up little Beech, glad to feel the warmth of his body against mine. He begins to tease the ribbons of my dress with his fat fingers and I can feel tears gathering – I suppose them to be tears of relief.

January 1563
Whitehall
Levina

The Queen is incandescent with rage and the reason is being whispered about the privy chamber: Katherine Grey is about to birth another baby. Levina wonders how the poor girl fares now she is kept under close lock and key. Sir Edward Warner has been replaced and they say Katherine has been moved to different quarters, but it is hard to get any news out. Lord alone knows what will become of her now. How they had hoped, as the Queen's life lay in the balance. Levina can't help questioning why God chose to spare her from the smallpox, remembering clearly how it was three months ago, the deathly hush over the court, everyone awaiting the announcement. But she rallied – she is tough as an old broiling fowl and has been in bad humour since. Levina admonishes herself silently for allowing such treasonous and ungodly thoughts to inhabit her.

She and Mary sit with a huddle of women near the hearth, where the Queen is in whispered conversation with Lady Knollys. Most are sewing, some are reading, leaning in close to the candles, others gossiping quietly. The weather is so icy their backs are left cold and occasionally one or other of them gets up and paces, rubbing her hands together to generate a little more warmth. Levina wraps her shawl tightly around her, looking to the window where she can see icicles a yard long hanging from the eves opposite. The winter light is so dim she finds it hard to see well enough for the fine stitchwork. She supposes it is all the portraits she has painted, the minuscule details worked with a three-hair brush, the tiny resin jewels, the almost invisible hatched shading, that has given her the eyes of an old woman. Lizzie Mansfield begins to strum at a lute, rather badly; Dorothy Stafford is attempting to teach her a new tune, eventually taking the instrument from her and demonstrating, beautifully, how it should be played.

Levina looks around at the company. Some old faces have gone, and new ones arrived, but little changes. Elizabeth simmers angrily in her velvet dress, a rich azure blue that serves to enhance the flame tresses of hair that escape from her coif. But she is gaunt and pale and rendered paler still by the white paint she rubs into her skin and the crude rouged circles on her cheeks that have a vaguely comical effect. She looks like an awful, white-faced parody of her coronation painting. It seems no one is prepared to tell her the truth and some have even begun to rub the same stuff into their faces as a kind of perverse homage or show of allegiance – both, perhaps. It is the smallpox that has taken its toll on Elizabeth's beauty. She has lost the fresh bloom of youth, and the hard edge that was always there, even when she was a child, that gave her an attractive robust air has crystallized into something akin to bitterness. Her mouth, set in a scowl now, turns down naturally and her face has begun to shape itself around it. Levina knows that face so very well, has scrutinized each line of it, can see the toll time and circumstance will continue to have upon it.

She counts on her fingers, working out the Queen's age – she will be thirty this year, not as old as she looks. She calculates other ages: Katherine is twenty-three; Mary soon eighteen – goodness, she is no longer a girl. How is it that time appears to crawl and then you turn round and it is all used up? She herself is forty-three, an age she never imagined reaching as a child. The Queen continues her murmuring with Lady Knollys. Levina tries to hear what is said but she is seated too far away to hear properly above the sound of the lute. Then Elizabeth bursts out, loud enough for the entire company to hear, 'There are some who seem bent on showing England how fertile they are, how easily they can produce sons. It is a slight on *me*, is it not?' She is talking of Katherine; that much is clear. 'I will not have such disobedience – it is treason, I say.'

Mary starts at the word 'treason' – it is hardly surprising – then settles back to her sewing with an air of blighted resignation. She must have hoped for the Queen's death more than any of them, though she never spoke of it. Levina watches as Mary's deft fingers stitch a pattern of hollyhocks along a border of fabric, pulling the needle through the cloth and back efficiently, her expression returning to intense concentration. Mary has learned to show a blank face to the world, has become quite the expert at it.

But now she sighs deeply and whispers to Levina, 'I don't think I can bear any more of this.' She drops her sewing to her lap and pinches the bridge of her nose with her thumb and forefinger as if she is in pain, then continues, too quietly to be overheard, 'I remember, Veena, before Maman died, she warned us that she' – she swivels her eyes slightly in the direction of the Queen – 'was . . . What was the word she used? That she was "more artful" than her sister. It was impossible to comprehend at the time. The old Queen had committed such monstrous acts it was hard to see how she could be worse, but now I see what Maman meant by it.'

'Yes,' says Levina. 'It is futile to even try and imagine what she will do next.' Levina is reminded, when she says this, of the old King Henry as he was at the end – his daughter is equally mutable. In moments of clarity she can see Elizabeth's fear; fear that she will make the wrong choice. Her judgement is clouded by it, making her unable to see that no decision can sometimes be worse than a bad decision, even to the point that she doubts her own judgement, her trust swinging back and forth from Cecil to Dudley like a game of tennis.

'What do you think will happen to Katherine?' mutters Mary. 'Oh, I know, no one can answer that, not even she.' Her eyes glance once more in Elizabeth's direction and she suddenly seems so very small and young. Levina remembers her promise to Frances; the promise founded on Jane's terrible death that has bound her, that has disintegrated her marriage, kept her at court. Her sense of failure crowds in – she may be a fair success as an artist but that only serves to mask the extent to which she feels she has failed as a human being.

Now Foxe's book is published in English and fanning the flames of the reformers even more. She thinks of her own involvement in that book. How passionate she had been then about spreading the word of the new religion – all those smuggled drawings, the terrible risks she had taken. She had wanted to make sense of Jane Grey's appalling death and the only way seemed to be to make a martyr of her. All those deaths, Latimer, Ridley, Cranmer, Jane; the list is endless – all for what? There is no making sense of any of it. She explores her soul and can no longer find even the last vestiges of grace there. Her faith hangs on a thread and that frightens her, for she has always felt God in her life.

Mary slaps a fist to her knee in a rare show of frustration, sending the box of embroidery threads crashing to the floor.

'If it wasn't for the refuge of Keyes's rooms, I think I would –' She stops.

'I know.' Levina pats her hand. She is grateful for Keyes; he is a compassionate man. Levina had worried at first that there had been some kind of ulterior motive behind his kindness to Mary, a political agenda of one sort or another, but it seems that he simply likes her company. Levina has watched him carefully and sees the way he springs to life when he is with her. It is nothing sinister; if anything he seems protective, and God knows Mary needs protectors these days.

The bell rings and they file up for chapel, following the Queen out. Levina stands, and sits, and kneels, and repeats the priest's words, and listens to the choir, and the interminable sermon – though she hears none of it. She had once thought that the world would be put to rights, if only they could all practise their religion in the way they wished without fear of persecution. Elizabeth gave that to England but it hasn't put an end to the dangerous machinations of the differing factions. The Queen likes to play them off against one another and sits on a fence of her own making. How naive Levina was to have thought the world so straightforward. Now she feels too distanced from her faith to make any sense of it. She looks to the front of the chapel where the Queen kneels at her prayer stand; even from behind she can see the anger still simmering in the set of her shoulders and wonders what her next move will be. It is impossible to predict. Hertford will be hauled before the Star Chamber, no doubt. She doesn't dare think beyond that.

August 1563
The Tower of London
Katherine

There is a single window in my chamber that looks over an inner court. This has been my entire world these last seven months: a square of sky, a cobbled area, a flower-bed sometimes bright with pansies, a bald patch of grass where daily I watch my dogs scamper when they are taken down for exercise. I may not go there, for I am kept tightly these days. I know not where my husband is housed, will not allow myself to imagine him in a lightless dungeon or worse, preferring instead to pretend he is still in his round tower room with a view of the river. Pretending has become more difficult and my optimism has shrunk to nothing these days.

Beech is stomping up and down between my two rooms wearing an old red cap of mine in imitation of a yeoman guard; the dogs follow him in a wagging pack but even the sight of that cannot bring a smile to my face. That is all he knows, guards and keys and a mother who clings to her sanity by a thread. My mind keeps turning, without permission, to Edward Courtenay, who it is said spent his entire youth shut away in this place because of his Plantagenet blood, then to the famous princes of a hundred years ago. Those boys entered this place and never left; no one knows to this day what became of them. Some say murdered by their uncle. Their fates were written in their blood, as was Jane's, as is mine, and I have passed the curse of it on to my sweet boys. My boys who have never known what freedom is.

I can hear baby Tom crying in the inner chamber. The nurse is fussing, calling me in to feed him, her voice cold and polite, all emotion erased by correctness. There is no wet nurse; I suppose it is meant as punishment that I must nourish my own infant, but the truth is, it is one of the sole joys I have left, though it is tinted by other, darker things. Hertford is gone, Nan is gone, Warner and his wife gone, Ball and Chain gone, and no explanation; no more letters are smuggled in and out. I have a rota of maids and nurses and guards who will not look me in the eye. I fear that I am already good as dead, my babies too – perhaps it would be better if we were. Sometimes I deliberately prick my finger with my embroidery needle to see if there is any blood in me. There is, of course, and I watch it pool on my skin like a jewel. I imagine bleeding myself, from the fat blue vein in the crook of my arm, as I bled the night before my wedding, until I am emptied altogether of cursed blood and can begin again.

Tom's cries become more urgent. I am not moved. I will not allow myself to love Tom as I love Beech, for when I fell in love with my firstborn I imagined a life for him, full and perfect. But now it is clear that will not be, and I cannot bear to love Tom too and see his little life similarly sucked dry of pleasure. Or, worse, watch him wrenched from me and disappeared like those princes.

Beech, tired of his marching, drops into my lap. I lift off the red cap and bury my nose in his soft hair. He smells like his father and the strings of my heart are stretched to breaking.

'Baby Tom cry, Mama,' he lisps. 'He hungry.' He stands and pulls at my hand until I heave myself up, walking with him through to the other chamber and my waiting infant. The maid is in a huff, pacing the room, jigging him up and down, exasperated with his howling. I sit on my bedraggled chair, which has been chewed and shredded by the pets, opening my shift. Tom is plonked on my lap and instantly his mouth searches out my breast. He latches on, causing the momentary sharp sting that makes me hold my breath, as my milk drops down. I try not to look at him but cannot help it and feel my heart melt a little with the bittersweet intimacy. Beech watches from the side of his eye; I smile at him, to remind him that it is him I love. He twiddles the rings on my fingers, the pointed diamond, the knot of secret might, and searches for the limning that always hangs from a ribbon about my neck.

'Papa.' He strokes the surface of the glass with little fingers, then looking at me with his head tilted to one side says, 'Mama cry.'

'No, Beech,' I say. 'I'm not crying. I have sore eyes, that's all.' I thought I had cried myself dry long ago.

He climbs up on to my lap, negotiating his way around his baby brother, stretching up to put a wet kiss beside my eye. 'Better now,' he says.

'Yes, all better,' I tell him. Tom has had his fill and is lolling drunkenly in my arms, his mouth swollen with sucking. I fear if I look too long at him I will fall under his spell, so I place him gently in his cradle.

I can hear the nurse talking to the guards outside, their low voices rumbling. She comes back in, glancing over at me before gathering the dirty linens. A foul stench drifts over from the slop bucket in the far corner; it hasn't been emptied today, which is unusual.

'Where is the slop boy?' I ask.

'Plague,' she says and I see then that what I had thought was sullenness in her face, is fear.

'There is plague in London?' She looks at me as if I am a fool. 'I am told nothing in here,' I add.

'Fifteen thousand souls taken in the city alone.'

'Fifteen thousand?' I am horrified, cannot believe what I am hearing. Then think of Mary and Hertford, wondering if they are safe.

'My husband?' I say.

The woman shrugs, and I search her face to see if she is hiding something from me, but her look is blank, revealing nothing.

I rap on the door for the guards. It is opened and I shout, 'Has the court left?'

'Months ago,' one of them says. 'We'd all be gone if we had a place to go to.'

'And my husband, is he stricken? My sister, is she with the court?'

The girl slides out with her pile of linens, looking at me askance, as if I am a lunatic.

'I would not be at liberty to relate news of your kin, even were I to know it.'

The door is shut in my face and I am alone once more. Surely, I try to reason with myself, I would have been informed if my sister had died, or my husband. My head spins and I feel the danger pressing on my boys and me. It is a mother's job to protect her children but I cannot. We are in here, unable to leave, the slop boy plague-ridden already and who next – one of the maids, one of the guards, one of my boys? Perhaps it would be better if we were taken by the plague, all three of us together, but what of Hertford?

They say it is the worst kind of death, the plague, and I cannot help my imagination from running away with me, showing me images of my husband in agony, fighting for his life in a cell somewhere. My breath is short, shallow, and I feel panic rise up in me like a flame set to kindling. Opening the window, I heave in lungfuls of air in an attempt to steady myself. But I will not be steadied and it is as if another woman is inside me shouting.

'Hertford, my Hertford, my Hertford, my love.'

Beech, thinking it a game, joins in, 'Papa, Papa, Papa,' falling into laughter when he becomes breathless from shouting. I look down, imagining grabbing his little hand and jumping from the edge, flying, falling – I am above the river pool, above the smooth stone slabs.

'My Lady.' It is a voice behind me, one of the guards. I continue shouting until I am hoarse – I cannot stop myself. He takes my arm; I struggle a little but know there is no point. 'The lieutenant is here to see you.'

'Warner?' I ask, feeling a sliver of hope slip between the edges of my panic.

'Not Warner, no.'

Of course, Warner is gone.

The lieutenant is hovering by the door of my chamber, with a woman standing behind him.

I hold Beech's sweaty little paw tight in my hand.

'You are to be moved,' he says, not bothering with a greeting.

'To where?' I make a list in my head of all the possible places: a dungeon; another room like this; house arrest somewhere in the country; back to court – no, he said 'moved' not 'released'.

'I cannot say, My Lady. But you are to gather your things and be ready to leave within the hour. The infant will go with you, and the older boy with his father.'

'Hertford lives?' I cry.

'Why would you think otherwise?' says the lieutenant, and I wonder if my mind is not breaking apart, for I believed his death as if I had seen it with my own eyes. But now I know Hertford is safe I am confronted by the other thing I have been told: Beech is to be separated from me. The woman takes Beech's hand and moves for the door.

'NOOOO!' I shriek, grabbing at his sleeve.

'Mama.' His little face is scribbled over with bewildered fear. 'Mama, come?'

The lieutenant pulls me away, holding me tight with one hand and slamming the door with his other. I can hear Beech's screams as he is carried down the steps, each shrill note gouging out a piece of me. I collapse to the floor sobbing, feeling the full force of my loss as if a great weight has landed on me and knocked all the love from my heart.

'I am sorry, My Lady,' the guard is saying. 'It is the Queen's command.'

August 1563
Windsor Castle
Mary

It is pitch black and I can hear the Queen tossing and turning in the bed. The court is in disarray owing to the plague, and lately I have often been required to spend the night with her – a duty I do not relish. These last months I have been perplexed by the warmth Elizabeth has shown me. Perhaps she feels it atones for what she has done to my sister. But there is no pleasure in it for me and I have no choice but to accept her attentions, bear these interminable nights in the royal bedchamber. But it did give me the chance to plead Katherine's cause when plague struck in London and beg that she be removed to a safer place. It has been done – I can scarce believe it. She is on her way to Pyrgo, which is surely better than the Tower. Though I remember well enough how Uncle John treated her last time we were there, that dreadful summer before she was arrested. I hope he finds a way to muster up a little sympathy for his least favourite niece.

I am not supposed to be aware that the Queen has fulfilled my request. Does she think if I know one thing has been granted me that I shall get above myself and ask for more? I am not such a fool. It was Keyes who got word to me that they were to be moved: Hertford and Beech to

Hanworth and baby Tom to Pyrgo with his mother. While I am glad they are away from the infected area, I know the separation will be as torture to Katherine, who could hardly even bear an hour parted from her favourite dog. I think of my nephews, wondering constantly what they are like, trying to get a sense of them; but they inhabit my thoughts like spectres, and I cannot imagine up any substance to them.

Keyes's letter was smuggled through, in spite of nothing or no one being allowed entry from London for fear of infection. Even the barges are prevented from passing by on the river, and visiting delegates must wait in quarantine a full four weeks before they are admitted to court. I fret for Keyes, who was required to stay behind at Westminster, though he tells me he keeps at a safe distance from strangers. I miss the sanctuary of his chambers, our games of chess and whiling away our precious spare time in conversation. He has become a stalwart presence in my life. I pray for his safety and am thankful, at least, that Levina is safely here at Windsor with the court.

'Mary? Wake up.' I feel the Queen's hand shaking at my shoulder. 'Wake up. I cannot sleep.'

'I am awake, madam. Can I be of service to you?'

'Fetch a candle.'

I drag myself out of the truckle and fumble for my gown, pulling it over my shift and, unable to find my slippers, make for the door barefooted. Outside, both guards have dropped off. They are exhausted from working double shifts as their number is depleted by the plague. One has his head back at an uncomfortable angle against the wall – chin up, snoring loudly – the other is slumped on a stool. His eyes half open as I appear and he hastily pulls himself to his feet, smoothing down his livery and straightening his cap.

'Have you a taper?' I ask.

He makes a little bow and digs about in a carton, finding one, lighting it for me, only then seeming to notice my naked feet and blushing hotly as if he is surprised to discover that I have ten toes like any other woman.

Back in the bedchamber I can hear the Queen relieving herself in the pot. I light some candles, pull aside the hangings and plump her pillows. When she is done she flops down on the bed with a loud exhalation, and I notice in the dim light how drawn and haggard she has become, with dark circles about her eyes as if she has been punched.

'Have you not slept at all, madam? Can I bring you a soothing drink?'

'Not a wink,' she answers. 'Come and sit up here with me, Mary.' She pats the bed next to her. 'And bring those comfits from the far table.' I fetch the dish and clamber up. We sit for some time without talking, while she satisfies her sweet tooth, popping the comfits into her mouth one after the other, as if she will never be sated. I can't help myself from watching her and she must feel that I disapprove, for she holds one out to me, saying, 'Where else shall I get my pleasure?' in a voice sharp with cynicism. I take it, touching my tongue to its sweet, crystalline surface. 'It won't poison you,' she says. 'Try a little indulgence, Mary. You might find you like it.'

'I could mix you a tincture to help you sleep, madam.'

'I have tried most things and none have any effect. My head is filled with worries of such great import. But I have never slept well, since I was a girl.'

'I suppose it both a blessing and a curse, to be Queen,' I say, and then regret it, thinking I may have offended, because she looks at me askance.

But then she smiles. 'That is the truth. Most wouldn't say

it to me, though. Only him.' By 'him' I suppose she means Dudley. 'I watch them – all my courtiers – minding their words so very carefully.' She stops for a moment, bringing another comfit to her mouth. 'And there is Cecil,' she continues. 'But he seems to think he knows better than I what is good for me. He becomes carried away.'

She doesn't explain herself and I do not ask what she means, but I wonder if she refers to my sister's wedding.

'I suppose you to be lonely, in a manner of speaking,' I say.

'Yes, lonely,' she repeats, as if it has never quite occurred to her. 'Yet always surrounded. I suppose marriage *is* the answer.' It is hard to tell, from her deadpan tone, if she means this, or its opposite. 'Since I was brought low with the pox, my council have been petitioning me to wed more than ever before. I have to invent increasingly ingenious ways of keeping them at bay.'

'They all think you follow your heart, but it is your head you follow.'

'Clever Mary. You understand it all, don't you?'

'Not all,' I say, lightly, implying I understand most things. She laughs at that.

'If I followed my heart our ship of state would be sunk.'

She picks up a gilt casket from the table beside the bed, taking some little packages out of it, unwrapping them to reveal a number of limnings. I have heard of the Queen's miniature collection, but never seen it. I suppose the likenesses Levina made of Katherine, Lettice and me are amongst them. I wonder if my sister's has been removed.

She holds one up. 'My Scottish cousin. You are one of those who believes *she* should be named as my heir, are you not?' I am surprised she remembers our conversation about primogeniture, so much has happened since. 'It was due to you, Mary, that I spared your sister's life. There were those who called for her execution.'

I want to remind her that my sister is hardly spared; she may have her life but she lives it in a cage, separated from those she loves. But I remain silent, respectful – obedient Mary, in the Queen's pocket. I am so full of bitterness now; I fear if I died and was opened up they would find me black to the core.

She passes me the tiny portrait, saying, 'Do you find her beautiful?'

I know what she requires from my reply; I am meant to say 'not as you are' but what I actually say is, 'I *do* think her a beauty.'

The Queen narrows her eyes and her mouth tightens. I prepare myself for an outburst of anger but she surprises me by saying, 'Honesty is a quality I greatly admire. It is true, she *is* a beauty.' She has taken another limning from the bed and is rubbing it between her fingers. 'I have wedding plans for my beautiful cousin. This is who I mean to send her way.' She tosses the portrait over to me. I pick it up.

'Dudley?' It is his face in the palm of my hand.

'Once he is made Earl of Leicester, he will be quite a suitable match for her.'

'You would do that?' I ask, finding a shred of begrudged admiration for the woman. I hear the first notes of the dawn chorus; a lone blackcap sings out and is joined then by the trill of a chiffchaff.

'It is you who said I follow my head, not my heart. He is the only one I fully trust. It would be for England.'

'I see.' What I see though, in a flash of clarity, is that this is some kind of revenge. I remember hearing of the scathing comments Mary of Scotland made about the Queen and her 'horse keeper'. It is Elizabeth's way to put her ambitious cousin firmly in her place – marry her off to the 'horse keeper'. A song thrush now makes itself heard. Does she truly mean to do such a thing?

The Queen gathers up her miniatures, replacing them in their box.

'Well, at least *you* will never be a threat to my throne, Mary.'

What she means is that I am the wrong shape for greatness and will not produce boys. I wonder if she intends to be cruel or if she is oblivious of the sharpness of her tongue, for she smiles as she says it and rubs my arm, as if she has paid me a compliment.

'In spite of everything I have become fond of you, Mary Grey.'

I try to return her smile, but find I can barely tease an upward lift from even the furthest reaches of my mouth.

September 1563
Pyrgo
Katherine

I am banished to deepest Essex. I know our destination is Pyrgo even before the house comes into view. I remember the great oak at the head of the drive. I used to climb in it as a child on visits to Uncle John and Aunt Mary. I recognize the dairy where we used to go for cups of warm milk fresh from the cows. I recognize the spinney where I once kissed one of Uncle John's pages, and I remember Uncle John locking me in the store cupboard for a full day and night to teach me a lesson. I fared better than the page, who was beaten and dismissed. Uncle John was nothing like Father, for where Father was sunny and gleaming he was sullen and sharp – jealous of his older brother, perhaps.

Uncle John and Aunt Mary are waiting for us on the step and I must look a fright from weeping the whole length of the journey, for Aunt Mary gasps when the litter curtain is pulled back fully. Uncle John helps me out with his mouth set in a taut line. Aunt Mary goes to take Tom from my arms, but I grip him tightly. I will not be separated from him too. They introduce me to the line-up of staff: three men, three women and a lackey, none of whom I have ever seen before. They are my household – my jailers, in truth. There is a big-breasted wet nurse too, grinning stupidly – so they mean to take Tom off me anyway. I fear that when that gurning girl with her pendulous breasts comes to take my boy, I will have no resolve left in me to fight to keep him; it is lucky then that I have not allowed myself to fall so deeply for Tom as I did for Beech, or so I tell myself. But I am a mother and any mother who has felt her infant suckle falls deep, whether she chooses to or not.

Uncle John lays down the law, his voice cold and hard as a slab of ice: I am not to leave my rooms, not even to walk about the house or stroll in the gardens, unless I am accompanied; I am to attend chapel twice daily to ask pardon for my sins; I may not receive any letters, visits or communication of any sort from outside unless first verified; I may only have sanctioned reading materials and nothing to stir my 'wanton emotions further', as he puts it; my baby is to reside with the wet nurse in the east side of the house and shall be brought to me once daily, and, finally, my pets are to live in the stables.

'Oh, and one other thing,' he adds. 'You are to write to the Queen begging forgiveness and demonstrate to her that you have seen the error of your ways. You have tipped our family into this mire and you will do all you can to make amends.'

Uncle John's icicle face looks as if it would shatter with the slightest smile and Aunt Mary's is not much better, though she has a crease of sympathy on her brow. I do not speak to them, nor to anyone, save to tell the stable boy the particular whims of my pets, as it is he who shall be caring for them – he alone has a smile for me.

I am taken upstairs to my rooms at the back of the house. These are the rooms I used to share with Jane and Mary on our visits here. I remember the tree that grows so close to the window it scratches against the glass in the wind and used to terrify us at night. It all seems so very long ago, as if that Katherine was another girl in another life.

There is a book on the bed. I place my sleeping Tom beside it, surrounding him with pillows in case he rolls off, and pick the book up. It is familiar, the worn leather binding, the well-thumbed pages – I have seen this book before. It is Jane's New Testament in Greek.

'Your sister sent it,' says Aunt Mary. 'We are not supposed to let you have anything from outside but we thought this could do no harm. It is God's word. It can only do good.'

I do not reply, do not look at Aunt Mary; I just sit on the corner of the bed and open the book. There is Jane's letter. It is Jane's book, *her* blessed fingers have touched the places where mine are now, Mary's too, even Maman's – the faintest shred of joy finds its way into me. Remembering Mary's words about asking Jane for guidance, I hold it to my breast and lie on the bed next to Tom, feeling his snuffling breath against the skin of my cheek, closing my eyes.

I wait for Aunt Mary to leave, but she clucks about for a time, telling the maids where to put my things. People come and go but I do not move, I am talking silently to Jane. I watch through half-closed eyes as someone comes with a plate of food, leaving it on the table. The smell of it makes me nauseous. Then the girl comes for Tom. I don't fight for him, don't even open my eyes to see him go; he is better off with the grinning wet nurse than with me now. I search myself for feelings but I have none left – I am all turned to dust inside.

When everyone has gone and I am alone, save for one of the girls who is snoring on the truckle, I light a candle and read Jane's letter: *It shall teach you to live and learn you to die. And learn you to die. And learn you to die.* I wish I could read the book and learn how to die from it, but Greek is worse than Latin even, just lines of dead spiders. I try and recall the stories from the New Testament I once knew so well, only really remembering the prodigal son and the story of the two loaves and the five fishes – there is nothing that will learn me to die there. I search my memory for snippets of sermons and a picture appears in my mind of the crucifixion, Christ's hands pierced and bleeding, his body wounded, his eyes filled with pain and love.

Seeing that I feel weighed down with sin, to have had all this visited on me – to have had each and every soul I have ever loved wrenched from me – I must have sinned most horribly. I get on my knees and find I have forgotten how to pray, do not even know how to speak to God. But when I fall asleep to the sound of the tree scratching at the window with its claws, I dream of Katherine of Siena and I am back in the chapel at Durham House, with Jane Dormer telling me the story of how St Katherine purged herself of her sins by allowing only the host to pass her lips, and with it God's pure grace.

I wake to a shuffling behind the bed curtain. The maid must be awake and dressing. She peeps in through the hangings and I pretend to be asleep. I hear the clank of dishes – more food, I suppose – and the curtains are whisked back to reveal Aunt Mary's stern face.

'You must be hungry, Katherine,' she says, even before she has wished me good morning. 'Here.' She places a platter on the bed – some manchet bread and a piece of cheese with a cut of meat. I feel like that saint who was tempted in the desert. She sits on the bed awhile, talking, wittering really, to fill the silence. I don't listen.

'Eat, dear,' she says.

I say nothing but find I am weeping once more, though I thought I had no tears left in me. She offers me her handkerchief, which is small and dainty and will go no way to wipe away the sea of tears that I can feel welling. I think of filling the room with them and drowning. They say it is a peaceful way to go, but how would they know?

She leaves eventually and I sit in the window looking out, hoping for a glimpse of my dogs in the park. Two of the women come to straighten the bed and get me dressed. I am like a doll. They try not to look at me. I look at the plate of food on the bed.

'Chapel now,' says one. I allow her to lead me there. I try to listen to the word of God, try to make sense of it, imagine I can hear Jane explaining it to me, but my sins are pressing down on me, making it hard to think. I push the hassock out of the way so my knees are on the hard flagstones. I wonder who is buried beneath me. I open my mouth for the host. My mouth waters. It is on my tongue, in my throat, in me, filling me up with God's grace. I ask His forgiveness – He hears me, I know it for I can feel Him all about me, emptying me of sin.

After chapel, Uncle John stands over me while I write to the Queen. The two women stand by the door watching. I dip the pen. The vinegar smell of the ink turns my stomach.

A drop falls on the paper. Uncle John tuts loudly, snatching it up, screwing it into a ball, placing another before me. He dictates, I write. *I dare not presume, Most Gracious Sovereign, to crave pardon for my disobedient and rash matching of my self, without Your Highness's consent, I only most humbly sue unto Your Highness, to continue your merciful nature towards me. I knowledge myself a most unworthy creature* . . . then I stop, put the pen down and sit in silence, my eyes streaming once more.

'You can finish it tomorrow,' he says, and calls for one of the women to take me back to my rooms, telling the other to fetch a plate for me from the kitchens.

She brings it up, putting it on the table, clearing her throat. 'Your uncle says if you eat you shall see little Lord Thomas, but if not he shall be kept from you until you do.'

I think of my dear sweet Tom, his tiny fist gripped about my finger, his long eyelashes in a perfect curve against his pale skin, his apple cheeks, and I ache with longing. I take a morsel of cheese and put it in my mouth, chewing it, swallowing it, then another, and another, coaxed like an infant by the woman. 'Three more pieces and little Lord Thomas will be with you.' But as I eat I feel each mouthful congesting me with sin. By the time my boy is brought to me, I am black to the soul and can hardly see his perfect small hand, nor his curve of lashes, nor his rosy cheeks, for I am clouded with wickedness.

When he is wrenched from me once more, I sit looking at the half-eaten plate of food, the remains of the cheese sweating droplets of oil, slices of ham striated with thick fat, sweetbreads doused in lard. My stomach twists and turns. It is only the manchet bread – white, clean, dry – that seems untouched. I break off a corner of it and wrap it in a square of linen, hiding it amongst my pillows.

One of the women returns with a box of candles, placing them in the sconces, lighting them, then leaves. They spit and flicker, sending out the stench of beef dripping – Uncle John has given me tallow, doesn't want to waste good beeswax on his disgraced niece, I suppose. The smell cloys, gets into the very pores of me. I blow them out and lie on the bed watching the darkness fall, listening to the tree claws scratch at the window. The clog of sin sits like a lead weight in my stomach.

I wake to hear Jane calling my name. *Katherine, I am here.* I feel a hand brush me and then see a glow, becoming brighter, so bright I fear it will blind me, and in the light a wound and, revealing itself about the wound, a body, hands pierced, bleeding, eyes brimming with love. I kiss those hands, that wound, press my face to the body, the flesh, and there is a voice in my head. *I shall bless your bread for you that it will become my body and you can eat without sin, Katherine.* In an instant he is gone.

'I have news of Hertford for you,' says Uncle John in a tight voice. 'He is at Hanworth with Beauchamp. Both are well and send this.' He holds out a book, which I take. It is a book of poems we used to read to each other.

'No note?' I look at him. We have barely exchanged a word in the month I have been here. It is not for want of him trying. It is I who has forgotten how to converse in the normal way.

He does not answer, which makes me think there was a letter with the book. 'I worry for you,' he says. 'You do not eat.'

But I do eat; I eat so I may see my boy. 'I eat,' I murmur, thinking of the stash of bread I have hidden in my bed – the only thing I can ingest that does not fill me with sin.

'Not enough,' he says, now pacing back and forth over the room. 'I only keep your boy from you that you will eat. I would not see you starve.'

I do not reply to this, but I suppose it might be true.

We sit silently like that until he says, 'There is no word from the Queen.'

He means there is no pardon. I know she will never pardon me now. But Uncle John is afraid to lose her favour – it is carved into him – afraid she will think he has not made me repentant. No wonder, when he sees in me what becomes of those who lose the Queen's good will.

'Write to Hertford,' he says. 'Just this once. I will make sure it gets to him.' I detect a little softness in his tone. He points to the table in the window where there is paper and ink. 'I shall leave you awhile.'

I look out of the window at the deer grazing in the park. There is a lake in the distance, flat like a silver shilling. I think about my sister, where she is, and then about my husband, at his mother's house, remembering how little the Duchess liked me. I try to imagine my precious Beech there, digging up the corridors of Hanworth from my past, and with them come vague beautiful memories of Juno. But I cannot conjure a picture of Beech in that place, and I will not imagine him in the firm arms of the Duchess. I begin to write, the words flowing from me:

> *It gives me no small joy, my dearest Lord, to hear of your good health. I ask God to give you strength, as I am sure He shall. In this lamentable time there is nothing that can better comfort us, in our pitiable separation, than to ask, to hear, and to know of each other's well-being. Although recently I have been unwell, I am now pretty well, thank God. I long to be merry with you, as I know you do with me, as we were when our sweet little boys were gotten in the Tower . . .*

I take my handkerchief and wipe my tears before they spoil the ink. I cannot bear to have him think I suffer.

September 1564
Ludgate
Levina

A full year on and the city is only just beginning to recover from the plague. There are still dozens of grubby-faced orphans lining the streets. They hold out cupped hands to passers-by, in the hope that someone will take pity and toss them a coin or a hunk of bread. Of the goldsmiths on Cheapside, half of them are still boarded up and the same goes for the cloth merchants and the other purveyors that used to line the streets. Levina's pigment supplier is gone and with him his entire family, as is the parchment dealer whose wife is struggling to re-establish the business, but the market at Smithfield is thriving once more, even if many of the old faces are gone.

She stops at the fish stall, casting her eyes over the splendid array spread across the trestle, picking out a pair of fat silver trout, a carton of cockles, and asking the vendor to tip a few handfuls of sprats into her basket. She counts out the coins, handing them over, telling the vendor to keep the change, and moves on to the poultry stall. Usually her maidservant would be doing this but Levina is preparing something special, for George is returning home. His first letter had come a month ago, begging her forgiveness. *And what of Lotte?* she had asked by return. *A terrible mistake*, he had called it, *and one I shall regret until the end of my days. Come home*, she had replied, *and we will never talk of it again*, adding in the postscript, *we are all entitled to our mistakes.* She has had more than enough time to think about things in the last three years. She can choose whether to spend her days resenting his absence, or to rejoice in his return. She has chosen the latter – life is short enough.

By her calculations, his boat should dock early this afternoon. She hurries home with her foodstuffs, feeling the excitement gather in her. Ellen is at the kitchen door when Levina arrives.

'There is someone here.' She nods in the direction of the door to the hall. 'From the palace.'

Levina's heart sinks. It can only be bad news. 'Who?'

'I have not seen him before.'

'Did you ask his name?'

Ellen mumbles an apology. 'I was busy with the boy. He came by, the painter.' She takes the baskets of produce from Levina's arms.

'What, Hilliard? What did *he* want?'

'Said he was leaving for France and came to bid farewell.'

'Farewell?' Hilliard hasn't spoken to her since she confronted him about the copied limning more than two years ago.

'He said he is sorry, that you were right. Said you'd know what he meant.'

Levina wishes she'd been here to accept his apology, would have liked to apologize to him too. Her outburst hadn't been charged only with anger about Katherine; there was envy beneath it too. She had ever known that he was the better painter. She supposes he will be studying with François Clouet in France. It was what he always wanted. He'd admired Clouet's work, much more than hers. Under his wing the boy would thrive.

'I suppose I must –' She takes a deep breath and opens the hall door, to find Keyes waiting there.

'Mistress Teerlinc.'

'Mister Keyes! What brings you here?' Her heart sinks, fearing the worst. 'Is Lady Mary sick?'

'It is not Lady Mary,' he says, proffering a stack of papers rudely tied together with twine, not quite a book but not a pamphlet either. 'I have come upon this.'

'What is it?' Levina asks.

'It is Club-foot Hale's tract.' His face is a mask of concern.

'I have never heard of such a person.'

'He has made investigations into the legitimacy of Lady Katherine's claim. It is all here. He makes a good case of it.'

'And this is published?' she asks.

He nods grimly.

'And the Queen?'

'She has seen it. Lady Katherine is to be moved from her uncle's care; the Queen thinks John Grey involved. She is to be more closely guarded elsewhere. Hales and Grey are to be sent to the Tower.'

Levina slumps on to a stool, despairing at her powerlessness. Thinking back, she can see that there was once a time, in the old Queen's reign, when she thought her actions could make a difference. But now she sees that even Foxe's book changed nothing; it was Mary Tudor's death that altered all their fates. Nothing she can say or do will change things for Katherine now. She wonders when it was that she lost hope.

'Is there nothing to be done?' She knows the question is futile. He shakes his head. 'I could at least petition for Lady Mary to reside here with me.'

'I don't think that will be possible. The Queen has become attached to her, these days.' Keyes's expression, the distant look in his eyes, reveals something Levina has long suspected about his feelings for Mary. She has watched the way he gazes at her, hanging on her words, the way he would do anything to make her grim life a little easier. Keyes has fallen in love with her.

'Why don't you marry her?' she says, surprising herself with her directness.

'Don't tease me,' he replies, jerking his face away as if she has slapped him.

'But I mean it.' She can see now that there is a way she might instigate a change in circumstance, for Mary at least.

'She is of the blood, and I am a nobody.'

'Exactly,' Levina says. 'Did you know Mary's mother married her groom in part as a way to extricate herself from court. As plain Mistress Keyes, she could never be perceived as a threat to anyone.'

'The Queen would never allow it; besides, what is there in a great grotesque oaf like me to attract one so' – he hesitates – 'one so perfect.'

It touches Levina to the core, hearing such a thing said of Mary; it is so rare for anyone to see beyond her shape. 'You might be surprised,' she says with a smile.

'I should be getting back.' Keyes puts his hat on, adjusting it carefully, as if it will prevent all his bottled emotion from finding a way out, and makes for the door.

Levina knows he will not ask Mary for her hand, but it was a pleasant thought.

Realizing the time, she rushes upstairs to change out of her plain dress, calculating how long it will take to get to the quayside in time for the boat, becoming caught up once more in the excitement of George's return. Sifting through her clothes, she hums a tune she picked up in the market, a lover's ballad, laughing inwardly at herself, a woman of forty-four behaving like a moonstruck girl over the return of her estranged husband. She changes her plain linen coif for an embroidered one and then again for one made of yellow silk, then climbs out of the scarlet kirtle she has just put on, replacing it with a damask one; she is reminded, with a jolt of sadness, of Katherine, who could not dress without changing her mind several times.

She is half in and half out of her kirtle when the door creaks, opening ajar. She stops her humming. 'Ellen?' she says. 'Why are you hovering without? Come in, you can help me with my laces.'

The door slowly swings wide and there is George standing before her, with a few more creases about his eyes, a few more streaks of grey in his beard, but George nonetheless.

'V-V-Veena,' is all he manages to say.

They stand looking at each other across the chamber, she holding her unlaced kirtle up in a fist, feeling the pump of her heart against her ribcage. He is both familiar and strange to her and she doesn't know what to say.

'I was coming to meet you,' she says when she finds her voice.

'We docked early.'

She moves towards him, her hand outstretched, taking his fingers.

'Am-am-am-am.' She waits for his words to form. 'Am I forgiven?'

'Entirely,' she whispers, close up to him now.

He brings her hand to his lips, kissing each finger in turn. 'You smell of paint.'

'Always paint,' she laughs.

'It is a wonderful smell,' he says.

Her kirtle has dropped and she feels awkward, worried that her porridge thighs will disgust him, and tries to tug it back up.

'Leave it,' he says.

Later they sit together at the table to eat and she listens as he describes his father's death. 'A man can lose himself a little when his father goes.'

'I know,' she replies.

'Tell me, then, what news at court?' He seems to want to change the subject, as if he is closing a lid on his time in Bruges. She listens for an edge of resentment or sarcasm in his voice when he mentions court, not finding either, and nor does it appear when she tells him of the plight of Katherine Grey. He takes her hand and gives it a squeeze, saying, 'I am so sorry, Veena. I know what those girls mean to you.'

'And I suppose you have heard that Dudley is made Earl of Leicester?' she says.

'So she did it, finally.'

'She did, and she is trying to broker a marriage between him and the Queen of Scots.'

'So court is as upside down as ever. Why would she offer the man she loves to her own cousin?'

'It is politics, George,' Levina says. 'She puts politics before emotion always, but it continues to amaze us all each time she does it. She wants Scotland in her pocket and how better than to wed its Queen to her trusted favourite.'

'And what thinks the Queen of Scots?'

'The rumour is that she would consider it, but only on condition of being named as Elizabeth's heir.'

'Abroad they all still talk of Elizabeth marrying the Archduke Charles.'

'*I* think she will not marry anyone. She says it, but none believe her. Mary Grey has always said so.'

They sit in silence for a moment, and something occurs to Levina that she had not fully realized until she articulated it – that for Elizabeth politics come before everything. That is how it must be if you are Queen regnant, your passions shut away in a box buried deep beneath the ground. It makes her think of her predecessor, Mary Tudor, who struggled so with that concept, and she surprises herself with a pinch of sympathy for these women who have to fashion a cold, hard face to show to the world.

'Father bequeathed me more than I expected,' he says after some time.

'So I no longer need to paint for money?'

'I will never expect you to stop painting, Veena. It is as much a part of you as . . .' He doesn't finish his sentence.

July 1565
Windsor Castle
Mary

'My oldest is Penelope.' Lettice is telling us about her daughters, as we make sugar fancies to cheer the Queen, for she has lost her closest companion, Kat Astley, who died quite suddenly. Kat Astley was as good as a mother to her. A burnt-caramel scent fills the room. 'She runs rings around her poor nurse,' continues Lettice.

'A naughty one, is she?' asks one of the women.

'A little headstrong.'

'It would profit you to curb that,' adds someone.

'I miss my darlings,' says Lettice. 'I think I shall return to Chartley. They grow up so fast.'

Frances Meautas clears her throat pointedly. We all know that it is not Lettice's choice to return to Chartley: the Queen has sent her away. For 'messing about' with Dudley, as Frances put it. I didn't probe further; it is none of my business what Lettice does or doesn't do. But I was surprised, for she is said to be with child, though it doesn't show on her. She reminds me a little of Katherine, she always has. She is the kind who has an exciting whiff of scandal about her. It is a full four years since I have seen my sister and a year since I gave up hope. After Hale's book was published and Katherine was moved from Pyrgo, I knew I would never see her again.

'The girls both have dark eyes and golden hair,' continues Lettice.

I cannot help but think of my nephews I have never met. There had been one or two letters from Katherine a year since, before she was moved. Strictly speaking she was not allowed to write. Uncle John had become lax, 'more sympathetic', she'd written. All I ever remember of Uncle John is his hardness, and if he had become sympathetic then I suspect it was not for Katherine's sake, but for the sake of her Tudor blood and what it might do to improve his own lot. I have become cynical, but it is no surprise. Her letters were sad enough to break my heart, were it not already broken – confused meanderings, talking of Jane and the Holy Ghost and the Body of Christ, only occasionally sounding like herself. I fear she has lost her mind altogether. But now Uncle John is passed away and Katherine remains under lock and key, tightly guarded in another house, and there will be no more letters.

I try to imagine my nephews, their round faces; maybe they are not round but long and slender, maybe they have pudgy hands, maybe not. In my mind's eye Beech is the image of his mother – this idea springs from the limning I still wear cached about my person, in which they are so very alike. His brother I have chosen to imagine as like Jane, conker-coloured hair and eyes to match, based on something Katherine wrote in a letter once. I yearn ceaselessly for the scattered fragments of my family to be reunited. Beech will be four soon and his brother three – all that time has dripped away while I was traipsing from palace to palace paying court to my fiery cousin – drip, drip, drip; the sound of my life. I was not designed for this, the constant coming and going, the up and down of it. All I ask is to be given leave to live quietly somewhere, but Elizabeth has her claws in me and the best I can expect is to grow old here amongst the poisonous courtiers.

When my despair is at its most profound, I still ask myself what Jane would have done. Jane would have faced her lot with stoicism, so that is what I do; I gather up the pieces of myself, lace myself tightly into my embellished dresses, ignoring the deep ache in my twisted spine, and do what is expected of me. But although that is what Jane would have done, Jane would have seen it as God's plan. Not I, for I lack Jane's depth of faith. I learned long ago that if I am to accept God's plan then I must acknowledge that, despite the new faith and the new covenant, I am still perceived as wrapped in the Devil's packing.

'Mary, you are daydreaming.' It is Peggy, in the doorway. She has caught me staring into space, spoon in mid-air, sugar burned. 'You were miles away.'

Frances Meautas sniggers. She is leaving court to be married soon – I shall be glad to see the back of her. I lift the pot off the burner, holding it with my sleeves to protect my hands.

'You have managed to ruin it,' says Frances. 'Is there *anything* you do well?'

Looking directly at her I take up a pitcher of water and, with slow deliberation, pour a stream of it into her pot. It sizzles, spitting drops of hot sugar over the table. 'Oh dear, yours appears to be ruined too.'

Frances makes an indignant gasp. Lettice laughs. I wonder how I am reduced to such spiteful idiocy and wish that I could rise above it, but that vindictive demon simmers in me still. Yes, it is a good thing Frances is to be wed but there will always be other women to replace her, who look at me and see something less than human. Peggy beckons me over and when I am close enough to hear her she whispers, 'Keyes wants to see you in the herb garden.'

'Keyes?' I ask. 'Why is he here at Windsor?'

'He didn't say, but he awaits you there.'

'Is it news of Katherine?'

She shrugs. 'I shall say you had to run an errand for . . . I shall think of something. Go – go on.'

As I make my way to the garden my mind twists and turns about what it could be that has brought Keyes all the way from Westminster. It may be good news, but it is more likely bad – I cannot remember the last time I heard good news. I think of all the possible misfortunes that could have befallen my sister or her boys and my body feels heavier and heavier. By the time I arrive at the gardens I am a dead weight and the effort of putting one foot before the other feels like an impossible task.

There is nobody about, just one or two weeders crouched over the beds in the knot garden, which I pass through and on, under the fragrant arch of jasmine that leads to the herb garden. Keyes waits on a stone bench in the shade of a yew hedge. He doesn't see me and I stop a moment, dreading what it is I am going to hear. He plays with a frond of lavender, pinching off the blue tips and rolling them between his palms then bringing his cupped hands to his face and breathing in with closed eyes. There is a gathering of finches twittering and flitting about in the hedge and I am struck by the charm of the scene before me, my concern abating a little – surely this is not a setting for bad news.

I make a small coughing sound and Keyes looks towards me, his face lighting up, then he stands, holding both arms out from his body. 'Lady Mary,' he says. 'Thank you for coming here.'

As I walk towards him I scrutinize him for clues about what he will say to me, but he is unreadable. 'Have you news, Mister Keyes?'

'No, not news,' he says, which confuses me. 'Will you sit?'

He offers me a hand to help me up on to the bench, before lowering himself beside me and we sit in silence for a while. I look at the angle of his knees, pointing up as if the bench is too small for him, his great feet planted into the ground, and then at my own legs, my feet dangling like a child's. 'So?' I say.

'My Lady,' he begins.

'Mary,' I say, reiterating what I always say, that he should use my given name. But each time he wants permission.

'Mary.'

'Yes?' I have noticed that he is folding and unfolding his hands, seems nervous. He is not the nervous type and I am assaulted once more by worry.

'Would you like to leave court?'

'I wish it greatly.' He has piqued my interest. 'But you are aware of that, Mister Keyes.'

'Thomas,' he says.

'Thomas,' I repeat, smiling now.

'I believe there is a way.'

'How?'

'Your . . .' He hesitates, seeming to try and straighten his thoughts. 'Your mother married beneath her and that way extricated herself from life at court, did she not?'

'If only . . .' I begin to say. 'Stokes loved Maman greatly and she him.'

'And if someone loved you?'

'What are you saying, Thomas? Speak plainly.' I watch a squirrel scamper over the path and up a nearby tree.

'*I* am a nobody,' he says. 'And I find I have . . . I am . . . Mary, you have got inside me and I can think of nothing else.'

'You are saying I should marry *you*?'

He is nodding and flushed and wears a desolate expression.

'I am so very sorry. I have over-stepped –'

'No!' I say, placing my hand over his. He appears to droop as if the stuffing is gone from him. 'You have not. But why would you marry *me*? I cannot give you a child.'

'I have grown-up children. It is *you* I want, not children.' He pauses again, looking at me, and I slip my hand beneath his, allowing him to hold it. Something awakens in the root of me, a feeling I do not recognize. 'Do you think you could grow to love a great oaf like me, even a little?'

I find I am looking at him differently, noticing for the first time the way his beard gathers into little whorls and the way his upper lip dips in a heart shape and the look in his eyes that I cannot describe, a blend of compassion and honesty. I find myself thinking not what would Jane do, but what would Katherine do – after all, she is the expert in things concerning love. I find I am swamped with this new feeling, giddy with it, and begin to understand what it is that has driven Katherine all these years.

'I think so,' I say. Then, suddenly, I see us as an outsider might – he, this giant of a man and I small like a bird beside him; we are quite ridiculous, like a mismatched pair from a comic masque. But then my mind turns to Heraclitus; I remember translating it from Greek in the schoolroom: *Opposites come together and from what is different arises the fairest harmony*. And I wonder if he is not the other half of my wheel and that his great size makes up for my smallness, so together we are a perfect whole. 'Are you requesting my hand, Thomas?' I am surprised by my boldness.

'I am, My . . . My Mary,' His voice is uncharacteristically timid and I understand how much courage it has taken him to ask this of me.

'Then my answer is yes.'

He makes a noise, not a word, but a kind of 'ahhh' that seems to be the sound of pure happiness.

'And what of the Queen?' I do not want to douse his joy, but it must be said.

'She will never give permission. She will laugh me out of court,' he says with a defeated sigh, as if this has not occurred to him before.

'Then we shall marry *without* her permission.' I have an image in my mind of Katherine smiling in approval. 'And I shall be Mistress Nobody.' It seems a perfect scheme. 'The Queen can hardly object. There is no threat to her throne in it. Indeed, quite the opposite.'

But then I am jolted to reality at the thought of the grotesque body I had momentarily forgotten, and the giddy feeling drops away with brutal suddenness. 'But . . .' I say.

'But?' I can see the joy begin to leak out of him, as if my 'but' has pricked him and he is deflating.

'My shape,' I say. 'It is not made for –' He stops my words, running a hand down my spine. All I have ever known are the matter-of-fact hands of women forcing my recalcitrant form into clothes that are the wrong shape for me, and hardly being able to bear even the lightest touch.

'Mary, in my eyes you are perfect in and out.' With this he takes a ring from his smallest finger and folds it into my palm. 'I am promised to you now. This is your proof.'

I take the ring, bringing it to my lips, kissing the rosy stone. I then, in the grip of some kind of wanton force, unpin my over-gown, letting it slip off my shoulders and unlace my high, ruffled collar. 'Touch me,' I whisper, holding his eyes with mine, hardly able to believe it is I saying such a thing.

His fingers creep behind my neck, and down to the part of me that is hunched into a great tight knot at my nape; then they slide down beneath my shift to the most misshapen part of me. Beneath his hands I am miraculously released from my skewed body; I am an oyster freed from its shell. I am crookbacked Mary Grey no more, and I shall be Mistress Nobody.

The Queen storms from the council chamber, surrounded by a group of clucking councillors, all on eggshells. 'Darnley, Darnley?' she is saying, almost shouting. 'That woman will be the end of me!'

I had been preparing myself to broach the fact of my marriage with her, but it would seem this is not the moment.

'I will hear no more of it. Let's have some music.' I watch the way the men melt back towards the edges of the room as the Queen settles into a chair at the centre. Cecil lurks, standing a little apart from them. A lutenist begins to strum an old familiar tune, one that I remember Maman humming to me when I was a child. The past looms.

'Darnley has wed the Scottish Queen,' whispers Peggy. So that is what this is about. Mary of Scotland has managed to outfox her cousin. Elizabeth's plans to marry the Scottish Queen to Dudley are thwarted and a match with the Catholic Darnley could well mean grave trouble for England. No wonder the Queen is in such a foul humour. I remember that night she first mentioned that planned match with Dudley to me, when I never believed she would do it.

'Mary Grey, let's have you on the virginals. I like your playing better than this idle strumming. Something uplifting.'

I clamber up on to the music stool and begin to play a frivolous little melody.

'That's more like it,' says the Queen, who begins tapping her foot and humming along. The tension begins to release from the atmosphere. But I am watching Frances Meautas, who is talking in the corner to Cecil, noticing the way she occasionally flicks her eyes in my direction. She is talking about me. It was only a matter of time before it got out and if there is gossip about, Frances will always catch it first. The hairs on the back of my neck stick up. I cannot read anything from Cecil's reaction. I miss a note, then another. Cecil moves over to the Queen, who waves him off with a shake of her head, but he persists. I focus all my attention on to the tune I am playing, so inappropriately jolly, given what appears to be happening. Cecil is insistent though and the Queen relents eventually, listening as he whispers something in her ear. I have a good idea what it is. I keep on playing, I don't know how; even when the tune comes to an end I start it up again. A few are clapping along with it. I am waiting, watching.

The Queen calls Frances over to her, asking her something. Frances is nodding like a drunk's puppet. My breath is shallow and I am trying not to think of what is about to happen, to think instead of my wedding day, my wedding night, of lying in the arms of my dear husband. As my fingers continue to play, I think about each of the fourteen days and nights I have been Keyes's wife, of each little kindness done, each blissful instant. I fear my moment in the sun is over.

Frances approaches me. 'Her Majesty would like a word.' She wears a smirk that I would wipe off her face were the circumstances different.

The room is silent and everyone has begun to wonder what is happening, throwing questioning looks at each other. I kneel before the Queen, head bent, eyes on the floor.

'Look at me, Mary,' she says.

I lift my eyes. Her expression is inscrutable.

'You are wed?'

I nod.

'To my Sergeant Porter.' I don't know if the look of distaste is more for the fact that I have married without her say-so, or the fact that Keyes is so far beneath me in rank – both, perhaps.

I can feel the room's attention bearing heavily on me.

'Have I single a cousin left who has not betrayed me?'

It is as if the room is in suspension, awaiting an explosion. I can hear a woodpecker's thrum from beyond the open window. It is summer outside. When the Queen speaks again she is quite calm, which is almost worse for its unexpectedness.

'You have defied me. What do you think I should do with you, Mary?'

In that moment I decide that I will not go off with my tail between my legs like a good girl – good little Mary Grey, good as gold. I will not give up my freedom without a fight.

'Your Majesty,' I say, trying to keep my voice steady. 'I am no threat to you. I cannot bear a child to claim your throne. I am barely a woman.' I open my arms as if to say, look at me, look at this useless body of mine.

I notice the Queen wipe a hand over her forehead and press her lips together. I think I see a drop of kindness there.

'I have made myself a nobody with this marriage,' I continue. 'I think you could give me a chance of happiness. It would cause no harm.'

She closes her eyes and opens them again slowly, and I allow myself to imagine I have appeased her.

'I beg of you, do not make me suffer for my sister's misdemeanours.'

She inhales deeply, then speaks very quietly. 'If only that

were possible, Mary.' Then louder, so the whole company can hear. 'If I allow this, all the world will think they can defy me and be forgiven.'

'But Your Majesty too has made youthful misdemeanours . . .' It slips out unbidden and I feel a knot of dread tie itself inside me. The Queen will not relish being reminded of her own weaknesses – that, I know only too well.

'Take her away!' is the command, spoken with her head turned from me.

A guard takes hold of my upper arm and hauls me from the chamber. Twisting my head back I shout, 'I hope it festers on your royal conscience, the misery you have visited upon us Greys!'

January 1568
Cockfield Hall
Katherine

The physician pierces the thin skin in the crook of my arm. I think of Christ's wound, a red flower opening in his white side, petals falling. I watch the ruby trickle slowly fill the bowl – all the cursed Tudor blood draining from me. I shut my eyes and try to hold the image I saw from the window yesterday, of Tom in the gardens, charging along, emitting peals of laughter, astride an upturned broom serving as a hobby horse, the dogs running behind him as if they were a pack of hounds after a stag.

In my mind it is summer but I can tell from the patterns of ice at the edges of the windowpanes that it is deep winter, and now I am confused as to when it was I saw my Tom in the gardens. I find I cannot hold things in my head, and wake sometimes thinking myself back at Pyrgo or in the Tower, with my Hertford but a few yards away. Then comes the wrench of knowing he is not there and the surprise of finding myself in an unfamiliar place. I have to ask one of the maids where I am. The image is fading away and the sound of Tom's bright laughter has become so quiet I can barely hear it.

'Hush,' I say to the maid, who is clattering about with the basin. 'I cannot hear my boy.'

'Lord Thomas is asleep, My Lady,' she says.

'Not in the gardens?' I ask, trying to untangle my thoughts, remembering it is winter now and that I was only seeing him in my imagination, realizing too that the doctor is gone and that my arm is bandaged. 'Oh dear, I am confused again. Tell me, Lucy, where are we?'

'I am not Lucy, My Lady. I am Maud and we are in Suffolk, at Cockfield Hall, in the care of Sir Owen Hopton.'

'Maud,' I say. I remember that I like Maud, but cannot make any sense of things otherwise. 'I thought we were at Ingatestone.'

'No, My Lady. We moved from there some time ago and have since been at Gosfield Hall and now here.'

'I am the King's mother.'

'There is no King, My Lady.' Her voice is soft. 'It is Queen Elizabeth on the throne, near on ten years now.'

'She is my cousin.'

'I believe she is, My Lady.'

'And Tom, where is he?' I feel panic rising.

She sits beside me, taking my hand. 'Fret not for Lord Thomas. He sleeps soundly next door.'

I am suddenly afraid that time is playing tricks on me. 'How many years have gone by, Maud?' I ask, trying to remember the places she talks of, trying to remember how old Tom is. 'What age is my boy?'

'He is five, My Lady. And a fine strapping lad he is too.'

'Five? Who stole the years?'

She takes a cup in her hands. I can see a feather of steam rising from it. 'Will you take a little broth?'

I smell it now – an animal smell that knots my stomach. The stench of it is filling me with sin. I shake my head slowly.

'Just a sip. You will feel better.'

'Maud,' I clutch at her arm. 'You will take care of him . . .'

I can tell by the stricken look on her face that she knows, as well as I, that I am not long for this place.

'I promise,' she says.

I am gripped with a sudden horror. I must face my own obliteration. Jane is whispering to me: *It will learn you to die . . . It will learn you to die . . . I will learn you to die . . .* I think of Christ – His skin is pearl white, luminous, and the red petals fall forever from His side. He smiles at me.

'Help me to the prayer stand, Maud.' As I say it, I wonder where I will find the strength to drag my carcass from the bed. I feel her capable arms about my waist as I stagger the few yards, collapsing to my knees on the hassock. Muttering out a prayer, I take the pellet of bread I have hidden in my gown and, eyes tight shut, holding the image of Christ steady in my mind, place it on my tongue. Water wells in my mouth and the pellet swells until it is bigger than a fist; bigger than a melon; bigger than my belly, great with child; as big as the earth itself. I swallow and I am replenished. 'Hear my prayer, O Lord, give ear to my supplications: in thy faithfulness answer me, and in thy righteousness . . .'

'I shall ask for the chaplain to come and pray with you, My Lady,' whispers Maud.

There are people hovering in the chamber like shadows. Jane is amongst them, at the foot of my bed, waiting for me, her small hand stretched out to take mine. Someone approaches.

It is Sir Owen. I can feel words collecting up in me, things I must say.

'How do you?' he is asking.

'Even now, going to God' – the words flow from me, a river of words – 'I beseech you promise me one thing, that you yourself with your own mouth will make this request unto the Queen's Majesty, from the mouth of a dead woman: that she would forgive her displeasure towards me, and that she would be good to my children, and not impute my fault on to them, and to my husband, for I know my death will be heavy news for him . . .' She must free him now, I am thinking, for when I am gone there will be no reason to keep him locked away. 'Maud,' I say, 'pass me the box where my wedding ring is kept.'

The box feels like a dead weight, heavy as a coffin. It takes all my strength to lift off the lid. Inside I feel for the pointed diamond. Handing it to Sir Owen, I say, 'Give this to my husband. It is the ring he gave me when I promised myself to him.'

'Your wedding ring?' he asks.

'No.' I take out the other ring and hand it to him. 'This is my wedding ring.'

He inspects it minutely, reading the inscription. 'Knot of secret might,' he murmurs. 'So it is true. Why did you not show this to the Church Commission?'

'I did.'

I can hear him exhale a great lungful of air. I don't want to have to remember all that, how they had decided not to believe me, before I even set foot in the Archbishop's Palace. I take one more ring from the box, bringing it close so my eyes can focus on it. It is the death's head ring I wore for Juno; its hollow sockets stare back at me. 'Give them all to Hertford. And this . . .' I pull Jane's Greek New Testament from beneath my pillow. 'This is for my sister Mary.'

I close my eyes, drained now, feeling the last vestiges of life leaking from me. I can hear Lady Hopton quite clearly, whispering to someone that if only I would eat something, my life would be spared. But I cannot keep Jane waiting. God has sent her to fetch me.

Images run through my mind and I am back in the gardens at Nonsuch with the music trickling from the banqueting hall, astride my Hertford, my face burrowed into his neck, breathing him in; I am in the Tower and there he is on the parapet, standing waiting for me as if it is an ordinary day; I am lying on my bed beside Mary, her small hand held against my belly, waiting for my baby to quicken; I am basking in the gummy smile of my dearest Beech; I am nursing little Tom, his mouth suckered to me; I am in Maman's arms, a babe myself; I am back above the river pool at Nonsuch, standing on the brink, Juno watching on as I throw myself into the air like I have wings. I look to Jane; she is not alone: Juno and Maman float either side of her, beckoning me.

A figure drifts towards me. It is my Tom. I touch his soft face. It is wet – a rain-drenched peach.

'Weep not, my precious. I go to the Lord's house. He is waiting for me.' His little shoulders heave as he plants a sweet, damp kiss on my cheek and I feel the threads attaching my heart to his thinning – one more tug and they will be broken.

September 1571
Bishopsgate
Mary

A blackbird sings outside my window and a breeze flutters the edges of my papers. I am writing to my husband. I think of him at Sandgate Castle, where he is now guardian, a position granted him by the Queen. Closing my eyes, I allow myself to imagine for a moment that I am there by the sea with him – the briny rush of air blows my hair from its ties, the gulls circle above, crying out to one another, the push and suck of the tide throw shells like precious stones up on to the wet beach. I am walking, barefooted, on damp sand, hand in hand with my husband.

I have a pile of his letters, tied with a ribbon that once fastened my sister Katherine's hair. It is one of two things I have from her. The other is Jane's New Testament. It was delivered with news of her death, three years gone. *So I am the last*, I remember thinking. But I am not the last, for there are her boys, my dear nephews, whom I still have never seen. Perhaps there will come a time . . . I do a good deal of thinking these days.

A pair of blue tits pecks at the crumbs I have scattered on the sill, flitting staccato movements, so pretty. Keyes's letters recount his time in the Fleet. His cell was so small he could not stand straight. He tells of how it was only thoughts of me that kept him from giving up on life. He tells, too, of his release and being joyfully reunited with his children. *It is only you, my dearest wife, that is still lacking from my life. And soon enough, I am sure of it, we will be together again. Look how I am favoured with this position. Is it not a sign, my love?* I do not need to read his words for I know them by heart. But I am not so hopeful. The words I spat to Elizabeth as I was taken away haunt me still. *She* will not have forgotten that, even six years on. Elizabeth does not forget a slight.

What cannot be taken from me, though, are those two blissful weeks I spent with him. I go over them in my mind, remembering his touch, how I was transformed beneath his fingers. I come back to my letter, dipping my pen, enjoying the satisfying scratch it makes against the paper. *Naught is easier than self-deceit; for what each man wishes, he believes to be the truth*, I quote Demosthenes. The ancients have been a great comfort to me in the times when I have felt deserted by God. Demosthenes in particular – who could not agree with him, when he says, *Whatever shall be to the advantage of all, may that prevail*?

My time is spent with my books in this chamber, so much time for reading. I watch the birds and once a day take leave to stroll in the cloistered garden below, from where I can feel the tight press of the city beyond the walls. It is not such a bad life and I sometimes think that I am like a nun from the old days, who has chosen to shut herself away in the service of something greater than herself.

I do not prevail upon the Greshams. Anne Gresham is not of an agreeable disposition and is a reluctant jailer, not because she is kind but because she is inconvenienced by my presence. I hear her argue with her husband about me. I see the disgust Anne Gresham has for me clearly. I know it well. It is the same disgust Frances Meautas had for me, the same, thinking far back, as Magdalen Dacre had also. There will always be those who think me an aberration. I do not fit with the perfect environment Anne Gresham seeks to design for herself here at Bishopsgate, her new-built palatial London house, where each fixture has been chosen for its prettiness and even the kitchen lads look like cherubim. Yes, I am not a pretty fixture for Anne Gresham's new house and when there are visitors I am kept away. I prefer it so.

The Queen was here in January. She had been to see Gresham's new exchange; they say it is a hub of commerce. He is a new man. Everything about the Greshams is new. Anne Gresham had bubbled with excitement for months over the Queen's visit, barking at the servants incessantly. She locked my door that evening, for fear I might cause some kind of trouble at her banquet. I occasionally slip a measure of salt into Anne Gresham's wine. Mary Grey's spirit is not entirely broken.

Someone has arrived below. I can hear the sound of horses and the shouts of the grooms. The great door thuds shut and there are voices and feet on the stairs. A knock, and my door swings open. It is Anne Gresham, wearing her usual look, as if she has smelled something rotten in my chamber.

'Someone for you.'

'For me?' I say. My surprise is genuine, for I am not permitted visitors.

'It is Doctor Smith.' I do not know such a person and she offers no explanation. She waits watching, while I cover my hair with a coif and tidy my skirts. I wonder what this doctor could possibly want. I am not ailing.

'My Lady,' he says. He attempts a smile, but seems not quite to manage it.

'What can I do for you, Doctor?' I ask, getting out of my chair to receive him.

'Please, do not stand on my account, My Lady.'

I remain standing and wait for him to speak. He seems unsure, passing his gloves from one hand to the other, and an uneasy silence cloaks the room with just the tick, tick of the clock to punctuate it. Anne Gresham hovers in the doorway and I see her husband too, out on the landing. Tick, tick, tick.

'Doctor Smith,' I begin, but simultaneously he says, 'There is news, My Lady.'

Something is not right. I can feel the hairs on my arms prickle.

'It is your . . . it is Keyes.'

'My husband?' I say.

'He is gone.'

'Gone where?' I ask, momentarily confused. But the man's bunched hands and downturned eyes tell me what I need to know. It is like a sharp punch to the gut. I am trying to remember him, those days we had together, but I cannot hold on to the memories that seemed so solid only moments ago; they are fragmenting; I am fragmenting.

'No,' I say. 'That cannot be right.' But I look at their faces and even flinty Anne Gresham looks stricken.

They all flash before me, those I have loved and lost. Jane first, Father, Maman, Katherine and now my beloved Keyes is dead – the thought is like a shadow so dark it obscures everything.

'He cannot be dead.'

Of those I love, just Levina is left to inhabit this world with me, and my nephews. The idea of my nephews is all I have to cling on to, although they are strangers to me. I think of them so I do not think of the thing which is crumbling my heart. I must force my mind on to those who live, think of little Tom and his older brother, Beech, whose tenth birthday is in a few days. The paltry facts I have of them do not make for much of a picture. I am trying to conjure up an image to fit them, but all I have to go on is the limning of Beech as a baby, and a few words my sister wrote; the rest is of my own invention. My throat is contracting, making it difficult to breathe. 'The easiest thing in the world is self-deceit,' I say, but my voice is a croak and full of tears. 'He is dead!'

'My Lady?' It is the Doctor. His voice sounds concerned; I suppose I am not hiding my grief very well. *Be stoic, Mary.* But my shoulders are heaving uncontrollably and the sobs are flowing from me unbidden.

Epilogue

June 1572
Beaumanor
Levina

Mary Grey is seated by the window with a book balanced on her lap. She is talking to little Bess Throckmorton, one of Stokes's thirteen stepchildren, explaining, in a simple fashion, Plato's allegory of the cave.

Levina is at her easel close by, trying to convey in charcoal the delicate dance of Mary's hands as she describes the flames of Plato's fire to the captivated child. The light is soft, kissing the edges of them in palest gold.

'Do you think, then,' Bess asks, 'that you are a shadow on the cave wall, distorted as shadows always are, and that if you could see it, there is a perfect you outside the cave?'

'That is one way to think of it,' Mary replies, with a smile. Levina knows Mary well enough to be sure that it will have pleased her to hear the girl talk with such frankness. 'My sister Jane described it as . . .'

Mary talks of the past as if it were yesterday. It is eighteen years since Jane died. So much time and, even so, Levina still feels a twist of horror when she remembers that girl on the scaffold, as if the years have collapsed and she is back there. She thinks of her promise to Frances; she has come to see that she couldn't have changed things. The best she has done for them is to have been a true friend.

'Heaven is the world beyond the cave, that us mere mortals can only glimpse at,' Mary continues.

The marks appear on Levina's paper as if some other hand is working the charcoal. There is a little girl, the roundness of childhood still in the curve of her cheeks, gazing intently at a woman in her middle twenties, a smiling woman whose eyes suggest something between kindness and defiance. That is Mary.

She feels George watching over her shoulder.

When she finally puts her nub of charcoal down he says, 'You have captured the scene exactly, Veena.' He has said this many times before. She slips her hand into his and he brings both his arms up to encircle her. She leans back into his body and they stand like that for some time in silence, looking from the drawing to the scene and back again.

'My George,' she murmurs. Thinking of those wilderness years. Somehow that separation, for all its pain, has served to make them stronger.

Levina's lurcher, Ruff, twitches where he lies sleeping drenched in a puddle of sunlight on the floor. His legs move as if he dreams of running and he whimpers a little.

'Ruff is chasing rabbits,' laughs Bess.

'Shall we take him outside, young lady?' suggests George. 'I'd like to stretch my legs and I have a feeling these two old friends would like time to catch up.'

When they have gone, the two women sit beside one another in comfortable silence. Something catches Levina's eye, a small object tucked into the corner of the room almost hidden in the gap where the skirting meets the floor. Curious, she leans down to pluck it from its dusty crevice. It is a wooden bead.

'Maman's rosary,' says Mary. 'Do you remember, Veena?'

'How could I forget?' Levina has the image of Frances fresh in her mind as if it were yesterday, ripping off her rosary, the beads scattering. 'This house is filled with memories.' Levina's head is assaulted now with images of her dear friend.

'My name is still inscribed on the door to my old chamber, Katherine's too, and I found some marks Maman made on the wall in her closet to record our heights. It is good of Stokes to take me in for the moment, since –' Levina supposes she means since she was released a few weeks ago. 'Is Hertford still at Wulfhal?' she asks.

'I believe so. He is no longer confined but leads a very quiet life, never goes to court.'

'He did truly love her,' says Mary.

'I think he did,' Levina replies.

'I don't suppose we will ever know if there was someone pulling the strings. And the boys remain at Hanworth with their grandmother?'

'So it is said.'

'I wonder –' Mary drifts back into silence, her expression unreadable, only after some minutes saying, 'You said you have found a suitable house for me.'

'Yes, in the parish of St Botolph's at Aldgate.'

'A house of my own.' Her smile has returned. 'And I will be close to you. You know, Veena, all I ever wanted was a simple life.' Levina supposes she is thinking of Keyes because she adds, as if talking to herself, 'It is enough to have known love.'

The silence slips around them once more, until Mary says, 'Tell me of your boy.'

'Marcus? He has returned to London with his wife. They have a baby.'

'You are a grandmother? Why did you not say?'

'I am saying.' They laugh and Levina thinks of the baby, his fat limbs, his wet chuckle. 'He is a fine boy.'

They talk on about how life will be and Levina describes the house she has found for Mary: 'It has a sizeable hall with linen-fold panelling and a view of the church.'

'I have not the means for anything much, Veena,' Mary says. 'The Queen is keeping me on a tight rein. She has not released any funds from my mother's estates. But I will have enough for a servant.'

'It is not a large house, but you will be comfortable, and you will see a good deal of me. I am almost never at court these days,' says Levina. 'Remember the boy, Hilliard? His limnings are quite in demand now.'

'I do remember him. He painted the copies of this.' Mary fumbles in her gown, retrieving the familiar portrait. 'He had a talent.'

'And a passion for the new religion, but little sense to go with it.' She stops, wonders if Mary is remembering that slap she gave him. She has never been so angry, before or since. 'As a limner he is good; better than me,' she says, adding wryly, 'He will be remembered for his work. And perhaps I will not. With age comes self-knowledge.'

'That is true. And the Queen is still getting rid of her cousins.' Mary refers to Norfolk, who was executed only this morning for conspiring to wed the Scottish Queen. *She* is Elizabeth's prisoner too, since Darnley died – another cousin. 'I remember Maman once saying of the old Queen that power corrupts. I have thought much on it and it seems to me that it is not power that corrupts, but the fear of its loss.' She pauses with a sigh. 'After all, Mary and Elizabeth Tudor were just girls once, not so different from my sisters, or any other girls, for that matter. It is fear that changed them.'

Levina feels the press of something unsaid, a weight of guilt she has carried with her for seven years. 'There is something –' she begins.

'Something?' Mary echoes.

'It was I who put the idea into Keyes's head, to marry you. I who brought all that suffering to your door, Mary. He would never have had the courage to ask had I not –'

'No, Veena, You did not bring me suffering.'

'But –'

'Veena, I will not allow this. It is thanks to you that I had my moment in the sun.' Mary touches Levina's hand lightly. 'In the scheme of a life, it is not the duration of something but its impact that is important. My short marriage, Jane's short life – those memories do not fade.'

Levina is struck, as she often has been over the years, by the depth of her friend's thoughts, of how she is never happy to slide upon the surface of something. She is like a painter trying to get to the heart of her sitter. 'I forgot, I brought something for you,' Levina says, fumbling in a satchel at her feet, passing Mary a roll of papers.

Mary pulls the ends of the string that ties them, allowing them to unfurl; they are drawings from long ago. There is one of Frances and several of Katherine – Katherine smiling that irresistible smile; Katherine laughing; Katherine sulking, the prettiest sulk you have ever seen; Katherine whispering something to Juno.

Mary sifts through them, finally coming upon one of Jane. She is there in a few lines: the stoic calm, that hint of a smile, her profundity.

'You have borne witness to it all, Veena, the great moments and the small. I suppose that is the role of a painter. I'd never really thought . . . the distillation of moments in time.' She looks for a while at the image of her eldest sister, her expression impossible to read. 'Might I keep this one?'

'They are all for you. It is your family, your past – they are yours.'

'Do you think, Veena, that if we – my sisters and I – had known what would happen, we could have changed the course of things?'

Levina doesn't answer immediately, ponders on it. 'No,' she utters eventually. 'It was your Tudor blood that damned your family. Mary of Scotland is full of it too, and so she is incarcerated as you and your sisters were. She will end up paying the ultimate price if Cecil has his way.'

'The ultimate price?'

'The Queen baulks at it. Mary of Scotland is an anointed queen after all. But Cecil – he usually gets what he wants.'

'You are right, Veena, our lives were written in our blood before we even came into the world. If one of us had been a boy . . .'

'A boy, yes! That might have been different.' She pauses and they both glance out of the window towards the lake. There is a swan driving upright across the water, wings flapping furiously, scattering a flotilla of ducks. It is comical, inelegant, not as a swan should be at all, and makes the two women laugh.

'I wonder who that is arriving?' says Mary. A party of riders have appeared, making their way up the drive. 'There are always comings and goings at this house.'

As if on cue, a door slams below as George and Bess make their boisterous return.

The two women settle back into their conversation, planning the future they will share.

The door opens ajar and little Bess's head appears.

'There are people here to see you, Lady Mary.'

'To see me?'

The door swings open to reveal two figures: two boys, dressed identically in blue brocade doublets and hats in the new style with high crowns. There is something familiar about them, an echo from the past.

'We are come from Hanworth, to visit Lady Mary Grey,' says the older one shyly, removing his hat. The other follows suit.

Levina sees it now; the older boy has the look of his mother, hair the colour of straw and bright sapphire eyes. The younger . . . well, the younger is the spitting image of Jane.

Mary gets to her feet, spreading her arms, her face opening in wonder. It is exactly the look of joyful astonishment Levina saw once on the face of a woman in a painting, who was visited by an angel.

It is the younger one, Tom, who first steps forward into her arms, then Beech, and Levina can hardly believe what is before her eyes – Mary Grey, who can barely stand to be touched, is enfolded in an embrace with her nephews.

Author's Note

This is a work of fiction, and though I have tried to adhere as faithfully as possible to the historical facts as we know them, it must not be forgotten that much from this period, and women's lives in particular, is unknown or disputed. Having said that, Katherine Grey's life is quite well documented and the story I tell of her is essentially correct, though her inner world is of course of my own making. We cannot know the extent to which she was involved in the campaigns that sought to have her named as Elizabeth's heir, and I have chosen to create her as a woman more driven by love than ambition, which does seem to fit with her character as it emerges from historical accounts of her life. Mary Grey's story is more vague; we have the basic facts of her life, her physicality, described by a poison-tongued ambassador as 'crook-backed and very ugly', and some detailed accounts of her marriage, incarceration and final years. The scene of her arrest, a version of which I describe in the novel, is not documented and her early years remain a matter of speculation, though we do know she was educated in the manner of her sisters.

It is largely the story of Levina Teerlinc that has required the full force of my imagination as so little is known about her. The idea of interweaving Levina's story with the Greys' derives from the existing portraits attributed to Teerlinc of Katherine Grey, and another image by her that is possibly of Jane Grey, or so David Starkey has argued. Susan James attributes the portrait of Katherine Grey as a girl to the

Master of the Marchioness of Dorset (Frances Grey's title before she became Duchess of Suffolk), and not to Levina Teerlinc, though it is generally recognized as Teerlinc's work and the V&A, who own it, describe it thus. This suggested to me that the Master of the Marchioness of Dorset and Levina Teerlinc were perhaps one and the same person, leading to my idea of Teerlinc's close relationship with the Grey family. So though it is a fiction, it is tenuously rooted in fact, and there is no doubt that Teerlinc knew the Greys. Her involvement with Foxe and the passage of accounts and images of the Marian martyrs to Geneva is entirely of my own invention, but her adherence to the new faith would chime with her links to the Grey family. Susan James even forwards the possibility that Teerlinc was first introduced to the English court via Katherine Parr's private secretary, Walter Bucler, who had been sent to Flanders on a secret mission with the hope of strengthening ties between England and the Protestant princes, which again supports my depiction of her as involved in the Reformation.

Levina's relationship as teacher to Nicholas Hilliard has been forwarded by both Sir Roy Strong and Susan James, who also makes a strong argument that an anonymous treatise on limning, published in 1573, is by Teerlinc – Hilliard went on to publish his own book on the art of the miniature some twenty-five years later. James even goes as far as suggesting that a good number of Hilliard's works, including the famous 'Pelican' and 'Phoenix' portraits of Elizabeth I, are Teerlinc's – I am not qualified to form an opinion on this but my instincts would suggest this is not the case. Specific details of the relationship between Teerlinc and Hilliard, and in particular his copying of the Katherine Grey limning, are entirely conceived by me. Though there are in existence a number of sixteenth-century copies of the portrait of Katherine Grey and her son, differing from the original in the manner I describe in the novel, none are, as far as I have been able to discover, attributed to Hilliard.

The most comprehensive source for information about the three Grey sisters is Leanda de Lisle's *The Sisters Who Would Be Queen: The Tragedy of Mary, Katherine and Lady Jane Grey*.

For further information on Levina Teerlinc's works, see Susan E. James's *The Feminine Dynamic in English Art, 1485–1603: Women as Consumers, Patrons and Painters*.

The Tudor Succession Explained

The Grey sisters' claim to the throne derived from their maternal grandmother, the first Mary Tudor, younger sister of Henry VIII. Her first husband was Louis XII of France; she was widowed only months after her wedding and then secretly married Charles Brandon, Duke of Suffolk. They had two daughters, Frances and Eleanor. Frances married Henry Grey (then Marquis of Dorset, later Duke of Suffolk) and gave birth to the three Grey sisters.

Mary Stuart's claim was also from her maternal grandmother, Margaret Tudor, the older sister of Henry VIII. Margaret was the wife of James IV of Scotland; their son, James V, and the French Marie of Guise were Mary's parents. On her father's death, and only days old, Mary Stuart became Queen of Scots. She was betrothed in infancy to the Dauphin and raised from the age of five at the French court.

In 1543 Parliament passed an Act reinstating Henry VIII's two daughters, Mary and Elizabeth Tudor, to the succession and a few years later Henry, in his last will and testament, excluded the Scottish Stuart line from the English throne. There were various reasons for this, one being the prevailing belief that English monarchs had to be born on English soil, but it was also because of the close ties between Scotland and France and the fact that both countries were in almost permanent conflict with England. According to Tudor historian Leanda de Lisle, the Grey girls were chosen by Henry because, unlike the Stuart line, they were not sufficiently strong candidates to threaten his son Edward's position. For Henry, however, this must have been a moot point, as he surely assumed that Edward would have heirs to continue the Tudor dynasty.

But Edward VI died aged only fifteen, having fathered no children. Under the influence of the Duke of Northumberland, Edward drew up a new Device for the Succession on his deathbed but it was never ratified by Parliament. This legislation echoed his father's wish to eliminate the Stuarts from the throne but also excluded his half-sisters Mary and Elizabeth on the grounds that their father had deemed them both illegitimate (a hotly disputed point). This placed Lady Jane Grey next in line, as her mother had set her claim aside, but not everyone was in agreement, particularly those supporting Mary Tudor. Jane was crowned but the popular support lay with Mary, who easily ousted her young cousin only nine days after she had been declared Queen.

By the time Elizabeth Tudor inherited the throne from her half-sister the two strongest claimants to succeed her were Katherine Grey and Mary Stuart, both problematically female, with the former dying in captivity and the latter executed. Although both had borne the sons that England had so desperately hoped for, Elizabeth failed for her entire forty-five-year reign either to name an heir or to produce one herself, much to the consternation of her advisors. In her final years, though, it became clear that James Stuart, the Protestant son of the Scottish Queen she'd executed, would succeed her, becoming James I.

Cast of Characters

I have listed characters alphabetically according to either first name, or that by which they are most often referred to in the novel. I also include interesting details about some of the minor characters that may not have made it into the story.

AMY ROBSART ⚘ *Lady Dudley; wife of Robert Dudley. She died in suspicious circumstances, which caused a scandal for her husband, who some thought had killed her in order to be free to marry Queen Elizabeth. (1532–1560)*

ANNE GRESHAM ⚘ *Wife of Thomas Gresham, who set up the Royal Exchange. Mary Grey was under house arrest at the Greshams' London house in Bishopsgate for some years, much to the dismay of Anne, who disliked Mary and resented having to take on the role of jailer as it curtailed her freedom. (c.1520–1596)*

ARUNDEL ⚘ *Henry Fitzalan, Earl of Arundel; Lord Steward of the Royal Household to both Mary I and Elizabeth I and uncle by marriage to the Grey sisters. Arundel fancied himself as a suitor of Elizabeth I and also of the much younger Lady Jane Seymour (Juno), though neither suit was taken with any seriousness. (1512–1580)*

Beech ⸭ *Edward Seymour, Viscount Beauchamp; born in the Tower of London, son of Katherine Grey and Edward Seymour, Earl of Hertford. (The eldest sons of earls reprised the lesser titles of their fathers, hence the appellation Beauchamp.) According to Henry VIII's will he should have been the heir to Elizabeth I but the Queen questioned his legitimacy and preferred the Stuart line. He married a cousin, Honora Rogers, and had six children, the eldest of whom, William, was imprisoned for marrying Arbella Stuart, the great-granddaughter of Margaret Tudor. (1561–1612)*

Bonner ⸭ *Edmund Bonner; Bishop of London under Mary I. He was imprisoned in Marshalsea prison under Elizabeth I, where he died. (c.1500–1569)*

Cardinal Pole ⸭ *Reginald Pole, papal legate to Mary I and the last Catholic Archbishop of Canterbury. (1500–1558)*

Cecil ⸭ *Sir William Cecil, later 1st Baron Burghley; Secretary of State under Elizabeth I and her most trusted advisor. Cecil was instrumental in creating a highly effective secret intelligence service, thus increasing his power greatly. Some believe he promoted Katherine Grey as Elizabeth's heir, preferring her to Mary Stuart, who was enmeshed with the French, though he distanced himself when she was imprisoned. Cecil worked tirelessly to bring down Mary, Queen of Scots, on Elizabeth's behalf. (1520–1598)*

Dorothy Stafford ⚜ *Lady-in-waiting to Elizabeth I and close friend of Mary Grey. (1526–1604)*

Duchess, The ⚜ *Anne Seymour (née Stanhope), Duchess of Somerset. She was the mother of ten, including the Earl of Hertford and Lady Jane Seymour, and wife of (1) Lord Protector, Duke of Somerset, (2) Francis Newdigate – thought to have been her husband's steward. As the Lord Protector's wife she claimed precedence, without entitlement, over dowager queen Katherine Parr. (c.1510–1587)*

Dudley ⚜ *Robert Dudley, Earl of Leicester; husband of (1) Amy Robsart, (2) Lettice Knollys; son of John Dudley, Duke of Northumberland; brother of Guildford Dudley, so brother-in-law of the Grey sisters. He was Elizabeth I's favourite and her Master of the Horse; his close relationship with the Queen spawned much scandal, particularly when his first wife died in suspicious circumstances. He secretly married Lettice Knollys in 1578, falling out of royal favour, but was forgiven, though Lettice was not. (c.1532–1588)*

Edward VI ⚜ *King Edward VI, 28 January 1547–6 July 1553; only son of Henry VIII and Jane Seymour. He came to the throne aged only nine and England fully embraced the reformed faith during his reign. His 'Devise for the Succession' named the Grey sisters as his heirs before his own Tudor sisters. (1537–1553)*

Elizabeth I ⚘ *Queen Elizabeth I, 17 November 1558–24 March 1603; younger daughter of Henry VIII with Anne Boleyn. Deemed illegitimate by her father, Elizabeth was subsequently reinstated to the royal succession. She controversially avoided marriage, turning her single state to her advantage, and so is remembered as the Virgin Queen. (1533–1603)*

Felipe of Spain ⚘ *Felipe (or Philip) II, house of Habsburg; son of the Holy Roman Emperor Charles V and Isabella of Portugal; husband of (1) Maria Manuela of Portugal, (2) Mary I, so King of England, (3) Elizabeth of Valois, (4) Anna of Austria. Spain reached the zenith of its powers during Felipe's reign, gaining territories far and wide – it was he who coined the term 'the empire on which the sun never sets' – though it was his great Armada of 1588, famously overcome, with help from the weather, off the coast of England, which became one of the glories of Elizabeth I's reign. (1527–1598)*

Feria ⚘ *Gómez Suárez de Figueroa y Cordoba, Count of Feria and later Duke; husband of Jane Dormer; briefly envoy of Felipe II to Elizabeth I. Hoped to arrange a marriage between Katherine Grey and Felipe's son, thereby strengthening the Spanish position in England. (c.1520–1571)*

Foxe ⚘ *John Foxe was the English author of* Actes and Monuments, *more commonly known as* Foxe's Book of Martyrs, *a hugely influential anti-Catholic polemic. He spent the reign of Mary Tudor in self-imposed exile in Geneva. (c.1516–1587)*

FRIDESWIDE STURLEY ⚘ *Also Strelly; lady-in-waiting to Mary I. (Died 1565)*

FRANCES GREY ⚘ *Duchess of Suffolk (née Brandon); wife of (1) Henry Grey, (2) Adrian Stokes – thought to have been her Master of Horse; mother of Jane, Katherine and Mary Grey; first cousin of Mary and Elizabeth Tudor. She was remembered – I think unfairly – as a harridan, mainly due to a single reported statement of Jane Grey's that she was beaten as a child. (1517–1559)*

FRANCES MEAUTAS ⚘ *Member of the household of Elizabeth I and the subject of romantic advances from Hertford at a time when he had been cautioned by Cecil to stay away from Katherine Grey. (Dates not known)*

GEORGE TEERLINC ⚘ *Born in Belgium (date unknown), the younger son of a well-to-do Blankenburg family, Teerlinc came to England around 1545 with his wife, Levina. He settled at the English court under the sponsorship of William Parr (then Earl of Essex) to become a member of the Royal Guard of Gentleman Pensioners, a post he held until his death. He was granted English citizenship in 1566. (Died c.1578)*

GUILDFORD DUDLEY ⚘ *Husband of Jane Grey; son of John Dudley, Duke of Northumberland; younger brother of Robert Dudley, Earl of Leicester. His marriage to Jane was organized when it became apparent that Edward VI was dying. Northumberland sought to tie his own family with the Greys, who had been declared next in line by the King. He was executed for treason on the same day as his wife. (1535–1554)*

HARRY HERBERT ⚜ *Lord Henry Herbert. Son of the Earl of Pembroke and Anne Parr (sister of Katherine), Herbert was first married, aged about fourteen, to Katherine Grey as part of Northumberland's scheme to gain power. Herbert's father, the Earl of Pembroke, was keen to firm his place close to the throne. The marriage was hastily annulled when it was clear that Mary Tudor would depose Jane Grey as Queen and Pembroke shifted allegiance. Some years later, in 1561, Katherine, desperate, pregnant and thinking herself abandoned by her secret husband, Hertford, approached Herbert in the hope of rekindling their relationship. He reciprocated her advances initially but on discovering the truth of what he termed 'her whoredom' threatened to make a public example of her. He did not make good his threats, probably due to his own pride. There are letters between them that testify to this but, alas, there was not space to fully explore the episode in this novel. He went on to marry (2) Lady Catherine Talbot and (3) Mary Sidney. (after 1538–1601)*

HENRY GREY ⚜ *Duke of Suffolk; husband of Frances Grey; father of Jane, Katherine and Mary Grey. He was executed for treason on the command of*

Queen Mary for his part in the Wyatt uprising of 1554. (1517–1554)

HERTFORD ⚘ *Edward Seymour, Earl of Hertford; son of the Duke of Somerset, Lord Protector, and Anne Stanhope. He secretly married Katherine Grey, and was imprisoned in the Tower of London, fathering two sons with her there: Edward, Lord Beauchamp, and Thomas Seymour. He remarried more than fourteen years after Katherine's death, in 1582, in secret again, to a Frances Howard and was arrested once more. After Frances's death in 1598 he married in secret yet again, by a remarkable coincidence to another woman named Frances Howard. (1539–1621)*

JANE DORMER ⚘ *Countess of Feria, later Duchess, wife of Gómez Suárez de Figueroa y Cordoba, Count of Feria. She was a confirmed Catholic and close companion of Mary I. (1538–1612)*

JANE GREY ⚘ *Lady Jane Grey; Queen Jane, 6–19 July 1553; eldest daughter of Frances and Henry Grey, Duke and Duchess of Suffolk; wife of Guildford Dudley; older sister of Katherine and Mary Grey. Jane had been thought of as a possible bride for her cousin Edward VI but when it became apparent he was dying she was matched with Northumberland's son as part of his scheme to gain power, as Jane had been named as heir to the throne by the young king. She was crowned but deposed only days later by her cousin Mary Tudor and executed on 12 February 1554 following Wyatt's rebellion.*

Though it was thirteen days from the death of Edward VI to the deposition of Jane she is remembered as the Nine Day Queen. (1536/7–1554)

JUNO ⚘ *Lady Jane Seymour. Named Juno for the purposes of this novel only, to avoid confusion with Jane Grey and Jane Dormer. She was the sister of the Earl of Hertford and daughter of the Duke of Somerset and Anne Stanhope. Lady Jane was Katherine Grey's closest companion and witness at her wedding, though tragically died and was unable to testify to the match. Jane was an author; her best-known work was* 103 Latin Distichs for the Tomb of Margaret of Valois, *a collaboration with her sisters, Margaret and Anne. (c.1541–1561)*

KAT ASTLEY ⚘ *Katherine Astley or Ashley (née Champernowne) was governess and mother figure of Elizabeth I, nearly losing her life in 1549 for attempting to broker a marriage between her young charge and Thomas Seymour. (c.1502–1565)*

KATHERINE GREY ⚘ *Lady Katherine Grey; second daughter of Frances and Henry Grey, Duke and Duchess of Suffolk; wife of (1) Lord Henry Herbert – annulled, (2) Edward Seymour, Earl of Hertford; sister of Jane and Mary Grey; mother of Edward, Lord Beauchamp, and Thomas Seymour. Katherine was not yet thirteen when she was first married (at the same ceremony as her sister Jane) and though she lived with her new husband's family the marriage was not consummated, making it easy for her father-in-law, the Earl of Pembroke, to gain an annulment when he changed allegiance. Aged twenty, she was imprisoned in the Tower of London on the order of Elizabeth I, having secretly married Hertford, and gave birth to her two sons there. Katherine was devoted to her numerous animals – it is documented that her dogs, monkeys and birds destroyed the furniture she had used while in the Tower. Later, under house arrest, Katherine refused food and fell ill, dying after almost eight years in captivity. There is the suggestion that Katherine starved herself to death, which is the approach I take in the novel, and it is clear from accounts of her final hours that she had entirely given up the will to live. (1540–1568)*

KEYES ⸭ *Thomas Keyes, Sergeant Porter to Elizabeth I; Captain of Sandgate Castle. He married Mary Grey without royal permission and was sent into solitary confinement at the Fleet prison as a result, which destroyed his health. He was known as being the largest man at court, with accounts stating his height as anything between 6' and 6'8". Cecil said of the clandestine marriage: 'The Sergeant Porter, being the biggest gentleman of this court, has married secretly the Lady Mary Grey; the least of all the court.' (c.1524–1571)*

LADY KNOLLYS ⸭ *Wife of Sir Francis Knollys (née Catherine*

Carey); officially daughter of Mary Boleyn and William Carey but was rumoured to be the daughter of Henry VIII, as Mary Boleyn had been his mistress around the time she was conceived. If true, this would have made her Elizabeth I's half-sister. Mother to fourteen children, including Lettice Knollys, Lady Knollys served as a lady-in-waiting to Elizabeth and was one of her most loyal and close companions. (c.1524–1569)

LATIMER ⸭ *Hugh Latimer, Chaplain to Edward VI. After 1550 he served as chaplain to Katherine Brandon, the Grey sisters' step-grandmother. Latimer was burned at the stake for heresy during Mary I's reign. He said at his execution, 'We shall light a candle which, by God's grace, in England, as I trust shall never be put out.' (c.1487–1555)*

LETTICE KNOLLYS ⸭ *Countess of Essex, Countess of Leicester; wife of (1) Walter Devereux, Earl of Essex, (2) Robert Dudley, Earl of Leicester, (3) Sir Christopher Blount. Lettice was one of the fourteen children of Lady Knollys and mother of Penelope, Dorothy, Robert Devereux, 2nd Earl of Essex, and Walter. She was exiled from court for secretly marrying Dudley, Elizabeth I's favourite, for which she was never forgiven. (1543–1634)*

LEVINA TEERLINC ⸭ *Daughter of renowned Flemish illuminator Simon Bening, wife of George Teerlinc and mother of Marcus Teerlinc. Levina was the eldest of five daughters and trained as an artist in her father's studio in Bruges. In 1548 she joined the English court, possibly at the invitation of Katherine Parr, serving as court painter for Henry VIII, Edward VI, Mary I and Elizabeth I and as gentlewoman to both queens. Her earnings in 1546 are recorded as £40 (more than Holbein). Though little of her work survives, there are two limnings of Katherine Grey, one alone (in the V&A collection) and another in which she is holding the baby Lord Beauchamp, and there is a further portrait by her that is possibly of Jane Grey. She is known to have painted Elizabeth I several times and was granted English citizenship in 1566. (c.1520–1576)*

LIZZIE MANSFIELD ⚜ *Member of the household of Elizabeth I. (Dates not known)*

MAGDALEN DACRE ⚜ *Member of the household of Mary I. Tall, blonde and pretty, she attracted the unwanted attentions of the Queen's husband, Felipe II. (1538–1608)*

MARCUS TEERLINC ⚜ *The only child of Levina and George Teerlinc. (Dates not known)*

MARGARET, COUSIN ⚜ *Margaret Clifford, Lady Strange, was the niece of Frances Grey and first cousin of the Grey sisters. Margaret openly declared her belief that her cousins had forfeited their right to the succession because of their father's treason, thus claiming that she was Mary I's true heir. (1540–1596)*

MARY I ⚜ *Queen of England, 19 July 1553–17*

November 1558; eldest daughter of Henry VIII with Catherine of Aragon; wife of Felipe II of Spain. Mary was deemed illegitimate by her father but subsequently reinstated into the royal succession. England was returned to Catholicism in her reign, and the brutal methods used to achieve this mean she is remembered as Bloody Mary. Desperate to produce a Catholic heir, Mary had a succession of phantom pregnancies, which caused her great distress. (1516–1558)

MARY GREY ⸭ *Lady Mary Grey, youngest daughter of Frances and Henry Grey, Duke and Duchess of Suffolk – sister of Jane and Katherine Grey. Mary married Thomas Keyes without royal permission, resulting in her imprisonment in 1565 on the order of Elizabeth I. She was released in 1572 after the death of her husband. Though described by a contemporary ambassador as 'little, crook-backed and very ugly', Mary was not hidden away but educated with her sisters and was thought to have been as precocious as Jane. (1545–1578)*

MARY OF SCOTLAND ⸭ *Mary Stuart, Queen of Scots, Queen of France; wife of (1) François II of France, (2) Lord Darnley, (3) Earl of Bothwell; mother of James VI of Scotland and I of England. As a Catholic, Mary Stuart believed herself to be the rightful Queen of England, rather than Elizabeth, who was the product of a marriage that was not recognized by the Catholic Church. Raised in the French court,*

Mary was returned to Scotland aged eighteen, after the death of her husband François. Elizabeth had hoped to control her and had even proposed her favourite, Robert Dudley, as a possible husband in order to do this, but Mary rashly married her cousin Darnley, who died in violent and suspicious circumstances. Once married to the unpopular Bothwell, who it was believed had murdered Darnley, Mary was forced to abdicate the crown and flee Scotland. She hoped for Elizabeth's mercy in England only to find herself arrested and eventually, after nineteen years of incarceration, executed for treason. (1542–1587)

MISTER GLYNNE ⚘ *Loyal servant to Lady Jane Seymour and Hertford. (Dates not known)*

MISTRESS POYNTZ ⚘ *Mistress of the maids during Mary I's reign. (Dates not known)*

MISTRESS ST LOW ⚘ *Also St Loe or Saintlow. She served in Elizabeth I's household and was arrested for questioning about the marriage of Katherine Grey, who had confided in her. Sometimes she is confused with Bess of Hardwick, whose third husband was Sir William St Loe. It is thought more likely she was a relative. (Dates not known)*

NICHOLAS HILLIARD ⚘ *Miniaturist of great renown working in the courts of Elizabeth I and James I. He possibly studied under Levina Teerlinc and later under Clouet in France. He was the author of a treatise on the art of limning (published 1589–1600) in which he stated that the art was not for women. Much of his very fine work survives. (c.1547–1619)*

NORTHUMBERLAND ✣ *John Dudley, Duke of Northumberland; father of Elizabeth I's favourite, Robert Dudley, Earl of Leicester, and Jane Grey's husband, Guildford Dudley. He was Lord President of the Council under Edward VI and was thought to have been instrumental in Edward VI's decision to name Jane Grey as his heir, which is not improbable given he had hastily wed her to his son. Northumberland was executed for high treason when Mary I was declared Queen. (1504–1553)*

PEGGY WILLOUGHBY ✣ *Margaret Willoughby, wife of Matthew Arundel; in childhood she was a ward of Frances Grey and lifelong companion of Mary Grey. (1544–after 1578)*

PEMBROKE ✣ *William Herbert, Earl of Pembroke; father of Harry Herbert. He was a courtier and soldier and known to some as 'Wild Will' for his antics on the battlefield. His wife was Anne Parr, making him the brother-in-law of Queen Katherine Parr. Though he was deeply involved in the power play that put Jane Grey on the throne, Pembroke managed to disassociate himself from Northumberland (partly by hastily annulling the marriage between his son and Katherine Grey, which had been an integral alliance in Northumberland's axis of power) and regained favour with Mary I. Pembroke may have been a ruthless and slippery character but he was beloved of his dog, who pined under his coffin, dying of a broken heart. (1501–1570)*

SIMON RENARD ⚘ *Spanish ambassador to Mary I, prior to her marriage. (1513–1573)*

SIR EDWARD WARNER ⚘ *Lieutenant of the Tower of London during Katherine Grey and Hertford's incarceration, he lost his post and was himself imprisoned when it was discovered Katherine had conceived another child on his watch. (1511–1565)*

SIR JOHN BRYDGES ⚘ *Lieutenant of the Tower of London during Jane Grey's incarceration. (c.1491–1557)*

SIR OWEN HOPTON ⚘ *Lieutenant of the Tower of London from 1570. Katherine Grey was under house arrest at Cockfield Hall in Hopton's care when she died. He attended her deathbed. (c.1519–1595)*

STOKES ⚘ *Adrian Stokes was the second husband of Frances Grey and so stepfather to Katherine and Mary Grey; their marriage caused some disapproval as he was beneath her in class – thought to have been her Master of Horse – and misrepresented as having been many years her junior, though in fact was only two years younger than her. He later married Anne Throckmorton. (1519–1585)*

SUSAN CLARENCIEUX ⚘ *Favourite lady-in-waiting to Mary I. (Before 1510–1564)*

TOM ⚘ *Lord Thomas Seymour; younger son of Katherine Grey and Edward Seymour, Earl of Hertford. He was born in the Tower of London; according to Henry VIII's will he should have been, after his older brother, Lord Beauchamp, the second in line to Elizabeth I but the Queen questioned his legitimacy and anyway preferred the Stuart line. (1563–1600)*

UNCLE JOHN ⚜ *Sir John Grey, brother of Henry Grey, Duke of Suffolk, and uncle of the Grey sisters who, with his wife, Mary, guarded Katherine Grey when she was under house arrest at Pyrgo. He was sentenced to death for his involvement in Wyatt's rebellion against Mary I, but was reprieved in exchange for his land and titles. He was rehabilitated under Elizabeth, who also gave him the royal palace at Pyrgo. Sir John again came under suspicion on the publication of 'Club-foot' Hale's tract, a pamphlet that demonstrated Katherine Grey and her offspring's rights of succession, but fell ill and died before anything came of it. (c.1523–1564)*

Acknowledgements

So many people have helped in the creation of *Sisters of Treason.* First and foremost I am lucky enough to have two exceptional editors, Sam Humphreys and Trish Todd, both of whom have helped me knock an unwieldy set of ideas into something approximating a novel; also Hana Osman, Stephanie Glencross and Katie Green, whose collective editorial input and fine-tuning I couldn't have managed without; my agent, Jane Gregory, who is one of the blessings I count daily, and Catherine Eccles, whose advice is sound as a bell. There are so many others whose unerring support makes my world as a writer turn: Liz Smith, Clare Parker, Maxine Hitchcock, Viviane Bassett, Chantal Noel, Francesca Russell, Merle Bennett, Anna Derkacz, Jessica Lawrence and Andrea de Werd to name but a few. I must also thank Lee Motley for her unparalleled cover designs, Trevor Horwood for his tact and insightful copy-editing, Deborah Dicks for her Latin expertise, Dr D. M. Turner for pointing me in the direction of research on disability in Early Modern England, and Leanda de Lisle for writing the book that inspired *Sisters of Treason.*

Further Reading

I am hugely indebted to Leanda de Lisle's wonderful *The Sisters Who Would Be Queen*, an exhaustive exploration of the three Grey sisters, which provided the initial inspiration for *Sisters of Treason* and is a must-read for anyone who seeks to dig a little deeper into the lives of Jane, Katherine and Mary Grey. Other invaluable works have been Anna Whitelock's *Mary Tudor* and *Elizabeth's Bedfellows,* both of which illuminate those two Tudor queens, bringing them into vivid life; Sara Gristwood's captivating *Elizabeth & Leicester* helped me understand that complex relationship between Queen and favourite, and Alison Weir's *Elizabeth the Queen* gave me, in astonishing detail, a perspective on the politics of Elizabeth's reign.

This should not be considered as an academic bibliography but merely a pointer to some of the texts of my research.

Alford, Stephen. 2012. *The Watchers: A Secret History of the Reign of Elizabeth I.* London: Allen Lane.

Alston, R. C. (ed.). 1969. *The French Garden, Peter Erondell.* London: Scolar Press.

Baldwin Smith, Lacey. 2006. *Treason in Tudor England: Politics and Paranoia.* London: Pimlico.

Baldwin Smith, Lacey and Reeder Smith, Jean (eds.). 1993. *The Past Speaks: Sources and Problems in English History*, vol. I: *To 1688.* Lexington, MA: D. C. Heath and Co.

Boorman, Tracy. 2010. *Elizabeth's Women.* London: Vintage.

Coombs, Katherine. 1998. *The Portrait Miniature in England.* London: V&A Publications.

Coter, Will. 2001. *Family and Kinship in England, 1450–1800*. London: Longman.

de Lisle, Leanda. 2008. *The Sisters Who Would Be Queen: The Tragedy of Mary, Katherine and Lady Jane Grey*. London: HarperCollins.

———. 2013. *Tudor: The Family Story*. London: Chatto & Windus

Dickson Wright, Clarissa. 2011. *A History of English Food*. London: Random House.

Doran, Susan. 1993. *The Tudor Chronicles 1485–1603*. London: Quercus.

———. 2008. *Elizabeth I and Religion 1558–1603*. London: Routledge.

———. 2000. *Elizabeth I and Foreign Policy 1558–1603*. London: Routledge.

Doran, Susan and Freeman, Thomas S. (eds.). 2011. *Mary Tudor: Old and New Perspectives*. Basingstoke: Macmillan.

Eales, Jacqueline. 1998. *Women in Early Modern England, 1500–1700*. London: UCL Press.

Emerson, Kathy Lynn. *A Who's Who of Tudor Women*. http://kateemersonhistoricals.com/TudorWomenIndex.htm

Fraser, Antonia. 1969. *Mary Queen of Scots*. London: Weidenfeld and Nicholson.

———. 1984. *The Weaker Vessel: Woman's Lot in Seventeenth-century England*. London: Heinemann.

Fry, Susan and Robertson, Karen (eds.). 1999. *Maids and Mistresses, Cousins and Queens: Woman's Alliances in Early Modern England*. Oxford: Oxford University Press.

Gristwood, Sarah. 2007. *Elizabeth and Leicester*. London: Bantam.

Haynes, Alan. 1997. *Sex in Elizabethan England*. Stroud: Sutton.

Hearn, Karen (ed.). 1995. *Dynasties: Painting in Tudor and Jacobean England 1530–1630*. London: Tate Gallery.

Hobgood, Allison P. and Houston Woods, David (eds.). 2013. *Recovering Disability in Early Modern England*. Columbus: Ohio State University Press.

Hutson, Lorna. 1999. *Feminism and Renaissance Studies*. Oxford: Oxford University Press.

Ives, Eric. 2009. *Lady Jane Grey: A Tudor Mystery*. Oxford: Blackwell.

James, Susan E. 2008. *The Feminine Dynamic in English Art, 1485–1603: Women as Consumers, Patrons and Painters*. Aldershot: Ashgate.

Julian of Norwich. 1998. *Revelations of Divine Love*. Harmondsworth: Penguin.

Kemeys Brenda. 2009. *The Grey Sisters*. London: Olympia.

King, John. N. (ed.). 2009. *Foxe's Book of Martyrs: Select Narratives*. Oxford: Oxford University Press.

Laurence, Anne. 1994. *Women in England 1500–1760: A Social History*. London: Weidenfeld and Nicholson.

Licence, Amy. 2012. *In Bed with the Tudors*. Stroud: Amberly.

Loades, David. 2003. *Elizabeth I*. London: Hambledon Continuum.

———. 2007. *The Cecils: Privilege and Power behind the Throne*. London: The National Archives.

———. 2012. *Mary Tudor*. Stroud: Amberly.

Logan, George M. (ed.). 2006. *The History of King Richard the Third, Thomas More*. Bloomington: Indiana University Press.

Markham, Gervase. 2011. *The Well-Kept Kitchen*. Harmondsworth: Penguin.

Metzler, Irina. 2013. *A Social History of Disability in the Middle Ages*. London: Routledge.

Mikhaila, Ninya and Malcolm-Davies, Jane. 2006. *The Tudor Tailor*. London: Batsford.

———. 2013. *The Tudor Child*. Lightwater: Fat Goose Press.

Mortimer, Ian. 2012. *The Time Traveller's Guide to Elizabethan England*. London: Bodley Head.

North, Jonathan. 2005. *England's Boy King: The Diary of Edward VI, 1547–1553*. Welwyn Garden City: Ravenhall.

Plowden, Alison. 1998. *Tudor Women: Queens and Commoners*. Stroud: Sutton.

———. 2003. *Lady Jane Grey: Nine Days Queen*. Stroud: Sutton.

Porter, Linda. 2009. *The Myth of 'Bloody Mary': The First Queen.* London: Piatkus.

Reynolds, Anna. 2013. *In Fine Style: The Art of Tudor and Stuart Fashion.* London: Royal Collection Trust.

Ridley, Jasper. 2002. *The Tudor Age.* London: Robinson.

Sim, Alison. 1996. *The Tudor Housewife.* Stroud: Sutton.

———. 1997. *Food and Feast in Tudor England.* Stroud: Sutton.

———. 2002. *Pleasures and Pastimes in Tudor England.* Stroud: Sutton.

———. 2006. *Masters and Servants in Tudor England.* Stroud: Sutton.

Somerset, Anne. 2004. *Ladies in Waiting: From the Tudors to the Present Day.* Edison, NJ: Castle Books.

Stone, Lawrence. 1990. *The Family, Sex and Marriage in England, 1500–1800.* Harmondsworth: Penguin.

Strong, Roy. 1983. *Artists of the Tudor Court: The Portrait Miniature Rediscovered, 1520–1620.* London: V&A Publications.

Weir, Alison. 1992. *The Six Wives of Henry VIII.* London: Pimlico.

———. 2008. *Children of England: The Heirs of King Henry VIII, 1547–1558.* London: Vintage.

———. 2008. *Elizabeth the Queen.* London: Vintage.

Whitelock, Anna. 2009. *Mary Tudor: England's First Queen.* London: Bloomsbury.

———. 2013. *Elizabeth's Bedfellows: An Intimate History of the Queen's Court.* London: Bloomsbury.

Loved *Sisters of Treason*? Then read on for the prologue of Elizabeth Fremantle's next novel,

Watch the Lady

Coming in summer 2015.

Prologue

October 1589
Leicester House, the Strand

The wax sizzles as it drips, releasing an acrid whiff. Penelope presses in her seal, twisting it slightly to make it unreadable, wondering if it – this letter – is folly, if it could be construed as treason were it to fall into the wrong hands.

'Do you think . . .' she begins to say to Constable, who is standing at her shoulder.

'I think you risk too much.'

'I have to secure my family's future. You know as well as I that the Queen is not a young woman. Were she to –' she stops and looks furtively about the chamber, though they both know they are alone as they had searched, even behind the hangings, for lurking servants who might be persuaded to sell a snippet of information if the price were right. 'There have been attempts on the Queen's life and she has no named heir. If one were to strike its target –' she continues in the quietest of whispers. She doesn't need to tell him that there are eyes on Elizabeth's crown all over Europe. 'The Devereux need an established allegiance.'

'And James of Scotland is the strongest claimant to the English throne,' he says.

'Some say so.' She closes the discussion firmly. Constable is not aware that this has been discussed endlessly with her brother – and their mother for that matter, who understands diplomacy better than all of them put together. 'I do it for Essex, not for myself. My brother is the one who needs powerful allies.' She hands him the letter, meeting his eyes briefly.

He runs his fingers over the paper as if it is a lover's skin. 'But should it fall into the wrong hands . . .'

He is surely thinking of Robert Cecil, son of Lord Treasurer Burghley who holds the reins of England. Cecil has a knife in every pie.

She meets his gaze with a half-smile. 'But this is merely a missive of friendship, an outstretched hand. And it comes from a woman.' She places her palm delicately to her breast and widens her eyes, as if to say a woman's words count for nothing. 'Secret communication with a foreign monarch might see Essex in trouble, but little me –' she tilts her head. 'Oh I think I can get away with it.' She hopes to God this is true.

Constable laughs. 'A mere woman.'

'You are sure you wish to accept this mission?'

'Nothing would give me greater pleasure than to serve you, my lady.'

She doesn't doubt it. Constable has penned near on a hundred poems for her, and he is not the only one. Essex is a magnet for poets and thinkers who cluster round him like iron filings, hoping for his patronage, prepared to go to any lengths to gain his favour. By flattering his sister they think they help their cause. She wonders at the irony that, for all those lines of poetry written in celebration of her beauty, repeating incessantly the same figures of speech – her black starry eyes, her spun-gold hair, her nightingale's voice, her marble skin – the man she is wed to has never got beyond his disgust of her. Beauty may make for pretty lines in a sonnet but it is eggshell thin, and as friable; it does not speak of what lies within. Besides, she is not what she was, though time has been kind to her; nothing can undo the quarter-century and more she has lived, and childbirth has taken its toll.

'You will give it straight into the hands of King James.' She is aware of the danger she might visit on Constable with this secret mission, but so is he, and she can almost hear him panting with eagerness. Besides, he is no stranger to espionage.

'But,' he begins, then hesitating, 'How can I be sure of admittance to the King?'

'You are a poet; use your velvet tongue. My seal will get you into the privy chamber.' She takes his hand and folds her signet ring into his palm. 'After all, I am the sister of England's most favoured earl, the Queen's great-niece – that counts for something, does it not?' Her tone is unintentionally sharp and he looks uncomfortable, as if admonished, so she offers him a smile.

'Keep the seal separate from the letter. And give him this, as further proof.' She opens a gilt box on the desk and takes out a limning, passing it to him. He inspects it a moment, his eyes swimming a little.

'Hilliard has not done you justice. Your beauty is greater than this.'

'Pah!' she says with a sweep of her arm. 'Beauty is as beauty does. It looks like me enough to serve its purpose.' She watches as he caches the miniature carefully inside his doublet with the letter.

Her spaniel Spero begins to bark, scratching at the door to get out, and they hear the clang of the courtyard gate, then the din of urgent hooves on the cobbles below and a frenzied bout of shouting. They move swiftly to the window just as the door is flung open and her companion Jeanne rushes into the chamber flushed and breathless, crying out, 'Come quick, your brother is wounded.' Her French accent with its soft lisp delays the impact of her words.

'How?' Panic begins to rise in Penelope, like milk in an unwatched pan, but she takes a deep breath to force it into submission.

'Meyrick said it was a duel.' Jeanne's face is ashen.

'How bad is it?' Jeanne simply shakes her head. Penelope takes the girl's elbow with one hand and gathering her own skirts with the other, calls to Constable, who is already halfway down the stairs: 'Send for Doctor Lopez.'

'If he is wounded then surely a surgeon is what's needed,' says Constable.

'I trust Lopez. He will know what to do.'

They get to the hall as Essex is brought in, supported by two of his men, the broad bulk of loyal Meyrick striding ahead, concern written over his freckled face, eyes darting about beneath invisible eyelashes. He wipes a hand through his hair; it has a smear of dried blood on it.

'A basin of hot water,' she barks at the servants, who have gathered to gawp. Jeanne is shaking: she cannot bear the sight of blood, so Penelope sends her to tear bandages in the laundry.

Essex, his teeth gritted, is heaved on to the table where he half-lies, half-sits, propped up on his elbows, refusing to succumb to repose.

'Just a scratch,' he says, pulling his cape away from his leg so Penelope can see the slash across his thigh and the blood that has stained his white silk stockings, down right into his boot.

'Meyrick, your knife,' she says to her brother's man.

Meyrick looks at her askance.

'To cut off his stockings. What did you think?' She checks the sharp tone that has appeared from nowhere. 'Here, help me with his boots.' She gets both hands around a heel and gently prises one boot away, while Meyrick works on the other, then takes up the knife and, pinching the bloody silk between her fingers, gently peels his stocking away from the wound. It has stuck where the blood is congealing, which causes Essex to wince and turn away. She then touches the tip of the knife to the fabric, slitting it from thigh to knee, revealing the full extent of the damage.

'It is not as bad as I'd feared – not so deep. You will live.' She kisses him lightly on his cheek, only now understanding how relieved she is.

A maid places a basin of steaming water beside her and hands her a clean muslin cloth.

'That varlet Blount,' Essex spits.

'Who challenged whom?' she asks, knowing it will have been her brother's rash temper that provoked the spat. She dabs gently at the wound. The blood is surprisingly bright and still flowing, but she can see that no serious damage has been done. An inch further towards his groin where the vessels cluster close to the surface and it might have been a different story.

'It was Blount's fault.' Her brother sounds surly. Penelope has seen Charles Blount at a distance once or twice at court. He gave the impression of being careful and measured. He is comely too, enough to give Essex some competition with the Queen's maids – and, most importantly, the Queen herself. She's heard that Blount has been attracting some favour and knows full well what her brother is like. He wants to be the only star in the Queen's firmament. 'He started it!'

'You are twenty-three not thirteen, Robin.' Her voice is tender now. 'Your temper will get you into serious trouble.' Penelope is his senior by less than three years but she has always felt older by far. She can sense his indignation at having lost in this ill-advised duel, when he supposes himself the foremost swordsman in the country. She wants to point out he is lucky to have got off so lightly, but doesn't. 'The Queen will hear of it. She will not be happy.'

'Who will tell her?'

She doesn't answer. They both know you cannot sneeze in the whole of Europe without Robert Cecil finding out and informing the Queen, before you've a chance to get your handkerchief out of your pocket.

'You will need to rest a day or two,' she says, rinsing the cloth in the basin where the blood billows out pink into the clean water. 'And your amorous intrigues will be curtailed for a week or so.'

Their eyes meet in silent amusement as he takes a pipe from inside his doublet and begins to stuff its bowl with tobacco.

Doctor Lopez arrives and, after a brief exchange of formalities, he gets to work, tipping a measure of white powder into the gash, 'to stem the blood flow', he says, offering Essex a length of wood to bite down on.

Essex refuses it, asking for Meyrick to light his pipe and saying he would rather be distracted by listening to his sister sing, so Penelope begins to hum as Lopez threads a length of catgut on to a needle. Essex blows strands of smoke from his nostrils and appears unperturbed as the needle weaves in and out, pulling together the mouth of the wound.

'Your gifts of stitching rival the Queen's embroiderers,' says Penelope, admiring the tidy sutures.

'It is a gift I learned on the battlefield.' He places an avuncular hand on her back and steps with her to one side. There is something honest about the close crop of his hair and beard, steely with age, and the way his smile reaches up to crease his eyes. 'Make sure he rests and keeps his leg up.'

'I will do my best, ' she replies. 'You know what he is like.' She pauses. 'And . . .'

'It will go no further, my lady,' Lopez says, as if reading her mind.

'I am grateful to you, Doctor.' It is not the first time she has felt gratitude for Lopez. If it were not for him she might have lost her first child.

Later they gather about the hearth, listening to Constable recite a new poem.

My lady's presence makes the roses red,

Because to see her lips they blush for shame.

Penelope is thinking of the letter to King James tucked in the man's doublet, imagining him riding up the Great North Road to deliver it, feeling a shiver of fear-tinged excitement at the subterfuge.

The lily's leaves, for envy, pale became,

For her white hands in them this envy bred.

'But you change tense there, Constable,' says Essex, who is seated with his foot propped on a stool. 'It should be "become" and "breed".'

'Don't tease him,' says Penelope. 'He does it so the rhyme scans. It is lovely.' She winks the poet's way.

'It's charming,' adds Jeanne, looking up for a moment, needle held aloft, pinched between thumb and finger. Her hands are delicate, small as a child's, and she has a frame to match. They are embroidering a row of hollyhocks on to the border of a shift, had started one at each end and planned to meet in the middle but Penelope's concentration has wandered off and her own needle hangs idly from its length of thread. Essex's teasing of the poet has silenced the poor fellow who stands awkwardly, not knowing whether to continue his recitation or not. Odd he has such thin skin, thinks Penelope, given he served as Walsingham's emissary for such a time. And to be part of that man's network of spies takes mettle.

'We'd love to hear the rest,' she says, distracted by Meyrick entering the chamber and handing Essex a letter with what appears to be the royal seal attached.

Constable clears his throat and glances at Essex, who is ripping it open.

The marigold the leaves abroad doth spread,
Because the sun's and her power is the same.

Penelope has stopped listening and is watching a flush take hold in her brother's cheeks. He screws up the paper and hurls it into the fire, muttering under his breath, 'I am banned from court. Disobedience. Huh! She thinks it is time someone taught me better manners.'

'A few weeks away from court is probably a good thing,' says Meyrick. 'You wouldn't want to flaunt that wound. People might taunt you for it.'

How good Meyrick is with my brother, she thinks. But then they *have* been close since boyhood.

Essex expels a defeated sigh.

The violet of purple colour came,
Dyed in the blood she made my heart to shed.

A page has popped his head around the door, beckoning Meyrick, who approaches him, listening to something the boy says, before returning to Essex and passing the whispered message on.

'Blount!' exclaims Essex. 'What the Devil does he think he's doing turning up here?'

Penelope holds up a hand to silence Constable and turns to her brother. 'I expect he has come to pay his respects and see that you are recovered. It is only out of respect, I'm sure.'

'Respect? The man has none.'

Meyrick puts his large hand firmly on her brother's shoulder. 'Leave Blount to me.' Penelope can see the tightly packed muscles of the man's neck tighten and a flash of brutality in those invisibly lashed eyes.

'You *ought* to see him, Robin,' she says. Essex brushes Meyrick's hand off his shoulder and begins to heave himself out of his chair. 'What are you doing? You need to keep that leg up.'

'If I am to receive the miscreant I will not give him the satisfaction of seeing me reposed like a milk-livered clotpole.' He limps over to stand beside the great memorial portrait of the Earl of Leicester, as if to gain strength from his illustrious stepfather. He positions himself, one hand aloft, fingers touching the gilded frame. His eyes are ablaze, which causes Penelope concern; she has seen that look before many times and it often signifies the onset of a bout of deep melancholy. That is Essex: wild fire or leaden heart but nothing in between. 'Send the villain in, then.'

As Meyrick leaves the chamber to fetch Blount, Penelope sees he has not yet washed the smear of blood from his hand.

Blount enters, dropping immediately on to his knee and removing his hat. 'Forgive me, my lord, if I interrupt your peace but I come to pay my respects and to return your sword.'

'My sword?'

'It was left at the scene, my lord.'

'So where is it?'

'My man has it outside. I did not think it proper to enter your presence armed.'

'Feared it might provoke another spat?' says Essex, then adds grudgingly, 'You did right, Blount.'

'Of the duel, my lord,' says Blount. 'It was nought but fluke that my blade caught you. It was you who had the upper hand. It should have been I who took the cut.'

Penelope catches herself staring and quickly pulls her gaze away, picking up her redundant needle, making busy with it.

'Get up, man,' says Essex, 'no need to stay on your knee on my account.'

Penelope thinks she can see the hint of a smile play at the edge of her brother's mouth. She knows only too well how he likes a show of humility. 'Get our guest a drink.' A page jumps to it and pours a cup from the flagon of wine on the table, handing it to Blount.

He raises his cup saying, 'Pax?'

'Pax,' replies Essex and they drink back, he a little more reluctantly than the other man. But he knows as well as they all do that if he rebuffs Blount's chivalry it will end with another duel.

Penelope's eyes have wandered back to Blount, taking in his halo of hair, dark as an Arab's, and the fine proportions of his face and the warm dark eyes. He is finer looking than she'd thought. He doesn't wear a ruff, just a flat lacework collar and a notched satin doublet, quite beautifully understated. He has clearly chosen his garb carefully so as not to outshine Essex. So he is a diplomat too. But a single earring hanging from his left ear adds an appealing touch of dash. She is thinking this man might be a good ally for her brother, makes a mental note to talk to Essex about it later, to make him understand that it is not men like this who are his enemies. It is men like Cecil and Ralegh who have powerful allegiances and the Queen's ear, men who would see him ousted, that he needs to watch out for. Besides, she would like to see more of Blount at Essex House. He glances towards her at that moment and she feels herself blush as if he can see what she is thinking.

'Do you know my sister?' asks Essex.

'I am honoured to make the acquaintance of one who has inspired such poetry,' he is back on his knee now, and reaching out for her hand.

She is wondering if he isn't spreading it a little too thickly, the charm, which he clearly has in abundance. She can see why the Queen has favoured this one. But he looks up at her and she can find nothing but sincerity in those eyes of his.

'Sidney's sonnets are unparalleled, my lady. They have transported me at times.'

'And what makes you suppose me to be the subject of Sidney's poems?' She has wondered often at the fame that arose from being the muse of a great poet, how it seemed to have so little to do with her and so much more to do with Sidney. What is a muse anyway, she has asked herself many times – no more than a cypher.

Her brother laughs. 'Everyone knows that you and Stella are one and the same.'

'When Nature made her chief work, Stella's eyes, In colour black, why wrapped she beams so bright?' recites Blount quietly. 'I recognize your likeness from his words, my lady.'

'Now there is *real* poetry,' says Essex, causing poor Constable to shuffle uncomfortably.

'None surpass Sidney,' exclaims the embarrassed poet.

'Enough of this,' declares Essex. 'Meyrick, fetch me my sword. Indeed, it is the very blade Sidney gave me.'

'And I'm sure he didn't intend that you use it for duelling,' says Penelope, trying to remain light hearted, but all this talk of Sidney is churning up painful memories, forcing her thoughts back to the girl she was eight years ago. She remembers arriving at court, imagining it to be nothing but romance and light-hearted intrigue. The woman she is now, restrained, secretive, political, is as different from that girl as an egg from an oyster.